When Love is True
A PRIDE AND PREJUDICE VARIATION

MELISSA ANNE

Copyright © 2024 by Melissa Anne

All rights reserved.

No part of this book may be reproduced in any form or by any electronic or mechanical means, including information storage and retrieval systems, without written permission from the author, except for the use of brief quotations in a book review.

This novel is entirely a work of fiction. The names, characters and incidents portrayed in it are the work of the author's imagination. Any resemblance to actual persons, living or dead, events or localities is entirely coincidental.

This is a work of fiction based on the characters created by Jane Austen in Pride and Prejudice. Ms. Austen created these characters, but like many others, I enjoy placing them in alternate circumstances and situations.

Cover Design by Pemberley Darcy

❦ Created with Vellum

For my husband and my family. Your support is necessary for me to have the time I need to write, and I appreciate your love and assistance in doing what I cannot.

Acknowledgments

I have a wonderful team of Alpha, Beta, and ARC readers who were tremendous helps as they read this story in all its iterations. From the very beginning when I posted it on FanFiction.net to multiple variations and multiple reads, I cannot say thank you enough. Many of you have read and commented on the story and given feedback on how it can be improved, on words I misspelled or misused, and so many other things. I could not write my stories without your support and I cannot tell you what it means to me!

Contents

Preface	ix
Chapter 1	1
Chapter 2	11
Chapter 3	17
Chapter 4	27
Chapter 5	34
Chapter 6	42
Chapter 7	50
Chapter 8	54
Chapter 9	62
Chapter 10	71
Chapter 11	79
Chapter 12	86
Chapter 13	93
Chapter 14	100
Chapter 15	107
Chapter 16	115
Chapter 17	121
Chapter 18	130
Chapter 19	136
Chapter 20	145
Chapter 21	152
Chapter 22	161
Chapter 23	167
Chapter 24	176
Chapter 25	179
Chapter 26	187
Chapter 27	193
Chapter 28	199
Chapter 29	205
Chapter 30	211
Chapter 31	217
Chapter 32	221
Chapter 33	230

Chapter 34	238
Chapter 35	244
Chapter 36	252
Chapter 37	259
Chapter 38	265
Chapter 39	272
Chapter 40	278
Chapter 41	284
Chapter 42	291
Chapter 43	297
Chapter 44	304
Epilogue	311
About the Author	315
Also by Melissa Anne	317

Preface

This story is a vagary, not a variation, meaning that our dear couple (ODC) and other characters differ from their canon counterparts in both age and personality. I also tend to make the Bennets even more flawed than in the original, so I apologise in advance if that bothers you.

Additionally, in this version, Mrs. Bennet displays many narcissistic traits. Today we might diagnose her with Narcissistic Personality Disorder, or possibly even consider her bipolar, but it's clear she suffers from some form of mental illness. Lydia as well, though perhaps not to the same extent. These things have likely always existed to some point, even during the Regency period, but women were more likely to be considered "hysterical" and treated in less than nice ways when diagnosed with such. I have tried to treat both these characters with respect.

FEBRUARY 1799

Eight-year-old Elizabeth Bennet followed her elder sister, Jane, sneaking as they made their way into the stables. "Jane," she hissed, "Papa will not be happy if he finds us here. The stables are always off-limits, especially when a mare is foaling."

"All will be well," ten-year-old Jane replied. "Besides, Papa never gets angry with you when you sneak into the stables."

"Papa warned me just this morning not to go to the stables today because a mare is foaling. Jane, you heard him. We must not go in. He will be very angry if we disobey him," Elizabeth replied.

"Lizzy, I have followed you without question on any number of adventures. This time, it is you who must follow me. Now, come," she demanded.

Praying they would not be discovered, Elizabeth reluctantly went with her sister into the stables. Nearly all the stable hands were standing outside the stall containing the expecting mare, their attention fully absorbed by the imminent birth. This distraction allowed the sisters to slip inside unnoticed.

The stables were faintly lit, the doors flung wide to let in air and light, and a few lanterns were lit at strategic locations to provide enough light so that those who needed to see could. The scent of hay and horses lingered heavily in the air. Jane, moved with a determined excitement, her eyes wide with anticipation. Elizabeth, on the other hand, felt a knot of anxiety tightening in her stomach. She glanced around nervously, half-expecting to hear the stern voice of their father or the disapproving tone of their mother.

Jane pressed forward, reaching the stall where the mare stood. The mare's sides heaved with each laboured breath, and the stable hands whispered among themselves, offering gentle words of encouragement to the animal.

"Look at her, Lizzy," Jane whispered.

Elizabeth nodded, her eyes darting between the mare and the stable entrance. The thought of getting caught weighed heavily on her. She replied quietly, "We should not be here, Jane. If Papa finds out-"

"He will not," Jane interrupted, her tone resolute. "We will just watch for a little while. Please, Lizzy."

Elizabeth sighed, her resistance weakening. She could not deny Jane this small joy, especially when her sister's enthusiasm was so palpable. "Just for a few minutes," she conceded.

As the sisters watched, the stable hands' murmurs grew more excited. The mare was getting closer to delivering her foal, and the anticipation in the air was almost tangible. Elizabeth found herself momentarily forgetting her worries, caught up in the miracle of new life unfolding before her.

The mare gave a final push, and the soft sound of a newborn foal hitting the straw-covered floor filled the stable. Jane clasped Elizabeth's hand in her own, her eyes shining with wonder at what she saw. Although they had known it was a messy business before, they were amazed by how easily the mare seemed to bear it and how naturally it all happened. For the most part, the men just stood back and watched, only ready to assist if necessary. They had not been necessary in this birth.

Suddenly, the girls were startled by an unexpected noise. Inadvertently, they had backed up and now stood directly in front of the stall that housed their father's stallion. The horse did not tolerate anyone except their father and one groom, and it did not like when anyone else approached. Elizabeth heard the noise and tried to pull Jane away from the door, but somehow, when the horse kicked, the door flew open, knocking Jane down.

Elizabeth scrambled toward her, trying to pull Jane away from the horse, but someone grabbed her by the waist, picked her up, and pulled her away from the stallion. The horse bolted toward the group of men, causing them to scramble, and bolted toward the open stable doors.

In just a moment, it was over. The stable hand holding Elizabeth set her down, and she rushed toward Jane. It was obvious her sister was injured, but Elizabeth could not be certain how bad it was from a distance. Jane's head was bleeding, so Elizabeth used her own skirt to apply pressure to the wound, attempting to stem the flow. Soon, others joined her, and Mr. Bennet scooped Jane up in his arms, carrying her into the house. "You should not have been in here," he said tersely to Elizabeth.

As soon as the group entered the house and Mrs. Bennet became aware of what had happened, she began shrieking. Seeing Elizabeth behind the others, she immediately began to berate her least favourite child. "ELIZABETH Bennet! You wretched, wretched child! I told you to stay away from Jane. And now look at what you have done. If my sweet Jane is disfigured, it will be your fault. You could have killed her!"

Elizabeth felt the injustice of being blamed for something that was not her fault. "No Mama, I didn't do anything. It was Jane. Jane, tell

Mama it was your idea to go to the stables. I swear t was not my fault."

Though Elizabeth begged Jane to explain what had happened to their mother, Jane closed her eyes and was silent.

Her eyes filled with tears as her mother's accusations continued to rain down on her. Mrs. Bennet's tirade showed no signs of abating, and Elizabeth knew from bitter experience that nothing she said would change their mother's mind when she was like this. Instead, she swallowed her retorts, knowing they would only make things worse. She stood there, taking the blame, as she always did, feeling a familiar mix of hurt and resignation.

The apothecary arrived soon after this, cutting off the tirade. For hours, Elizabeth sat in the hallway outside Jane's bedroom awaiting news. Mrs. Bennet had been sedated long ago—her cries and incessant complaints were distracting, and her presence in Jane's bedroom was in the way of those who needed to give her care. Elizabeth heard only small snippets of conversation, but it seemed they all largely ignored her presence. At one point, the housekeeper chided her to go change her soiled clothing.

Eventually, the house stilled, the apothecary left, and Jane was assigned a maid to sit up with her. Elizabeth attempted to sneak in to see her sister.

"She is well, Miss Lizzy. Mr. Jones gave her some laudanum, and she will sleep well tonight. I think she will have some pain tomorrow, but she will recover," the maid assigned to watch over her said.

Relieved, Elizabeth thanked the maid for her reassurance and went back into the hallway. Her tears, which she had held back all day, finally spilt. Jane would be well.

The day after the accident, Elizabeth made her way into Jane's room. "Jane," Elizabeth said softly, "do you want me to sit with you for a time? Perhaps I can read to you?"

Jane hesitated, then shook her head. "I am tired, Lizzy. I would like to go to sleep."

Elizabeth watched her sister for a moment, a lump forming in her throat. "Sleep well, Jane," she whispered, before leaving the room and shutting the door quietly behind her.

Mrs. Bennet continued to resent her second daughter for Jane's injury. When Jane was recovered enough to finally make some token protest to her mother's invectives against her sister, Mrs. Bennet quickly brushed it aside.

"You are a good girl, Jane. There is no need to try to protect Lizzy. You would never have disobeyed your father and gone to the stables if Lizzy had not made you go with her. She is a bad influence on you, and you must stay away from her from now on. I do not know why God gave me such a troublesome child. Sometimes, I think she must be a changeling. The fairies came and took the boy I should have had and gave me that unnatural child in its place."

Elizabeth tried once more to explain what happened, but Mrs. Bennet would not listen.

"Do not lie to me, Elizabeth Bennet! I know exactly what happened. You, with your unnatural ways, climbing trees and spending time in the stables. Well, I will not put up with it any longer. This is the last time I will permit you to harm my Jane. You are no longer welcome in my house. I will have your father turn you out. That is exactly what I will do." Mrs. Bennet pushed Elizabeth out of her way and marched from the room, screaming for Mr. Bennet.

Upon hearing her mother's threat to send her away, Elizabeth became hysterical. "Why did you not tell Mama, Jane? Why did you not explain that going to the stables was your idea and that you insisted I come with you?"

"Oh, Lizzy, I did not wish to make Mama more upset. I will tell her when she calms down."

"It may be too late, Jane, she is going to send me away! Oh, help me, Jane!"

"Do not worry so much, Lizzy. She will not send you away. All will be well."

Mrs. Bennet's shrill voice could be heard throughout the house, and everyone present witnessed her harsh demands to Mr. Bennet that Elizabeth be sent away. Unfortunately, her father's voice was quieter, and it was impossible to know what he said in response.

From this point on, life changed at Longbourn. Jane began to spend more time with her mother, and less with her younger sisters, especially Elizabeth.

Elizabeth felt even more alone, for she had lost her closest companion, her confidante, and her playmate. Jane's absence left a void that Elizabeth did not know how to fill. She missed the way Jane's eyes sparkled with excitement, the warmth of her smile, and the comfort of knowing she always had a friend by her side.

Instead, she spent time with the younger girls, especially Mary, who was more than a year and a half younger than her, but Mrs. Bennet still found ways to berate Elizabeth constantly. This continued for weeks after the accident, and Jane only grew more distant.

"Jane, would you like to go for a walk in the garden?" Elizabeth asked one day early in the spring, her voice hopeful that her sister might have finally forgiven her for whatever she had done to cause the rift between them.

Jane looked up from her sewing, her expression distant. "No, Lizzy, I think I prefer to stay here," she replied softly.

Elizabeth's heart sank. "But the flowers are beginning to bloom. You always loved seeing the flowers."

"I know," Jane said, forcing a small smile. "Perhaps another time."

Elizabeth nodded, trying to hide her disappointment. She missed the Jane who would have eagerly jumped at the chance to explore the garden, who would have laughed and chatted with her as they strolled among the flowers. Now, Jane's polite refusals and lack of enthusiasm were like a constant reminder of how much had changed.

As painful as Jane's withdrawal was, it also meant that Mrs. Bennet's treatment of her second daughter grew worse. Mrs. Bennet, always quick to find fault in Elizabeth, seemed to take out her frustration and fear over Jane's injury on her more than ever. Every minor mistake Elizabeth made was met with sharp criticism. Every attempt to defend herself or explain was dismissed out of hand.

"Enough of your excuses!" Mrs. Bennet snapped. "Why can you not be more like Jane? She never causes me such trouble."

Elizabeth bit her lip, feeling the sting of her mother's words She tried her best to avoid doing anything that might provoke her mother's ire, but it seemed that no matter how hard she tried, she could never do anything right in Mrs. Bennet's eyes.

One evening, after yet another scolding, Elizabeth found herself in the kitchen, helping the maid with the dishes, a punishment for some perceived wrong she had committed during dinner. The warm, soapy water was soothing, and she found comfort in the simple, repetitive task.

The door opened behind her, and Elizabeth turned to see her father enter the room. He looked at her with a mixture of concern and sadness. "Elizabeth," he said gently, "how are you, my dear?"

"I am well, Papa," she replied automatically, then sighed. "I just do not understand why Mama hates me. I did not do anything wrong. It was Jane who was determined to go to the stables, I only followed to convince her not to go. Jane even admits to that. But Mama will not listen and continues to blame me for what happened."

"I know, Lizzy. I am sorry you are having such a difficult time," Mr. Bennet said, stepping closer and placing a hand on her shoulder.

Finally, as the spring turned into summer, an unexpected guest arrived at Longbourn. Elizabeth was pleased to see her Uncle Gardiner when she saw him step out of his carriage, though his own expression was stern and serious. She felt a flicker of hope—perhaps he would intervene in the situation between her and her mother, perhaps he would make things right. When he noticed Elizabeth standing there, his face lightened somewhat as he smiled gently at Elizabeth and told her to go pack her things.

"You will be coming to London with me for a time," he said. "Your aunt and I want you with us."

Elizabeth stared at him, her heart pounding. "Why, Uncle? Is Mama sending me away like she threatened?" she asked, her voice trembling.

"It has been decided that a change of scenery would do you good," he replied, his tone leaving no room for argument.

Elizabeth did as she was told but saw her uncle's face turn angry again as he burst into her father's study without so much as a knock. After asking Mrs. Hill to bring a trunk down to her room and begin packing her things, she slipped into the small room by the stairs, where she could overhear what was said in the study.

She heard her father's voice first. "Fanny will not allow her to stay any longer, not after Jane was injured again in her presence."

"From what I heard you say, Elizabeth did not cause the injury. Both she and Jane insist it had been Jane's idea."

"It does not matter whose idea it was. Fanny wants her gone. She refuses to let Jane to spend time with her and is constantly referring to her now as a changeling. She is making life intolerable here."

"For God's sake, are you unable to control your wife? I know she is difficult, but it is your place to resolve this."

"Gardiner, I cannot be vigilant every second of the day. Things have deteriorated so much that I am afraid Fanny will actually injure Elizabeth, as her anger has only worsened. I think she is expecting again, which is perhaps contributing to her uncertain emotional state," Bennet replied tiredly.

"Bennet, just so we understand each other, if I take Elizabeth, it will be for good. She will not return to this house. I want it in writing," Gardiner demanded

"Of course, whatever you say," her father said. Elizabeth gasped at his easy acceptance, though she hid it well.

"I had my solicitor draft this agreement before I came. She will continue to receive one hundred pounds per annum in your lifetime. You owe it to her to give her at least that much."

"I will do as you insist."

"There is no going back on this once it is done."

"Yes, yes, she is yours. Call her Elizabeth Gardiner if you like. Fanny would certainly prefer it."

"Will you write to her?"

Nothing was said, and Elizabeth assumed her father had declined. He never wrote any letters that he did not absolutely have to.

"Sign the damned paper, Thomas. Elizabeth is now my daughter, not yours. You will never have a claim on her again. If she is not allowed here, then neither will I visit."

"You will cut off your sister and her family?"

"You are allowing her to cast off her child. Elizabeth will not be welcomed back here; you have said as much. You cannot expect us to leave her in London to travel here. If you wish to send any of her sisters to London, you are welcome to do so. I will, of course, not limit your ability to correspond with Elizabeth, but I will read any letters from you or your wife before giving them to Elizabeth."

Bennet shrugged at this. It was unlikely he would expend the energy to write to Elizabeth once she left, but he might wish to one day. "I suppose you are correct that you could not leave her in town to come here. When will you be leaving?"

"As soon as Elizabeth is packed."

With that, Elizabeth turned and ran toward her room, where Mrs. Hill was packing her things in a second trunk. Many things had already been packed, as Mrs. Bennet no longer wanted the two eldest girls to share a room and intended for Elizabeth to move into a small bedroom upstairs, near where the servants stayed.

"I am going to London to live with the Gardiners," she informed the housekeeper when she entered the room.

"I know, Miss Lizzy."

"Papa says I will not come back. Ever."

"I know, dear."

"Why does Mrs. Bennet hate me?"

Mrs. Hill shook her head. "I have never understood it, my dear. But you will be happy with the Gardiners. They are very good people. It will be better for you there."

Elizabeth nodded. "Thank you, Mrs. Hill."

It did not take much longer for the rest of Elizabeth's things to be packed into two trunks. Mr. Hill carried them downstairs and had them attached to the back of Mr. Gardiner's carriage, and soon, the two were on their way south to London.

Chapter Two

SUMMER, 1804

As Mr. Gardiner had promised when he took her from Longbourn, Elizabeth was treated as though she were the Gardiners' own daughter. Though Mrs. Gardiner was expecting her first child at the time, it did not change the fact that Elizabeth was now regarded as their eldest.

Though treated with the love and care of a daughter, Elizabeth always remained conscious of the fact that she was, in fact, their niece and that her first family had cast her aside. She knew they were caring for her out of kindness, not obligation, and this awareness drove her to prove herself worthy of their generosity. She approached her studies with diligence, quickly surpassing the governess who had been hired to teach her the typical accomplishments of young ladies. Recognising her potential, the Gardiners hired additional tutors to teach her subjects more commonly reserved for young men, such as mathematics and the sciences. They never hesitated to provide her with the best masters in any area in which she showed interest.

As a belated celebration for Elizabeth's fourteenth birthday, the Gardiners planned to take a trip to the Lake District. However, last minute business concerns made such a lengthy trip impossible, so they opted for a fortnight in the Peak District instead. They would stay in the village of Lambton in Derbyshire, where Mrs. Gardiner had grown up. She had been the daughter of the rector there before meeting and marrying her husband. Although her father had died a few years after her marriage, and her mother had moved to London with Mrs. Gardiner's brother, she still had friends in the area she wished to visit.

The Gardiners left their three children with the nanny, as it was easier not to travel with them. They travelled slowly, stopping frequently to visit several places along the way, and reached Lambton on Friday. They visited a few of Mrs. Gardiner's friends on Saturday and met with others at church on Sunday.

Elizabeth had heard much about the beauty of Derbyshire and, after nearly a week in the carriage, she was eager to explore its charm on foot. Her uncle ascertained from the innkeeper that the area was generally considered safe and reluctantly allowed her to go for a walk provided she did not stray too far and remained on paths.

Stepping out of the inn, Elizabeth felt invigorated by the crisp morning air. Lambton was nestled in a lush, green valley, surrounded by gently rolling hills and meandering streams. As she walked along the cobblestone path that led out of the village, she passed by charming cottages with their thatched roofs, their gardens bursting with colourful blooms. The scent of roses and lavender filled the air, mingling with the fresh, earthy smell of the countryside.

Beyond the village, the path opened up to a sprawling meadow, dotted with wildflowers in every hue imaginable. Butterflies fluttered from blossom to blossom, and bees buzzed industriously, collecting nectar. The sky above was a brilliant blue, with only a few fluffy clouds drifting lazily by. Elizabeth paused for a moment, breathing deeply and taking in the serene beauty around her.

Continuing her walk, Elizabeth followed the path along a clear stream. The water babbled over smooth stones, and she shed her boots to traipse over the rocks, mimicking the flow of the stream. Tall trees lined the banks, their leaves rustling gently in the breeze. She noticed a family of ducks paddling by, the ducklings trailing closely behind their mother.

The path took her through a small, wooded area. Sunlight filtered through the leaves, casting dappled shadows on the forest floor. The cool, refreshing air was filled with the scent of pine and moss. Elizabeth heard birds calling and small animals rustling in the underbrush.

Emerging from the woods, Elizabeth found herself at a tranquil lake. The water was so clear she could see pebbles and fish below the surface. She walked to the shore and sat on a large rock, dipping her fingers into the cool water. The lake was surrounded by lush greenery, with gently rising hills in the background, covered in fields and hedgerows. In the distance, she could see the top of what was surely a large house. Idly, she wondered if it was the famed Pemberley she had heard so much of in Lambton.

As she sat, she allowed herself to think about all that had occurred over the last years. When she first left Longbourn, her father and Jane had written occasionally, no more than once a month. Mary, who was just learning to write, infrequently included a line or two to the letters, mostly speaking of what she was learning at that time, but she received nothing from her mother. However, about eighteen months after she left, the letters had become more infrequent, until they finally ceased entirely.

For the last four years, she had heard nothing from her family. Her Aunt and Uncle Phillips wrote to the Gardiners once a month or so, telling the news from Meryton. Her uncle had known many of these people for years and enjoyed hearing about his former neighbours. By mutual consent, the letters from Mr. and Mrs. Phillips included very little about the Bennets, though occasionally the mention could not be avoided.

After a while, Elizabeth noticed the position of the sun in the sky. Rising from the spot she had discovered, she donned her boots and returned to the inn to tell her aunt and uncle what she had found.

Over the next few days, Elizabeth rose early each morning to make her way to the lake she had discovered. Her uncle permitted it, knowing that Elizabeth had always enjoyed her time outdoors. While she had never complained, she missed living in the country.

For three mornings, she met no one as she walked between the inn and the lake. However, after sitting by the lake for several minutes on that third morning, she turned upon hearing a noise and saw a gentleman approach on his horse.

"Good morning, miss," he said, his voice pleasant, but something in his eyes made Elizabeth wary.

She nodded in greeting. "Good morning. If you will please excuse me, it is time I return to my relations."

"Leaving so soon?" he asked, in a teasing tone that set Elizabeth's teeth on edge. "We have not had a chance to get to know one another yet. I have watched you these last several days as you explored the grounds. Tell me, what do you think of the estate's grounds?"

"My family is expecting me back," was all Elizabeth would say as she began to make her way toward the path. Something about this man, and the fact that he had been watching her on her previous visits, made her extremely uncomfortable.

He dismounted from his horse and put himself in her way. "They would be delighted to know you were with me," he said. "You must not be from here."

"I am not," she replied, attempting to sidestep him and go around him. He was making her uncomfortable. "Please allow me to pass."

"Forgive me for not introducing myself sooner; most people here already know me. I am Fitzwilliam Darcy," he said. "I am the master of

Pemberley, or will be soon. Have you seen it yet? Come with me and I will give you a tour. That will give us an opportunity to learn more about each other."

"I do not care who you are as I have no intention of remaining. We have not been properly introduced and your actions do not make me want to know you at all."

She nearly shrieked when he put his hands on her arms to hold her still.

"That is not very nice," he said. "Stay."

"No," she replied, stomping on one of his boots. Unfortunately, she was too slight to cause him pain, though she did make him angry.

"Stupid chit," he cried. "You'll scuff my blasted boots and then where will I be?" He smacked her across the face, and she immediately reached up and returned the favour, scratching his cheek in the process.

"Bitch," he cried out as he further accosted her. "I would have made this good for you, but now, I will make sure it is unpleasant. Now, I will ensure I ruin you and your whole family."

"Let me go," she cried as she continued to struggle. Her hands clawed at his face and neck, and he slapped her once again before grabbing the neck of her gown and pulling at it, causing it to tear.

She kicked at him then and attempted to free her arms from his grasp. He turned her so her back was toward him as he attempted to subdue her.

Just as Elizabeth began to think all was lost, another man rode up. He quickly jumped down from his horse and, after taking a moment to determine what was happening there, without a word to anyone, struck her attacker across the jaw, forcing the man to release his grip. For several long moments, she watched the two scuffle, each landing several punches, when suddenly, her attacker stilled and did not rise again.

She turned to look at her rescuer and found herself staring into the most beautiful blue eyes she had ever seen.

Chapter Three

Darcy had arrived home from Cambridge only the day before. He had worked with his instructors to finish early, allowing him to read for his exams early since his father had been unwell for much of the last year. By finishing sooner, he would be able to be at home with his father and provide what assistance he could and spend his father's final days with him.

That morning, Darcy had argued with his father about his godson, George Wickham. Wickham had run up yet another large debt in Lambton, and Darcy was trying to convince his father to stop enabling his godson's reckless behaviour. Wickham had a habit of accumulating debts he had no intention of paying and ruining the lives of servants and tradesmen's daughters. Darcy knew of two women Wickham left with child, abandoned and cast off from their families. He had managed to help them find decent men to marry, but his father remained unmoved. Nothing Darcy said could convince him to cast off the scoundrel.

Since his father refused to listen, Darcy stormed from the house in frustration. Naturally, he turned to the stables and saddled his horse without asking for help, intent on a bracing ride to work out the frustrations which would no doubt grow as the summer progressed.

He had ridden for perhaps forty-five minutes when he heard a woman's cry. Stopping, he quickly dismounted, discovering Wickham attempting to force himself on a young woman. Judging from her clothing, she appeared to be a gentlewoman, and she was obviously not a willing participant. Darcy was taken aback by how fiercely she fought against Wickham, and he was horrified to discover that his former friend actually seemed to be enjoying her struggles.

Without a word, he struck Wickham across the jaw. Wickham fell away from her, leaving her legs exposed, which she quickly attempted to cover.

They exchanged several blows, but soon Darcy landed a decisive blow to the man's temple, causing him to black out.

"Come, miss, I will take you to my home where we can explain to my father what has happened and then see about returning you to your family. I promise you, my father and I will say nothing of this, but I admit, as much as I am sorry for what has happened to you, perhaps it might be enough to finally convince my father of Wickham's misdeeds."

At first, Darcy did not think she would respond to his command, but slowly, she nodded. He led her toward his horse, intending to help her onto its back so she would not have to walk. He knew his servants would be discreet, and she appeared young enough that no one would assume the worst.

Elizabeth shied away from the horse. "I ... I cannot." Her voice trembled visibly, her terror at the idea evident.

"I will ride behind you, Miss. I will keep you safe. There is no need to worry."

"I cannot mount."

"You must. Otherwise, Wickham will wake and arrive at Pemberley before me. If he does that, your reputation will be ruined, and mine will likely be ruined along with it."

Taking a deep breath to steel herself, Elizabeth nodded, grimacing. "Very well."

He assisted her into the saddle and quickly mounted behind her. They promptly returned to the house-they had not been that far away, and Darcy led her directly to his father's study. He had stopped only once, speaking to the housekeeper in low tones to briefly tell her what had happened and to ask for her assistance. Mrs. Reynolds wanted Wickham gone from Pemberley almost as much as Darcy himself.

"Father, I found this young lady being assaulted by Wickham. I asked her to tell you for herself what happened, praying you will finally believe me and realise the menace he has become."

The elderly man stared at his son for a second. "I cannot believe you would go this far in an attempt to make me believe you. What is the meaning of this farce? Have you found a woman to lie for you to persuade me?"

This infuriated Elizabeth and she moved to stand defiantly before the older gentleman. Her voice was strident as she made her displeasure known. "Am I correct in assuming that you are Mr. Darcy and that this is your son, also Mr. Darcy?" At the senior Mr. Darcy's nod, Elizabeth continued. "Sir, I find it difficult to believe that the master of Pemberley makes decisions without an understanding of the facts of a situation. Surely, you will listen to what occurred to me today before you dismiss me as a fraud. However, if you are set in your determination that I am a liar, I will take my leave of you without further delay. You have only to inform me which it is to be."

"Go on, let me hear your tale."

"Very well. I do not know what lies between you, your son, and this other man, but I can assure you what I am about to tell you is the absolute truth." She took a deep breath and continued. "I guess about an hour ago, I was sitting by the lake when I encountered a man who informed me he was Fitzwilliam Darcy, the master of Pemberley. When I refused his offer to give me a tour of his estate and attempted to return to my relations, he blocked my way and assaulted me. As you can see, he ripped my dress, and he hit me in the face. I tried to get away, but I was no match for a man almost twice my size. If your son had not come upon us when he did and rescued me, this man, who I now know to be a Mr. Wickham, would have ruined me completely. I fought as hard as I could-see the blood under my nails from where I scratched him? Your son has no injuries on his face or arms from my scratching him. The other man will have these injuries. That should tell you who the culprit is, even if you refuse to believe me or your son. I do not know what is happening here, nor do I want to be a pawn for any of you. No one paid me anything to make me tell this story. You can choose to believe me or not, but I was promised assistance and safe passage back to my relations in Lambton."

Both Darcy men were amazed at this girl's courage and poise as she described her ordeal. The elder Darcy had a hard time believing that Wickham was as evil as his son always tried to claim, but he could tell from her appearance that she had been assaulted. Even now, she was pale and despite her bravado had obviously been frightened. Bruises were already developing on her cheek and arms and her gown was torn. He also acknowledged that the girl's presentation of evidence in the form of scratches to the perpetrator's face would incriminate Wickham if he had attacked her. Instead of facing the bigger issue of Wickham, he decided to ask the easier question for now. "Where are your relations?"

"We are staying at the inn in Lambton. My aunt was Madeline Chambers, the daughter of a former rector there. She now lives in London with my uncle. We travelled to Derbyshire this summer so she could visit some old friends. I apologise if I was on the estate in a place where I should not have been. Apparently, young women alone are not safe on Pemberley lands. I was assured that it was so, or I would have never strayed so far from my relations."

Mr. Darcy pulled the bell cord, and Mrs. Reynolds bustled in a moment later. "Please help this young lady. Ensure the servants do not gossip about her state, though do let me know if she needs to be seen by anyone." He gave his housekeeper a pointed glance and she nodded in understanding. The housekeeper quickly bustled her off. "Did you get her name, son?"

Darcy laughed mirthlessly. "No, we never got that far, but she certainly is an interesting sort of girl. Do you believe her? Or me? You must know I would never force myself on any woman, much less a mere slip of a girl, but I will show you that I have no scratches anywhere on my person. My knuckles are bruised because Wickham and I fought, but I am not scratched."

"I would not believe you capable of such a thing. As much as I hate to think ill of my godson, I find myself convinced without going to such extremes, Fitzwilliam. I intend to hear George out, but I am inclined to believe the young lady's account of events. I will also speak to the servants to see what they have seen that I have missed." The gentleman sighed heavily at this admission.

"But not my account? Had I not convinced her to accompany me and tell you what happened, would you still be convinced I was 'mistaken', as you have claimed so many times before?" Darcy's voice rose in frustration. For years, he had attempted to persuade his father to listen to him about Wickham's behaviour, or at least to make inquiries of others if he would not trust his word, but he had never before listened.

"No, Fitzwilliam, it is … it is …" He trailed off, uncertain how to continue. Before he could collect his thoughts, his son spoke again.

"Father, I cannot understand why, for all the years we have been in university, even before really, you have always been willing to believe everything that reprobate says to you, always claiming that I misunderstood the situation, or I was mistaken in some way. I have shown you the debts in both his name and my own-the young lady just informed you that, yet again, he used my name in an attempt to blacken it. Would you have thought me the villain had she gone back to the village and claimed I assaulted her? Time and time again I have shown you the forged notes Wickham has written, claiming I had authorised him to borrow in my name, and you have never believed the proof I brought you. Why is this girl's story so much more believable than mine? You met her once. I am your son!"

His father's head dropped, shaking it for a moment, but he made no answer. Still angry, the younger Darcy stalked from the room, glad to have at least finally convinced his father of Wickham's true nature but unable to understand why his word had not been trusted in this matter.

He had not gone far before he ran into the girl. "Excuse me, miss. Did Mrs. Reynolds take care of you?"

"I am well, but I am ready to return to Lambton. The servant stepped away, and I thought I would attempt to find my way to the entrance, but this house is much larger than I realised," the girl responded, her voice and tone indicating she was still affected by earlier events.

"Allow me to show you the way and arrange a carriage to take you into the town. Do you need me to accompany you to explain to your relatives what happened?"

She sighed. "Perhaps it would be best. There is no one here to introduce us and doing so would be easier if you knew my name. I am Elizabeth Gardiner." She stuck out her hand in a way more common to gentlemen than ladies, and surprising him, grinned pertly. He took her hand, and returning her grin, raised it to his lips instead.

"I am honoured to make your acquaintance, Miss Gardiner. As you have no doubt already realised, my name is Fitzwilliam Darcy. The other man you met is George Wickham, my father's godson. I believe you have finally convinced him of what George really is; I have been attempting the same for years. I suppose I should applaud you for managing to do what I have long attempted."

"I am sorry."

"For what?"

"That your father did not trust you. I ... I understand a little of what you must feel."

"Truly?"

Elizabeth hesitated for a moment before she continued. Seeming to recognise that this young man faced similar struggles to what she had experienced as a child, she found herself telling him far more than she ought to confess to a stranger. "My mother never believed a word I said. I was ... I was sent to live with my uncle after my mother unjustly blamed me for causing my older sister an injury. It ... it was why I was unwilling to ride your horse; my father's horse was to blame. Well, that and the fact that we were where we should not have been. But my mother insisted it was my fault. She ... she did not love me, did not even like me. She called me a changeling because, apparently, I should have been born a boy but was a girl instead." He watched tears form in her eyes. "Forgive me again. My aunt and uncle have encouraged me to leave it behind, and I have taken on their name instead of my father's. I am no longer that girl. I have been blessed by being placed in my aunt and uncle's home and have benefited from it far more than had I remained at Longbourn."

"Your father is a gentleman? But you now live in London with an aunt and uncle?" Darcy asked, intrigued by this girl's story.

"Yes, my uncle is in trade. He does well for himself, and I was fortunate that he took me in when my father ordered me cast out from my former home."

"While my father always seemed to prefer Wickham and never would believe what I said about him, I have never believed him capable of replacing me with another, whatever Wickham may have said. I cannot imagine casting off a child or despising her for not being a boy," Darcy said sympathetically

Again, Elizabeth debated telling this stranger too much about her family, but decided it felt right to tell him all. "My father's estate is entailed. My mother bore five daughters; I was the second. I am not certain why I was hated in particular, but my mother took out her frustration at not bearing an heir on me. My elder sister, Jane, is blonde like my mother, while I have the darker hair of my father's family. I always supposed that was part of it. Mrs. Bennet considered me troublesome since I preferred the outdoors to sitting quietly inside."

Suddenly, they arrived at the front hall. Darcy spoke, changing the topic to one less personal with servants about: "Here we are. Let me ask for a maid to join us in the carriage. I assume from your clothing that you are not yet out, but it is still necessary to protect your reputation, and mine."

"My uncle will appreciate your thoughtfulness," Elizabeth replied

The two engaged in lighter conversation during their journey into Lambton, the presence of the maid limiting the topics they could broach. Darcy accompanied Elizabeth in the inn to meet her aunt and uncle.

After exchanging pleasantries, Darcy took Mr. Gardiner aside and spoke to him about what had transpired earlier. He explained the situation with Wickham and how he had intervened to protect the young woman from harm. Mr. Gardiner listened attentively, his expression grave as he took in the details of the encounter.

"I am grateful for your intervention, Mr. Darcy," Mr. Gardiner said solemnly. "It seems we owe you a significant debt of gratitude for protecting our niece."

Darcy waved away the thanks, his expression serious. "I could not stand by and allow Wickham to harm her or anyone else," he replied. "I only hope she is unaffected by this event."

Mr. Gardiner nodded, his eyes flickering with concern. "We will see to it that she receives any assistance she may need," he assured Darcy. "And I trust you and your family will make sure Wickham faces the consequences of his actions."

"I hope this incident will finally open my father's eyes to Wickham's true nature. For years, I have tried to persuade him to withdraw his support, but I have always failed. Your niece, however, was far more convincing. I pray that my father now realises what a menace Wickham truly is."

Gardiner clasped his hand on Darcy's shoulder. "It is sometimes difficult for a man to admit when he has been wrong and that his inaction has harmed another. Give your father some time to accept what is right in front of him."

Darcy sucked in a deep breath. "It *is* difficult, sir, but I appreciate the advice. My uncle has said something similar before; that one day, Wickham would show his true colours in a way that even he could not brush it aside. I am uncertain what will happen to him after this, but at the very least, I hope my father will withdraw his support at Cambridge and here in Derbyshire."

"Would he accept my call tomorrow to discuss what happened to my niece? If your father is protecting him, perhaps being confronted by the guardian of one of his intended victims will help reinforce what his inaction might cost. I am uncertain as to whether I would be able to bring charges against him without harming my niece's reputation, but since she is not out yet, and frankly, of little importance in the society hereabouts, it could be done. She is a gentleman's daughter, and he is not a gentleman," Gardiner suggested.

"Wickham's actions are well enough known in Lambton that it might be easy to protect your niece from harm should you decide to press charges against him. May I think on it and speak to you tomorrow when you visit? If your wife and Miss Gardiner would like to visit, we would enjoy having you all, though I realise Miss Gardiner may not want to be seen in public for a few days." Darcy was nearly holding his breath, hoping the gentleman would accept. Miss Gardiner was far too young to think about seriously, but something about the young lady drew his attention.

"I will ask my wife and send a note in the morning to let you know if I will call alone or if we will all come. Elizabeth is a brave girl and may not wish to hide, especially as your staff already knows what happened today," Gardiner replied.

Feeling a weight lift from his shoulders, Darcy thanked Mr. Gardiner once more before rejoining Elizabeth and her aunt, feeling a sense of release and gratitude for the unexpected turn of events. After only a few more minutes, he took his leave, first from the gentleman and then from the ladies. His eyes lingered on the young lady for a few minutes, trying to assess for himself if she were well before he finally departed.

He rode back in the carriage, wishing he had his horse with him so he could ride again. After all that had transpired, he needed a hard, bruising ride for the second time that day and he briefly wondered if the entire summer would be this way. Though, if Gardiner pushed this idea of holding Wickham legally accountable, then perhaps his father would be compelled to take action.

Chapter Four

Upon returning to Pemberley, Darcy went directly to his rooms. He was still in the dirtied riding clothes he had donned that morning, having not had time to change after encountering Wickham and Miss Gardiner earlier. As he washed his knuckles in the basin set up by his valet, he winced at the pain, as they were still cracked and bloodied from fighting Wickham.

"Your father asked for you to come to his study as soon as you are ready," Carson stated when Darcy was dressed in clean attire. "He was concerned when he heard you left the house, though I think he was relieved when he learned you had escorted the young lady back to her family."

Darcy nodded, his thoughts racing. What had occurred in his absence? Had Wickham returned to Pemberley and attempted to accuse him of what he had done? Did his father confront Wickham?

Worried about these things and more, he slowly made his way to the study in an attempt to calm himself enough to meet his father and whatever awaited him.

He knocked on the study door, and upon hearing his father's voice call for him to enter, he stepped inside. His father stood at the window, reflecting while gazing out of it. Taking a deep breath, he approached, knowing that the conversation ahead of them would be difficult.

"Father," Darcy began, his voice steady but laced with tension underlying it. "We need to speak about George Wickham."

Mr. Darcy turned to face his son, his expression equally grave. "Yes, Fitzwilliam. I believe we do."

Their conversation started slowly, with Darcy recounting Wickham's various misdeeds, first as a boy and later as a young man at Cambridge. He told his father of the many debts his father's godson had accumulated, many of which he had paid himself, and cited examples of his dishonesty and inappropriate behaviour with women, laying out the evidence piece by piece. Each revelation seemed to deepen the lines on his father's face.

"I have tried to explain this to you before, Father," Darcy said, his frustration barely contained. "But you always dismissed my concerns, thinking I was driven by jealousy that he had what ought to have been mine. I never minded you supporting him at Cambridge, but you were doing him no favours by not holding him accountable in any way."

Mr. Darcy sighed heavily. "I realise now that I was wrong to do so. That young lady's account of her interactions with Wickham has opened my eyes to what he has become. I also spoke to several of the servants after you left, including Mrs. Reynolds, who told me additional stories about him that were extremely distressing."

Darcy felt a mix of relief and lingering frustration. "Wickham's behaviour is not just irresponsible; it is dangerous. When I tried to warn you, you brushed me away. I cannot understand your loyalty to your godson ... unless he is more than that?"

Mr. Darcy blanched and briefly closed his eyes. "No, nothing like that," he replied, his voice harsh and gravelly in evident surprise. After a moment, he nodded slowly as he further acknowledged his son's words. "I see it now for how it must have appeared to you and perhaps others as well. Today, I am truly listening to you, Fitzwilliam. My only regret is not doing so earlier."

Encouraged by his father's openness, Darcy continued, detailing the latest incident involving the young woman in Lambton. "Father, Wickham was attempting to force himself on an innocent woman. If I had not arrived when I did and intervened—"

Mr. Darcy held up a hand, his face pale with shock. "That is enough. I understand the gravity of the situation. We cannot allow Wickham to continue in this manner unchecked. What did her uncle say when you informed him of what had transpired?"

"It is obvious that Mr. Gardiner desires to protect his niece, but he would not hesitate to press charges against him if he could find a way to do it without affecting Miss Gardiner's reputation. She is young and not yet out, and we are far enough from London that people there would not speak of it. The family is in trade and unknown amongst the *ton*. If you withdraw your support from Wickham and let that be known in Lambton, I am certain others will come forward. Many were too afraid to take action against him because of your influence."

"I wish I had known—" he stopped when he saw his son's face looking at him in disbelief. "Forgive me. You have told me often enough, and I have brushed it aside. His father was such a good man, and I had hoped that his son would be like him."

"What will you do? I invited Mr. Gardiner here tomorrow to meet with you about the incident. His wife and niece might accompany him, but he was uncertain if Miss Gardiner would want to be seen in public after today's events. I informed him that our staff will be discreet and, of course, we will say nothing about her bruises. Several have already seen them, of course."

The elder Darcy held up a hand. "Then I will send a note to the inn, adding my own hope that the entire family will come tomorrow. I will see you at dinner and let you know if I receive a reply."

Darcy understood that he was dismissed and left the study, choosing to pay a brief visit to his sister in the nursery. Georgiana had only recently turned nine and was more than a decade his junior. He quite doted on her, especially since their mother had died when she was small. To his surprise, he found himself telling his sister about the young lady he had met that afternoon. While he did not mention what happened with Wickham, he did tell his sister about the boldness of the young lady and encouraged his sister to meet and befriend the girl if she arrived on the morrow. Darcy spent an hour with his sister, until her own dinner arrived, at which point he returned to his chambers to dress for dinner. He joined his father just before the meal was announced, and the two ate mostly in silence, speaking only of one or two matters related to the estate.

Before his father took his leave from the dinner table, he spoke once more. "I received a message from Mr. Gardiner. He, his wife, and his niece will all arrive tomorrow morning at eleven for luncheon and intend to remain for tea. As far as I know, George has not returned to the estate, but I have sent a note to the magistrate, asking him to join us mid-afternoon. After today's misdeeds, I will withdraw my backing from my godson and make it known that young Wickham no longer has my support or protection."

Darcy nearly sagged in relief at this news. Though Wickham would no doubt be upset by this change in fortune, perhaps now steps could be taken to mitigate the harm he could cause to others in the future. "Father, when Wickham learns this, it is possible he will act against our family or the Gardiners. We will need to take steps to prevent this."

George Darcy paled. "You cannot think ..." he trailed off, uncertain how to continue.

"Father, I have seen how he reacts when crossed. When he learns you will no longer support him, he will be angry and will blame me, in particular. Perhaps he will also blame Miss Gardiner, if he learns her identity, believing her somehow at fault. Might we invite the Gardiners to remain at Pemberley for the remainder of their stay?"

His father's brows reached his hairline. "Did you not tell me that Mr. Gardiner is in trade? It would be most unusual to invite such a person to Pemberley."

"You permitted me to invite my friend Bingley to stay last summer."

"Bingley is not actively engaged in trade," his father protested, though he stopped when his son fixed him with an incredulous look. "Yes, I know even I am actively engaged in a trade of sorts and that I have interests in several businesses that many in our society would look down upon if they knew. We can ask the Gardiners to stay, but we cannot be certain they will. If the gentleman is as intelligent as you say, perhaps he will not turn down an invitation to stay at Pemberley, thus saving him the cost of the inn." This last was said with a wry smile, which Darcy returned.

"Thank you, Father," Darcy said.

"Miss Gardiner will lead some man on a merry chase in a few years," his father said next, perplexing him at the sudden change in topic.

"She is young, but I believe she will be rather pretty in a few years. Her uncle will not find it difficult to find a match for her," Darcy replied after a moment's hesitation.

"Many men will not appreciate her assertiveness. She will need someone exceptional, a man who sees her as an equal," he reflected. "After what she endured this morning, entering my study unaware of the tensions at play, she only seemed to grow stronger. Rather than wilting or crumbling as many women might in such circumstances, she stood her ground. Few women, let alone a young girl, would have confronted me the way she did."

Darcy grinned. "I am uncertain whether to call her a Valkyrie or an Amazon. Her dark hair makes me lean more toward an Amazon, though she is far too short for that designation. Perhaps a nymph of some sort?"

His father laughed. "She quite impressed me. Perhaps, in a few years, she might make a good wife for *you*?"

That caused him to start. "Father, I am scarcely ready to think about marriage, and Miss Gardiner is much too young."

The elder Darcy fixed his son with a probing gaze that made him struggle not to squirm. "I am not saying you should marry her tomorrow, son, merely that she might make a good wife for you someday. You are right, you have several years before you are ready to contemplate marriage, but so does she. When she comes out, perhaps both of you will be ready then. You, at least, are old enough to begin contemplating what you desire in a partner. A woman such as her would not allow you to dictate to her and would force you to listen to her point of view. She is unlike many of the women you will meet in town."

"Just a moment ago, you were hesitant about inviting her family to stay at Pemberley, and now you suggest I might marry her in the future?" Darcy asked incredulously.

His father laughed at that. "Silly, is it not? She is a gentleman's daughter, or so I understand. Did her parents die? Is that why she is living with her aunt and uncle?"

Darcy's face darkened as he recalled what the young lady had revealed to him in the carriage. "No, her parents are alive, and yes, she is a gentleman's daughter. Miss Gardiner shared a bit of her circumstances, and it appears to me that she is better off where she is."

Once again, his father assessed him before speaking. "What happened?"

"When Miss Gardiner was eight, there was an accident in the stables that injured her elder sister. The girls should not have been there, and her mother blamed the younger sister for the elder's injuries, which were, ultimately, rather insignificant in nature. However, the mother felt that her second daughter was a troublemaker, calling her a changeling, and demanded her husband cast her out of the house. The father contacted his wife's brother, Mr. Gardiner, and sent the girl to live with them. They have not returned since, and while the father and elder sister did write for a time, they stopped writing when the mother demanded it. She has not heard from her family in over five years," Darcy explained.

"It was very good of the Gardiners to take her in," his father replied thoughtfully.

Darcy simply nodded, and his father did not speak further, bringing an end to the conversation. The gentlemen parted ways, each retreating to their rooms. Once alone, Darcy settled in his adjoining sitting room, a book resting idly in his lap as his thoughts wandered over the events of the day and what the following morning might bring.

Chapter Five

The Gardiners arrived precisely on time the next day. Much to his surprise, Darcy found himself anxiously awaiting their arrival, in particular looking forward to seeing Miss Gardiner again. Georgiana was to join them, at least for a part of the visit, and Darcy wanted his sister to meet this young lady. Though they were several years apart in age, Darcy felt Georgiana would benefit from befriending the older girl.

"Welcome," Darcy said as the Gardiners disembarked from the carriage. After Mr. Gardiner helped his wife down, Darcy stepped forward to assist Miss Gardiner and led her into the house. Once inside, servants helped them remove their outerwear, and Darcy noticed the slight bruising around Miss Gardiner's wrists and on one cheek. Her hands were clean, though like his, they possessed a few defensive wounds. Once again, Darcy felt an immense sense of release that he had come upon her and Wickham the day before and even more so that he had arrived before Wickham could have caused more damage to the young girl.

This done, Darcy escorted his guests into the drawing room where his father and sister waited. He performed the introductions, and soon, the elder members of the party were in a deep discussion, while Georgiana and Elizabeth spoke of accomplishments Georgiana was only beginning to learn.

Since Darcy was not directly involved in either conversation, he quietly observed his guest and his sister as they spoke. To his astonishment, Miss Gardiner effortlessly drew out his usually reserved sister, and a quick friendship blossomed between them. He had noticed this same quality in Miss Gardiner the day before, when they travelled to Lambton. Despite their brief acquaintance, their conversation had flowed with surprising ease, putting him at ease in her presence.

Darcy was unaccustomed to feeling so at ease with a lady upon first acquaintance. The sensation was unfamiliar, yet being around Miss Gardiner felt natural, almost instinctive. Before he could dwell on the matter any longer, someone addressed him directly, pulling him from his thoughts.

"Brother, Miss Gardiner has never learned to ride. Do you think you could teach her while she is in the area?" Georgiana looked at her brother, her eyes filled with anticipation, even eagerness, as she made her request.

"Miss Gardiner, I would gladly teach you if you care to learn. My father suggested last night that we invite you and your family to stay with us at Pemberley for the rest of your stay. I have little doubt that this is the subject of their conversation even now. If you wish to learn, it could easily be arranged," Darcy offered.

He saw trepidation in her face, and he reached out to touch her hand. "Miss Gardiner, the decision is entirely up to you, but I can guarantee that we will take excellent care of you."

"If my uncle agrees to your father's request, I will allow you to teach me. I am uncertain how good of a student I will be, but I will try. I do not have a riding habit, so I do not know if that will prevent me from learning," Elizabeth said quietly, in a voice less confident than the one she ordinarily used.

"You will not need a riding habit. Do not let that stop you from learning. It is a useful skill and even living in London, you may find there are opportunities for you to ride at other times," Darcy implored, and Elizabeth nodded her agreement.

Just then, the elder Darcy stood and walked to where the young people were standing. "Miss Gardiner, your uncle agreed to my request that you all stay at Pemberley for the rest of your visit. However, I have a few questions for you, and I would like you to join your uncle and me in my study. Son, I would appreciate it if you would join us as well. Mrs. Gardiner has offered to keep Georgiana company while we speak."

Darcy looked over at his companion before speaking. The only thing that betrayed her anxiousness about this conversation was a slight indrawn breath that she could not hide. Intuitively, he realised his father had not noticed it. He offered the young lady his arm as he led her to his father's study behind the others. It quavered slightly, and he lifted his free hand to apply light pressure on hers in a comforting gesture.

"All will be well," he whispered, his voice soft but reassuring. "I spoke with my father yesterday after returning from delivering you to your uncle. At last, he listened to what I have been trying to tell him for years about Wickham. Your uncle is determined to hold Wickham accountable, without bringing undue attention to you or tarnishing your reputation. I am certain this is what all of this is about." He paused, concern evident in his eyes. "How are you holding up after everything that happened yesterday?"

She drew in a breath and Darcy watched as she closed her eyes for a moment. Without thought, his free hand once again came up to press hers. "You do not have to speak of the incident if you do not wish it."

"I am well enough," she breathed. "Although I spent most of my childhood wandering the countryside near my family home, I never imagined that I would encounter a situation like that. My uncle warned me to be careful when I was out walking, but the innkeeper assured me I would be safe enough. He did not cause any lasting harm to me."

Darcy scoffed. "While I have little doubt the outward signs of your encounter will not be lasting, I feel certain you will remember this far longer. Acting as though it never happened will not help you heal."

Elizabeth tilted her head to look at the man standing beside her. "How do you know that?"

"Though I was only fourteen when my mother died, the memories of her loss have never faded. Pretending that I was well only prolonged the pain. It was Mrs. Reynolds who taught me it is better to confront such wounds rather than hide them away."

"I am grateful for my aunt and uncle," Elizabeth began softly, "but I have often felt like an orphan, a burden rather than a true part of their family. It has been difficult, being cast aside by my own parents as I was, and I have not wanted to trouble others with my concerns." Once again, she found herself confiding in Darcy with an ease that surprised her.

A silence settled between them, filled with the weight of shared vulnerabilities. As they reached the study, Darcy gave her hand a final reassuring squeeze before releasing it. The elder Darcy and Mr. Gardiner had already taken their seats, awaiting the pair.

"Miss Gardiner," Mr. Darcy began with a gentle but firm tone, "our purpose here is to ensure justice is served and your honour is preserved. Your uncle and my son have spoken to me about what happened with my godson yesterday, and I agree it is wise to speak to the magistrate on your behalf. The magistrate may want to speak to you, but your uncle will be there with you when he does so. Your uncle will also move your family to Pemberley, so we might offer our protection until Wickham is caught."

Elizabeth could not hide her gasp at that statement. "Am I in danger?"

"It is merely a precaution, Miss Gardiner. We can better protect you and your family here at Pemberley, should Wickham attempt to get his revenge once he learns my father will no longer support him," Darcy spoke before his father could.

Elizabeth nodded, her expression resolute yet vulnerable. She looked first at the younger gentleman beside her as though for reassurance, before nodding and turning to speak to the father. "Thank you, Mr. Darcy. I appreciate your kindness and assistance in this matter."

Mr. Gardiner leaned forward, his face etched with concern. "Elizabeth, you must know that none of this is your fault. We will handle this with the utmost discretion to preserve your reputation. We are far from London, and it seems that people in Lambton and the surrounding areas are well aware of Wickham's behaviour."

Elizabeth's eyes flickered with gratitude. "Thank you, Uncle. Your support means more to me than I can express."

Darcy's father nodded. "You are under the protection of my family now, Miss Gardiner. We will see this through together."

As the conversation turned to practical matters of dealing with Wickham, the young Darcy watched Elizabeth closely. Despite the gravity of the situation, he felt a glimmer of hope that he had not felt since his mother died. When he looked into her eyes, he silently vowed to stand by her, no matter what challenges lay ahead.

After luncheon, the magistrate arrived as invited and he spoke first to the elder Mr. Darcy and Mr. Gardiner, before inviting the younger Darcy and Elizabeth to join them. The two young people shared their versions of what happened the previous day while the magistrate took notes.

"Fortunately, George Wickham is well known in this area and has few friends," he said, casting a wary glance at the Master of Pemberley. "Once it becomes known that Mr. Darcy is withdrawing his support, there will be several others who will be interested in helping ensure he is caught quickly and punished," the magistrate said once Elizabeth finished telling her story. "It is possible that what he did to you will not even need to be mentioned in light of these other claims."

Darcy noticed his father's face at these words and wondered if he was feeling shame or some other strong emotion. He wondered how the conversation between his father and the magistrate had gone earlier and felt grateful that he had not been a party to it. Knowing his father prided himself on being a good landlord and diligent landowner, it must be difficult for him to hear that the people in town had known of Wickham's misdeeds but feared saying anything to him about them because of the perception that he would protect his godson over them. Darcy was unsure if he could broach this topic with his father later, but hoped his father would bring it up so he would not have to.

Soon, the magistrate departed, and Mr. Gardiner returned to the inn to arrange payment and for their belongings to be packed and brought to Pemberley. His wife accompanied him, but Miss Gardiner and Georgiana made plans to walk around the gardens. The younger Mr. Darcy joined the girls, both to provide protection, but also because he enjoyed their company. The three walked around the gardens of Pemberley for an hour, speaking of the flowers they saw, the history of the estate and gardens, and anything else of interest to the trio.

They returned indoors when they saw the carriage with the Gardiners and their luggage arriving. A servant showed Elizabeth to her room, where she dressed for dinner, and then she joined the family again for dinner. Dinner was lively and interesting, as the two families became better acquainted.

After the meal, they gathered in the library since it had been mentioned at dinner how much Elizabeth enjoyed reading. She and the Gardiners were astounded by the collection of books in that room.

"You may have to drag me from this room when it is time to leave," Elizabeth said with a smile at her host. "I have never seen such a grand space, filled with so many books. I cannot decide whether I prefer it to Hatchards, but at least here I might be able to look at any book I like!"

The elder Darcy grinned. "You are welcome to read any book you wish, and even take them to your chambers to read them there instead of being confined to this room. We have a similar library in our house in town, although perhaps not quite as large, and when we are in town, you should visit us. Fitzwilliam will be at Cambridge for a time, so we will travel to London in the autumn. Georgiana and I will stay for a month or two before returning to Pemberley for the holidays, and we will all be in London again for the spring. We will invite your family for a visit when you are in town, and we would be delighted to have you all come again next summer. Perhaps then you will bring your other children, Gardiner."

Darcy was surprised by this invitation but did his best to mask it. When Mr. Gardiner nodded, he stood and made his way toward Elizabeth.

"I do hope you will visit us in London," he said. "The library there is not as large as this one, but still, it is enjoyable. Might I make a recommendation for something to read?"

He suppressed a smile when Elizabeth smiled up at him in reply, and he led her to a shelf containing several novels he had read to Georgiana. "I know that you mentioned enjoying reading novels. Have you read *Robinson Crusoe*?" he asked.

"I started it once, but I was not able to finish it," she said, her voice saddened, causing Darcy to look at her carefully. Right as I had started it, I was forced to leave Longbourn. I had not picked it back up since my uncle did not own it, but perhaps now would be a good time to start it again."

"Georgiana and I read it last year and thoroughly enjoyed it. It is a favourite of my father's as well, so it would be enjoyable if we read it aloud in the evenings. Of course, you are welcome to read it on your own, if you prefer."

Her smile warmed him. "I would be delighted to hear it read aloud. You and your father have similar voices, and I think they could be rather soporific when reading a novel."

He laughed lightly. "I am uncertain I have ever been told I am boring quite so charmingly," he teased.

Elizabeth brought her hand up to cover her mouth as she giggled. "That is not at all what I meant, sir."

"Come, Miss Gardiner, I will make the suggestion to my father and see what he says. If our elders agree, then we might read for an hour or so before we all retire."

Chapter Six

The Gardiners extended their visit to Pemberley for a full fortnight, during which the relationship between the Darcys and the Gardiners deepened. Several business discussions also took place among the gentlemen. Before the visit concluded, Mr. Gardiner shared that the elder Mr. Darcy had signed a contract promising a significant investment in his business. Both Mr. Darcy and Elizabeth were involved in these conversations since Elizabeth occasionally assisted her uncle with his bookkeeping.

Fourteen-year-old Elizabeth found a sense of home at Pemberley she had never quite felt in London. She missed her childhood home of Longbourn, or at least she missed the freedom she once had to wander through the fields and forests. Together with Fitzwilliam and Georgiana Darcy, she felt some of that freedom again as the siblings showed Elizabeth around the estate. The three were often together, and despite the disparity in their ages, they found much in common. Elizabeth was in between the two in age, helping to bridge any gap between them, and they each helped her as she learned to ride. Though not fashionable or strictly proper, Georgiana's brother had taught her to ride astride, so Elizabeth was taught the same. She attempted riding side-saddle but found it less comfortable and less steady, so she grew to prefer riding astride, though her uncle informed her it would not be permitted in town.

Georgiana, with her shy demeanour, gradually opened up to Elizabeth's spirited companionship. Fitzwilliam, though initially reserved, showed a kindness and patience with both her and his sister that Elizabeth would not have expected a brother to show. He joined them on their rides, offering tips and encouragement while providing additional protection in case Wickham sought them out.

One afternoon as they rode through the countryside, Elizabeth revelled in the sensation of the wind blowing through her hair. The rhythmic motion of the horse beneath her made her feel more alive than ever before.

"You are becoming quite the accomplished rider, Miss Gardiner," the younger Darcy remarked with a rare smile, displaying his dimples.

Elizabeth grinned back at him, though her cheeks heated slightly at the appearance of said dimples. "Thank you, Mr. Darcy. I have had excellent teachers in you and Georgiana."

Georgiana, riding alongside, nodded in agreement. "Indeed. I am glad we could share this with you, Elizabeth. I have always wanted a sister, and I have so enjoyed having a female companion this last week. I know your aunt and uncle must depart, but I wish you could remain." The young girl pouted a little since she had been told already that it could not happen.

"Your father has invited us to return next summer, and he mentioned to my aunt and uncle that we might see you in London in the autumn and spring. You must write to me, Georgiana. It may not be the same as seeing each other, but it will at least allow us to stay in touch until we are again in the same town," Elizabeth suggested.

The three stopped for a few minutes as they reached the top of the small hill they had been ascending. "This is beautiful," Elizabeth cried.

"I do not know how you ever leave it," she said, turning to smile at her companions.

They returned her smiles, and the three spoke for several minutes about the view of the distant peaks. Before long, they turned their mounts and began to ride back toward the manor. Elizabeth slowed slightly, and Darcy did the same, allowing Georgiana to go on with the groom riding behind her.

"Are you well, Miss Gardiner?" he asked.

She turned to him; her smile gone. "We are to leave soon, and I have heard nothing more about the man who accosted me." She paused briefly as she took in the look on her companion's face. "I did not know whether Georgiana knew what happened and so did not want to mention it in front of her. I have also hesitated to say anything to my uncle. Can you tell me anything?"

It took a moment for Darcy to answer, and Elizabeth watched as his face grew stonier the longer the silence lasted. "Forgive me if I have upset you," she said quietly.

"You are not to blame, Miss Gardiner. I was momentarily lost in thought. You have become like a … sister to me, so I suppose that makes me angrier at what Wickham attempted with you," he paused and sighed before continuing. "Wickham was discovered three days ago attempting to steal a horse and some other things from a farm near Derby. He was caught since he also attempted to injure the farmer's daughter in the same manner he did you, but he did not count on her having several brothers who arrived home just as he struck her to silence her. One brother attended to the injured girl while the other two took him behind the barn and beat him severely. If he recovers from the beating, he will hang. Once again, Wickham attempted to claim that he was Fitzwilliam Darcy, so the magistrate sent a note to my father informing him of events and letting him know Wickham's fate. They knew he was lying since both my father and I are well-known in and around Derby."

"So, he will be punished for his misdeeds?"

Darcy nodded, taking a moment to think before he answered. "We were friends once. It pains me to see what he has become and to know that his life will soon end. Despite everything he had done before, my father offered to sponsor him in a career, with a promise of funds once he completed an apprenticeship, but he refused. He has been given so many chances to better himself, yet he chose this path. Even after he was beaten and arrested, he attempted to use my name in the hope of injuring me one more time. I suppose I feel sorry for what he could have been; I know the thought plagues my father."

Elizabeth leaned slightly in her saddle and patted his hand. "He made his own decisions, Mr. Darcy."

"Why is it that you call my sister by her name, and even call my father Uncle George, yet you still call me Mr. Darcy?" he asked, the suddenness of the question surprising Elizabeth.

Laughing at the abrupt change, Elizabeth squeezed his hand for a moment. "Because they have asked me to call them such while you have not," she trilled.

"Miss Gardiner," he said loftily, a hint of teasing in his eyes, "would you please allow me the honour of calling you by your Christian name? I would like it if you would address me as my sister does and call me William."

"I would be happy to call you William though I suppose if we do see each other in town as your father plans, we should return to formality of address," Elizabeth replied.

"Only when in company, and truly since you are not out, it should make little difference. Though perhaps in London, I could refer to you as Miss Elizabeth?" Darcy replied.

Elizabeth turned to smile at him. "I would like that," she said simply. Shaking off whatever feeling was seeming to overwhelm her, she continued. "Georgiana has told me on several occasions that she views me as a sister. Perhaps we ought to call you my brother or another cousin, then our informality might be excused."

"I think I could benefit from another cousin," he said slowly, and Elizabeth felt an unexplainable sense of relief over his claiming *that* relationship.

The Gardiners left for London shortly after this conversation. Over the next year, they met with the elder Mr. Darcy and his daughter several times in the city, but they saw the younger Mr. Darcy rarely until he finished at university shortly after Christmas.

AT TWENTY-ONE, Darcy was already considered quite a desirable catch in London society. A naturally quiet and reserved man, he was uncomfortable with the attention of matchmaking mothers, their daughters, and the occasional brother or father keen to encourage a match between the heir of Pemberley and their titled, well-dowered, highly accomplished, or well-connected sister or daughter. Darcy struggled not to retreat behind a mask when attending the events his aunt, Lady Matlock, and his father insisted he attend.

He found relief in his books, his daily rides, and his frequent visits to the Gardiner home. The presence of Mr. and Mrs. Gardiner, whether at their house on Gracechurch Street or at Darcy House in Mayfair, did much to ease his tension when he was forced to be in town during the Season, but it was their niece who provided the most support during this time. His father was steadily declining—his illness was becoming apparent even to those who did not know him well. Unfortunately, that only thrust him further into prominence within society and caused even more women to attempt to gain his attention.

The Gardiner home became a place where he could forget many of the troubles that plagued him. Even Darcy House became less of a retreat, as visitors dropped by at all hours, and his father's increasing reliance on him for business matters was, at times, overwhelming.

Additionally, he had to put on a brave face for his sister when he was there; soon, it was only in Gracechurch Street when he felt he could relax. Though Gardiner still discussed business with him, it felt more like a partnership than it ever did with his father.

During this time, Elizabeth was an excellent companion, offering just the right balance of support and teasing. She seemed to instinctively understand his needs, skilfully coaxing him out of a sour mood when necessary. She knew when he needed quiet and when he required a gentle nudge to start speaking.

One evening, after an especially trying day, Darcy sought refuge at the Gardiner home to escape his responsibilities. He was weary, burdened by his father's illness and the relentless pressures of society.

As he entered the drawing room, Elizabeth looked up from her book and immediately sensed his distress.

"Mr. Darcy," she said with a warm smile, "you appear as though the weight of the world is on your shoulders."

Darcy attempted a smile in return but failed. "Some days it feels as though I do, Miss Elizabeth."

She stood and walked over to him, placing a comforting hand on his arm. "Come, let us take a turn in the garden behind the house. The fresh air will do you good. You did not leave your study today, did you?"

He nodded, grateful for her understanding. They stepped outside into the cool evening air, the garden bathed in the soft glow of twilight. As they walked, Elizabeth chatted lightly, her voice a soothing balm to his troubled mind.

"Tell me what you are reading," she prompted, knowing how much he loved to read as a way to calm his troubled mind.

As Darcy spoke of the history he was currently engrossed in, his expression softened. Elizabeth listened attentively, her presence a steadying influence. She asked questions, made insightful comments, and gradually, he felt the tension ease from his shoulders.

After a short time, they came to the bench in the middle of the garden and sat down. Elizabeth turned to him; her eyes filled with genuine concern. "You are carrying too much on your shoulders, William. It is not wrong to lean on those who care for you."

He looked at her, struck by the sincerity in her gaze. "It is difficult, Elizabeth. My father relies on me more and more, and society's expectations are relentless. By society, I mean my Aunt Matlock. And my Aunt Catherine …" Darcy shuddered at the recollection of her last letter in which she demanded a formal announcement of his engagement to her daughter. His father had repeatedly told her over the past two years, both in person and through letters, that there was no such arrangement and that he would not force his son to marry his cousin no matter what the 'Great Lady Catherine de Bourgh' claimed. In fact, Lady Catherine had insisted so often, that he included a clause in his will explicitly denying the match and actively discouraging it.

"You have friends and family who wish to support you," she insisted gently. "Do not shut us out."

Darcy nodded, moved by her words. "Thank you, Elizabeth. Your friendship means more to me than I can express. I am worried about so many things, most particularly my father's declining health. But even there, my motivation is selfish—I am certain I will fail as master of Pemberley when he passes."

She smiled, her eyes sparkling in the fading light. "Your friendship is valuable to me as well, William, and to my aunt and uncle. You will not fail; you are well prepared for this position. For the last year, you have been the person in charge of the estate and even before then, were helping your father make decisions. He has prepared you very well."

In that moment, Darcy felt a profound sense of gratitude for this young girl. Here, in the presence of someone who truly understood him, he found a measure of peace that he rarely felt elsewhere. As they sat together in the quiet of the garden, he realised that as long as Elizabeth and the Gardiners were in his life, he would not fail since they would always support him.

His family would aid him, particularly his uncle, Lord Matlock, but without his father there to be the figurehead in charge of Pemberley, everyone would turn to him for advice and support. Not having his father there would hurt. But Elizabeth had already eased that fear, at least a little.

Chapter Seven
LONGBOURN

After Elizabeth's departure, life at Longbourn settled into a new routine. Jane felt the loss of her sister acutely, especially as it meant their mother could now focus more attention on her. Even though Jane was only ten years old, she frequently heard discussions about how she was expected to "save the family" through her marriage. As Jane grew older, this talk intensified. By the time she turned fifteen, she was 'out' in Meryton and attending social events. However, in such a small community, the only men she encountered were those she had grown up with, and neither the Lucases nor the Gouldings could support the entire Bennet family alongside their own.

Recalling the Gardiners' promise not to deny their daughters a visit, Mrs. Bennet sent Jane to London for a visit in the spring of 1804. She did this without advance notice, relying on her uncle's sense of familial duty to house his niece when she showed up with only the barest of warnings before her coach arrived at his home one afternoon.

Jane found the Gardiner household was not to her liking since they did not cater to her every wish, nor would they take her to the finest modiste in London. Neither would they take her to the balls and other events as she had hoped, nor could they introduce her to wealthy men. The family attended the theatre one night while she was there, but even that was met with complaints. Jane did not like that Elizabeth accompanied them, and that her uncle did not rent a box as she insisted. After a fortnight of constant complaining and of not getting her way, she wrote to her mother asking to return home. Her aunt and uncle were happy to send her back, though they did not escort her there, but returned her in the same manner she arrived.

Initially, Elizabeth was pleased to see her sister, though she was disheartened when she realised how shallow Jane's interests had become. Despite her initial excitement at being reunited, their conversations quickly grew tiresome. Jane showed little interest in Elizabeth's life in London or in any of the broader world topics Elizabeth enjoyed discussing. Instead, she focused on trivial matters and local gossip. Though Elizabeth was familiar with some of the people Jane discussed, she did not care for Jane's attitude toward them.

Despite her not visiting Hertfordshire, Elizabeth was familiar with several of the families there. After receiving his knighthood, Sir William Lucas brought his family to London once or twice each year. Edward Gardiner and William Lucas were friendly as children, so each year when Sir William came to London, he visited with his former friend. Through these visits, Elizabeth had become acquainted with the whole family, but in particular Charlotte Lucas, who despite their difference in ages, proved a good friend to the young girl.

Charlotte and Elizabeth wrote to each other often, so when Jane visited, she did not care for how her sister tore down the Lucas family. In many ways, Charlotte was more an older sister to Elizabeth than her own sister, so it bothered Elizabeth to hear her friend spoken of in such a way.

"Jane, I cannot understand why you speak so of Charlotte," Elizabeth said on one of the first mornings her sister was in town. "Charlotte visits my aunt and uncle with her father often, and I find her to be an interesting and delightful friend."

Jane sniffed at her sister's words. "It is nothing more than what Mama always says," she insisted. "The Lucases are quite the conniving family, always seeking an advantage. It was ridiculous that Sir William was elevated as he was for such a small matter and 'Lady Lucas', as she insists on being called, lords it over Mama whenever she can."

No matter how much Elizabeth tried, she could not understand the depth of the animosity toward the Lucases by her sister, and presumably, her mother as well. When Jane finally left London, Elizabeth felt more of a kinship with the Lucas family than her own.

Jane returned home full of criticisms for her sister and the Gardiners. She could not understand why her aunt and uncle had not taken her out as often as she wished, and Mrs. Bennet was annoyed with her brother for not introducing Jane to wealthy men. The only potential suitors Jane met during her visit were tradesmen, and Mrs. Bennet did not think them at all suitable for her beautiful daughter.

Unbeknownst to Elizabeth, Mrs. Bennet wrote frequently to her brother to complain about this and other matters. Though she begged him to allow Jane to visit again each spring thereafter, Mr. Gardiner refused to house her again, claiming that if Jane arrived, she would be sent right back to Longbourn.

The next several years brought little change to the Bennet estate. Jane continued to grow more beautiful, and Mrs. Bennet used whatever funds she could persuade her husband to part with to dress her in the best Meryton could afford. Of the other girls, Mary was largely ignored since she lacked the beauty of her eldest sister. However, she was interested in the church and frequently visited the rector's wife, Mrs. Allen, for piano lessons and a few other lessons her parents did not see fit to teach her. These did not occur as often as Mary might have wished, but she did receive more instruction in these matters than the other girls.

At nearly nine years of age, Lydia was already spoiled and nearly uncontrollable. Both she and Kitty had been taught the basics of reading and mathematics, and of course, were taught to sew and embroider, but little else. Mrs. Bennet did not worry about things such as deportment or manners, not seeing anything wrong with their youthful liveliness.

Mr. Bennet thought his daughters silly and ignorant, not bothering himself to worry about their education. He paid enough attention to his estate to keep it running and to keep its income at the same level it always was, though the lack of improvements did mean his income fell a little from one year to the next. The stables declined to the point that he sold off the horses, for after Elizabeth was sent away, he lost all interest in the stables, using the money gained from those sales to purchase additional books for his library. As the years passed, he spent more and more time in his library reading, avoiding his family when he could.

As a result, the Bennet family floundered after Elizabeth's departure. Neither Mr. nor Mrs. Bennet took the trouble to ensure their daughters were prepared for the future. Mrs. Bennet continued to pin her hopes on Jane marrying well, though she also considered what else could be done to prevent the family from suffering too greatly in the years to come.

Chapter Eight

SUMMARY, 1805

Once again, the Gardiners were travelling north, but on this occasion, they were joined by two Darcy carriages, one containing Fitzwilliam Darcy and another with servants who would work at Pemberley for the summer. His father and sister had returned to Pemberley a month prior, but business kept him in town longer. Therefore, when it was time for the Gardiners and the children to head north, Darcy chose to accompany his friends and travel with them.

The family travelled in two carriages, including the Gardiners' three children, who were now five, four, and two years old. The extra carriage made the journey more comfortable for the children, allowing them to switch between carriages at each stop, and even ride in the servants' carriage when needed, so they could be separated as necessary.

Charles Bingley accompanied Darcy to Pemberley on this occasion. A few years his junior, Bingley had yet to complete his studies. Despite their contrasting personalities, the two were friends. Bingley was the son of a successful businessman who left him a substantial fortune, and the desire to purchase an estate to elevate the family into the landed gentry. He had two sisters, each with a considerable dowry. His elder sister, Louisa, was engaged to a minor gentleman, and they were set to marry soon in Scarborough. Bingley planned to stay at Pemberley for a fortnight to learn about estate management before continuing on to his family home for the wedding in September.

Bingley's younger sister, Caroline, was constantly hounding her brother for an introduction to his friends, particularly Darcy. Caroline had heard about the Darcy estate and wealth and was keen on making a match with the man. She would have preferred a title but would settle for the reputed wealth and connections of the Darcys.

So far, Darcy had managed to avoid the introduction and the Bingley townhouse by citing business. He met his friend at the club when necessary and invited Bingley to accompany him only after his sisters had already departed London.

As the carriages rolled along the well-worn roads, Darcy found peace in the familiar company of the Gardiners—their niece in particular. Gardiner's conversations were always engaging, offering a respite from the relentless social obligations he was leaving behind in London. Additionally, Gardiner possessed a keen intellect and a curiosity about the world, making their discussions rich and varied. The older man was a mentor of sorts to young Darcy, and whether they were debating the latest political developments or delving into the intricacies of business, Gardiner's insights were always thought-provoking and enlightening. While he had learned much from his father, his conversations with Gardiner provided an insight that always made him view any issue from a different angle than he initially considered.

Likewise, Mrs. Gardiner's warm presence provided a comforting, motherly attitude that Darcy deeply appreciated. She had an innate ability to make everyone around her feel at ease, her gentle manner and kind words a balm to his often-strained nerves. Her affection for her family was evident in every gesture. This was in contrast to his aunts, one of whom spent most of her time directing Darcy how to interact in a society he abhorred, and the other who attempted to dictate her own desires to Darcy and everyone around her. Mrs. Gardiner was the gentle influence he needed, and she frequently reminded him of his own mother, Lady Anne Darcy.

Despite this, it was Elizabeth who drew his attention the most. At just fifteen and not yet out, her lively spirit and quick wit were a constant source of fascination for him. She had a way of looking at the world that was both pragmatic and hopeful, a balance he found himself admiring. Her laughter was a bright counterpoint to his serious demeanour, and her ability to find joy in the simplest moments was infectious. Darcy marvelled at how she could effortlessly shift from a playful tease to a thoughtful companion, sensing what he needed at any given moment.

Their conversations, though often light-hearted, carried a depth that Darcy found rare. Elizabeth challenged his perspectives, made him reconsider his opinions, and pushed him to be more open and reflective. She seemed to understand his need for solitude and never pressed him to speak more than he wished. Instead, she offered her companionship in a way that was unobtrusive yet undeniably comforting.

During one of their stops at a charming village inn, Darcy found himself walking with Elizabeth along a creek, a gentle breeze rustling the leaves. They spoke of books and travels, and Darcy was struck once again by her keen insights.

"William," she said, her eyes sparkling, "tell me, what is it about Pemberley that you hold most dear?"

He paused, considering her question. "There are many things, Elizabeth. The beauty of the land, the history of my family, the responsibility of stewardship. But more than that, it is home. It is where I feel most myself. As you know, I detest London though I do appreciate the culture one can find there. If there were a way to transport the bookshops, the theatre, and the museums to Derbyshire, I would be content."

Elizabeth nodded thoughtfully. "I see why you would cherish it so much. I have lived in London for most of my life, or so it seems, but I miss the life I lived as a child in the country. If I still lived on an estate, I would no doubt know every tree and hill just as well as you do those at Pemberley. I look forward to riding again on the estate and hope you will have time to join Georgiana and me. I have not ridden very often since last summer."

"You would remain outdoors all the time if your aunt would allow you. I have little doubt you would be familiar not just with the trees and the hills, but with every woodland creature who lived nearby. You are closer to a nymph than a girl at times," he teased, a broad grin on his face as he watched her. "And I look forward to reacquainting myself, and you, with all the delights of the park at Pemberley. Do you still wake early?" At Elizabeth's nod, he continued. "Then you must join me for my morning ride. Georgiana will never rise so early, but if you can be in the stables at seven, I will take you with me. Unfortunately, I am uncertain I will have much time later in the day, judging from the correspondence that has crossed my desk in these last weeks.

Her smile was warm. "I would be delighted to join you." However, after only a moment, her smile faltered. "How is your father? Has he grown worse?"

Darcy drew in a deep breath as he thought about how to answer. "His letters indicate little change, but the letters from the steward and Mrs. Reynolds indicate he is not well. I am afraid he is rarely stirring from his rooms these days. Georgiana will occupy much of your time at Pemberley, I am afraid. She will need your support, and that of your aunt, while you are there. I know you write to her already, but I hope you will continue to do so. She has so few friends …" he trailed off, emotion choking his voice.

Elizabeth stopped, bringing her hand up to rest on his arm. "It will be well, William. Even should the worse come, you will be well. Your father has taught you well, the steward already trusts you, and your uncle and mine will assist you when you need it. There are many who are willing to be of aid to you, but you are prepared to step into your father's shoes. You already have. Georgiana and I will continue to tease you so that you will not be so serious all the time. I will include lines in her letters for you since I am unable to write to you directly."

"We are cousins, are we not?" he asked lightly. "It is not improper for you to write to me directly. Perhaps I ought to ask your uncle if it is acceptable. If not, I will include lines to you with Georgiana's letters, and perhaps in letters to Gardiner as well. I find it difficult to think that Wickham has ever done anything to aid me, but in doing what he did, he brought you into my life."

"You have not mentioned that man in ages. You no longer feel guilty about what happened to him?" she asked.

Sighing heavily, Darcy shook his head and moved Elizabeth's hand from his arm to clasp it in his own. "Between you, my father, and Bingley, I have come to realise that there was little more I could have done. I did what I could, but others enabled Wickham to become what he was. He got what he deserved, and I am at peace with that."

With a smirk, Elizabeth retorted: "Good, because I would hate to have to convince you of the error of your ways. Your cousin Richard has shown Georgiana and me several methods to convince men to see things our way," she said with a sly grin.

Darcy raised his brow at this, having known that Richard intended to teach Georgiana and Elizabeth a few methods to defend themselves, but wondered what else he might have taught them. "Should I be worried?" he inquired.

"Very," Elizabeth replied confidently. "I am certain that if Wickham had attempted what he did with me last summer now, I would have him on his knees in moments. Though Richard would not actually let us strike him, so it is only hypothetical."

"I will have to ask Richard about his methods," Darcy replied, wondering if Elizabeth meant what he thought she did. If so, she would definitely have been able to harm an attacker, but whether she would be able to escape afterwards was less certain to him. Regardless, with Wickham gone, it was unlikely she would encounter such a thing again.

Darcy felt a sense of protectiveness surge through him. He attributed that feeling to her close relationship with his sister, but it occurred to him that he felt in no way brotherly to her. In fact, the mere idea caused his stomach to revolt—or was it his heart?

Shaking aside these thoughts, he focused his attention back on the girl in front of him. Their conversation shifted to other matters, including making a definite plan for their morning rides.

BINGLEY and the Gardiner children added much frivolity to their party while Darcy remained busy and troubled. The only time he felt truly at peace was during his morning rides with Elizabeth. When they were together, he always felt a sense of peace wash over him. It did not matter whether they were talking or not, as Elizabeth was one of the few people in his life who understood his need for silent contemplation, especially during troubled times. She quietly waited for him to share whatever was on his mind and listened attentively, without interrupting or pressing him for details. Her patience and understanding were qualities Darcy found comforting.

Elizabeth had an uncanny ability to create a space where he felt safe to express his thoughts and feelings, no matter how complex or difficult they might be. She was young, but both his father and her uncle had occasionally referred to her as an "old soul", and Darcy agreed with this assessment. He knew she had already dealt with significant loss in her life; her parents were not dead, but they had sent her away from her family. Yes, the Gardiners had welcomed her into their family, but she was essentially an orphan, separated from parents who had cast her aside. Her grief over this loss provided her with a perspective that often helped him as he faced the sorrow of losing his mother several years ago and, soon, his father.

When his mother had died, Darcy had been forced to be strong. His father's grief was so deep that it was his son, though only fourteen at the time, who had helped with Georgiana as often as he could, providing the familial affection that was missing with Lady Anne gone. For nearly a year, his father's grief had been all-consuming, forcing the son to take charge of managing the estate, although he received considerable help. His uncle, Lord Matlock, provided advice and assistance, particularly when young Darcy was away at school. Eventually, he took his brother-in-law in hand, urging him to shake off his overwhelming grief and re-engage with the world.

Upon returning home from his final year at Eton, Darcy found a father who had once again taken charge of the estate. The young man remained involved in its running, though not as much as he had been for the previous year, and the two resumed a more normal father-son relationship. Despite this, the elder Darcy had never completely returned to himself, depending heavily upon his son and ensuring he was prepared to take over the estate's management. This became far more important now that he was truly dying.

Elizabeth was a beacon amidst the turmoil in his life. While many would view Bingley as his closest friend, in truth, Elizabeth understood him far better. She knew more about his thoughts and feelings than anyone else, even more than Bingley, who was far more likely to avoid serious topics than listen to Darcy share his burdens. Bingley was jovial and pleasant to be around, but it was Elizabeth whom he turned to when he was frustrated or uncertain.

A fortnight into the visit, on the Saturday before Bingley was to depart for the north on Monday, an unexpected carriage arrived at

Pemberley while much of the family, including the Gardiner children and Georgiana, were on the front lawn enjoying a few games. Much to everyone's surprise, a tall, thin young lady disembarked from the carriage, accompanied by a maid, and she eyed the manor and park greedily. She was quick to hide her displeasure at the frivolity that was taking place in front of her, though as soon as she spotted her brother standing next to her prey, she began to make her way toward the pair.

Chapter Nine

"Charles," the lady called in a piercing voice as she descended from the carriage, "Louisa sent me to collect you and take you to Scarborough for you were expected days ago. The wedding cannot proceed without your presence since you must sign the settlements and give her away. I knew that, given your closeness to Mr. Darcy, you would be reluctant to leave as scheduled."

Bingley frowned when his sister's words reached him. "I am scheduled to leave on Monday and have already made preparations to do so. There was no reason for you or Louisa to collect me, as I had already sent several letters, each clearly stating my intentions to arrive on Wednesday. As you have come to Pemberley uninvited, what is your plan for the next two days? You cannot travel on a Sunday, which you must have already known."

She scoffed, "Surely Pemberley is large enough that you could impose upon your friend to beg for a room for your sister to stay until we can leave on Monday. Though, perhaps, the Darcys would wish us to stay a few extra nights. There is still above a fortnight before Louisa's wedding, and she seems to have it all well in hand."

Bingley sent a pleading look to his friend, requesting his aid in this situation. "I will ask Mrs. Reynolds to prepare a room, but you must impress upon her that she is not an invited guest, and she is never to attempt this again. I suppose I must agree to an introduction, though I am loath to reward her presumption in this way," Darcy replied, his voice quiet and obviously displeased.

Mrs. Gardiner stepped forward to offer her assistance. "William, would you like me to escort this young lady into the house while you speak to the housekeeper and inform your father of your unexpected guest?" Her tone was kind, but there was something in it that made Caroline Bingley flush.

"Thank you for your assistance, Mrs. Gardiner," Darcy replied, grateful for the offer. "Bingley, if you would please go with them to handle the necessary introductions. Miss Bingley, kindly go with Mrs. Gardiner. She will make sure you are settled while I speak to the housekeeper and my father about your arrival. You and your brother will depart as scheduled on Monday. I will extend you some small measure of hospitality based on my friendship with your brother, but your arrival is an imposition. Do not repeat such an action again." His voice was firm and once again, Miss Bingley could not help but flush, this time with shame at being reprimanded.

Caroline Bingley, though visibly annoyed by the perceived slight, nodded and followed Mrs. Gardiner toward the house. Darcy watched them go, a sense of unease settling over him at this guest. He turned to Bingley, who looked both apologetic and frustrated.

"I am sorry, Darcy," Bingley said quietly as he began to make his way toward the house behind his sister. "I did not anticipate her arriving or acting in such a way. She has not been introduced to you or your family; even she must recognise this as a serious breach of propriety."

"It is not your fault, Bingley," Darcy reassured his friend. "But we must ensure she understands the boundaries. Pemberley is not a place for such presumptions. She will not be welcome to join the family for meals or entertainment though I suppose she ought to be permitted to attend church with us. Other than that, she will have to stay confined to her rooms. She may visit the grounds accompanied by a footman or a maid, but she is not to wander the house unaccompanied. A footman will be assigned to stand outside her rooms, and her maid's activities will be likewise restricted."

Bingley nodded, looking genuinely contrite. "I will speak to her, Darcy. I promise I will tell her what you have said and make your displeasure, as well as my own, known to her. I cannot believe that Louisa encouraged this behaviour and wondered how she managed to travel so far."

Darcy watched his friend make his way into the house behind his sister before heading that way himself. He needed to speak with Mrs. Reynolds about the restrictions on the lady and inform his father of their unexpected guest. Still, he could not help but feel a sense of irritation at today's events. Caroline Bingley's blatant attempt to insert herself into their plans was unwelcome, and he could only hope that her stay would be uneventful.

Back on the lawn, Elizabeth watched the scene unfold with a mixture of curiosity and concern. She had not missed the tension in Darcy's expression or the way Caroline Bingley had eyed him with clear intent. Though she was not yet out, she had heard enough stories about avaricious women who sought to tie themselves to a man for fortune and connections, and even she recognised that Pemberley itself would be a significant draw for most women. She listened when the men spoke and knew that despite what was commonly reported in society, the Darcy family brought in far more each year than most people knew.

As Mrs. Gardiner and Caroline disappeared into the house, Elizabeth followed and approached Darcy as he sought out the housekeeper.

"You will be cautious around Miss Bingley, will you not?" she said as she came up behind him. "I may be young, but I can recognise a mercenary woman when I see one. Is not Mr. Bingley's family from trade? I think his sister desires to use you to raise her status."

Darcy whirled around to glare at Elizabeth. "You are far too perceptive for your own good, Elizabeth. But yes, I intended to take precautions. I will let the staff know Miss Bingley is not to be anywhere in the house unescorted, aside from her own rooms, and her maid is to be watched as well. I will station a footman outside her rooms and another at the entrance to the family wing."

"And the servants' hallways in these areas?" Elizabeth inquired.

Frowning, Darcy stared at Elizabeth for another moment. "Perhaps I will have another footman stationed in the back hallway near mine and my father's rooms. It may be presumptuous, but I suppose in this instance, it is better to be overly cautious."

"I struggle to believe that any woman could truly act in such a way, but I have heard the stories about ladies who attempt to compromise men to force them into a marriage. For years, I watched the relationship between my parents, and more recently, I have seen how my aunt and uncle relate to one another, and I would infinitely prefer a marriage made for mutual love and affection. My father would not stand up to my mother and allowed her nerves and complaining to dictate his actions. There was no love there—not for his wife, and certainly not for his children. Had he loved any of us, he would have stood up to my mother and demanded that she love their children equally. My Aunt and Uncle have that sort of relationship, one based on mutual love and respect for the other. They have been married for more than a decade, and their love has grown stronger as they have faced life's difficulties together. When I marry one day, if I marry, I want a marriage like theirs," Elizabeth concluded.

Darcy nodded. "Fortunately, I have spent little time in society so far, having been largely spared that experience due to my father's illness. I attended a few events this season when required, but they were quite miserable. There were far too many people, and everyone seemed focused solely on a person's monetary or social worth. No one showed interest in my character, likes, or dislikes. I have no desire to make a match based on wealth and connections, and my father shares that sentiment. I remember discussing it with him last year, and he encouraged me to find someone who sees me as a person, not someone who merely sees the Darcy name with its Fitzwilliam connections. My Aunt Matlock has been continually pushing me to seek the most well-connected and well-dowered young lady, but that is not what I want. Not that I am contemplating marriage. If my father dies before summer ends, as we suspect, it will be at least a year, if not longer, before I even consider looking for a wife."

Elizabeth grinned at him. "I am uncertain if I wish you to be married or unmarried when I come out in society. Uncle Gardiner has said that he will find someone to sponsor me when I reach the proper age—my aunt wishes me to come out in two years, though I have tried to argue that I should wait until I am eighteen."

"Your birthday was in May, was it not?" Darcy asked.

She laughed. "Yes, and you were at my birthday dinner, sir, so I am astounded that you could forget. Aunt Gardiner says that since I turn eighteen in the middle of the season, I should not wait until the following year but begin attending events at seventeen. Since Uncle Gardiner is in trade, I will attend fewer events, and likely few of the same events that you attend, but I do hope you will partner with me a time or two when the time comes."

"It would be a pleasure, Miss Gardiner," he said formally, with a bow that made her giggle. "In fact, might I ask for your first dance, whenever and wherever that may be, after your dance with your uncle, of course?"

She curtseyed with equal formality. "I would be delighted to accept your invitation, Mr. Darcy," she replied, though she let out another laugh as she answered. Their *tête à tête* was interrupted by a cleared throat behind them.

"Sir, I was informed that you were looking for me," Mrs. Reynolds said, her tone filled with warmth. Although she appeared displeased—most likely due to her encounter with their uninvited guest—she clearly adored the two people in front of her, and her affection was evident in her voice as she spoke to them.

"I was, Mrs. Reynolds. I take it from the look on your face that you have already met our ... guest," Darcy stated tiredly.

"Yes, and Mrs. Gardiner told me a few things about the woman. I have already tasked one footman to be on guard outside Miss Bingley's chambers and another stationed in the family wing. There will be others in the servants' passages in that wing, and I have informed the staff that the lady's maid is to be escorted everywhere. Neither she nor Miss Bingley will be able to go anywhere within the grounds of Pemberley without being observed by someone."

"Thank you, Mrs. Reynolds. I intended to ask you to do exactly as you have already done. As usual, it seems you have anticipated my thoughts and ensured that everything is taken care of as it should be. Please have someone assigned to serve Miss Bingley all her meals, as I do not wish for her to join the family at those times either. She will have to attend church with us in the morning, but she will ride with her brother in their carriage, not in mine. They will not sit in our pew; it will be full on the morrow," Darcy finished.

"I met the woman only briefly, but she is the sort to cause trouble, if allowed. Her brother will have a time finding someone to marry her, and she obviously wishes it to be you or someone like you. I will ensure your father is well looked after as well, though I do not think she would try anything with him. Your father would refuse to marry her even if she managed a compromise, as he still views himself as married to your mother," Mrs. Reynolds said, flushing when she realised how bold she had been in speaking to the almost-master about a guest, even one who was uninvited.

No one saw Bingley again until that evening. It was obvious from his demeanour that he had a difficult afternoon while speaking with his sister. "Darcy, I cannot say enough how sorry I am for my sister's actions. She was quite displeased to learn that she would not be able to ingratiate herself into your presence and was livid when the maid arrived to bring her the meal. I was unfortunately passing by her room when the maid scurried out of the room, carrying the ruined tray. Caroline will not be satisfied until she has made a fool of herself. I am astonished that the younger sister I once knew could have turned into such a harpy, but I am afraid that school did more to ruin her than to help her."

Darcy, who was sitting with Elizabeth, stood and clasped his friend on the shoulder in silent acceptance. "Has she entered society yet?"

Bingley shook his head. "No. Our mourning for our father has only just ended. That is why Louisa is finally to marry; she and Gilbert Hurst preferred to wait until the mourning period was over, so no one thought ill of us for rushing things. Caroline finished at the girls' school my father enrolled her in just this past spring and has decided, based on what she had heard me say, that you are the ideal suitor to raise her standing within the ton. She was insistent that once you met her, you would be convinced she is the perfect woman to become the mistress of such a grand estate."

"After her behaviour today, especially arriving as she did, it is unlikely I would have ever considered her for such a position. It is likely I will soon be in mourning myself and do not intend to seek a bride for several more years. When I do, it will be with a woman I can genuinely care for and who values me more for myself than for Pemberley," Darcy told him. "From the look in her eye when she stepped down from her carriage, Miss Bingley desires Pemberley for itself, and could not care less about the man who comes with it."

At this, Elizabeth trilled a light, happy laugh. "I am uncertain about that, William. I noticed her expression when she first saw you. While she might be eager to take Pemberley regardless of its owner, she certainly seemed quite taken with your handsome appearance this afternoon."

When Darcy's face turned a brilliant shade of red, Elizabeth laughed cheerfully again. After a moment of stunned surprise, first Bingley, then Darcy joined her in the laughter. The Gardiners and the elder Mr. Darcy were surprised at the sounds they heard coming from the room when they joined the young people.

"Here now," the elder Mr. Darcy said insistently, "what is the cause of all of this mirth? I expected to find the lot of you in an ill-humour after our unexpected arrival, and while I am pleased to find you in good spirits, I am curious to know what caused it."

For some reason, this statement made Bingley laugh harder and it was Darcy who finally found his voice and responded to his father. "It is probably not that amusing, sir, but Miss Elizabeth here mentioned how pleased Miss Bingley was at my appearance. It disconcerted me somewhat, and then we all found it rather amusing."

Elizabeth's uncle frowned. "Were you impolite, Elizabeth?"

Elizabeth shook her head, but before she could defend herself, Darcy interjected. "Not at all, sir. I usually find Miss Elizabeth's opinions and her direct way of expressing them quite refreshing, and that was certainly the case this time as well. She simply caught me by surprise, that is all. She is a remarkably astute young lady, very skilled at reading others and getting to the heart of the matter."

Gardiner merely nodded, eyeing the young man and his niece for several long moments. Concluding nothing was amiss, he continued: "Bingley, how was your conversation with your sister? I gather that she was not pleased to learn her machinations would not work?"

Once again, Bingley hung his head slightly and shook it as though to clear a memory. "I am convinced that school did her no favours. Caroline believes that a man will overlook her status as a tradesman's daughter and wish to marry her for her accomplishments and her fortune. While that might be true in some cases, almost all the men she desires to wed—for she believes she is destined for a wealthy gentleman at least, if not a member of the peerage—would find it difficult to accept her as a bride, unless he direly needed that fortune, due to her status as the daughter of a tradesman. Forgive me, I do not mean to speak ill of anyone, but I know, Darcy, that were it not for your friendship with me, I would not be as accepted as I am in society. There are simply too many well-dowered and much better-connected women available for men like you to choose from. Caroline has little to offer a man like you, but you are precisely the kind of man she desires."

"As I said earlier, Bingley, your sister is the opposite of what a man like me wants in a wife. And that has little to do with her status," Darcy replied.

"Let us change the topic to a more pleasant one," Mrs. Gardiner interjected, believing this conversation had gone on long enough. "Mr. Bingley, you are to depart on Monday for your sister's wedding, are you not?" At his nod, she continued. "Then we should make tonight's dinner something of a farewell. I have a feeling tomorrow will be eventful. Your gardeners warned of a summer storm on the morrow and informed me and the children that they are a sight to behold."

With this, the conversation turned more general, and the topic of Caroline Bingley was avoided for the rest of the evening. The party soon moved to the dining room, where they enjoyed a sumptuous meal, before retiring to the music room, where Mrs. Gardiner and Elizabeth both graced the party with music.

Chapter Ten

That night was the last dinner with Mr. George Darcy. The summer storm that came through late Saturday night and lasted into Sunday morning prevented the party at Pemberley from attending church. Miss Bingley was seriously displeased by her stay at the grand estate and left with her brother the following day. She expected a far greater welcome than what she had endured, having believed she could use her brother's welcome to engender her own. She did not seem to understand that her actions would make others view her as grasping and impolite and so was unable to account for how they treated her or why her brother was angry at her now.

The elder Mr. Darcy suffered from a summer cold, caused by the dampness of the storm on the Sabbath. When he did not stir from his bed after two days, the apothecary was summoned from Lambton. His son was saddened to hear the dampness appeared to have settled into his father's lungs, more so when he began to worsen quickly. Within a fortnight of his first acquiring the cold, the elder Mr. Darcy passed from this earth, rejoining his wife for whom he had pined since her own death eight years previously.

However little he liked it, Mr. Gardiner found it necessary to leave Pemberley to return to London only a few days after his friend became ill. He had spoken to both Darcy men and explained the circumstances, during which the elder Darcy asked the tradesman to help his son as he made the transition to master.

"Fitzwilliam is well prepared for the task of managing Pemberley, however little he may believe it himself. In truth, he has been the one making decisions for Pemberley for the last several years, despite his being in school. I have only assisted though my son believes it to have been the opposite. He has proven to be a good judge of character, and I was a fool for not believing him about George Wickham sooner than I did. I am sorry he nearly injured your niece, but I am glad that his actions brought my family together with yours," the elder Darcy said, his words slow as he attempted to say to his friend what desperately needed to be said.

He turned his eyes toward his son, who was sitting on the other side of him. "Fitzwilliam, you are a good man, and you will do well. You saw through George Wickham when I did not. My own opinions of him were coloured by the belief that he was more like his father than he turned out to be. After … after your mother died, it was simply easier to be with George than it was to be with you. You … you reminded me so much of your mother, and I was lost without her. Young George was lively and jovial where you were serious. I know you were affected by the loss of your mother just as much as I, but it was difficult. Regardless of the reason, I should have tried harder to be the father you needed and should have trusted your word. Forgive me," he pleaded.

"Of course, Father," young Darcy replied.

"After I am gone, you must lean on Mr. Gardiner and your uncle, allowing them to advise you. Be cautious of those who would use you; your friend Bingley is a good man, but I fear the influence of his sister and what it may do to him. I have told you before that I think Miss

Gardiner is well suited to you; despite her youth, I think she will make you an ideal wife in a few years."

When Gardiner made a small noise in surprise, the dying man stopped to look at his friend. "You and I have spoken of the matter, Gardiner. Elizabeth is just fifteen at present but is far older in spirit than her years indicate. I am not suggesting that the two of them wed at this moment, but in two or three years, when they are older and if they both wish it, I believe they would do well together. Since I know how the *ton* can be, I have left your niece a legacy of fifteen thousand pounds. Use the interest from the funds to provide for her education and other necessities as she grows older. I have asked my sister, Lady Matlock, to sponsor her when it is time for her to debut in society, and if she cannot help you, she will find someone who can. I am uncertain whether she will be able to be presented, though if she becomes Mrs. Darcy as I hope, she would be presented then. Regardless, the Matlocks will support my son's decision to wed her, should he one day decide to do so."

"Mr. Darcy, this is too much: both the legacy and the suggestion of my niece marrying your son. They are not of the same status; surely you do not expect Fitzwilliam to agree to this," Gardiner protested.

"Mr. Gardiner, my father and I have spoken of this before. Your niece is a gentleman's daughter; therefore, I would not be marrying below my station. With the legacy from my father, which is a surprise to me, she will be the equal of many in society, certainly the superior to a woman such as Miss Bingley. I consider Miss Elizabeth a friend, and while she and I are too young to truly consider marriage at this time, I am not averse to the match should she prove amenable at a more appropriate time. I question my father's certainty that she is the ideal bride for me, but I believe she needs time to grow up before either of us are asked to decide."

Gardiner nodded, unsure how to react for a few moments. As he sat there contemplating the matter, a slow grin began to break out across his face. "Actually, I can easily imagine my niece wed to you,

Fitzwilliam. She has a knack for encouraging you to be livelier than you might otherwise, and she is constantly challenging you. Without her in your life, you would be set upon by ladies who would agree with everything you say, whereas Elizabeth would argue with you for the mere joy of it."

All three gentlemen laughed at this thought. "Elizabeth certainly has no qualms about arguing with me and has been known to argue a different standpoint just to extend a debate. Were she allowed to go to Cambridge, she would drive the professors there mad with her questioning and arguing, likely even trounce many of them out of sheer stubbornness. As her husband, I fear I would never win an argument ever again," Darcy barked out after a few minutes. The slight smile on his face as he said this surprised Gardiner although it did not surprise Darcy's father. He had seen the look that occasionally passed over his son's face when he spoke to or about Elizabeth Gardiner and knew the two would someday fall in love. In his opinion, the basis of a good relationship was already there, yet neither were presently aware of it.

When Mr. Gardiner departed a few days after this conversation, he left his wife and children at Pemberley to support Darcy's children during the inevitable loss of their father. The Matlocks arrived a few days later, but by that time, George Darcy was already insensible. Lady Matlock and Mrs. Gardiner did everything they could to assist Georgiana, working together to help Mrs. Reynolds prepare the house for mourning.

Lord Matlock worked with Fitzwilliam Darcy to ensure all was ready for the transition of power. In truth, there was little to be done, but his uncle merely confirmed that what he was doing was right and threw his weight as an Earl behind his nephew when required. The Darcy family was well respected in Derbyshire, so this was not truly necessary, but it gave young Darcy the boost he needed to get through these days.

However, Elizabeth's companionship aided Darcy the most through this difficult time. The couple still rode out each morning, their rides getting longer the worse the gentleman's father grew. Elizabeth was sitting with both Darcy men, holding the son's hand when the elder Mr. Darcy finally passed from this world, and she remained with him until his father's valet finally came to begin preparing the body for burial. Since it was summer, the burial would occur quickly. Notices were sent to the newspapers in London, as well as to all those in Darcy's family who had not already been informed.

Lord and Lady Matlock assisted as much as possible, and Lord Matlock himself wrote and sent the letter to his sister informing her of their brother's death, much to Darcy's relief.

> Catherine,
>
> To my great sorrow, I write to let you know that George Darcy has died. I know that both George and Fitzwilliam have written to you about his poor health over the last year, so this should come of little surprise. We are all saddened by the loss.
>
> As I am in close proximity to Pemberley, I am already here assisting our nephew with the arrangements. By the time you receive this letter, George will have already been laid to rest, as it is not prudent to wait for your arrival for his burial. I also want to assure you that there is no need for you to come to Pemberley. I will ensure that all of George's final wishes are carried out, and if he left anything for you or your daughter, I will see that you receive it. Additionally, I want to remind you that George stated repeatedly that his son and your daughter are not engaged, so do not presume that his death has changed that situation.
>
> Do <u>not</u> journey to Pemberley at this time. When you are needed, you will receive an invitation, but as Pemberley is now in mourning, Darcy does not wish for additional guests.

He will travel to London in the spring to take care of any necessary business then; I will join him on his annual visit Rosings at Easter. Georgiana is well, having been left to the guardianship of Fitzwilliam and my Richard. The two have always been good friends, almost as close as brothers, and I do not question George's wisdom in leaving his daughter to the two men who love her most.

Sincerely,
Reginald Fitzwilliam
Earl of Matlock

Darcy smiled when he read the letter by his uncle, only nodding before refolding it and handing it back to his uncle. "Do you think she will obey your demand that she remain where she is?" he asked.

Lord Matlock scoffed. "It is doubtful. I will remain a sennight further, and then Lady Matlock and I will return to our home on the following Monday. That way, if she arrives as I expect, we will be here. Regardless, if she arrives after, we will be less than half a day's journey away since we will not return to London until October. How much longer will Mrs. Gardiner and her children remain?"

"Part of me wishes they could remain through the winter. The house is livelier with the children in it. I appreciate what you and my aunt are doing, but Georgiana is very grateful for the company of a friend during this time. Elizabeth has been an excellent friend to her."

Lord Matlock examined his nephew for several minutes without speaking. Darcy held his eye and did not so much as flinch. "She is a good friend to you as well," he said finally.

"She is," was all Darcy would say in reply.

"Your father left me a letter and mentioned her in it," he sallied again.

"I know."

"Then you also know that your father wished my wife to sponsor Miss Gardiner in society when she makes her debut. She has a dowry of fifteen thousand pounds left to her by your father, and he is very much interested in advancing the match between you and Miss Gardiner in a few years," Lord Matlock stated.

"I am aware of it. My father discussed the matter with me on at least two separate occasions and shortly before Mr. Gardiner left for London, spoke of the matter with him. We are not engaged at this moment, nor have we promised to be so in the future. I have promised to consider her when she is old enough though if I fall in love with another or either of us decides we do not suit, we are not bound to the other."

Lord Matlock frowned. "No contracts have been signed?" he asked again.

"No."

"You must extricate yourself from this family then. Send them back to London; give Miss Gardiner the money your father left her if you must but have nothing else to do with them."

"No," Darcy stated, more firmly this time. "Elizabeth is a good friend to both my sister and me. I have little wish to forsake her friendship, nor that of the Gardiners for that matter. They have asked for nothing, demanded nothing. My father trusted them and even spoke to Mr. Gardiner of his wish that I offer for his niece one day. He could have demanded a formal contract be signed immediately—he could have asked for many things, —but attempted to persuade my father that the match was unwise. However, my father argued against all of his objections, insisting that he at least consider the idea before rejecting it out of hand."

The earl watched his nephew for several moments. "She is young—too young for you to have already decided in her favour."

"I have not decided. At present, she is a friend. I feel comfortable speaking with her, and she has been an enormous support over the last months as we have dealt with Father's illness. She is also a good friend to Georgiana and has been helping her through the grief. I am in mourning and will be for the next year. Elizabeth is only fifteen and has two or three more years before she will enter society. At that point, I will decide whether I wish to court her. She will write to Georgiana which will be our only contact for the next six months or until I return to London. You are worried about something that might or might not happen two years in the future. Should I decide to offer for her, she will accept me only if she loves me in return, and I will know she accepts me for who I am, not for what I have. If I am satisfied with that, and I am following my father's wishes in the matter, how can you object, Uncle?"

Scowling, Lord Matlock agreed that his nephew had a point, however little he liked it.

Chapter Eleven

A few days later, too soon for the letter from Lord Matlock to have reached Kent, Lady Catherine de Bourgh descended upon Pemberley. Immediately upon her arrival, she began to make demands and offer complaints to everyone in the household.

"I am most seriously displeased, brother, that neither you nor your nephew felt it necessary to inform me of my brother's ill health until after he had passed away. Nor can I understand why these interlopers have been allowed to remain in this house which ought to be a house of mourning. It is unseemly to have guests in the house who are unrelated to the family," she said upon being introduced to Mrs. Gardiner and Elizabeth.

"Lady Catherine–" Darcy began but was cut off by his uncle.

"Catherine, why are you here? You have known of George's ill health for some time and while we were all surprised at the suddenness of his death, we have known for months that it was inevitable. Had you truly wished to see him again, you would have come at the beginning of the summer when you were asked, or even visited him while he was in London in the spring," her brother asked in an equally haughty tone.

"I have come to ensure that Fitzwilliam does his duty and marries my Anne. I have had my solicitor draw up a marriage contract, and since you are here as well, you and Fitzwilliam should sign it, making the engagement official. It was the dearest wish of my sister Anne that our children marry, and now that Fitzwilliam has inherited Pemberley, he can marry Anne immediately. She can remain here with him, and I will return home to Rosings."

"Aunt–" Darcy began again, only to be interrupted by his uncle.

"You have wasted a journey then, Catherine since Anne never agreed to such a betrothal, and Fitzwilliam has no intention of marrying your daughter. You knew this, you have been told this multiple times by me, by Fitzwilliam, and even by George. We have repeatedly informed you, through verbal communication and letters, that Anne never agreed to such a betrothal, and that Fitzwilliam has no intention of marrying your daughter. Despite this, you chose to ignore everything we said.

"Fitzwilliam cannot wed until his year of mourning has passed. George and I spoke of the type of woman he wanted his son to wed, and he hoped his son would marry for love. Should our nephew fall in love with your daughter or decide on his own he wished to marry her, I would not object, but I will not allow you to bully him into a marriage based solely on your wishes. Other than you, Anne spoke of her desire for her son to marry your daughter to no one—not her husband, not her brother, not my wife, and not her son. You are the only person who believes she wished for the match," Lord Matlock stated.

"She did. We spoke of it when both children were still in their cradles. Fitzwilliam is now the master of Pemberley; it is the perfect time for the two to wed. Anne is not yet of age, but she will do as I command."

"Catherine, I hope your men have not unloaded your carriages just yet. My wife and I were to depart for Matlock shortly; you and your daughter will accompany us there. I will not allow you to harass our nephew in an attempt to force him to comply with your wishes in this matter when he is already dealing with so many other things." He turned toward his nephew and spoke quietly. "Darcy, I will write to you but let me know if there is anything that you need from me. I suppose other matters will have to wait for the moment, but we will speak again when I see you in London in the spring, if not sooner. For now, I will escort Catherine to Matlock myself; please inform my wife that I have departed and to follow me soon with our things. She will understand my haste."

And with that, he escorted his sister into the hallway and back out to her coach, where the carriages were not unloaded, nor did anyone seem to be in a hurry to do so. With a brief wave to his nephew, he helped his sister and niece back into the carriage and instructed the driver to take them directly to Matlock.

Mrs. Gardiner and Elizabeth remained at Pemberley a fortnight after Lady Catherine's visit. Though Elizabeth wished to remain longer to stay with her friends and support them, Mrs. Gardiner was anxious to return home to her husband. Reluctantly Elizabeth agreed with her aunt, and the two departed for London, along with the Gardiner children, who were equally disappointed to depart from the country for smelly London.

"Please write to me often," Georgiana pleaded with Elizabeth as the two stood in the great hall on the day the Gardiners were to leave. "I have so enjoyed having you all here and will miss your company. I know we are in mourning, and should not be having fun, but the house will be so quiet without you all here with us. William will be eternally busy, and I will have so little company."

"Georgiana," Darcy scolded gently. "Mrs. Gardiner needs to return home, as do her children. They intended to remain only a month and have been here nearly twice that long to be of use to us during our time of need. Mrs. Gardiner and the children miss their father, and it would be inappropriate for Elizabeth to remain here without them. We will see them again in London in the spring, though it is possible we will have a reason to journey there in the autumn."

"Truly, William?" she asked excitedly.

"I cannot say for certain yet, Sprite. But it is possible I will need to travel to London in October or November. You know that Uncle will be in town for the beginning of Parliament then, and we will be just entering half-mourning near Christmastide. I am uncertain whether I would prefer to be at Pemberley or in town for the holiday, but we will decide nearer to the time and see what might occur. Regardless, we will certainly be in London in the spring. In the meantime, you can write to Elizabeth and use my messenger when it is feasible."

"Thank you, William," she gushed, then turned to her friend and said in a hushed voice: "Write to me often," she repeated before watching her brother step out the main door with Mrs. Gardiner on his arm. "Write to William as well since I feel certain your letters will help to brighten the frown he wears perpetually since our father's death. He is so busy now that he is the master of the estate; I cannot recall Father working quite so hard."

"Hush, Georgie," Elizabeth reprimanded gently. "Your brother has had a significant burden thrust upon him, and he wants to do what is best for the estate and all those who rely on him. He is scarcely less busy now than he was at the beginning of our visit; it is only your perception of his work that has changed. Although you are only ten, you can help him by refraining from scolding him for working hard and by doing what you can to assist. You should focus on your lessons and perhaps play for him occasionally. You are quite skilled on the pianoforte, and you know he enjoys listening to you."

"I fear there is little I can do to help him," she whispered.

"Ask him about his day. Do not pressure him. Go riding with him on occasion and force him to leave his study. Even try rising early, at least once a week, to join him on his morning rides. If he does not leave his study, tell me, and I will scold him in a letter or have my uncle do it. I know it is difficult, Georgiana, but you can lighten his load by attempting to be cheerful yourself. You both miss your father, and I promise, it is equally difficult for him."

Her voice was almost inaudible when she said: "He had Father for longer; I feel like I had so little time with him. And I cannot remember our mother at all."

Elizabeth pulled the younger girl in for a hug. "I do understand what you are feeling, Georgie. We cannot control these things; we can only do the best with what we have. You had ten years with an excellent father and now you have an excellent brother who will do everything in his power to be what you need. You have your aunt, Lady Matlock, and my aunt to support you, and me to be your friend. Truly, Georgiana, you have much to be thankful for. Be grateful for the time you did have and remember how much he loved you."

"I will do my best, but you will need to remind me on occasion, Elizabeth. I will miss you."

"And I will miss you. Now, come, let me say goodbye to your brother and then we must depart. My aunt is anxious to return home because she misses her husband." She took her friend's hand and led her toward the front stairs where the rest of the party waited.

The children and Mrs. Gardiner were already in the carriage, having said their goodbyes earlier. Darcy was standing by the carriage door, having helped the children in first and was still exchanging a few final words with Mrs. Gardiner.

"Elizabeth, we must go, my dear. Say your goodbyes quickly," her aunt called.

Darcy took a few steps to meet her and stood in front of her. "I will miss you, Elizabeth. You have been a good companion on my rides. I fear Georgiana will not be as willing to accompany me in the mornings."

"I have become quite the horsewoman this summer. It is too bad I will have little chance to ride while in London, but I hope to return to Pemberley someday. You may have to endure my poor riding a third time since I will no doubt have forgotten all I learned by then," Elizabeth said brightly, though in truth, she was very sad to be leaving both of the Darcys. They had become even more dear to her during this visit, and she wished she could stay with them in the country.

"I would gladly suffer through more lessons with you if it meant you could join me on my rides as you have. I will miss you."

She smiled up at him, her smile not quite reaching her eyes. "Georgiana told me to write to you. I have not forgotten our conversation about how it is not improper since we are cousins, of a sort. Do you still wish to me to write to you?"

"I do," he said, his smile happier than she had seen in some time. "Your uncle approved our writing to each other in his last letter. Since your uncle and my father approved our friendship, I have no qualms at all about continuing it in this manner. In fact, I have a letter for you to read on your way to London."

This time, her smile did reach her eyes. "How scandalous, sir," she teased. "Not yet out, and already receiving secret correspondence from a gentleman. I have told Georgiana to accompany you on your rides in my place, at least occasionally. Do not isolate yourself in your study and forget everything else. She is hurting, and I know you are as well. Lean a little on each other. Speak of your father, and your mother, for Georgiana knows little about her. I think it was too painful for your father to speak of her, but now Georgiana is missing her too and feeling a little lost that she is an orphan at such a young age."

Darcy nodded. "You can sympathise with her, can you not? Perhaps you can advise me on this through your letters as well. She is so much younger that I am sometimes uncertain how best to approach her."

"Just spend time with her. I know you are busy but make a deliberate effort to spend a little bit of time with her each day. Perhaps have dinner or breakfast with her a few times a week as you can. If you need ideas, you can write to me, and I can make suggestions."

"Thank you, Elizabeth; I will do as you ask," Darcy said, before gently pulling her in for a hug and pressing a chaste kiss to her forehead. "I will see you soon." After helping her into the carriage, he shut the door and latched it, remaining where he was. Elizabeth watched him until the carriage crested the hill, and she could no longer see him.

Chapter Twelve

SPRING, 1808

For the next two years, Elizabeth corresponded frequently with Georgiana Darcy. She also exchanged letters with Fitzwilliam Darcy, usually included inside a letter to Georgiana or sent under the cover of her uncle's letters. This limited the number of letters the two were able to exchange. Additionally, due to a variety of circumstances, Darcy did not see Elizabeth in person during this time.

Problems at Pemberley kept the Darcy siblings in Derbyshire the following two springs, and when they did journey to town for essential business, circumstances prevented the Gardiners from visiting their friends. During the first summer, a difficult confinement kept Mrs. Gardiner at home, and Elizabeth had to assist with the children and her aunt, which prevented any visits between the friends. The following summer, Darcy came to town for a fortnight, but the Gardiners had taken Elizabeth and their children on a short trip into the country for a brief respite.

During the autumn of 1807, Darcy was in town, but Elizabeth was away in Bath attending a girl's school for a brief time to prepare for her introduction to society. Mr. Gardiner did have an opportunity to call on the young man during this time and reported to Elizabeth that he seemed well enough, though Elizabeth was concerned that he was working too hard. She conveyed this thought in her letter and received a teasing note in response, placating her, though she remained worried for him.

The early part of 1808 was spent preparing for Elizabeth to come out in society. Lady Matlock had agreed to sponsor her in society, even going so far as to obtain her a voucher for Almack's and to agree to host a ball in her honour. She claimed Elizabeth as a distant relation, the daughter of a school friend, as a reason for her sponsorship.

Once again, Darcy's journey to London for the season was delayed though he promised faithfully to attend the ball hosted by Lady Matlock in Elizabeth's honour. He arrived in town on the day of the ball and rushed to prepare himself that evening. Though he was pleased to see his friend again, he was less excited about being forced to attend a ball so soon after his arrival. Since becoming Master of Pemberley, he was highly sought after by all the matchmaking mothers and their insipid daughters, perhaps more so because of his infrequent attendance at such events and his reluctance to dance with any of the women.

However, this night he could not enter late and remain on the edges of the ballroom as he preferred since he had requested a dance from Elizabeth. He had been granted her third; her first was claimed by her uncle and her second by his. He had also requested that Elizabeth reserve the supper set for him while promising not to hold her to it if she found another gentleman she wished to dance that set with.

Darcy imagined her laughter when she read that line in her letter, as she had written back with:

> *"Do not think you can escape your duty so easily, sir. Your aunt has told me how much you detest dancing in*

general; since you have requested this set from me, I will hold you to it. Perhaps your dislike of the activity has much to do with your dislike of making small talk with others. You might therefore practice on me during our two sets and perhaps find a way to enjoy dancing more."

It was easy to imagine her laughing at his attempt to get out of dancing since her letter caused him to laugh out loud, something he rarely did except when time he received a letter from *her*. He was looking forward to seeing her again in person, recalling the girl he knew from the last summer she had spent at Pemberley.

When Darcy arrived at Matlock House, the receiving line had already formed. He quickly spotted his aunt and uncle in the gathering crowd, but he was stunned when he saw the young woman standing beside his aunt. Surely this stunning beauty could not be his friend Elizabeth —the same girl who had ridden across the estate with him on horseback and played games with him and Georgiana in the nursery. In the two and a half years since he had last seen her, she had blossomed into a strikingly lovely woman, and there was no mistaking the way his body reacted to the sight of her.

Her hair was artistically coiffed on top of her head with little ringlets framing her face. Diamond and pearl hairpins added a touch of sparkle and contrast to the chocolate-brown richness of her hair without appearing ostentatious. Her green eyes seemed even brighter, accentuated by the emeralds that adorned her neck. Finally, Darcy allowed his gaze to take in the rest of her appearance. She wore a white dress, as all debutantes did for their presentation balls, trimmed with green ribbons to complement the jewels she wore.

The dress fit perfectly, accentuating her slender waist and flowing gracefully to the ground. Under the light, the delicate fabric shimmered softly, enhancing both her natural elegance and pleasing figure. The emerald ribbons added a touch of vibrant colour, drawing attention to her graceful movements. Darcy could not help but admire how the entire ensemble showcased her beauty and poise. The gown had a modest cut, yet it revealed more of her graceful neck than he had seen before.

It took several moments for his feet to obey his command to move forward. He hoped no one had noticed his dumbstruck expression as he gazed at her, utterly captivated. His heart raced, and he silently prayed for the strength to regain his composure before anyone could see the effect she had on him. Judging from the amused expression on his cousin Richard's face, whom he had not noticed until that very moment, it had been. "Well, cousin, what do you think of the fair Miss Gardiner now?" Major Richard Fitzwilliam, second son of the Earl of Matlock, asked as he approached Darcy.

"She is lovelier than I could have imagined. I have not seen her since the summer my father passed away, and I will admit to being surprised at the change from the girl I knew to the woman who stands before me now. I am extraordinarily pleased that I have already claimed two dances with her, the third and the supper."

Richard grinned at his cousin. "About that, Darcy, Mother informed me that you had claimed the supper set but had given Miss Gardiner the opportunity to decline. I hate to tell you, but she chose me for her partner for that dance instead. You will have to find another young lady to ask for that set."

"Not a chance in hell, Richard. The supper set is mine, and I meant to claim it. I have it from Elizabeth's own pen that she intends to hold me to my promise to dance that set with her, and I will not allow her to recant on her promise," Darcy said in a rare show of possessiveness. The idea that Elizabeth would prefer his cousin to him angered him in a way that he had never before experienced, and he intended to spend whatever time he could in Elizabeth's presence that night.

Richard laughed. "Are you smitten so quickly, cousin?"

For a moment, Darcy halted in his steps toward the receiving line. He was uncertain what he felt; he had always viewed Elizabeth as a friend but seeing her now and hearing Richard attempt to take her from him had him feeling out of sorts. "I do not know what I am," he admitted softly after a moment of reflection. "There is no question that we are friends, but just now, I felt a possessiveness toward her that I have never felt for another person. I did not like the idea of you taking her attention away from me."

That admission just made his cousin's grin widen. "You are smitten. How will you woo the fair lady?"

Again, the question made Darcy falter. "I have no idea, Richard." He contemplated the matter for a moment and quietly continued, "Do you know that my father spoke of me marrying Elizabeth shortly before he died? Actually, that was the second time he mentioned it; the first was shortly after we met her, when she stood up to him about Wickham. He was so insistent that she would make a good match for me that he left her a bequest to serve as her dowry to aid her when she entered society. He knew she would have a difficult time with her relations being in trade but thought that having a respectable dowry would make things a little easier for her."

Richard nodded. "Father told me when I returned home a month ago and met her again. Apparently, he thought I acted too familiarly with her, and he informed me that she was intended for you."

"Truly?" Darcy asked, astonished that the earl was supporting the match. "I had believed he was against the idea, but I admit that we have not spoken of it since shortly after Father died. She is an intriguing young lady; perhaps she found a way to win him over."

This made Richard laugh. "Father adores her. I think he has begun to believe Mother's claim that they truly are related. He often refers to her as his 'ward' in company and is nearly as proud of her as Gardiner is. You know he has claimed her second dance and tried to insist that he should be allowed to lead her out for the first instead of her own uncle. He might disown *you* should you fumble the courtship."

Darcy let out a laugh, causing several eyes to turn in his direction. His eyes immediately sought Elizabeth's, and he instantly knew when she saw him in return. The smile she gave him was brilliant, and their eyes locked. Time stretched on as Darcy's surroundings faded away, leaving only Elizabeth.

A hand grasping his shoulder halted his involuntary movement forward. "You mustn't appear too eager for the lady, Darcy, or she will know the power she has over you."

He promptly shook it off. "Richard, you are a fool. I have not spoken to Elizabeth in two and a half years, and I intend to do so now, whether or not you approve. I may know nothing of 'wooing' a lady, as you call it, but if there is anything I do know, it is how to speak to Elizabeth."

Leaving his cousin behind, he perfunctorily greeted first his aunt and uncle, before moving to stand in front of Elizabeth, clasping her hands in his. He found his claim that he knew how to speak to Elizabeth to be false, and it took him a moment to form the words. "You are beautiful tonight, Elizabeth," he whispered huskily. He cleared his throat in an attempt to dislodge whatever was there. "I am happy to see you again; you have become a striking young woman, and I am inordinately pleased to have already arranged two dances with you tonight. My cousin over there tried to claim he had stolen your supper set from me, but I will not allow such a thing, as I already know I will enjoy dancing with you tonight."

"What if I am a terrible dancer, Mr. Darcy?" she asked with an impish look at him.

"Then we will dance terribly together, but I will not care, because I will still be able to speak to you throughout." He lowered his voice and whispered for her alone: "And what is this Mr. Darcy business? I thought I was William?"

"We are in London, and I am now out. Your aunt told me I should not address you so informally in public."

He frowned slightly. "Perhaps we should not, but might I retain your permission to address you as Miss Elizabeth instead of Miss Gardiner? I would not care to treat you as a stranger now; we know each other too well for that."

Her laughter soothed him. "You are right. When no one can hear us, I will still address you as William unless you prefer I do not."

"No, Elizabeth, I admit that I enjoy hearing my name on your lips. Now, I have just arrived in town this afternoon with barely enough time to arrive here, and I know that I cannot claim all of your attention tonight, however much I might desire it. I brought a mount with me from Pemberley that will be suitable for you to ride, and since you told me you have practised a little, I hope to have you out riding with me in the mornings when we can. You are staying with my aunt at Matlock House?"

Elizabeth nodded. "Since she is sponsoring me, she thought it would be best. She has also taken me to her modiste and purchased far more dresses than I can imagine ever needing or wearing, but she insisted it was absolutely necessary. When will we ride?"

"The day after tomorrow," Darcy said, before giving way to the next arrival who stood behind him, annoyed that Darcy was taking up so much of the guest of honour's time.

Chapter Thirteen

After what felt like hours of greeting guests, it was finally time for the dancing to begin. Elizabeth moved gracefully across the dance floor, first with her uncle and then with the earl. Finally, it was time for her dance with Darcy. When he took her hands in his, a jolt of electricity seemed to pass between them, somehow marking her as his. It was a heady feeling, completely unfamiliar, and it seemed to occur only with him.

They smiled at each other as they took their places and began moving through the steps. Just as had happened when she saw him for the first time across the foyer a few hours ago, their gazes locked, and the rest of the room seemed to fade away. It was as if only the two of them moving across the dance floor, their steps in sync as though they had practised together many times before. Barely a word was spoken between them, but much was communicated regardless.

The music flowed around them, creating a perfect harmony that matched their movements. Darcy's touch was firm yet gentle, guiding her effortlessly through the intricate patterns of the dance. Elizabeth felt a familiar sense of familiarity, one she had often felt when they rode together across the fields at Pemberley.

As the dance continued, Elizabeth could not help but marvel at how natural it felt to be in Darcy's arms. Admittedly this was their first dance, but still, his presence was both comforting and exhilarating, and she found herself lost in the moment, completely absorbed by the man before her. The intensity of the connection was undeniable, and it left her feeling breathless.

When the music came to an end, they stood facing each other, their hands still clasped. The spell was broken when they heard the sounds of those around them clapping, but the effects of the dance lingered. Darcy's eyes held hers, and in that moment, Elizabeth knew that something profound had shifted between them.

"Thank you for the dance, Miss Elizabeth," Darcy said softly, his voice filled with genuine emotion.

"The pleasure was all mine, Mr. Darcy," she replied, her heart pounding in her chest as she took the arm he offered her to escort her back to her aunt and uncle.

"I cannot recall if I mentioned it before, but you look lovely tonight, Miss Elizabeth, utterly captivating. You have always been lovely, but I was astounded at the change from the girl I knew into the beautiful young woman who stands before me."

She felt her cheeks grow warm. "Thank you, Mr. Darcy. You look very well also; I daresay your valet found it challenging to have you presentable so quickly after arriving from Derbyshire."

This made Darcy laugh. "I have little doubt that he was cursing me for cutting it so close. I did at least send him ahead. He arrived yesterday as I had intended to do, but I was delayed somewhat by a letter just before we were supposed to depart. As a result, I left the day after my staff and rode most of the way so I would arrive in time."

"You rode all the way from Derbyshire?" Elizabeth asked, surprise evident in her tone as she turned to look at him.

"I rode a bit the first two days but rode most of today. My travelling coach arrived at my townhouse just as I was leaving the house to come here, so it was fortunate I did so. I suppose I could have still been ready, but I would have arrived at the last moment. I did not want to cause you concern."

"I am glad you made it on time, for I would have hated to have missed our dances. However, I prefer that you remain safe and well; you took a chance riding so far, did you not?"

"I was at least as safe riding my horse as I would have been in a carriage. I was not alone since I had a groom riding the horse I brought for you keeping me company. Do you worry for me, Miss Elizabeth?"

The almost flirtatious tone surprised Elizabeth in his voice. She had heard other gentlemen attempt to flirt with ladies before, and a few had attempted the same with her, but she was astonished that her friend William was acting in such a manner towards *her*. Knowing his distaste for society, she wondered what would cause him to act in such a way. "Of course I would worry for you, William. You are a dear friend."

They arrived at the side of her relatives, so he greeted them once more. Soon, Richard came to claim Elizabeth for the next dance, leaving Darcy standing beside her uncle. Elizabeth noticed that the two men appeared to be engaged in a serious conversation, and her partner observed her inattention.

"Are you well, Miss Elizabeth?" he inquired kindly.

"William and my uncle appear to be rather deep in conversation, and I wondered what could cause them to be so serious at a ball. I suppose William is frequently this way; he has not danced with anyone tonight."

"Except for you," Richard emphasised.

"Except for me," Elizabeth replied in a near whisper.

"William admires you, always has, but I think seeing you again after such a long time took him by surprise," Richard told her.

The dance separated them, allowing Elizabeth to think about what the gentleman meant by his comment. Finally, she returned to him and asked; "Whatever did you mean when you said I took him by surprise?"

"When my cousin last saw you, you were a girl still, too young to think of as other than a friend. Perhaps he is seeing you in a different light after not seeing you for so long."

Elizabeth stared at her partner, not speaking for several more turns. "I think you are implying something, sir, though I am uncertain if you are attempting to warn me off your cousin or encourage me toward him. If you are implying that he sees me differently now and is contemplating … what exactly? I know he is an honourable man, but surely with my connections to trade, I am far too low for him to contemplate marrying. Besides, as you have said, we have not seen each other in the last two years."

"But the two of you have corresponded. Perhaps not as frequently as you have with Georgiana, but I feel certain my ward would have shared each of your letters with her brother. He knows you very well and would not dream of offering anything less honourable than marriage, should he decide he wished it. Nor would he allow your family or his to separate you. Again, I am speculating, but you should not discount yourself. You may have relations in trade, but they are here tonight, are they not? My parents are not at all dismayed by the connection. My mother is sponsoring you in society; she would not object to you."

Shaking her head as though to clear it, Elizabeth retorted. "I do not even know why you broached this topic. If William—" she paused, shaking her head again. "—If Mr. Darcy desires to pursue a relationship with me other than friendship, then allow him to speak in his time. Your trying to put ideas in my head or confuse things between us will do no one any good. It is best you do not interject yourself into this and raise hopes before it is time. I like William—Mr. Darcy—very much, and consider him a good friend. For now, that is enough. If either of us decides to pursue something different, then allow *us* to sort things out."

The gentleman's laughter surprised her. "You are right, Miss Gardiner, and I will say no more. I do hope you will set William straight in the same manner, should he ever require it."

It was her turn to laugh. "You have not heard of the day we met, have you? I was rather direct with both Mr. Darcy and his father that day. Despite the events of that day and their potential for a very different ending, I cannot regret what happened, for it brought me into contact with this family. I like your cousins and your parents very much."

Again, it surprised Elizabeth when Richard laughed at her gibe. "But it also brought me into your life, though perhaps that is not as pleasant a subject after tonight. Regardless, I will endeavour to show you why I am Darcy's favourite cousin, and perhaps one day you will agree with him."

Fortunately, the dance ended, and Richard said nothing else when he escorted Elizabeth back to her uncle. Darcy was still standing there, and he gave his cousin a menacing glare. Richard only smirked in reply. Before Darcy could inquire of Elizabeth what he said to her, her partner for the next dance came to claim her. This pattern continued for several more dances until the supper set, when Darcy could reclaim her once more.

"Did my cousin upset you?" he asked immediately after taking her hand to place it on his arm.

Elizabeth sighed. "Not exactly. I was uncertain of his intentions which irritated me a little. I am unsure what he was seeking to accomplish, but I believe he will not importune me again. I *think* that after what I said to him, we might be friends … eventually." She laughed as she said this which eased Darcy's concerns somewhat.

"What was he speaking about?" he asked again, clearly noticing how Elizabeth seemed to blush at his questioning.

"He … he," she stammered, before sighing as the dance once again separated them. When they came back together, she blurted: "He hinted that you were attracted to me tonight. I told him not to attempt to raise hopes that could not possibly be fulfilled, and then he told me that no one in your family would object should you and I … I do not know what exactly he was attempting to say. He claimed he was not warning me away from you, and the more I say aloud, the more ridiculous the whole matter seems."

They were once again separated by the dance, and she noticed how Darcy sought out his cousin with his eyes and glared at him. Uncertain of the meaning, she faltered a little in the dance, and Darcy noticed, quickly pulling her out of the line of dancers. "Are you well?" he asked. "Do you need a drink, some fresh air? Is there anything I might do for you?"

As he was speaking, he led her toward a balcony that would give them a scant amount of privacy. "I am well," she said firmly. "It is just … as I said, I do not know what his purpose was, and it unsettled me. I told him that whatever there might be between us, it was best for us to sort through it all and that I was happy to be your friend, that if you desired for things to be different between us, that you could speak for yourself."

"Damn Richard," she heard him murmur, making her laugh though she was uncertain if it was in relief, in embarrassment, or because of another emotion entirely.

"He is an idiot, but I think he was attempting to be helpful. Elizabeth, we have been friends for many years, and, yes, when I saw you tonight, I think some of those feelings toward you shifted into something else. However, I do not even know what that means at this moment, so clearly, I had not intended to speak of this. I have always cared for you, not in a familial way since my stomach always revolted at the idea that you could be like a sister to me. I did not want you as my sister even when you were still a girl, or at least less of a lady than you are now. We have had a connection ever since we met. I hoped that we could come to know each other again as friends now that we are together in person, which was the purpose of me asking you to ride with me. If I were to ask you for a courtship, that would change things between us too soon, I think, and I am reluctant to do so. Not because I do not wish to court you, but I did not want your uncle to put the restrictions on me that he would if we were publicly courting. Am I making sense at all?"

Elizabeth laughed at this. "Yes, you are, William. And I would like to get to know the person you are again as well. I have also never felt particularly sisterly toward you; toward Georgiana, yes, but not toward you. That was why we decided to be cousins, was it not? I do not want to ruin the relationship we do have, our friendship, by forcing things to change before they should. So I agree. We should spend time in company with each other and get to know these new versions of ourselves before rushing into any decision about the future."

She almost laughed again when she noticed Darcy seeming to sag in relief. "Thank you, Elizabeth. As usual, you have said it better than I could. If only we had a glass of something so we could toast our friendship."

Laughing, the pair re-entered the ballroom, unaware of the jealous eyes watching Elizabeth charm the elusive gentleman by her side. Lady Matlock discreetly whispered in a few ears about Elizabeth's dowry of fifteen thousand pounds, ensuring that word of her eligibility would spread throughout the *ton*. This resulted in a few jealous eyes casting glances in Darcy's direction as well.

Chapter Fourteen

Just after eleven the following morning, Darcy paid a visit to his aunt's home, hoping to see Elizabeth. It was too early for morning calls since most of the visitors would wait until mid-afternoon to begin their visits. An early riser, Darcy struggled with the timing of events in town, which was yet another reason he avoided it as often as possible. He hoped that by calling early, he would have a chance to see and speak with Elizabeth privately, or as privately as could be managed with his aunt there.

"Good morning, Darcy," his aunt greeted him when he entered the drawing room where she and Elizabeth were sitting. Elizabeth smiled at him but was unable to speak. "I told Elizabeth that we would likely see you this morning. Your timing is fortuitous, for I wished to speak to you of our plans for the next several weeks."

"I do hope those plans include outings to museums and the theatre, else I will have to decline," Darcy replied dryly.

His aunt turned a shrewd eye on him. "You will attend several events a week with me and Elizabeth since we will need your assistance in squiring her about town, at least for the beginning of the season. She

WHEN LOVE IS TRUE

has a few friends, but I would prefer that you attend events with us, especially when my husband or sons cannot."

Darcy attempted not to roll his eyes. "I will attend whatever events you tell me I must, but I beg that not all of them are dinner parties and balls. You know that I detest events when I am forced to make small talk for hours on end."

"I do know, nephew. And fortunately for you, Miss Gardiner prefers to go to museums, the theatre, and the opera, along with a litany of other cultural and musical events. While she seems to enjoy dancing, she has already complained several times about the late nights required during the season."

Elizabeth laughed. "I am an early riser. While I have lived in town for years, I have never fallen into the routine of so many society matrons, like you, Lady Matlock. Country hours are a far better fit for me."

This statement made Darcy grin at her. "Yes, I recall how much you enjoy mornings. Speaking of which, Aunt, I have asked Miss Elizabeth to join me for a morning ride whenever possible while we are in town. I know you keep to town hours, but I know Elizabeth's penchant for rising early and her need for frequent exercise. While not quite as early as I would normally prefer, might I come by at nine in the morning to collect Miss Elizabeth for our first ride?"

Lady Matlock looked between the two young people. "Elizabeth, you will need to take a footman with you, but I will give the order for one to be available to accompany you. Darcy, do you have a mount appropriate for her to ride? Side-saddle, not astride, as you allow Georgiana to do at Pemberley?"

Darcy grinned. "I do. And I assume you have had Miss Elizabeth prepared with a riding habit appropriate only for riding side-saddle? I taught her to ride both ways at Pemberley though it has been a while since I have been able to ride with her. I hope you have practised occasionally without me?"

Elizabeth frowned. "I have not had much opportunity to ride except on holiday last summer. My uncle and I rode for a brief while, but the mounts he acquired for us were far from Pemberley's standards."

"You will like the mount I brought for you. She is an Arabian, light of foot and energetic. I think even you cannot exhaust her, at least, not while in town. At Pemberley, I think she could ride all day long without tiring," Darcy told her.

"Perfect. Then an hour's amble through Hyde Park will be a very enjoyable form of exercise, especially after so many days spent in boredom and forced stillness. Do you know that your aunt has required me to purchase more gowns within the last month than I likely owned in my entire lifetime, William? She adores shopping apparently and believes that I must accompany her on all of her trips to the shops," Elizabeth complained, laughing as she did so and causing the others to laugh with her.

"My dear Elizabeth, you know that you cannot be seen in a gown more than once while in town. However, now that we have acquired a wardrobe for you, you can have some of those gowns repurposed at the end of each season. Until you marry, that is, at which point you will need an entirely new wardrobe."

Elizabeth groaned. "Then I will never marry, for I do not ever want to have to endure this torture ever again."

Once again, this elicited a laugh from the others. "Perhaps, Miss Elizabeth, you will meet a man who entices you enough that you will willingly submit yourself to the modiste once again. If not this season, then in the next?" Darcy teased.

Elizabeth did not rise to the bait. "Never, sir," she repeated. "For I would have to find a man as good as my Uncle Gardiner, and I am not sure he has an equal."

"And what does Gardiner do that makes him such an excellent man?" Darcy inquired, genuinely interested in how she would answer.

Elizabeth thought for a moment, and then responded seriously. "He brings my aunt her favourite delicacies, treats her as an equal in his business and family, spends time with her, fights battles on her behalf, and generally puts her above all else in his life. When Aunt Maddie needs him, he is willing to drop everything else in order to do what she requires. Obviously, there are moments when the children or the business take priority, but if she were to ask him of it, he would drop everything on her behalf. I suppose I want a man who puts me first—something my father refused to do."

Darcy simply nodded at her list. He had witnessed Gardiner make similar decisions before. When Darcy's father passed away, Gardiner had wanted to bring his wife and children back to London with him. However, at her insistence, Mrs. Gardiner had chosen to remain in Derbyshire. Though Gardiner would have preferred to keep his family together, he respected his wife's judgement and ultimately agreed to her wishes, trusting her instincts.

Darcy already knew that he could be the person Elizabeth needed. However, despite their friendship, she was not yet willing to see him as a partner in her life, or at least he did not believe she was. It was challenging to read her feelings on this matter, and he wondered if he would be brave enough to broach the topic soon. Though he was only twenty-four and had not planned to marry so young, he was seriously considering making Elizabeth his bride. He asked himself how long he would need to wait. She would turn eighteen in just a few weeks, but he questioned whether they were both too young to contemplate marriage. Since his father had approved of Elizabeth, he did not doubt her suitability but was not certain she was ready to hear his intentions just yet.

He spent several minutes in contemplation as the conversation between his aunt and the woman he admired continued. Finally, Elizabeth's laughter drew him out of his ruminations.

"Are you still with us, William?" Elizabeth's cheerful voice called to him. "Or are you dreaming of your horses or estate? I have seen you smile that way only when at Pemberley."

Darcy shook his head as though to clear it. "I was contemplating something pleasant, but not Pemberley in this instance. I was actually recalling something my father said to me shortly before he died, and it was a good memory. Elizabeth, I look forward to riding with you in the morning, and I will arrive at nine to collect you. Aunt, I would like to join you for tea later, but first, I think I must speak to my uncle. Is he at home?"

Both ladies looked at him inquisitively for a moment, but after a brief pause, Lady Matlock answered. "Please do return after you have spoken with my husband. We expect guests in a few hours, but the house should be empty for a while longer. Yes, he is in his study and will not mind you disturbing him for a few minutes."

Darcy nodded and stood, bowing to both ladies before rushing from the room.

Elizabeth watched him depart, wondering what had occurred to him that caused him to rush out of the room as he did. "That was odd," Lady Matlock said after a moment, voicing the same thought Elizabeth had.

"It was," she replied thoughtfully. "I have not seen William in over two years, but even then, he was always contemplative—reluctant to speak until he had fully worked through whatever troubled him. That last summer, when we rode the estate, he would often fall silent for long stretches, only to speak later when he was ready. Perhaps it is something like that now—a problem he is trying to solve, one where he seeks his uncle's counsel to help him find the answer."

"Well, if that is the case, he will speak of it when the time is right. For now, let us review these invitations and decide which events you would like to attend and which ones we will require Darcy to accompany us to." Lady Matlock gestured to the stack on the table, and the two spent the next half hour discussing their various entertainments. Considering Elizabeth's preference not to be out every night, they selected two or three events to attend each week for the next month, along with outings to the theatre and opera. They also chose a few musical evenings, and soon the ladies had filled their social calendar with events for the next fortnight, along with tentative plans for the following weeks.

Elizabeth carefully copied out the list of events with dates that Darcy was expected to accompany them. The first of these was that very night for an informal dinner at Matlock House with the Gardiners. Darcy had seen Mr. Gardiner occasionally in the last two years, but he had not seen Mrs. Gardiner at all during this time. That night, Georgiana and the Gardiner children were invited to dinner—a rare invitation, but one that they occasionally made and always enjoyed. The Matlocks had two sons who were both unmarried, and though they hoped for grandchildren eventually, they had not yet been so blessed. The Gardiner children were presently standing in, something which both of the Fitzwilliam sons appreciated since it lessened the pressure from their parents to wed.

When Lord Matlock and Darcy returned an hour later, both men were smiling. Darcy practically beamed when Elizabeth handed him the list of events. They men found tea and coffee waiting for them, and the four of them enjoyed a quiet half-hour of conversation before the first guests were announced.

"That is my signal to depart," Lord Matlock said as he rose to his feet. "Come, Darcy, I will escort you out. If the guests see you at the door with me, they will not think you are merely avoiding them. Elizabeth, I am glad to have you here, as I do not have to hear my sons complain about their mother's matchmaking since she has turned that on you this season."

Everyone laughed at his comment, though Darcy and Elizabeth both flushed slightly at the mention of matchmaking. That Darcy was left out of the schemes was not lost on the gentleman, but he knew that it was because of the discussion he had just had with his uncle.

Chapter Fifteen

The next morning, Darcy arrived at Matlock House with two horses in tow. One was ridden by a groom who would accompany the pair, and one was riderless, already saddled with the side-saddle Elizabeth would need to use while in town. Nearly as soon as he knocked, the door opened, and he saw Elizabeth walking toward him, pulling her gloves onto her hands as she walked.

"Good morning, William," she said cheerfully.

"Good morning, Elizabeth," he replied. "Are you ready for a bracing ride?"

"Ha," she scoffed. "I cannot go on a bracing ride in town, and well you know it. I cannot ride like I do at Pemberley because I am forced to ride side-saddle in town. Between that and this ridiculous skirt, the horse would likely spook if I attempted to make her go beyond a canter."

Darcy grinned at her. "Perhaps you are correct. Then I will go for a bracing ride and return to you to tell you about it. How does that sound?"

She scowled at him in return and swatted his shoulder. "Silly man. You cannot do that as you must accompany me. Therefore, you must keep to my pace and remain near me the entire time. You will have to take me to Pemberley if you want a bracing ride."

"I would adore that, my dear Elizabeth," Darcy replied, his voice deeper than usual. He cleared his throat. "That will have to wait until the summer for I have been assured that I must remain in London at least until June. After the Derby, we will be allowed to depart, and I will plead with the Gardiners to come with me this year. I have invited your family the last two summers as well, but your uncle was forced to decline the invitations."

Elizabeth sighed. "I know. I was able to escape town for a few days last summer, but it was not the same as being at Pemberley. I already told you about the horses my uncle managed to hire for us that were not nearly of the same quality as the horses you keep at your estate."

"Well, yes, Pemberley's horses have been bred carefully to ensure both stamina and strength. We have an excellent stable and stablemaster."

She laughed at that. "I recall. He thought it nothing less than shameful that I had never been taught to ride at the 'advanced' age of fourteen."

Darcy laughed, as Elizabeth had known he would. That a lass from the country had not been taught to ride as an infant had shocked the old Scot. "Aye, and a shame it is," he had said to the pair when they had gone to the stables to find a gentle mount for Elizabeth. "Such a bonnie wee thing as you should ha' been on a pony from the time ye could walk."

"Allow me to assist you," Darcy said after a moment, and quickly grasped Elizabeth by the waist to help her onto her mount. She gasped in surprise at his sudden action, one he had done many times before, but never before had it felt so intimate. Elizabeth's cheeks reddened as she put her own hands on his shoulders to steady her, feeling his closeness acutely.

Their eyes met, and for a brief moment, as it had the night they danced, the world around them seemed to fade away. Darcy's touch was firm yet gentle, and Elizabeth could not help but notice the warmth and strength in his hands. Her heart raced, and she struggled to compose herself when his hands moved away.

"Thank you, William," Elizabeth breathed, her voice and breathing both unsteady.

Darcy stepped back, his own emotions equally unsettled. He attempted to calm his racing heart as he spoke: "It was my pleasure, Elizabeth. Shall we begin our ride now?"

As they rode side by side, the memory of his touch lingered. Darcy's presence was both comfortable and strange, and Elizabeth found herself stealing glances at him. They were both quiet, his expression unreadable. However, there was a softness in his eyes that made her heart flutter. Typical for them, they rode in comfortable silence. They had ridden together many times in the past, most often in the countryside surrounding Pemberley. While each was aware of the other, they did not let the strangeness of this encounter affect them, and after some time, they began to speak as they had in the past.

"Do you remember when we stumbled upon that old ruin near Pemberley?" Elizabeth asked with a hint of a smile. "You tried to convince me it was haunted."

Darcy laughed, easing the tension between them a little more. "You were so easily convinced! In fact, I believe you encouraged the notion. When you told Father what we had found, he glared at me first and then told you it was all a lie."

"I was so disappointed. We had such a grand time making up stories about what could have been haunting it. You were not as good at coming up with ideas as I was, but once I had given you the notion, you were able to carry them much further than I."

"You have always had a better imagination, but I had the knack for storytelling," Darcy replied, his tone warm. "Despite my age, you still managed to make even the most mundane outings feel like grand adventures."

They continued to reminisce as they rode through Hyde Park. Soon, any earlier awkwardness dissipated as they slipped back into the easy camaraderie they had always shared at Pemberley. The conversation flowed effortlessly, filled with light-hearted banter and genuine laughter.

When they finally returned to Matlock House, Darcy dismounted first and swiftly moved to help Elizabeth. This time, she was prepared for his touch, but the same intimate feeling coursed through her as he guided her down.

"I have enjoyed our ride this morning, William. When will we be able to repeat it?" Elizabeth asked.

Darcy took a moment to respond. He would like to repeat the activity every morning, but after his conversation with his uncle yesterday, thought it wise to limit it to a few times a week. "Day after tomorrow?" he suggested. "We have a dinner to attend tonight and will return home quite late." Elizabeth agreed and looked forward to their time together.

THIS PATTERN CONTINUED over the next two months. Darcy tried to avoid early morning rides after attending events that kept them out late, though the pace of the season did not seem to affect Elizabeth as much as it did her sponsor. He even discovered that he enjoyed the season far more when he was escorting Elizabeth, partly because her presence calmed him and made it easier for him to be sociable.

Toward the end of May, before the Derby that marked the point that Lady Matlock would allow Darcy to return to Pemberley, he asked

Elizabeth Gardiner for a courtship which her uncle quickly approved. The family celebrated this announcement along with Elizabeth's eighteenth birthday.

Shortly after the first ball, Darcy invited the Gardiners to spend the months of July and August at Pemberley and offering a second carriage to convey the children on the journey. Darcy himself would leave for Pemberley earlier, in mid-June, but he hoped the Gardiners would not be far behind them. He had already decided he would propose to Elizabeth when they were all at Pemberley that summer.

Gardiner accepted the invitation, making the suggestion that he send his wife, Elizabeth, and the children with Darcy when he headed north for the summer. In mid-July, Gardiner would follow since he could not be away from his business for so long. With these plans in place, Darcy began to plan for his proposal to Elizabeth, and their frequent rides in Hyde Park, along with their reminiscences of the past, had given Darcy an idea how to make the proposal special.

Not long after Mr. Gardiner arrived at Pemberley, Darcy put his plans into place. That morning, he would take Elizabeth on a ride to the ridgeline with a perfect view of the estate. Now that Elizabeth was out, a groom customarily accompanied them, but in this instance, he had her uncle's permission to take her out alone. If Elizabeth noticed his absence, she did not mention it, and the two rode in companionable silence until they reached their destination.

Darcy dismounted and moved toward Elizabeth's side to help her dismount. She allowed him to assist her, smiling gently at him as she stood a beat longer than necessary in his almost embrace, revelling in the feeling. This happened every time they touched, yet Elizabeth never tired of it.

"Elizabeth, come, I have something to show you," Darcy said, taking Elizabeth's hand in his, leading her toward the ridge. A blanket and a small picnic were awaiting them which surprised her given the early hour. Darcy led her toward it and helped her sit before taking the seat next to her. He opened the basket and pulled out a flask of tea and several scones, accompanied by clotted cream and strawberry jam, Elizabeth's favourite.

"This is lovely, William," Elizabeth exclaimed. "How very thoughtful of you to arrange all this."

"I wanted to do something special for you this morning, my dear Elizabeth," he said, before pouring her a cup of tea and handing her a plate with a scone that he had cut in half so she could top it with jam and cream. The two ate in silence, though Elizabeth noticed that Darcy appeared slightly anxious.

"Is something troubling you this morning?" she asked after she had finished eating. Darcy was still fiddling with his own food, which was unlike him.

"No," he said abruptly, surprising Elizabeth with his terseness which he must have noticed from her expression for he immediately apologised. "Forgive me, my dear, I did not mean to be short with you. There is something that I did wish to say, and I am having trouble finding the best way to do so."

Elizabeth furrowed her brow, looking at him in concern. "Tell me, William. What is bothering you?"

He smiled and reached out to pick her hand up in his. "We have been courting now for several months, have we not? And I have cared for you nearly since we first met and you stood up to that vile reprobate, and then again to my father and myself. We became friends that first summer and deepened our friendship the following summer.

"Then we did not see each other for the next two years. We exchanged letters, but did not see one another for all that time. When I saw you again in London this spring, you were different; you looked different from the girl who had been my friend and supported me when my father died. It took a moment to reconcile those two people in my mind, but it did not take long before I realised that I was falling in love with the woman you had become. You were still the girl who had been my friend, but those feelings grew deeper the more time we spent together."

During this, he had been staring at her hand, but now, he lifted his head to look her in the eye as he made his final confession. "I am in love with you, Elizabeth. What I brought you out here today to ask is —" he paused, shifting once again to take both her hands in his, "— Elizabeth, will you do me the honour of granting me your hand in marriage? Since the day we met, despite the circumstances of that day, I have felt at ease when I was with you. My father told me after we met that you would be the perfect wife for me, but you were too young, and I was too young, at the time. However, I think I always knew you would one day be my wife. Now, before I make an even greater fool of myself, what is your answer? Will you marry me?"

His eyes had dropped once again after he had asked the question and continued speaking, and when he looked up, he saw that tears had pooled in Elizabeth's eyes. "Elizabeth, darling, what is wrong? Have I offended you in some way with my request? Forgive me..."

"No," Elizabeth's voice cut him off, and he stopped completely, uncertain what to say next. "You did not offend me, and nothing is wrong, William." She paused to wipe her eyes and regain her composure. "Yes, I would be honoured to marry you. I love you, too, William. These tears are happy tears for while I hoped you would ask, I was uncertain if that was your intent this morning. I was a little afraid that you were bringing me here to tell me you viewed me as too much of a sister."

Scrambling to his feet, Darcy pulled up Elizabeth behind him and immediately into his arms. "Not a sister, Elizabeth. Not familial at all, unless as a wife. You will be my wife?" he asked again, hesitating a little, still not quite believing that she had accepted him.

Elizabeth laughed. "Yes, dear William, I will be your wife. Now let us seal our promise with a kiss, or I will have to be angry with you, and that would not bode well for our marriage."

Smiling fondly at her, Darcy shook his head even as he dipped down to bring his lips to hers. Their lips touched briefly before pulling away only for a moment. Her eyes were still closed, so Darcy brought his lips to hers once more, lingering longer this time.

Chapter Sixteen

As soon as they returned from their ride, the Gardiners were waiting at the house for news. Neither believed Elizabeth would reject Darcy's suit, but nonetheless, they were waiting to see the couple as they returned to offer their congratulations.

That Darcy's suit had been successful was obvious when they returned to the house. The Gardiners and Georgiana immediately embraced the couple, offering their congratulations and asking questions that they had not yet had the time to answer.

"Do you wish to marry in London from our church, Elizabeth, or here at Pemberley?" Aunt Gardiner asked.

Elizabeth turned to look at Darcy, who shrugged. "While a part of me wishes we could marry here, many of our family and friends could not attend if we did so. If we married early in October in London, we could invite the Matlocks, as well as some friends I have made in town during my time there. What do you think, William?"

"Elizabeth, as long as the result is that we are married, I care not. If it pleases you to be married from London, then that is what we will do.

It is late July now; do you believe it will take three months for you to be ready to marry?"

Mrs. Gardiner laughed at this statement. "From the man's perspective, no, it does not take three months to prepare for a wedding. However, as the bride, there are far more things to consider, including where the wedding breakfast should take place. I will need to meet with your aunt as soon as I can to discuss the matter with her since I am certain she will have ideas about it. In fact, she has already begun to make plans, if I am not mistaken."

Darcy looked at her in surprise. After a moment, though, he said thoughtfully. "I suppose she views me as a son, in some ways. She has been anxious for her own sons to marry, so I am unsurprised that she is looking forward to mine. I thought it was typically the bride's family who planned the wedding breakfast."

"In most cases, I believe it is. However, your aunt is a countess, and that may make a difference. Since Lady Matlock sponsored Elizabeth in the season, I think she would prefer to have some say in the proceedings," Mrs. Gardiner replied.

Sighing heavily, Darcy agreed that she definitely would. "My aunt does adore planning parties. However, Elizabeth, if you feel the need, be sure to remind her that it is *our* wedding. I know you prefer smaller parties, and my aunt will likely desire to make this a large event requiring months of planning. My only request is that the wedding take place in the early part of October, or even late September, if it can be arranged, and that she not be allowed to push it back beyond that."

Elizabeth smiled and patted his hand. "We will certainly be wed by the middle of October, William, even if I have to put my foot down with your Aunt Matlock. As my aunt said, she is expecting our engagement to occur although she and your uncle would not have known precisely when you would ask.

Mrs. Gardiner smiled her agreement. "The modiste already has your measurements, and if you recall, Elizabeth, I asked you to work with her to design your ideal wedding gown toward the end of the season. I will send her a letter telling her to begin construction on it so that it will be ready for a fitting when we return home next month. That will allow the process to be much easier, and she can also begin designing dresses for you in your new status as Mrs. Darcy. You have worked with her for several years now, and she is familiar with your preferences."

"Thank you, Aunt," Elizabeth said, and the conversation then drifted to other topics related to the wedding, as well as plans to occupy their time at Pemberley.

Before the day was done, letters had been sent to Matlock and London, and another note dispatched to the rector in Kympton where Darcy attended services when he was home. Gardiner sent one to the rector of the church they attended in London, so the reading of the banns could begin there as well.

During the next weeks at Pemberley, the residents occupied themselves with various pursuits, some of which were related to the wedding while others were not. Elizabeth did visit the dressmaker in Lambton to order some dresses appropriate for her role as Mrs. Darcy, made up in the heavier fabrics that would be needed for a winter in Derbyshire. Elizabeth and her aunt also inspected the mistress's suite, which had been thoroughly aired and cleaned by the servants, before deciding how to update the room.

The Matlocks joined the party at Pemberley after hearing the news of the couple's engagement. After much discussion, Elizabeth and Darcy planned to visit the seaside for a fortnight after the wedding before returning to Pemberley to spend the winter in their home. Lady Matlock recommended a girls' school for Georgiana to attend this autumn, as she had several friends who sent their own daughters there.

Unlike the seminary attended by the Bingley sisters, this one did focus on teaching useful accomplishments to young ladies. There was still an emphasis on rank and social status, but it was nearly impossible to find one that did not. Regardless, it seemed to everyone involved that it was in Georgiana's best interest to attend school for a year or two, and so she would begin this autumn after the wedding. Her aunt and uncle's promise to take her to the school not long after Darcy and Elizabeth's wedding pleased Georgiana.

The newlywed Darcys would return to London in the spring to attend the season. Lady Matlock had already begun to plan a ball to occur a few days after the wedding before the couple departed for the seaside.

Shortly before the entire party was to depart for London, Bingley arrived with his sisters and brother-in-law in tow. Bingley had been expected—the others had not. As he had done before, Darcy made his displeasure known about the additional guests arriving uninvited and without warning in spite of Bingley's claim of having written to inform him of the additions to his party. Knowing his friend's poor penmanship, he suspected the letter had gone astray.

Reluctantly, Darcy agreed to house his party for a day or two as they were *en route* to their family home in Scarborough but not without a serious discussion with his friend about the presumption of showing up as he had. Bingley and Darcy had maintained a correspondence over the last few years though they had seen one another rarely. Unlike the correspondence between Elizabeth and Darcy, the letters exchanged between the two gentlemen were far more superficial and had done little to advance the friendship.

Elizabeth met with the Bingleys and Hursts on a few occasions in London. She knew she was disliked by Caroline Bingley, mainly because Elizabeth had Darcy's attention whereas the other lady did not. However, neither Elizabeth nor Darcy was aware of the extent to which Miss Bingley disliked Elizabeth, for Miss Bingley came nearer to hating Elizabeth than merely disliking her. She believed she deserved the attention of her brother's friend, and despite the rumours of Elizabeth's dowry being almost as large as her own, she felt that Elizabeth was beneath her, both in beauty and in wealth.

It was not widely known that Elizabeth's dowry surpassed the fifteen thousand pounds left to her by the elder Mr. Darcy. In the two and half years since receiving the legacy, it had very nearly doubled, between the investments made by Mr. Gardiner on her behalf and having added the interest on the accounts back into it, enabling the funds to grow to closer to twenty-five thousand pounds. Of course, Gardiner himself had been setting aside small amounts to be used as Elizabeth's dowry ever since she came to live with them, for Elizabeth had proved to be rather adept in suggesting investments that did well and enabled her to prosper.

When Miss Bingley and her sister entered the drawing room where the party was gathered for dinner, she sidled up to her prey almost as soon as she entered the room, grabbing at his arm and attempting to ingratiate herself with the gentleman.

As soon as he could, however, he moved away from her and came to sit next to Elizabeth, boldly taking her hand in his own. "Bingley since I have not had the chance to write to you of my news just yet, I would like to announce that Elizabeth and I are engaged. We are to wed in London in October, and my aunt, Lady Matlock, will be hosting our wedding ball to celebrate the event."

Bingley immediately stood and went to shake his friend's hand. "Congratulations, Darcy, Miss Gardiner. I must say this is quite unexpected. I had believed your interest lay in another direction." He said this as he looked toward his sister, who was struggling to control her expression at this news.

Darcy could only blink at his friend in surprise. "I cannot understand what you could mean, Bingley. I have been courting Miss Gardiner for several months now. In fact, as soon as we saw each other again at the ball my aunt hosted in her honour, I knew I would marry her. She is the only woman who has ever drawn my interest."

Such a statement confused Bingley and irritated the gentleman's sister. She had been feeding her brother lies for months, telling of his friend's apparent interest in her and speaking of Darcy's frequent calls on her at the Hursts townhouse in London that spring. If Bingley was surprised to have never encountered his friend on one of these calls, he never questioned it, but had believed his sister's claim that the gentleman was courting her.

"But Caroline said you were calling on her," Bingley asserted, turning to look at his sister in confusion.

"Bingley, all of London knew that I was courting Miss Gardiner, especially since she was staying at the home of my aunt and uncle, who wholly favoured the match. I do not know what your sister's scheme is, but I have never once called on her. The only time I have visited the Hursts' house on Grosvenor Street, I was in your company. Not only that, but had I been calling on your sister, do you not think I would have spoken to you about the matter?" Darcy demanded.

Bingley turned to glare at his sister. "Caroline?"

The lady could only glare right back at her brother. "You are mistaken, Brother. Mr. Darcy, please forgive my brother for his apparent misunderstanding. Miss Gardiner, I suppose congratulations are in order?"

Elizabeth smiled knowingly at the bitter, jealous harpy. "I suppose they are, Miss Bingley. I suppose you will be quite disappointed to miss the wedding since you will be with your family in Scarborough when we marry." Elizabeth knew what the lady was about with her comment and answered in a similar fashion. Mrs. Gardiner fixed her niece with a look; in fact, everyone in the room, except perhaps for Mr. Bingley, understood the slight Elizabeth intended by her comment.

No further discussion took place about the wedding that evening. Darcy persuaded his friend to leave the next day, and soon peace returned to Pemberley.

Chapter Seventeen

The rest of the party departed from Pemberley for London only a few days later. With August coming to an end and the wedding to take place in a little over a month, they spent much of the journey discussing the plans that had already been made and what was left to do.

Upon their return, Elizabeth was introduced to the staff at Darcy House as its future mistress and began planning any changes to her suite that would need to be done before the wedding. The mistress's chambers had not been occupied in many years, so the rooms would need to be cleaned and aired, and the bedding changed, along with the curtains. The furniture appeared to be in good shape, and only a few items needed to be changed out based on Elizabeth's preferences.

Elizabeth spent nearly a full day going through Uncle Gardiner's warehouses along with her aunt and Darcy's to select fabrics for the curtains and the bedding in her rooms, along with many other fabrics for dresses that still needed to be created. Elizabeth's dress for the wedding was nearly done—a note from the modiste was delivered the day of their arrival from Pemberley requesting Elizabeth come try on the dress and ensure all was as it should be. She also had fittings for the rest of her trousseau, which required Elizabeth to spend two full days at the modiste being poked and prodded. The end result was quite a few dresses that Elizabeth truly did like, though she hoped she would not have to endure such an event again.

A fortnight after their return to London, Elizabeth had a rare day at home to rest. Her uncle was at his office, and Mrs. Gardiner needed to visit several friends she had been neglecting since her return. Elizabeth had the rare opportunity to stay at home and rest, as she did not need to accompany Mrs. Gardiner on her outing, and the children were being taken care of by their nurses and governess.

She sat in a sitting room in the back of the house, reading and waiting for her intended. Darcy would call on her early that afternoon, for he had business with his solicitor that occupied him in the morning.

When the post arrived, the butler brought it directly to her since she was the only one at home. Upon sorting through it, she noted that there was a letter for her, addressed in a somewhat familiar hand. There was another letter for her uncle which she laid aside, staring at the one addressed to her.

"Please, take these to my uncle, but ensure he sees the one on top. Ask him to come to me when he has read it, or to send for me, if you will," Elizabeth requested, still staring at her own letter, uncertain and a little worried about what it might contain.

In all the time she lived with the Gardiners, she had never received a letter from her father. This was the first and she doubted it contained good news. Elizabeth did not believe anyone in Meryton knew of her upcoming wedding.

There had been no announcement of their engagement published in any of the London newspapers and though the connection between Elizabeth and Darcy had been speculated about in the papers' gossip columns since they first met again at her debut, little had been written that overtly mentioned the engagement. She knew this in part because of the letters Darcy received from his aunt, Lady Catherine de

Bourgh, complaining about the frequent mention of him in company with 'some tart' as she called Elizabeth, though she did not know who the lady was. Despite the confrontation at Pemberley shortly after George Darcy's death, Lady Catherine still attempted to claim Darcy was engaged to her daughter, but all the family merely rolled their eyes at her insinuations before correcting her, yet again. Still, it seemed odd, and more than a little concerning, that Mr. Bennet would write to her so close to the wedding date.

Slowly, she opened the letter. It contained no greeting, only a few words:

> *Elizabeth, it is time for you to return home to your family. We expect you to arrive no later than Michaelmas. Sincerely, Thomas Bennet*

Darcy was announced into the room only moments later. He must have seen some of what she was feeling in her face, for the greeting seemed to die on his lips and he immediately strode in her direction.

"Fitzwilliam," she breathed, her voice tremulous as she saw her intended standing in front of her.

IMMEDIATELY, Darcy moved to Elizabeth's side, his worry mounting when he noticed the tracks of the tears on her dear face. Upon realising they were alone, he knew whatever it was must be serious. Quickly, he took the seat beside her, capturing her hand with his own and bringing it to his lips for a kiss. "What is it, my darling Elizabeth? What is wrong?" It was then he noticed the letter in her hand. She held it warily, and barely looked from it.

"You have a knack, sir, for arriving at precisely the moment when you are most needed." Elizabeth breathed, causing Darcy to move his arm around her waist to provide comfort.

"May I?" he asked gently as he nodded toward the letter.

Elizabeth only nodded, extending her hand so he could take the piece of paper from her. He took it from her, but before he read it, he pressed a light kiss to her cheek. "Whatever it is, we will face it together, my love," he whispered, squeezing her waist slightly as he looked down at the piece of paper now in his own hand. It did not take him long to read the message it contained, and he frowned down at it.

"William," she repeated, sighing heavily as she leaned into him. "My … my uncle received a letter as well. I assume it also demands my presence at home within the next fortnight."

His hands clutched hers firmly. "Will you go? Will you do as your father commands? He has not been much of a father to you in recent years; did not Gardiner say he had practically disowned you?"

Elizabeth scoffed. "There is no 'practically' to it. He told my uncle to take me and never bring me back. Not only that, but when my uncle demanded he sign my guardianship over to him, he agreed without question and told my uncle that I was no longer his daughter or his concern. Thomas Bennet has ignored me for almost ten years, ever since he sent me to live here, and I do not think he should have the right to suddenly demand my presence. I confess I am a little frightened because I do not obtain my majority for another three years and my letter seems to imply I am expected to remain there."

"If you truly believe that, you cannot possibly go."

"You are right. I have no reason to return, yet I am concerned what Mr. Bennet will do if I do not comply. After all, just because he made uncle my guardian does not mean he cannot withdraw his consent. But why would he? Why is he suddenly interested enough in me to bring me back to Longbourn? I simply cannot understand it."

Elizabeth was correct. Legally, her father had the right to rescind the authority he had given her uncle to act as her guardian. It did not matter what documents he may have signed, there was little to prevent him from demanding that his daughter come home if he wished it. Of course, Elizabeth could refuse to travel on her own, but if Thomas Bennet were to come to London and force her to return with him, her uncle could not prevent it.

Darcy would not let that happen. His mind was already racing for a solution to protect Elizabeth from her family, should she need it, and also to ensure nothing delayed the wedding. They were scheduled to marry in just over a fortnight; in truth, their banns had already been called both in Derbyshire and in London. There was nothing to prevent their marriage from taking place earlier than planned.

Her words interrupted his thoughts. "I really do not wish to go. And yet, I am extremely curious as to the reason for the summons to Longbourn. I cannot imagine he wants to apologise and restore our relationship. It is more likely he has somehow learned of our engagement and intends to interfere with or even prevent our wedding to obtain some material gain in return for permitting us to marry. I should not think such things, but still…"

Darcy embraced her, drawing her to his chest. They both remained silent for several moments, lost in contemplation. "You have a fortnight before you are expected?" he asked again quietly.

She sniffed. "Yes."

"I have an idea," he murmured, lifting her chin so he could look her in the eyes. "The banns have been read. Considering your valid concerns regarding your father's summons, we will simply move our wedding date forward. Let us plan to marry on Monday. Then, after a week of honeymooning," he gave her a lascivious grin that made her giggle, "we shall travel together to Meryton and pay a call on your father. Perhaps there is a small inn, or a cottage, where we can stay while we are there."

Elizabeth leaned back and gave him a teasing grin. "I like the way you think. It would please me greatly if we are already married when we arrive. Mrs. Bennet will be furious that I married before her beautiful darling Jane. Even better, she cannot attempt to claim you for Jane."

Darcy shook his head, smiling tenderly. "I do not think I have ever told you, but you stole my heart nearly from our first meeting, my dear girl. I was intrigued by you the moment you stood up to my father. You were young when we first met, and I appreciated your friendship in the years following my father's death. When I saw you again this Easter, well, I knew you owned my heart for certain."

"You had mine far longer," she whispered. "You stole my heart when you first rescued me as a girl and never surrendered it. I did not quite recognise my feelings for what they were back then, but I thought of you so often in the years we were apart. I was worried you would find someone else to marry before my come out and I was stunned when you began to court me in earnest this spring."

"Did you know my father approved of you as my wife? It was not long before he died, and although you were only fourteen at the time, he told me I should consider you when it came time for me to marry. He remembered how you visited the tenants at Pemberley with Mrs. Reynolds during that visit and how interested you were in reading and learning. You were quite forceful in expressing your opinions and debated with me frequently. It was at his recommendation that the Gardiners sent you to school; did you know that? I remember laughing at my father when he said it, but after I saw you as a woman instead of the girl you had been, I was inordinately pleased to recall his words to me."

Elizabeth chuckled. "Four years have certainly had their effect on you as well, Fitzwilliam. You have changed quite a bit yourself."

He shook his head, smiling fondly. "Are you concerned about marrying such an old man?"

Smiling lovingly at him, she shook her head and reached up to caress his face. "You are hardly old, sir, at twenty-four, but you are far more serious than the twenty-year-old I first met. I am thankful that I knew you before you became the Master of Pemberley since I sometimes think you would not have found it as easy to fall in love with me had we met now. I know how much these last years have affected you."

"It would have been far worse had I not had your friendship and that of the Gardiners. Bingley has been a friend, but you and the Gardiners have done far more to help me feel comfortable in my new role. You recognised that large groups of people made me uncomfortable and did not force me into company as he so frequently did. Georgiana benefited from your friendship, and I was grateful for their advice in raising a much younger sister. I would have been a very different man if I had not met you."

Elizabeth leaned her head against his shoulder. They had had this same conversation numerous times, but at this moment, it reassured her. He wrapped an arm around her and drew her more tightly to him. They remained in this attitude for some minutes. Eventually, he let out a sigh and spoke again. "We have drifted from the primary concern, my dear. What do you say to getting married on Monday? That way, when you return to Hertfordshire, it will be as my wife. Your father will no longer be able to command you, but you will still honour his request to visit."

Elizabeth thought for a moment as she firmed her resolve. "My Uncle Gardiner is more of a father to me than Mr. Bennet ever was, and that is the relationship I choose to honour. Yes, we will marry on Monday, but then I will allow you to decide if we should venture into Hertfordshire and for how long. My father does not have the right to object to our marriage now and should not be permitted to interfere with it in any way."

For a moment, Darcy also wondered if the Bennets had somehow learned of Elizabeth's pending nuptials and resolved to go to the Gardiners' church and his own as soon as possible. It was unlikely, but he wanted to ensure Mr. Bennet had not sent a letter objecting to the match if he had somehow learnt of it. Mr. Gardiner did have a written document giving him guardianship of Elizabeth and had provided for her for most of the last decade. Her father's lack of involvement in her life should prevent him from interfering, but he wanted to be certain.

"What will your uncle say about this letter?" Darcy asked after they had been silent for several more minutes.

"I believe they will agree with your suggestion of moving the date forward. This way, if I must face my father, I will do so with you at my side. As my husband, you will have the right to speak for me, and my father cannot demand that you return me. The settlement has been signed, and all the legalities have been arranged."

Darcy nodded. "They have been generous in giving us so much time to talk privately. Should we call them in so we can share our plans?"

Elizabeth shook her head. "My uncle should arrive home soon. But for right now, William, we are quite alone. Kiss me," she whispered. "Remind me of your love."

He could not deny her request. He stood, pulling her along with him, and wrapped his arms around her waist. Hers immediately went around his neck, and her fingers toyed with his hair at his nape. For several moments, they merely stared into each other's eyes. "I love you, Elizabeth. I will always love you, and I will not allow anyone to separate us," he whispered, then lowered his lips to hers.

Lightning seemed to shoot through them both, and the kiss lasted several minutes. They had never kissed like this before, and it felt ... wonderful. Finally, panting and breathless, they broke apart. Darcy rested his forehead on Elizabeth's as he sought to catch his breath. "I am glad we will not wait, my darling. Monday, it seems, cannot come soon enough. Come, let us find your relations before I embarrass myself or thoroughly ruin you."

"Mmm," was all Elizabeth could manage. "Yes, Monday seems very far away."

He laughed lightly, dropping a kiss on her nose before separating from her more fully. "I ... I need a moment, my darling. Can ... will you go find out if your uncle is home and ask him to come here if he is? Slowly?"

Elizabeth's eyes dropped to his waist and slightly below. Her cheeks coloured when she saw the distension in his breeches. She and her aunt had discussed such things before, and Elizabeth knew in general terms what to expect from the marital bed. On occasion, she had felt this ... hardness ... against her belly when they kissed, but this was the first time she had seen evidence of it. Instead of frightening her, it only made her look more forward to their wedding and all that would follow.

Darcy caught her gaze as she stood transfixed. "Elizabeth," he groaned, "you must go. Staring at it like that, with that look in your eye, does not help it go away." He nearly laughed as he watched the flush, which had started to fade, begin to deepen at once. He noted that it encompassed not only her cheeks but also her chest and décolletage. That image did not help his condition in the least. "Go, Elizabeth," he commanded.

With a giggle, she flashed him an impertinent smile and hastily departed the room.

Chapter Eighteen

Elizabeth found her uncle in his study, just having finished reading the letter that had arrived earlier. "Staunton said you received a letter as well. Your father is insisting you return home, but I have no intention of making you. I heard Darcy arrived soon after you received the note, so I left the two of you to discuss the matter. Is he coming?" Gardiner asked his niece as soon as she entered.

"He sent me to find you and ask you to join us, Uncle. And yes, I shared the letter with him. Mr. Bennet commands me to return home," she laughed derisively. "However, William has an idea for how to thwart him. Promise me you will hear him out." Her voice had turned pleading, as though she were concerned her uncle would not, though in all reality, he was typically very understanding. "I have asked for tea to be served in the sitting room; will you join us, or should I call for him to come to you?"

Her uncle eyed her for a moment and Elizabeth struggled not to blush under his scrutiny. "I will hear whatever he has to say, Elizabeth, but I suppose the two of you have come up with a solution that I might not approve. Let us go to the parlour where your aunt will probably join us before too long."

Elizabeth could do little but shrug at this as she led her uncle toward the room where Darcy was waiting.

Before Darcy could say much, Mrs. Gardiner was shown in. Immediately, she seemed to pick up on the tense atmosphere in the room. "What has happened?" she asked.

"Mr. Bennet sent a letter demanding Elizabeth return to Longbourn," Gardiner said to his wife with a look that Elizabeth was not certain she wished to interpret. She had not seen the letter to her uncle, and now she wished to know what his had said.

"He sent a note to me as well, telling me it was time for me to return home and that I should return by Michaelmas which is slightly over a fortnight from now. However, Fitzwilliam has a suggestion for how to handle his demand," Elizabeth said. "But, Uncle, will you not tell us what your letter said?"

Gardiner looked uncomfortable "I would prefer not to at this time, Elizabeth." He held up a hand before she could protest any further. "Elizabeth, trust my judgement in this. It is best that you do not see what he wrote. However, I will say that he said to me roughly what he said to you: you have been away long enough, and that it is time for you to do your duty and return to Longbourn."

Her eyebrows raised at this. "Do my duty?" she questioned. "Does he have something in mind for me to do? Surely, he has not arranged a marriage for me or anything of the sort. He cannot have done so! Since he has not been in contact with any of us for the last several years, he cannot even know for certain that I am yet unmarried. He cannot truly expect me to return or to feel that I owe him anything at this point."

"I agree, Elizabeth," her uncle said soothingly. "I sense my sister's hand in this, and there is no way of knowing what either of them might be thinking. Over the last few years, she has written on occasion to demand something from me or my wife, but those letters were always consigned to the fire nearly as soon as they were received."

Elizabeth turned astonished eyes toward her uncle. "I never knew."

"It was not worth you knowing," her aunt said in a sympathetic tone. "That is beside the point. Now, what is William's suggestion for how we ought to handle this matter?"

Elizabeth and Darcy looked at each other for a moment, then Darcy spoke. "We should marry as soon as it can be arranged instead of waiting until the end of the month as we planned." He continued explaining the rest of his plans including renting a house near Meryton that would enable them to visit her family while remaining at a distance from them. If the meeting went well, they would be close enough for regular visits, but if not, they would be far enough away that they would not have to see the Bennet family again. "Elizabeth has mentioned wanting to visit Meryton before, of wanting to pay a call on some of her friends who are still in the area and even to visit her Aunt and Uncle Phillips," he finished. "Taking a house nearby would allow us to do that while not interacting with the Bennets if we do not wish to."

This time, it was Mr. and Mrs. Gardiner who shared a speaking glance. While they were reluctant to move the wedding date forward, they could not deny that doing so would prevent Mr. Bennet from preventing the wedding from occurring or delaying it. Reluctantly, Mr. Gardiner acknowledged that if Elizabeth was already married when she ventured into Hertfordshire, she would fall under her husband's protection rather than her father's and there was nothing Mr. Bennet could do about it.

"The document he signed giving me guardianship of Elizabeth is legal and binding currently, but once Elizabeth is in Mr. Bennet's presence, he could easily terminate the guardianship and resume his inherent authority over Elizabeth. However, as her husband, Darcy you will usurp any authority Mr. Bennet expected to have over Elizabeth upon her return." He raised his hand before Elizabeth could object. "In the eyes of the law, my dear. You know that a woman is essentially the property of first her father and then her husband. You may not care for the idea, but it is the truth."

Unhappily, Elizabeth silenced whatever protest she would have made about being some man's chattel. Their discussion ended with the Gardiners agreeing that moving the wedding forward was the best way to protect Elizabeth. At that, Darcy departed for home to prepare for the dinner party arranged for that night. On his way, he stopped to meet briefly with the rector of his London parish to confirm that Thomas Bennet had not written to object to the wedding. If he did object at the wedding, he assured Darcy that he planned to ignore it as nonconsequential given the proof that the man had given up his guardianship over his daughter to the Mr. Gardiner ten years before and that Mr. Gardiner did approve the match.

Darcy did not look forward to telling the Matlocks about the change in plans. Though there was little they could do about it, he knew his aunt would be unhappy.

Later, when the Gardiners and Elizabeth arrived at Darcy House for the dinner with Darcy's family, Mr. Gardiner informed Darcy of his own visit to his church, which had garnered similar information. Additionally, the rector had agreed, given the circumstances, to move the wedding forward to Monday at ten in the morning. Darcy was pleased with this knowledge, as was Elizabeth. She greeted him with a brilliant smile that left Darcy momentarily dumbstruck.

Dinner passed pleasantly. Since their initial meeting at Pemberley before George Darcy's death, the two families had been frequently in company. Both Lord and Lady Matlock viewed Elizabeth nearly as a niece already and were pleased to be truly welcoming the girl into the family through her marriage to their nephew. While Lord Matlock may have initially hoped for Darcy to marry a titled lady, he had grown to adore Elizabeth, especially during the weeks Elizabeth lived with them during the Season. That George Darcy had met the young lady and approved the match only further strengthened their pleasure.

Despite this, it came as a great surprise to the couple when Darcy announced the change to the wedding plans and its reason. "Nephew, I protest. You cannot move up your wedding for such a flimsy reason. Society will think you have compromised your bride and will believe that a child will come too soon," Lady Matlock complained.

Darcy tried not to roll his eyes at his aunt. "It is not a flimsy excuse, Aunt. Mr. Bennet's demand that Elizabeth return to Longbourn weeks before our wedding is suspicious, especially with the letter to Gardiner claiming he wants her to 'do her duty' to the family. Remember, it will be several years before Elizabeth reaches her majority. This is the only way to ensure Mr. Bennet cannot prevent or delay our marriage. If we are already wed when Elizabeth arrives, he can do nothing about it, and we can circumvent any plans he might have made. As no child will come early, any gossip this creates will be easily disproved soon enough."

"Will you return to town for a time after this visit?" Lady Matlock asked. "You refused to allow me to celebrate with an engagement ball, so now you must allow me to hold a ball to celebrate your marriage. I can plan a ball for early November, and, after that, you may depart for Pemberley. You will need to inform Georgiana of the change in plans. Now, do you still intend to marry from your parish, Elizabeth?"

Elizabeth nodded. "My wedding dress is ready. All the rest of my clothes will be delivered directly to Darcy House when they are completed. We wanted to wait to speak to you about the matter since you had originally intended to host the wedding breakfast. I hope you will still be able to do so, but my aunt is able to host a smaller breakfast if you cannot adjust your plans so quickly."

"We will host the wedding breakfast at Matlock House. A wedding breakfast at our home will show the world that we support your marriage. Madeline, I do not mean to overstep, but I do believe this is best."

Mrs. Gardiner nodded, while Darcy groaned. "Please keep it small, Aunt. You know very well that I despise being the centre of attention."

"I will keep your preferences in mind, nephew," his aunt replied, grinning at him and watching him squirm slightly in his chair.

Elizabeth leaned against him, drawing his attention to her. "William, you are mistaken. You will not be the centre of attention; I, as the bride, will be. You are just a … an accompaniment." She grinned up at him pertly.

"An accompaniment," Lord Matlock barked. "That is telling you, lad."

Darcy laughed as well, sliding his hand around her waist to pull her into a quick hug. "Yes, you will, and I do not doubt you will be radiant, my love. Thank you for reminding me of my place."

She slipped her free hand into his and squeezed, resting her head against his shoulder. Conversation flowed around them while they were lost in each other for several minutes. It grew late, and soon, the Gardiners departed for home.

Chapter Nineteen

Monday morning and the wedding arrived quickly, and Elizabeth dressed in the wedding gown she had chosen at the modiste a little over four months before, even before Darcy had proposed. While she had not thought she would need it so quickly, she was thrilled that it had been ready in time, despite the change in their wedding date.

"Aunt Maddie, thank you so much for all that you and Uncle Edward have done for me. If you had not taken me in when you did, I am uncertain where I would be today without your love and your guidance."

"Hush, Elizabeth, we have adored having you with us. You have been a tremendous help to us, a big sister to your cousins, and we will all miss you dreadfully when your new husband takes you away. Of course, we adore him too, and we will still see you often. I am only sorry that we have had to rush this day due to your father's sudden insistence that you visit him."

Elizabeth sighed heavily. "While I prefer not to think of the Bennet family too much today, I cannot complain that his interference means that I will marry my Fitzwilliam that much sooner."

Her aunt pulled her into a hug. "You are loved, Elizabeth, very much, by so many. Do not worry about what the Bennets may say to you when you go to Longbourn. Rely on Fitzwilliam to support you through this and everything else you will face in your married life. He is a very good man and will do right by you."

"I know, Aunt. Now, let us finish getting ready so I might finally be wed to him. I feel that I have waited years for this moment," she said with a grin.

Laughing, her aunt moved to help finish arranging her hair before assisting her with the jewellery Fitzwilliam had given her to wear for their wedding. It was a lovely pearl necklace, interspersed with emeralds, with a matching bracelet and earbobs. She had exclaimed over the set when he had given it to her Saturday evening and had reprimanded him for spoiling her with his purchase.

"Not at all," had been his reply. "I was not the one who purchased it, but my father. He had it commissioned the last winter he was in town and told me to give it to my bride. Recall that he hoped my bride would be you, and know that it was chosen specifically for you."

Elizabeth had been uncertain how to respond to that, and so had only pressed a kiss to his cheek. "Then I thank your father," she finally managed, tears pooling in her eyes. She had not seen her intended again since Uncle Gardiner had decreed that he could not visit on Sunday, allowing the Gardiner family one final day with her before he carried her off. He had laughingly agreed, for after this day, she would never be parted from him again.

THE WEDDING WENT off without a hitch. A handful of close friends and family gathered to watch the nuptials take place. Darcy's cousin,

Colonel Fitzwilliam, acted as Darcy's witness, and Mrs. Gardiner signed as Elizabeth's. Georgiana stood up with her, delighted to be gaining a sister, but she was too young to sign the register as a witness.

As soon as the couple signed the register affirming their marriage, they quickly departed the church, with Darcy assisting his new bride into the waiting carriage. Few words were exchanged as the carriage made its way to the Matlock home near Grosvenor Square, and half an hour later, a slightly dishevelled pair laughingly excited the carriage.

After enduring the wedding breakfast, the newly married couple were finally free to return to their home and to finish what they had begun on the earlier carriage ride. Likewise, they took advantage of their week of solitude at home, rarely venturing from their apartments, although they did make a couple of trips to visit the library to find something to read to each other. Several books from the top shelf of the library were relocated to a locked bookcase in their private sitting room, and the couple were occasionally found studying them intently.

While they ignored most correspondence during this time, they did spend a bit of time in the study, discussing where they could stay for a few nights when they went to see Mr. Bennet. Uncle Gardiner had sent a letter to his brother Phillips, asking him about lodging in the area and he highly recommended a dower house near Longbourn that was available to be let for a few nights. Uncle Gardiner put Darcy in touch with Mr. Phillips and Darcy had been communicating with him almost daily to make the necessary arrangements for the house to be ready.

The dower house was on a nearby estate, located on the other side of Meryton from Longbourn. Fortunately, it was far enough away that no gossip had reached the town of its expected inhabitants. Darcy's servants had already been dispatched to begin preparing it for the couple's arrival. It would be ready to be occupied on the Monday following the wedding.

So it was, that exactly a week after their wedding, the couple boarded a coach to head north into Hertfordshire. Neither was particularly looking forward to the visit; Elizabeth dreaded meeting with her parents, and both were feeling a little anxious about their reception by Elizabeth's family.

Regardless of what they might suffer on this visit, Darcy was thrilled to have Elizabeth by his side on the journey. She was sleeping, snuggled against him, with his arm draped across her shoulders and her hand resting on his chest. Darcy smiled, kissed her forehead, and fell asleep himself, realising they both needed to catch up on some of the sleep they had lost over the last week.

They arrived at the dower house shortly after two in the afternoon. It was on the small side, though the manor house was significantly large and well maintained. Darcy had a passing acquaintance with the family who resided there, but they were away from the house at present, visiting their primary estate near Northampton.

For the first day of their visit, the couple spent their time acquainting themselves with the house and peeking into rooms. The largest suite was prepared for the two of them to occupy, though, as a dower cottage, it had only one bed chamber. This suited the couple well, for they had decided immediately after their wedding to share one bedchamber, shocking the housekeeper of the manor house who had come to greet the couple. That lady apologised for the lack of separate bedrooms and had been scandalised when they told her it was unnecessary.

Laughing, after being shown into the primary rooms of the house, they took up residence on a comfortable sofa in the well-stocked library and spent the rest of the afternoon enjoying each other's company.

The following morning, the Darcys rose late, or at least late for them, and requested breakfast delivered to their shared sitting room. Just after eleven, the couple mounted the horses that had been sent ahead of them and travelled the countryside. After their engagement, they had explored much of Pemberley together on horseback, accompanied by a groom for propriety. As with so many other things, Darcy was thrilled to be able to go for a ride without the chaperone and took advantage of his wife's sole company.

After a brisk ride and a picnic atop the highest spot they could find, they returned to their leased home where they readied themselves for a visit to the Bennet family.

"Mr. and Mrs. Darcy to call on Mr. Bennet," Darcy said to the housekeeper when she answered the door.

"Miss Lizzy?" the lady asked, staring at the young lady on the gentleman's arm.

"Yes, Mrs. Hill. But I am Mrs. Elizabeth Darcy now. This is my husband, Fitzwilliam Darcy of Pemberley in Derbyshire."

Mrs. Hill shut the door with the three of them on the outside. "You shouldn't have come, miss." She looked between the couple momentarily, finally seeming to have understood what had been said. "You are married?"

Elizabeth nodded, surprised at the mode of greeting clearly shown on her face.

"Then perhaps it will be well. The master will not be pleased, but at least you are already married."

"Why did Mr. Bennet summon me here?"

"He intends for you to marry his cousin and Longbourn's heir to ensure your mother never has to leave the house. Jane is 'too beautiful,' and her mother claims she is being courted by someone, so she decided that you must come home and do your duty to the family. The man has a son older than you already, but his wife died a little more than a year ago, and now he wants another. He decided one of you girls would suit and figured Mr. Bennet could not turn him down."

Elizabeth should have been surprised, but sadly, she was not, not since her father had cast her from the house so long ago without care. She turned to look at her husband, and when he nodded, she spoke again. "Well, that is quite impossible since I am already married. Please show us into the drawing room, Mrs. Hill, but do not announce my married name or that of my husband."

Darcy was proud of his wife. He had always known she was strong, especially after the incident that first summer at Pemberley. What would have been a fatal blow to most women seemed only to glance off Elizabeth. He knew she would need comfort later, but at the moment, she was strong. He was there to offer support, but she was there to confront her parents.

Mrs. Hill showed the pair into the drawing room where the ladies of the family were gathered. "Miss Elizabeth is here, madam," Mrs. Hill said, curtseying to her mistress before hurrying from the room to let Mr. Bennet know of the arrival.

"Lizzy Bennet, you were expected home days ago. Why have you waited so long to arrive?" Mrs Bennet demanded, her tone shrill and grating. Elizabeth remained standing, just inside the door, her husband behind her and shadowed. Those in the room could not see him, and he deliberately held back, as he and Elizabeth had discussed before arriving.

"I have not been Lizzy Bennet in some years, madam," Elizabeth said. "When I was cast from my childhood home and disowned by my family, I became Elizabeth Gardiner."

"There is no need for you to act all high and mighty now, Lizzy. You have finally come home to your family, and you will do your duty to save us from the hedgerows. I suppose your uncle has given you some money for you to be dressed as well as you are. When your trunks are unpacked, you will have to allow your sisters to look at what you brought, for you will not need all those fine things when you are wed," Mrs. Bennet began.

"Who exactly am I to wed, madam? I know of no engagement that has been entered into on my behalf. Why should others claim the dresses that were purchased for me? What right do they have to what my uncle gave me?" Elizabeth asked, maintaining a calm and cool demeanour despite her rising anger. Knowing that her husband was behind her, silently lending his support, did much to cool her frustration; that and knowing that none of the plans the Bennets had for her would come to fruition.

All four of Elizabeth's sisters were surprised by her sudden appearance in front of them and were shocked at her defiant words and stance. While Jane and Mary remembered their sister, Kitty barely recalled that she had another sister. Lydia was the least surprised since she had been privy to her mother's plans for Elizabeth though she was a little surprised that this sister actually arrived. For most of her life, she had heard her mother only complain about her second daughter and knew her mother planned to force her to marry Longbourn's heir as a way to 'save the family from the hedgerows.'

For the last several months, after intercepting a letter meant for her husband, Mrs. Bennet had corresponded with the future heir of Longbourn. Through these letters, she hatched a plan meant to ensure her status as Mistress of Longbourn even after her husband's eventual death. But it was necessary for the man to marry one of her daughters, and she had determined that Elizabeth was to be the sacrificial lamb.

"You shall marry the heir to Longbourn, your father's cousin, Mr. Patrick Collins. He is a little older than you, but I am certain he will make you a good husband. I will train you to be a good wife and the mistress of this estate in the month before your wedding, and you and your husband will live in the dower house. We have already begun refurbishing the cottage; it is a little small, but it will do for you. The estate will pay for you to have a few servants, but you and your husband will likely spend a great deal of time here since Mr. Collins wants to begin learning how to manage the estate," Mrs. Bennet explained.

"Unsurprisingly, your plan is illogical. Is not Mr. Collins nearly as old as Mr. Bennet?" Without waiting for a response, Elizabeth asked. "Why in heaven's name do you believe he will live longer than Mr. Bennet? What will happen to you should Mr. Collins die before Mr. Bennet or only survive him by a few years? You will still be homeless." Mrs. Bennet gasped and prepared to rebuke her daughter, but Elizabeth merely shook her head and waved her hand as though it did not matter. It did not. "It is irrelevant. Nothing you say or do can make me marry this man."

Mrs. Bennet stood, her anger rising toward her second eldest child. "You will do as you are told, Lizzy. You will not defy your mother in this way."

Elizabeth's eyes snapped; her anger and frustration at the way her mother had always dismissed her coming to the fore. "My name is Elizabeth, madam. I have not been Lizzy since I left here. When you cast me aside, I chose to take a different name since I no longer wanted any part of the person I was before."

"That is absurd, Lizzy; you are my daughter, and nothing will ever change that. It is about time you and your uncle came to your senses, but I am thoroughly vexed that you did not come home sooner. I gave you a fortnight, yet you had the audacity to wait until the very last moment to show yourself," Mrs. Bennet snapped, waving her hand dismissively.

Elizabeth shook her head in disbelief, and the movement prompted Darcy to step forward. Feeling his presence behind her, she took a deep breath. "Mrs. Bennet, you are the one being ridiculous if you think I owe you anything or can be forced to do your bidding. I will not lift a finger for your comfort and marrying the man you suggest is out of the question."

She was cut off before she could introduce Darcy. Mrs. Bennet spied him standing behind her and began shrieking. "Lizzy Bennet, you travelled from London alone with this man? Has my brother reduced you to a common trollop or allowed you to become some man's mistress? You will ruin yourself and your sisters by gallivanting around in this way. How dare you show up here with your, your, paramour?"

"Madam, cease this caterwauling at once," Darcy commanded, his deep baritone catching the attention of everyone in the room. "Had you allowed your daughter to finish the introductions, you would have heard who I was and my connection to her. Instead, you choose to cast aspersions without thought—"

Again, Mrs. Bennet was not listening and cut him off. "That girl is no child of mine. I would never allow such a girl in my home. I insist you leave at once. Lizzy Bennet is dead to me and is never again welcome in my home."

"Then it is a good thing I have not been Lizzy Bennet for a decade, madam. My name is Elizabeth Darcy. I married the man standing beside me several weeks ago. And I can promise you that I will never step foot in this house again, so long as you are the mistress here."

Chapter Twenty

This announcement was met by shocked gasps from all the ladies. Mrs. Bennet scanned the two strangers standing in her drawing room and quickly concluded that Elizabeth must have married well, if she was indeed married. Too late, she recognised the value of holding her tongue and remained silent.

The other girls were equally surprised and could not speak. Lydia, knowing her mother's plans for the daughter she had cast aside, furrowed her brow, wondering what would happen now and which of her sisters would be forced to marry that man. Kitty was merely shocked at what had transpired in their drawing room.

Jane was shocked that her sister had married before her and to such a handsome husband. She suddenly regretted not treating Elizabeth better.

Before the couple could leave, Mr. Bennet entered the room. "So, you have finally come; have you, Lizzy? Well, your mother has decided you are to marry, and your intended is to arrive shortly. You have a little more than a month to begin learning all you need to so you might one day take over as mistress to this great estate." He spoke with not a little irony and the trademark sardonic wit Elizabeth recalled.

"I have no interest in becoming the mistress of this estate. You have not wanted me in nearly a decade; it can be of no concern to you what I do now," Elizabeth retorted.

"That is no way to speak to your father, girl," Mr. Bennet's typical lackadaisical attitude fell away, replaced by a brief flash of anger.

"You are no longer my father, sir. Uncle Edward has acted as my father since the day you signed away all rights to me to him."

"Lizzy ..." he began.

"I am not Lizzy; my name is Elizabeth Darcy, and you should address me by my married name. I have little interest in allowing you such informality with my name," she stated, interrupting him.

"Elizabeth Bennet, you will stop this foolishness. You cannot be married; you are underage, and I have not given my permission for you to do so."

"I assure you, sir; my marriage is perfectly legal and an unalterable fact."

Mr. Bennet scowled and addressed Darcy. "How dare you take advantage of my daughter! I will have this travesty set aside since Lizzy is underage."

Darcy laughed. "You are welcome to try. It will be my pleasure to know you are wasting your time and money doing so. You have absolutely no grounds on which to object to our marriage, sir. My wife's uncle, with whom she has lived for nearly a decade, was authorised by *you* to be Mrs. Darcy's guardian in your stead. Mr. Gardiner gave his permission to my suit and signed the marriage settlement. The rector at both my church and hers were advised of Mrs. Darcy's guardianship, found no fault in proceeding with Mr. Gardiner's consent, and the banns were read in each of our parish churches the requisite three times without objection."

"Your marriage is invalid as you were already betrothed to the heir of Longbourn, Mr. Collins. You will be the mistress of this estate someday," Mr. Bennet insisted.

"You are mistaken if you believe a prior engagement invalidates a legal marriage. Sadly for you, my marriage ends any nefarious plot you may have had to sell me to a man twice my age," Elizabeth said, her tone frosty.

"What you say is impossible. You must marry Mr. Collins. If I do not give him my daughter in marriage, he will claim I have broken the contract and take Longbourn from me."

"You should not have signed such a contract naming a daughter over whom you no longer exercised authority," Darcy replied unsympathetically.

"Where will we go?" Bennet cried. "What will I do about Mr. Collins?"

Neither Darcy was inclined to care. "That, sir, is your problem." They turned to depart but were startled by the loud voice of the matron of the house. "Lizzy Bennet, you will do as you are told. I do not know who this man you are wantonly accompanying might be, but I am certain he cannot be your husband. You will marry Mr. Collins. He agreed to allow me and my daughters to live here if we gave him a daughter as a wife. You were always my greatest disappointment, and it is your duty to protect your family."

"I believe this is a madhouse," Elizabeth murmured to her husband before turning to face the irate woman. "Unfortunately, you will have to find someone else to do your bidding, Mrs. Bennet. I owe you and your family nothing. You are pathetic if you thought this scheme of yours would work even if I had not married. Had I been forced to marry this man, I would never have let you continue as mistress of this house. I would have thrown you into the hedgerows myself, that is if this Mr. Collins actually survives my father. I can assure you, this is an enormous joke to Mr. Bennet. He will laugh all the way to his grave at this convoluted mess you have created."

Elizabeth began to leave again but then turned to face her mother one final time. "Let me be clear to ensure you have no continuing expectations of me. No one from your family will be permitted to enter my homes unless I have extended an invitation to visit in writing. If you show up uninvited you will be turned away. Any letters you or your husband send me will either be returned to you or discarded unread. Mrs. Bennet, do not promise your daughters that I will buy them anything, sponsor them in Town, give them a season, or provide them dowries because I will do nothing of the kind. They are your responsibility, not mine. And do not expect me to care for you after Mr. Bennet dies. I will not house you or give you funds, so, if you have not saved for that eventuality, you should start now. Finally, let me caution you and your family against trying to use a connection with me to your advantage or spreading tales about me or my family. If I learn that you have done so, I will ask my husband to sue you for defamation. You are dead to me, madam." Elizabeth smiled at Mrs. Bennet. "Have a good day." And with that, she turned on her heel and left, followed closely by her husband.

BEHIND THEM, the room erupted. Elizabeth heard her mother exclaim: "Mr. Bennet, Mr. Bennet, If Lizzy cannot be made to marry Mr. Collins, whatever will we do?" She shook her head as she continued walking toward the door, her husband trailing behind. They stopped only when they were once again outside the house, when Darcy pulled Elizabeth to him and embraced her tightly just outside their carriage.

Their embrace was soon interrupted by a soft voice. "Elizabeth, I am glad you have returned, even if only for a moment. I am truly sorry that Mama and Papa sent for you like this. Had I known, had I any way to have done so, I would have warned you not to come. I have often wondered how you were, but I was wary of mentioning you to either of my parents. Suffice it to say, neither cared for the reminder of their second daughter."

Elizabeth turned and was surprised to see her sister Mary behind them. Her next younger sister had always been a quiet girl, and too young to participate in the games she and Jane played. She had been a gentle presence in their home, occasionally joining in on the older girls' lessons with their father. "I understand, Mary. Even had you known, it would have been difficult for you to warn me of what they were planning. There was nothing you could have done to prevent this from occurring."

"It does not change the fact that I wish things could have been different. I was seven when you left, but I knew enough to realise our parents and Jane changed for the worse once you were gone. Do you ... do you think I could write to you now? I am uncertain if Mama would allow me to receive letters, but perhaps we could find a way?"

Elizabeth reached out to clasp her sister's hand, but before she could respond, Jane joined them. "Lizzy, it has been a long time," she said, her tone icy.

"It is not as though I could have returned, Jane. Not when our parents cast me from the house and disowned me. I did write to you, for years. Long after you stopped writing back. And you were miserable to me during your one visit to London."

"Mama made things ... difficult," Jane said slowly.

"Yes, Mrs. Bennet is quite proficient at that," Elizabeth said, glancing at the front door and worrying who else might exit from it. She could still hear her mother screeching her displeasure, and did not want to encounter her or her father again that day. "We received an invitation tonight for dinner at the Lucases. I understand the entire neighbourhood was invited. Perhaps we will be able to speak more there. However, at the moment I think it is best that we depart. If we do not see you tonight, we will call on the Phillipses tomorrow morning. Good day."

Elizabeth curtsied in the direction of her sister and was helped into the carriage by her husband. As the carriage pulled away, she saw the front door open and heard Mrs. Bennet demand her daughters return to the house to attend to her.

"Are you well, my darling?" Darcy asked as the carriage pulled away.

Closing her eyes and sighing heavily, she opened them to see her husband's concerned eyes fixed on hers. "I will be. Foolishly, I did not expect a confrontation to occur as it did, but I suppose my showing up here after all these years and already married surprised them. Mrs. Bennet still has little use for me other than how my existence might benefit her. I should not have been surprised by this." She sighed and leaned into him as she spoke, and his arms immediately came up to surround her.

"Your hope for a restoration to your family is not foolish, dearest; some people are simply unable to see beyond themselves. We will pay the visits we had already planned, but then we can either return to London or simply remain holed up in our cottage until we are obligated to return for my aunt's ball," Darcy said, holding his wife tightly to his chest and pressing kisses to her forehead.

Elizabeth relaxed into him, and the two remained quiet the remainder of the way to their leased cottage. Upon reaching their lodgings, Darcy escorted his wife to their chambers, where they continued to speak. "What will you do about your sisters?"

She shrugged. "I do not know. If we see them again before we leave Meryton, I suppose we will have to judge them based on their reactions to seeing us. Jane seemed angry with me while Mary was ... I do not know, regretful. She seems to have missed me, and I wonder if forming a relationship with her is possible. If any of my sisters were to write to me, I would be willing to correspond with them. However, if their letters are self-serving or demanding, I will be reluctant to continue the relationship. I realise they are not the ones who cast me aside, but I no longer know them as I might have had I grown up with them."

Darcy nodded at this. "That is wise. Know that I will support you in whatever you decide, Elizabeth, and will be as encouraging as you would like me to be."

"Thank you, William. I admit that I cannot imagine having anything to do with either Mr. or Mrs. Bennet at this point. I am uncertain if anything would make me want to have a relationship with either of them again."

"I do not believe anyone could fault you feeling that way, Elizabeth. Your parents do not know what a treasure you are, and they do not deserve you. I cannot imagine what either of them were thinking, demanding you return to marry the heir to the estate."

Elizabeth laughed scornfully. "Nor can I. I do not remember much, but I believe the heir is a distant relation of my father's. It has been years since I heard him mentioned, but when I was a child, I recall him being spoken of as a contemporary of my father's. Hill said he was older than me and had a son around my age." She shuddered. "Even had I remained at home with my parents all these years, I cannot imagine willingly marrying a man more than twice my age. Of course, there is no telling what kind of person I would have been had I been subjected to the influence of the Bennets for all these years. I was taught by my father, but Mrs. Bennet always complained about the time I spent with him. Jane would have eventually listened to her and stopped reading, but I do not believe I would have. I wonder if we would have met had I remained at home."

This thought made Darcy take his wife in his arms once again. "I cannot imagine ever not loving you, Elizabeth. Without you," he visibly shuddered, "without you, I cannot imagine the man I would have been." The two remained tightly embraced for some time following this, and nearly all conversation came to an end.

Chapter Twenty-One

Some hours later, the two boarded the carriage to take them to Lucas Lodge for the party that was taking place that evening. When Darcy began making arrangements for their stay in Meryton through Elizabeth's uncle, Phillips had mentioned this gathering and obtained an invitation for the couple to attend. Only that afternoon, Elizabeth sent a note to her friend explaining how she had come to be wed, including ensuring that her and her husband's attendance that night would not cause any problems.

The return note informed the pair that Mr. and Mrs. Bennet had sent their regrets for the party that afternoon except for Jane and Mary would still attend. Elizabeth scoffed a little at this since it was outside the bounds of propriety for the two young girls to attend without some sort of chaperone, but Darcy attempted to excuse it, claiming that it was likely the families were so well acquainted, the Bennet parents had not thought it would matter. Elizabeth acknowledged that might be true but was hopeful that the two attended because they wanted to see her again.

Both suppositions proved to be correct, though in varying forms. Even Lady Lucas acknowledged the impropriety of the two arriving unchaperoned, but several others offered to perform the office in the absence of their parents. Jane and Mary did seek out Elizabeth on several occasions throughout the evening, always separately and it was obvious they had very different purposes in doing so.

Whereas Mary approached Elizabeth almost immediately and sought to discover what she could about the sister she had not seen in nearly a decade, Jane waited to seek Elizabeth out until dinner was finished.

Shortly after they arrived, Darcy was cornered by Mr. Phillips.

"My brother came to see me earlier, not long after you departed the house, I believe. Like the short-sighted fool he can be, he signed a contract with the heir presumptive of Longbourn, promising an unnamed daughter as a wife in exchange for a promise to allow Mrs. Bennet and her remaining daughters to live there after his demise. If he fails to meet the terms of the contract, the heir can claim that he has forfeited his estate, at least, is what was written. I am uncertain it is enforceable as it is, but he is obviously concerned about it now. It is unusual for him to exert himself so much as to actually seek me out, rather than sending for me to visit him," Phillips said. "Apparently, Mrs. Bennet was the one who read the letter from Mr. Collins and, after corresponding with the man in secret, demanded her husband sign the contract without ever ascertaining if the stipulations it contained were legal or even if the contract made sense. Bennet signed it without question," Phillips said, shaking his head as though he could not believe the words he said.

"No man of sense could sign a contract without reading it first and then being certain he could fulfil it. Before he agreed to give his daughter in marriage, he should have ascertained that she was free, particularly one he had disowned and had not lived with him in years. Though, a wise man would not have sent his daughter away in the first place," Darcy replied.

Phillips laughed derisively. "You are not wrong, nephew. Bennet is intelligent but unwise. Mr. Collins is the same age as Bennet and there is no reason to believe that Collins will survive him. My sister obviously did not comprehend that the arrangements she negotiated would not secure her future, yet Bennet capitulated to his foolish wife when she demanded he sign the agreement; he has always done what was easiest instead of what was wise."

"It was short sighted of him. However, he has made his bed and will have to live with the choices he has made. There is little that can be done about it now," Darcy replied.

"Returning to the point at hand, although it is my professional opinion that the contract Bennet signed with Collins is unenforceable, there are too many variables for me to make an accurate prediction of how this will be resolved. Since I am unaware of any correspondence that was shared beyond the contract, it is difficult for me to determine what promises may have been made. Part of it depends on how reasonable a man he may prove to be. He may demand another wife in Elizabeth's place, or he may recognise that something can be done to assist both families. Truly, all of my nieces are too young to marry a man who is nearly the same age as their father, but apparently, he wishes for a young bride."

Darcy grimaced at that. "That does not speak well of the man or his motives. I cannot imagine any of my new sisters wishing to marry such a man, though I do not know any of them well. Did not someone say he has a son nearly the same age as Miss Bennet?"

"His son is twenty-three, as I understand it, and has recently finished at university. Fanny claims he intends to seek a position as a curate since he hopes to take orders while he waits to inherit either from his father or his distant cousin," Phillips replied.

"I have experienced too many of my aunt's rectors to believe that everyone who is ordained is worthy of being so," Darcy retorted.

"However, if he proves competent, I may be able to aid him in finding a position. Once you meet him, let me know your opinion."

Phillips nodded and offered his thanks to the gentleman. The two spoke a little longer about the matter before separating to join the ladies. It was then that Darcy encountered his new sister speaking poorly of his wife, and the previous conversation was nearly forgotten.

In the meantime, Jane approached Elizabeth once the women were settled in the drawing room with their tea. "Well, Lizzy, it appears you have done quite well for yourself."

She eyed her sister warily. "What do you mean?"

"Your husband. Not only is he rather handsome, I understand from our neighbours that he is very wealthy," Jane said, eyeing her with a mixture of disdain and envy. "How did our uncle arrange that?"

Elizabeth inwardly sighed. It should not be a surprise to learn that there was already talk about her husband's wealth. The Lucases were vaguely familiar with him, and she supposed that others would have heard his name when they attended events in London. While none of them were of the same level of society as her husband, his family and wealth were well known. After a moment, she spoke: "Our uncle did not arrange anything. Fitzwilliam and I met several years ago, but did not see each other for some time after that. When we met again in April, we recognised our growing feelings for each other. He proposed when we visited his estate this summer," Elizabeth stated coldly.

Jane smirked at her sister. "And what did you do to convince him to offer for you?"

"I did not 'convince' him," Elizabeth began, but was cut off by the men entering the room.

"She did not have to convince me. I knew the moment I saw her at her coming out ball that I wanted her and no other for my wife," Darcy said, his tone gruff and icy. Elizabeth had never heard him so cold.

Jane put on a look of pretended innocence. "Forgive me for thinking otherwise. Mama simply thought that Uncle Gardiner must have arranged the match. None of us would have expected Lizzy to marry well and certainly not to a man like you. With her looks ..." she trailed off, fluttering her eyelashes at Darcy.

Darcy was displeased to have to defend his wife to this spiteful woman. "My wife is beautiful. Surely you would not imply anything else. I first met Elizabeth when she was fourteen, a mere slip of a girl, and I knew even then she would be an exceptional beauty. Even my father adored her before he passed. Not only is she lovely on the outside, but she is equally lovely on the inside. Not every woman can say that," he said pointedly.

It seemed that was enough to silence the eldest Miss Bennet, and Darcy was displeased to have had to defend his wife to this spiteful woman. "Elizabeth, your uncle asked me to bring you to him when we entered the room. I think your sister Mary is over there as well. Would you join me?" And with this, they nodded at Jane and left to find Mr. Phillips.

"That was badly done, Jane," Charlotte hissed. She and Jane were not particularly close, largely due to the gossip Mrs. Bennet and her eldest daughter enjoyed spreading about Charlotte Lucas and her status as a spinster. It did not matter that Charlotte's unmarried state was more due to her intended passing away before they could wed than her somewhat plain appearance. For some reason, Mrs. Bennet preferred to focus on appearances rather than Charlotte's many good qualities.

For instance, Charlotte Lucas did far more to assist the tenants at Longbourn than either Mrs. Bennet or Jane Bennet did, as well as assisting the poor in the parish. Lady Lucas may not have been born a gentlewoman, but neither had Mrs. Bennet. Instead, it was Lady Lucas who had taken the lead in the community providing aiding those who needed it.

"What would you know, Charlotte Lucas? You are a spinster and will remain in this insignificant town your entire life. Now that Lizzy has managed to marry so well, I will go to London and be introduced to wealthy and handsome young men. It will not be long before I am wed and far higher than you could ever aspire to."

"Who will take you to London, Jane?" Elizabeth asked, having returned when she saw Charlotte speaking to Jane. "For it will not be me, not when you seek to insult me and attempt to flirt with my husband. I expected better of you, Jane, though perhaps I should not have. I still recall how you treated me and my aunt and uncle the one time you visited."

"Mama will make you take me in," Jane retorted.

Elizabeth laughed at this. "The woman you call Mama is no mother to me. The only mother I have had in more than a decade is Mrs. Gardiner. If you think I would do anything because Mrs. Bennet demands it of me, you are sorely mistaken. Given what she must have told you, I am certain you now think that you are so beautiful that no man would reject you. Let me assure you that is not the case. I have met many gentlemen and ladies in town, and Jane, you would scarcely stand out among them. Moreover, many men seek to marry a lady with some wealth of her own, and short of that, one who has something to recommend her beyond her looks. Few men would marry a woman for beauty alone despite what your mother has told you. No, they will seek a woman who can benefit them in some way, and you, dear sister, have nothing to offer. You seem to be as spiteful and rude as many of the so-called ladies I have encountered in the *ton*, but that is not enough to recommend you."

Jane had no response to that, but tears formed in her eyes. Elizabeth and Charlotte shared a look, each assuring the other that there was no real cause for concern, and together, they strode off toward the other side of the room. They did watch, however, as a seething Jane moved toward the exit, and soon they heard a carriage departing, likely carrying her away from Lucas Lodge and toward home.

Elizabeth patted Mary's hand. "Mary, Fitzwilliam and I will assure you are taken home this evening. It is best if you wait a bit, although Jane will surely tell her mother what I have said. I am sorry if things will be difficult for you as a result."

"It will likely be little different than any other evening. I am typically ignored, and I am uncertain if they will even notice I did not return home. Mrs. Hill will of course, but Mama and Jane are unlikely to do anything tonight other than to commiserate with each other over you foiling their plans."

"Mary, I do hope you will find a way to write to me or to escape from Longbourn. I would like to get to know you as a sister. Perhaps Mr. Phillips can send and receive letters on your behalf. Or even the rector? I recall a little of Mr. Allen from before; is he still the rector of the Meryton church?"

"He is," Mary told her. "And I will ask Uncle Phillips first if he can help me correspond with you. I recall a few arguments in the years after you left about letters arriving from you and do not think that Mama would allow me to keep any letters you sent me. She would expect me to ask you for clothing and expensive trinkets, as well as to take all my sisters under your wing and take us to town."

"Mary, I must tell you that Mrs. Bennet will receive nothing from me, nor will I give in to any demands she may attempt to place on me. She had me sent away from my home at the age of eight, and up until the day she demanded I return home to marry a man twice my age, she has ignored me entirely. If she wishes to apologise for her behaviour, I will listen, but it will take time before I am willing to have anything to do with her or Mr. Bennet. The same goes for my sisters, Mary. I will gladly correspond with you and any of my sisters who desire it, but it will take time to build a relationship."

"I do understand, Lizzy, or would you prefer I call you Elizabeth, or even Mrs. Darcy? I have not seen you in many years and am uncertain if you will welcome the intimacy of sisters."

"I have not been 'Lizzy' since I left Longbourn. The Gardiners and William use my Christian name since I wanted to forget any reminders of that time. The nickname 'Lizzy' was one of those things that we changed first, that and my surname. Before I became a Darcy, I was a Gardiner, not a Bennet. It may sound terrible of me, but when my father agreed to disown me because he would not stand up to his wife about her treatment of me, I wanted nothing to do with the name Bennet."

"I do not know if others in my family would understand, but I think I can. I recall little of how Mama treated you, but after you left, I became the one she complained about. Jane and Lydia are her favourites—Jane for her beauty and Lydia for her liveliness. At thirteen, Lydia is quite spoilt, and Kitty follows her. I am largely ignored, but occasionally she will blame me for something that is wrong," Mary admitted.

Elizabeth frowned at that. "I am sorry, Mary. I know there is little I could have done, but I do hate that my being forced to leave made life more difficult for you." She took several minutes to look at her sister. "Do Kitty and Lydia favour Jane? You and I have the darker hair and eyes of our grandmother. It was a frequent complaint I heard as a child. Mrs. Bennet preferred the girls who looked like her."

This caused Mary to flush. "They do. I have been compared unfavourably to my sisters all my life. Kitty favours our mother though not as much as the other two. She gains attention mostly because she follows Lydia's example. Fortunately, they are too young to be much in company at present, but they are wild and unchecked already. I worry about them."

Mrs. Phillips reached them before anyone could speak further. "Jane left in the Bennet carriage a few minutes ago, Mary. Why did you not accompany your sister?"

"She grew angry with Elizabeth's reluctance to agree to Mrs. Bennet's demands that she take Jane to London immediately and left. I do not think she remembered that I was here with her," Mary said.

Mrs. Philips looked at her niece. "My sister has already demanded that you take Jane to London? I did not think today's meeting went well. Mr. Bennet met with my husband earlier, and they spoke of the marriage contract that was signed. He was a fool to sign the document without bringing it to my husband to review, but my sister was insistent that it was the only way to save the family. I do not think either of them read the document all the way through."

"You are correct that our meeting did not go well. They seemed to think that I would set aside my legal marriage so I could marry Longbourn's heir, and, naturally, I refused. Jane approached me this evening to tell me that Mrs. Bennet will demand I take my sisters to London to introduce them to wealthy men, also implying I won my husband by compromising him. She flirted with him right in front of me; I assume because she believes she can win him away from me. I informed her that none of those things would happen, and she grew angry with me."

Mrs. Phillips took a minute to allow the information to sink in. "Oh," she said after a moment, needing to absorb all the information that had been shared with her. "I believe my husband spoke to yours about what the Bennets have done, and I am certain they will soon realise they have made a mess of matters. Of course, my sister will be reluctant to admit it, and I worry about what she might scheme next. Come with me, Mary, I will ensure you arrive safely home tonight."

And with that, the older lady took Mary by the arm and led her to gather her husband before directing them all toward their hosts for the evening. The three departed, followed not long after by the Darcys themselves.

Chapter Twenty-Two

As Darcy waited for his wife to prepare herself for bed and join him in their chamber, he thought over what he had learned that day.

The confrontation with the Bennets had been unpleasant, but not unexpected. He knew from the letter his wife's uncle had shown him that the family expected Elizabeth to essentially sacrifice herself on the family's behalf, and they had guessed marriage was intended to be the method. Elizabeth was likewise unaware of a second letter sent to Gardiner emphasising the importance of Elizabeth's returning home. Darcy had wanted to share both letters with his wife, but Gardiner had been insistent he not do so.

Gardiner also told the younger man of the letters he had received through the years from Fanny Bennet. There were only a few, perhaps one or two a year, always making demands and speaking ill of the daughter she had cast aside. Neither his niece nor his wife was aware of these, and he doubted the lady's husband was aware of them either, but he had kept them as proof of her hatred for her daughter.

"I cannot say why I have kept these over the years, and have, on occasion, thought to confront Thomas and Fanny with them, but saw no reason to do so. However, I will turn these over to your safe keeping, in case it becomes necessary to remind my sister of what she has said. Once she discovers Elizabeth is married to such a wealthy man, she will likely begin demanding the world."

"Elizabeth hopes for a restoration, but if it is as you say, she will want nothing to do with them. She looks forward to seeing her sisters and hopes she can forge a relationship at least with them," Darcy replied.

The Darcys remained at their cottage the day after this meeting but went into the village the following day to take tea with Mrs. Phillips. They arrived in town early and decided to peruse the shops for a short time before they needed to arrive at Elizabeth's aunt.

As they were leaving the milliner's, they encountered Elizabeth's sisters. Accustomed to London, they were surprised to see all four Bennet daughters in town without any sort of servant. The two younger girls barely acknowledged their sister, while Jane and Mary stopped to speak with the couple. Mary seemed genuinely pleased to see them, whereas Jane subtly moved closer to Darcy in an attempt to flirt with him.

"Mr. Darcy," she cooed, before turning toward her sister, "and Lizzy. How pleasant it is to encounter you two in town today. Might we join you in your shopping this morning?"

"We are nearly done with our shopping," Darcy said, stepping away from the cloying lady and bringing his wife's arm more firmly to his side.

Elizabeth murmured her agreement. "Yes, we are due at our aunt's very soon. I think we have completed our shopping this morning since we were mostly engaged in looking in windows to see what the shops have to offer. We also enjoyed our chance to walk through town and speak to those we have encountered."

WHEN LOVE IS TRUE

"Oh, in that case, perhaps we can join you at Aunt Phillips's house. She will not mind the additional company for tea. We did not have the opportunity to converse much at Lucas Lodge the other night, and I would love to hear about your time in London," Jane said, her voice simpering toward her new brother.

Darcy and Elizabeth glanced between each other. They knew one of their purposes in meeting with the Phillips was to discuss how matters stood at Longbourn. "William, perhaps you can join my uncle in his office while my sisters and I join my aunt in her parlour. I cannot imagine you enjoying too much conversation about the season in London, given how much you detest the experience," Elizabeth said with a teasing glint at her husband.

He sighed in evident relief. "Yes, I will greet your aunt and then join your uncle, that is, if you ladies do not object."

Mary quickly agreed, forcing Jane to do the same, because if she did otherwise, she would appear petulant. After gathering the younger Bennet girls, the party headed across the street to the Phillipses. If either Mr. or Mrs. Phillips were disturbed by the additional company, neither showed it.

Once the gentlemen were able to separate from the ladies, Phillips immediately began. "I wanted to speak to you about your new sisters, Darcy, though I had hoped to include Elizabeth in this conversation. I am afraid their father neglected them as they grew up; his lack of resolve, which led to Elizabeth being sent away, seemed to drain any remaining desire to do better. Before that, he had taught her as he might have a son, including Jane in many of these discussions at Elizabeth's urging, with Jane showing some interest. For months after Elizabeth left, he rarely left his study, preferring to immerse himself in his books. The estate nearly fell into disrepair, and several horses had to be sold. I believe that jolted him back to reality, prompting him to at least do the bare minimum to keep the estate running and solvent, though little else. Any funds he had saved for the girls' dowries were used to restore the estate, and he never bothered to replace them.

"As a result, your new sisters are unruly and, frankly, rather wild. Lydia is very young yet, only thirteen, though she is already the subject of much gossip in our little village. They ought to have a governess to guide and instruct them, but neither my sister nor brother can be persuaded to restrict their spending enough to hire one."

Darcy sighed at hearing this but halted Mr. Phillips before he could continue further. "Phillips, I am truly sorry to hear this, but please help me understand why you think I should know this. Elizabeth has not been a Bennet for nine years. She had heard nothing from Longbourn in that time until this summons to return when she was informed that she was expected to 'rescue' the Bennets from their own laziness. I am truly sorry for my new sisters and wish they might have had someone to care for them and guide them as their parents should have done, and there is little I can do about the matter. As you said last night, perhaps it would be best to settle Mr. Bennet and his family elsewhere while Mr. Collins takes over the estate. The younger girls could perhaps be sent to school, and I would be willing to help with that. Not to mention, it seems likely that Mr. Collins will desire to sue Mr. Bennet for breach of contract. He may insist that Elizabeth be replaced by another daughter, thereby honouring the contract. The eldest Miss Bennet seems to be the only one of age to marry; however, even she is not entirely suitable to act as mistress of the estate at the moment from what I have observed."

Mr. Phillips shook his head. "Mrs. Bennet will not agree to Jane marrying the man. He is at least forty-five, if not closer to fifty, and my sister believes Jane deserves 'better'. Bennet mentioned it yesterday when he came to show me the contract, and I made the same suggestion. Last autumn, the man who leased Netherfield had paid your eldest sister a small measure of attention, so Mrs. Bennet decreed they would marry. However, it came to naught, but my sister still feels that Jane deserves to marry a wealthy man. Elizabeth marrying you will only further cement that in her mind."

Darcy snorted. "How will she meet this wealthy man who is destined for her? Elizabeth has not grown up on an estate except for her early years, and she will have much to learn when it comes time for her to take on the role. Miss Bennet does not seem interested in learning what will be required; she has flirted with me both times I have been in her company so far. Perhaps that has coloured my impression of her, but she does not seem like the type of woman who would be willing to learn what is necessary. Not to mention, her lack of dowry will make her far less interesting to the type of man she seeks to attract. Few men will marry a woman based solely on her appearance. Does she have accomplishments to speak of?"

Phillips shook his head slowly. "No, my sister has convinced Jane that all she needs to do to attract her husband is bat her eyes at him and smile. She can sew fairly well, mostly because to do otherwise would mean she did absolutely nothing. The tenants of Longbourn are among the poorest in our parish and require the most assistance from the church and the community. None of the Bennets take any interest in assisting them. The rector's wife has attempted to hint at matters to Mrs. Bennet, and a few of the gentlemen have spoken to Bennet outright about the matter, but neither seem to think anything of it."

With a grimace, Darcy looked at his new uncle for several moments. "It seems that nearly any other owner for Longbourn would ultimately be better than the existing master. Can any of the girls be encouraged to help the tenants, even a little?"

"I think Mary could be persuaded, but my wife does not know enough to help her. I suppose the rector's wife could; she already helps the poor in the parish a great deal, and I believe she was the daughter of an estate owner. If Mary began meeting with her on occasion, they might be able to do something for the tenants to ease some of their suffering," Phillips said thoughtfully.

With a heavy sigh, he continued. "I also wanted to put you on your guard. Your new mother will learn who you are and what you have and will expect your assistance both monetarily and in advancing the other girls in society."

Darcy returned the sigh. "Yes, I can imagine she will. However, I cannot imagine Elizabeth will desire to give into those demands. In fact, that was the point of the argument between Elizabeth and Miss Bennet last night; she informed her sister that she owed her family nothing. I think Elizabeth intends to treat her mother as her mother has treated her for much of the last decade by pretending she does not exist. I will ignore any letters she sends and have no desire to allow her in my home. If she approaches me, I will ignore her. She cannot have the ability to travel to Derbyshire so she will be unable to disturb us there."

"Will you share what we have discussed with Elizabeth?" Phillips asked.

"I will. I cannot say that any of it surprises her, but based on our conversations from yesterday, I know that Elizabeth will not easily give in. She will accept any letters from her sisters but will wait to determine what kind of relationship she will have with them based on the correspondence," Darcy replied.

Phillips nodded. "That is wise. I would not expect the younger girls to write, but Mary and Jane have appeared to be interested. I am uncertain what Jane might intend, but from what I have seen, Mary appears to be more interested in forming a real relationship. I am afraid that Fanny has ruined the other girls. Mary shares Elizabeth's looks so she has been largely ignored by both her parents. She spends a fair amount of time with my wife, the Lucases, and even the rector's wife."

Darcy nodded. "Elizabeth has enjoyed her conversations with her younger sister. Other than a moment at Longbourn, today was the first time she had seen her younger sisters, and they had little to say on that occasion."

The gentlemen then turned the conversation to less personal topics as they waited for the ladies to finish their tea in the parlour.

Chapter Twenty-Three

Elizabeth was uncomfortable in the other room. She did enjoy speaking with Mary, and to some degree Mrs. Phillips, but on this occasion, neither was able to say much. Instead, the two youngest girls asked questions about the London season, fashion, and similar topics without allowing Elizabeth time to answer. Jane was quiet but appeared to listen intently to the conversation when Kitty expressed her excitement about the prospect of attending the season herself in a year or two. However, before Kitty could say too much on the topic, Elizabeth held up her hand to stop the conversation.

"Who will sponsor you for this season you are hoping for? Neither Jane nor Mary have had one, so I cannot imagine Father will be willing to take you to town for that," Elizabeth stated matter-of-factly. She was willing to help her younger sisters to some extent, but they would need to prove themselves deserving of her assistance. They could not simply assume that just because their mother demanded something, Elizabeth would readily comply.

Kitty tilted her head and stared at her sister in confusion. "You will," she stated directly.

"I will not," Elizabeth stated firmly, wanting to ensure that all in the room understood. "First of all, you are fourteen and would not come out in London before seventeen, if not older. Young ladies do not come out in London until they are properly educated and prepared, and you would have much to do before you would be considered ready. Second, I do not know you. You were very young when I left home, when I was cast from our home and disowned, so for you to assume that I will do for you all of what you are proposing is insulting. Since Mrs. Bennet was the one who demanded I leave the only home I had known at the age of eight, and Mr. Bennet willingly went along with it, I owe no allegiance to *them*. I will gladly exchange letters with you, and should we form a friendship, I may invite you to visit at some point, but you should not assume I owe you anything."

"But Mama said—" Kitty began.

"What Mrs. Bennet said has no effect on me, I owe her no allegiance and I will not do anything that she demands of me, unless I choose to do it. I am your sister, not your parent, and I have no obligation toward you," Elizabeth said, a sense of finality to her words that a more astute person should have picked up on.

However, most of the girls raised by Fanny Bennet were not astute and had been raised believing they were owed whatever they wished.

"Mama always said you were not good for anything," Lydia said tartly. "After you left the other day, she looked over several of Papa's newspapers and found information about your husband. With your looks, she is astounded that you managed to find any husband, but she was shocked to learn that your Mr. Darcy is reportedly fabulously wealthy. Mama says you must have tricked him into marrying you somehow, or Uncle Gardiner did. You may not be willing right now to do as Mama says, but she will ensure you do. If you have ensnared such a handsome and wealthy husband, then surely I will marry a duke."

Elizabeth laughed derisively at the thought. "Lydia, you have many years before you are ready for marriage, and you are unlikely to ever even meet a duke. My husband may be highly placed in society and might move in exalted company, but even he rarely encounters anyone that high. Not to mention, there are presently no unmarried dukes and none younger than our father's age."

"But they must have sons, and once you take me to London and dress me in the finest silks and satins that are offered, I will have men desperate to marry me," Lydia sing-songed.

"As I told Kitty, you presume far too much. Unless you are willing to behave properly, I would never consider taking you to London. You still have many years to learn, being only thirteen, so I suggest you focus on acquiring accomplishments and learning to conduct yourself with propriety. There is no point in discussing it now, as any such trip is far off in the future. For the time being, I would like you to write to me once my husband and I leave the area. We have not been in each other's company for many years, and I would be glad to reconnect with you through letters for now," Elizabeth said kindly.

"Mama expects you to take Jane with you to London," Kitty informed her sister. Jane had the sense to blush at those words although she appeared ... smug, Elizabeth thought, as though she knew Elizabeth would comply with their mother's wishes. "She has already commanded Jane to pack her things so she might return with you to London."

"I will say this once more, for my husband and I do not intend to visit this town again beyond today. We hoped to visit my family and learn what the summons to Longbourn was about, but we are newly married," Elizabeth said, trying not to blush at the amused looks her youngest sisters cast at this statement. "I am happy to learn more about my sisters through letters at this point and will issue no invitations to London or to Pemberley for some time. Due to the separation enforced on us by Mr. and Mrs. Bennet, I do not know any of you well. Nor am I under any obligation to do as your parents' command, for I was disowned many years ago. As such, I have considered myself an orphan for much of the last decade and owe no obligation to anyone named Bennet. However, I know that you four had nothing to do with what happened and am willing to try to create a relationship with you. I make no promises aside from that." She fixed each of her sisters with an intent look, willing them to hear what she was trying to say.

"Should you persist in making demands of me, I will cut off contact with you. So long as the letters remain focused on getting to know each other better, I will be happy to correspond. At an appropriate time, if I offer an invitation, it will be because I desire to spend time with you, not out of obligation or some sort of demand. Am I rightly understood?"

Mary appeared to fully understand the sentiment, and neither she nor Mrs. Phillips said anything other than to nod in acceptance of her words. Kitty was taken aback at such a violent refusal, as was Jane but her eyes indicated ... defiance, or perhaps anger. Elizabeth was unsure what emotion shone in her elder sister's eyes. Lydia was more obviously displeased, but she rarely allowed anyone or anything to dampen her desires. If anything, her gaze only became more determined.

The conversation shifted then to easier topics with Mary and Mrs. Phillips, together with Elizabeth, able to guide the conversation. Kitty contributed little, and Lydia occasionally attempted to steer the conversation back into uncomfortable territory. However, Jane remained silent, long after both Elizabeth and the rest of the Bennet sisters departed from their aunt's.

When Mary stepped into her uncle's office, instead of following her sisters, none noticed. Mary was almost the forgotten daughter in her family. "Uncle, I do not want to be forced to marry the heir," she stated quietly once he turned to look at her.

"My wife and I will think of some way to protect you, Mary. I am uncertain what we can do at the moment, but I will write a letter to the Gardiners to see what they think might be done. They might be able to help you in London, but I cannot be sure your parents would allow you to go. Do remember that no one can force you to wed Mr. Collins, as the vicar will not marry you if you do not agree, but they can make it impossible for you to remain at home. If that happens, we will allow you to live with us or ensure you are taken care of," Phillips reassured his niece.

"Do I not have an obligation to obey my parents?" Mary protested.

Phillips closed his eyes as he considered it. "If your parents are making choices in your best interest, I would say you do. However, in this case, I do not think they would be taking into account what is best for you. Your mother is doing this to secure her own future, without regard to the impact on any daughter she tries to coerce into marrying Mr. Collins, and your father is unwilling to stand up to her and force her to do what is right. He has also been indolent and has allowed Longbourn to fall into a decline over the last decade. Had he saved funds to provide dowries for you and your sisters, none of you would need to marry Mr. Collins. Mary, I cannot answer religious questions. For answers, I suggest you stop and speak to the rector to see what he says about parents forcing a child to marry."

Mary nodded, sitting down in a corner and pondering what her uncle had said to her. "Why has Lizzy never returned home before now?"

Phillips looked at her in surprise. "She was not permitted to come home. After Jane was injured in the barn, Lizzy was sent to live with the Gardiners. Your father signed a letter giving Elizabeth into your uncle's care, surrendering all connection to her."

"I did not know. Mama always said that Lizzy asked to go to the

Gardiners because she did not want to be part of our family. I questioned this, but I had no way of knowing any differently."

"You could have asked your aunt and me, and we would have explained. We have kept up a correspondence with the Gardiners and would have helped you write to her," Phillips said softly.

"I never even considered it. I was surprised when Elizabeth arrived at Longbourn yesterday and then to hear what Mama had planned for her. It was odd to hear her mentioned when her name had not been spoken by any of us in years. I was not certain Kitty or Lydia even remember her."

"Lydia does. Lately, she has made a few comments that indicate she has been very aware of your mother's plans for your sister. My wife found her laughing a few times about the plan for Lizzy to marry 'an old man' and how your mother intended to continue running Longbourn even after Mr. Collins inherited. The two of them had big plans for what they would do when they were in charge."

"Lydia is awful. I wish I could get away from Longbourn and Mama. I would nearly volunteer to marry Mr. Collins just to get away, but since Mama thinks she will remain as mistress no matter what happens to Papa, I am uncertain that would be the escape I hoped for," Mary concluded sadly.

Her uncle did what he could to comfort the girl, but he was not particularly adept at the task. Soon, Mary left and thoughtfully made her way to a second location.

"Mrs. Allen, is the Reverend home?" Mary asked.

That lady nodded and invited the girl in. "Would you care for tea or cakes? Mr. Allen and I were just about to sit down for a small repast."

"Thank you; tea would be lovely," Mary replied, following Mrs. Allen into the parlour. Once all were served their tea and pleasantries were exchanged, Mary finally spoke.

"I have a ... theological question, Mr. Allen. I was hoping you would be able to help."

Mr. Allen was accustomed to Mary asking such questions but found her manner in this case unusual. Of course, he recalled that the girl's older sister had returned to the area recently and wondered if these questions had something to do with that.

"Of course, Miss Mary," he replied. "I am always happy to answer any of your questions."

"When does one's obligation to obey and honour a parent cease?" she asked.

Mr. Allen was taken aback by the question. There was gossip that the Bennets had intended to force the cast-off daughter to marry, but since the daughter in question had appeared already married, he wondered if Mrs. Bennet was now pushing another daughter to marry the man. Mr. Collins visited Longbourn once more than a decade ago, and the reverend seemed to recall the man was close to Mr. Bennet's age.

"Children are commanded to obey their parents; that is stated several times in the Bible. However, parents are also admonished not to 'provoke their children,'" Mr. Allen sighed heavily as he pondered how to continue. "Mary, may I be blunt with you?"

Mary nodded slowly, wondering what the rector might say. "Please do, Mr. Allen."

Rubbing his hand across his face, he blew out a breath before he began. "Your parents are selfish creatures. Their insistence that one of their daughters marry the heir to Longbourn is born from your mother's selfishness. Of course, she could be sure of having a secure future if she would only restrict her spending and make a deliberate effort to save. Your father goes along with her and does not force her to save because, frankly, it is too much effort for him to control her. Your parents have been married for more than two decades. Had they saved even one hundred pounds per annum, they would have over two thousand pounds. But they could not be bothered to do so. The situation is made worse because the income from Longbourn has decreased over the last years. Mr. Bennet has not made the effort to do better. His tenants all need his assistance, and while they stay, most would leave if they had an option. Your mother and sisters make no effort to improve their lives, leaving it for others to provide aid. Aid they would not need if the master and mistresses did their duty to their estate."

"If you are asking me whether, under these circumstances, you must honour your mother and follow her command that you marry a man against your wishes, the answer is no. Legally, no one can force you to wed. You can refuse to say the words even if you are not of age. However, your parents can also force you from their home if you do not obey them. It could place you in a difficult position.

"Uncle Phillips has promised his assistance, at least as much as possible. However, if I refuse to marry Mr. Collins, it would be best that I do not remain in Meryton. I am too young to seek a position, and I am uncertain what support I can expect from my family in London."

The Allens nodded their agreement, and silence resulted for several minutes until Mrs. Allen spoke. "Mr. Allen, did not a classmate write to you not long ago, stating that he was looking for a young lady who could be a companion of sorts for his daughter? Would Miss Mary suit?"

Mr. Allen considered this, steepling his fingers in front of him for several minutes. "She might. Of course, it is not a paid position, but a friend of mine has a young daughter in need of a friend. I am uncertain of her age, perhaps a year or two younger than you, but the family lost a daughter to illness a little over a year ago, and they are hoping having a friend would help her recover. The two girls were very close, and she has been melancholy since. There are not many young ladies nearby, so they wrote to ask if I knew anyone who could visit. Let me write to him this afternoon. I will send it by express, and we should have an answer in a few days. If things at Longbourn come to a head before I receive a response, you may come here or go to Phillips. Both of us will do what we can to protect you until we can send you north."

"Miss Mary, while you remain in the neighbourhood, would you like to begin to assist me as I help the poor amongst the neighbourhood? It would give you a reason to be away from Longbourn on occasion and also help prepare you for your future, whatever that may be," Mrs. Allen offered, sensing that the girl needed some occupation away from Longbourn.

"I would enjoy that, Mrs. Allen," Mary replied quickly. "I have read much about charity but have never thought to ask what I might do to help those around me. Mama would not have looked kindly at my asking."

"My usual days to visit the parishioners are Tuesday and Friday. I try to leave the house at precisely nine for that is typically when Mr. Allen works on his sermon at the church. If you arrive before that time, we can go together. It is also early enough that no one should notice you leaving your home."

"I will … I will try. Mama will not be downstairs that early, and I should be able to slip out."

After a little more conversation, Mary departed and continued on her way home thinking over what she had learned that day. She knew she wanted to begin corresponding with her estranged sister and hoped that she might be able to build a relationship with her.

Chapter Twenty-Four

Patrick Collins had been pleased when his cousin's wife responded to his letters instead of his cousin. He knew Thomas Bennet to be an indolent man, and when he had written to ask for his help, he had been uncertain the endeavour would be successful. However, Fanny Bennet had written back offering a daughter in marriage in exchange for allowing her to remain mistress for her lifetime.

Collins was looking for financial assistance and did not care what form it took. If he could persuade his cousin to house him for the foreseeable future, who would be mistress of the estate after his cousin died really did not matter. He was in dire straits with his worthless son having chosen to pursue a career in the church instead of choosing something more lucrative.

Over the last two years, the farm Collins had lived on all his life had fallen into disrepair with increasingly poor harvests. This was as much the result of poor management as it was the weather and other factors, but Collins had never been particularly adept at maintaining it. In the last few months, he had sold the small farm and just as quickly ran through the funds on liquor and other vices. Now, he was in the unenviable position of needing support, and since his son had yet to find a position as curate, the letter from his cousin's wife had seemed to be a godsend.

He was a few years younger than his cousin, having been forced to marry a local farmer's daughter when she was found to be with child after a brief interlude one evening. When the girl's father learned who sired the child, he had arrived at the Collins farm and demanded the two marry. While it may not have been the marriage his father wished for his only son, the girl was pretty enough and came with a small dowry that was used to benefit the farm. She died in childbirth with her second child, who sadly did not survive the birth either.

Collins had managed to marry a second time nearly a decade later, this time to a childless widow. However, that lady also died in childbirth a few years into the marriage. A widower for several years now, he was thrilled by the promise of a young wife. He already had his heir, but the idea of a young woman who would be at his beck and call, along with the promise of room and board for the rest of his lifetime, was pleasing.

Years before, prior to either of their marriages, Collins had fallen out with his Bennet cousin over something no one could quite remember. Most likely, the problems had been compounded when Collins not only married first but sired an heir while Mr. Bennet managed to produce only daughters. However, it had been this fact that led Collins to reach out to his cousin in the first place, offering a promise to care for his widow and daughters in return for financial assistance after Collins lost it all.

In truth, Bennet had little reason to agree since it was possible that Collins would die before Bennet, but that had not mattered to Mrs. Bennet. She responded and was delighted with his promise to ensure that the Bennet progeny would be cared for upon Mr. Bennet's death. With the promise of not only room and board, but also a wife at his beck and call, Collins had seen little reason to deny his cousin's wife.

Still, he was surprised when the signed agreement was returned without additional questions. The country solicitor who drafted it had raised his brow at some of the unenforceable promises that were included, even pointing those out to him as he listed them. Collins had only shrugged, insisting for their inclusion as a way to leverage some of the more enforceable conditions—primarily the ability to live on the estate and receive at least a small allowance of at least 500 pounds per annum to support him.

With all of these thoughts in his mind, he packed his things and hired a carriage to convey him and his son to Meryton. They were presently living in Kent, just south of Maidstone, but they would be taking all of their belongings with them when they travelled to meet his cousin. His son, William Collins, had grimaced in distaste at the idea of his father marrying one of his cousin's daughters, a mere girl barely of marriageable age, but he knew not to protest his father's decisions.

Young William had been on the receiving end of his father's displeasure one too many times to intentionally attempt it. Perhaps he would have a better chance persuading Mr. Bennet to rethink the arrangement, but in all honesty, he could think little of a man who was willingly giving his daughter away in marriage in such a way.

Perhaps it was not atypical of the time to arrange a marriage for monetary reasons, but still, he would like to think that the father would want to know more of the character of the man he was giving his daughter to. They would remain nearby, therefore giving Mr. Bennet the opportunity to see his daughter regularly, but he could do little to protect her once she was given in marriage to another man.

Chapter Twenty-Five

The Darcys' arrival at their London home was, miraculously, unheralded. They slipped in from the mews, retired directly to their chambers, and remained there for several days before they were discovered.

They spent that time in blissful solitude, talking and laughing about many things, including their first impressions of each other. It was a subject they had rarely discussed, as the day they met had been overshadowed by so many other challenges and distractions.

"I was impressed that, despite your youth, you stood up to him, to me, *and* to my father without fear," Darcy said, his voice soft with admiration as he reflected on her bravery. Elizabeth had just finished telling him how terrified she had been that day.

Elizabeth laughed, though the sound was tinged with disbelief. "You must be joking; I was so afraid," she said, shaking her head, "I would have thought everyone could hear my knees knocking together when I stood in front of your father. Women, especially young women, are rarely believed or given much consideration when attacked as I was. Though I was not yet out, if what happened to me had become known, I would have been ruined. I w*ould* have been ruined in truth, had you not come along when you did."

Her laughter faded, and her face fell as she remembered the terror she had felt. "I was angry, yes, but I would not have been able to hold him off much longer."

Darcy's heart clenched at the sight of her distress. The memory of that day had left scars on both of them, but it pained him to see how deeply it still affected her when she spoke of it. He reached out, gently tucking a loose curl behind her ear.

"I collapsed in my aunt's arms not long after you departed from the inn that afternoon," she confessed quietly, her voice barely above a whisper. "I was holding it all in until I could no longer."

Her words tugged at Darcy's heart, and without hesitation, he drew her into his arms. His embrace was tender, protective, as though he could shield her from the pain of the past even now.

"I think fate smiled on me that day," he murmured against her hair. "While I wish with all my heart that you had never had to endure such an ordeal, it accomplished two significant things. It finally convinced my father that his godson was as awful as I had always claimed, but most fortuitously, it brought you into my life."

He pulled back slightly, just enough to meet her eyes, his gaze earnest. "Were it not for your friendship, I would have struggled far more after my father's death. Your letters to Georgiana, and the lines you wrote just for me, regularly lifted my spirits when I felt overcome by grief and melancholy."

Elizabeth's eyes softened, and she smiled faintly, though the shadow of the past still lingered. "I never knew they meant so much to you."

"They did," he said earnestly. "More than you can imagine. Even then, I think I was beginning to fall in love with you." His fingers traced the line of her jaw, and his voice dropped to a near whisper. "I owe you more than I could ever express."

For a moment, the weight of everything left unsaid hung between them. Then, without another word, Darcy pressed his lips to hers, a kiss filled with all the love and gratitude he could not convey in words.

After several moments like that, she leaned back and smiled, caressing his cheek with her hand. "You have said that before, but I can scarcely credit it. Most of what I sent was meant to provoke, as I was certain you did not care for me. We seemed to always argue when we spoke at Pemberley that second summer."

"I was delighted by our debates. I was so impressed with your knowledge and understanding, and your compassion in helping my sister and Mrs. Reynolds with Pemberley's tenants. You know, they still speak of you with something like reverence, and I have received word from my steward that they are delighted that you are now their mistress."

"But I did so little," she protested.

"You were empathetic and kind. Pemberley had not had a mistress in several years at that point, and they appreciated the effort you took to know them. Mrs. Reynolds did visit as she could, but she was unable to do much. I know that you did not know much about the role of a mistress of an estate at that time, but you were approachable and merry."

Elizabeth laughed again. "I still do not know much about the role of mistress. Despite being born a gentleman's daughter, I have lived most of my life in the house of a tradesman. I do not recall anyone at Longbourn visiting tenants or doing half of what Mrs. Reynolds does, and I know I am far from prepared to be the mistress of such a grand estate as Pemberley."

Darcy kissed her forehead. "You will be exceptional, my love. I have complete faith in your abilities to do what is required. What you do not know, you will learn quickly enough. You have proven that you are a fast learner."

In response, she kissed him and relaxed into his embrace. They remained this way for several minutes before an idea struck Elizabeth, and she sat up slightly. "What made you finally decide to court me? We had not seen each other in years when I attended the ball at the Matlocks, and it was only a few days later that you asked for a courtship."

Darcy smiled broadly, his eyes sparkling with amusement. "Do you not know, my love?"

When Elizabeth shook her head, he laughed softly and pulled her closer, wrapping his arms around her as though he could not bear to be separated for even a moment. "I had not seen you in more than a year and knew of you only through your letters to my sister. We had a cheerful battle of wits in those letters, and I enjoyed the novelty of it, but in my mind, you were still a young girl."

Elizabeth raised an eyebrow at this, though she remained silent, her curiosity piqued.

"That night at my aunt's, well … my darling wife, I was utterly stunned," he continued, his tone deepening with sincerity. "You were so incredibly lovely, and I was instantly attracted to you. It took me a moment to realise that you were the very Elizabeth Gardiner I had traded barbs with for all that time."

He smiled at the memory, his expression softening as he recalled the moment. "When I realised it was you I was seeing, I was taken aback. Do you not recall that I struggled to form the words to ask you to dance?"

Elizabeth's eyes warmed, and she looked up at him fondly. "I thought you were annoyed to be forced to dance with me that night," she confessed, a hint of amusement in her voice. "I think we have spoken of this before, but I had admired my 'rescuer' for years. When you fumbled over your words, I thought it was because you were disappointed in me. Imagine how surprised I was when you called on me at your aunt's the next day."

"No, Elizabeth," Darcy said with a chuckle, his eyes filled with affection. "I fumbled because I was shocked. I remembered the impertinent little fourteen-year-old you had been and did not expect you to be the breathtaking woman who was standing before me. I was utterly unprepared. Ask Richard what I said, for he teased me all evening about being smitten with you."

His gaze lingered on her, his hand lifting to gently brush a stray curl away from her face. "And I must tell you, my darling, you have only grown more beautiful with time," he murmured, his voice low and full of emotion.

Before Elizabeth could respond, Darcy leaned in and captured her lips with his own. The kiss was tender at first, but quickly deepened with passion, their connection growing more intense with each passing moment. Elizabeth melted into him, her arms twining around his neck as their breath mingled, each of them lost in the love they felt for one another.

By the time they finally pulled apart, both were breathless, their foreheads resting together as they shared a quiet moment, the world outside their embrace forgotten.

SOON AFTER THEIR RETURN, Elizabeth received two letters from Hertfordshire. From Mary's letter, she learned how Mrs. Bennet had taken to her bed shortly after Elizabeth departed Longbourn, crying and complaining about her nerves and how "that foolish girl" had ruined all her plans for their futures. Mrs. Bennet spent much of the next several days bemoaning the lack of a son for Longbourn and that without Elizabeth there to marry the heir, all the girls were destined for the hedgerows.

Though I hate to say it of my own relation, I struggle to understand Mama. She and Papa could have provided for our future by restricting their spending. Regardless, she is quite upset by your appearing at Longbourn already married, and, I admit, her frustration is exacerbated by learning how well you have married. You should hear the rumours that have circulated since you left. I hate to say it, Elizabeth, but she is vexed that you are married while Jane is not, and she blames her brother, Papa, and everyone else she can name for it.

Apparently, she has decided that I am now the sister to marry Mr. Collins. I am anxious at the thought of it; the man is not only much older than I, but I feel I am not prepared for marriage.

Since you departed, I have begun spending less time at home and more time with Charlotte Lucas and Mrs. Allen, the rector's wife. In my conversations with her, I have learned that Longbourn's tenants are among the poorest in our parish, for Mama does not act as she should and does not do anything to aid them. Papa has raised the rents on our tenants to make up for the loss of income in other areas. The estate is failing, and Papa will do nothing to help. I am concerned that someday all Mama's cries about us ending in the hedgerows may be truer than any of us would like.

I do not say that to beg for assistance, for I know that neither Mr. Phillips, nor even Mr. Gardiner would allow us to live in penury, but should something happen to Papa, we would lose much of the status we currently enjoy as the daughters of a gentleman. Mama is worried that Mr. Collins will not allow us to live at Longbourn without either Jane or me marrying him, and even should that come to pass, he may *still be unwilling to do as our mother wishes. The man is to arrive soon, and I worry what will happen when he comes.*

Forgive me, Elizabeth, for I know my letter rambles. I have taken the lessons of Mrs. Allen to heart and have begun joining her as she visits the poor in the parish, many of whom are our tenants. Jane accompanied me once but found it too uncomfortable for her and has no wish to continue. According to Mrs. Allen, this is what young gentlewomen ought to do, and we ought to have always been doing it. Had you remained at Longbourn, perhaps we would have, or at least I think that may be the case. Regardless, I am finally learning what I ought to have known, and that will make me a better wife for someone whenever that comes to pass. I hope it is not soon.

Elizabeth sighed upon finishing this letter. "What is it, dearest?" Darcy asked, looking up from his own correspondence.

"Mary. Things at Longbourn are as bad as we supposed. Part of me wishes to offer my assistance, but another part of me asks myself why I should. They wanted nothing to do with me before. I can give Mary and my next younger sisters a bit more grace, but Jane I cannot understand. She has also written, but mostly to complain about the lack of opportunities for her in Hertfordshire and to beg for an invitation to come to town. I will wait before I reply to her. However, I do feel badly for Mary. It seems she has had her eyes opened to our parents and wishes for better."

"It is a shame that neither her mother nor her father never took enough of an interest in her to teach her what she ought to know as a gentleman's daughter. I know you did not live at Longbourn for many years, but even when you were first at Pemberley, you seemed to have some inclination of what was expected by the mistress of an estate. I remember you speaking to Mrs. Reynolds and even my father about some of the problems you noticed when you traipsed through the estate," Darcy said with a grin, obviously remembering that time. "Father was amazed at some of the problems you pointed out."

She grinned back at him. "My aunt always spoke to me about what was expected of someone of my station. She was the daughter of a gentleman although her father did not own an estate. Her father was a second son, but she did spend some time on the family's estate. My grandmother also spent a little time with me before she died. In fact, she died not long before I was sent to London which I think was one of the reasons that Mr. Bennet finally gave in to Mrs. Bennet's demands. Before that, my grandmother protected me. I have always been observant of things, and my aunt always encouraged me to choose charitable pursuits. Helping with the tenants at Pemberley just seemed to be an easy way to provide assistance where I could."

Darcy nodded, and the couple sat for several moments in silence. Finally, he spoke. "Perhaps your Aunt Gardiner would be willing to allow Mary to join them in London for a time. I am hesitant to invite her to join us, at least not directly from Longbourn. From what you have said, I feel certain others would attempt to turn anything we do for one sister into a way to use us. Mary would benefit from the companionship of Mrs. Gardiner."

Elizabeth sighed. "If it becomes untenable for her at Longbourn, I will suggest it. For now, it seems that the rector's wife and my friend Charlotte are aiding Mary. I hope to hear more about this Mr. Collins and what happens with him. If Mary is forced to accept an engagement to him, I will not hesitate to act. Also, I will speak of this to my aunt when she visits, for she would likely want to know how she might be of aid if it is required."

Chapter Twenty-Six

Three days after this discussion, Lady Catherine arrived on the Darcys' doorstep. Despite being told frequently that Darcy and her daughter would never marry, the grand lady had not ceased her insistence upon it. When she learned in the paper that her nephew had married the former Elizabeth Gardiner, she was incensed and did not hesitate to make her way to London to let her nephew know of her displeasure.

Though Darcy had informed his aunt of his courtship and subsequent engagement through letters, her daughter Anne had somehow prevented her mother from reading these and, therefore, kept her mother from knowing any of it. Unfortunately, she was unable to prevent her mother from finding the wedding announcement posted in the Times and the letter from her Uncle Matlock that announced the news.

Both the letter and the newspaper did not arrive for more than a fortnight after the wedding had taken place. To say that Lady Catherine was displeased was an understatement. Anne did her best to mitigate her mother's anger by telling her that she was not upset by the so-called 'betrayal', but it did not matter to her mother. She was upset that her own plans were wrecked.

Lady Catherine liked being in charge at Rosings and wanted to remain in charge. As it stood, Anne would inherit upon her twenty-fifth birthday, now less than a year away. Had Lady Catherine got her way, Darcy would have married Anne and carried her to Pemberley, leaving her to remain in charge of Rosings.

Anne flatly refused to accompany her mother to London to confront Darcy. "There is little point, Mother. Even had I wanted to marry Darcy, he is already wed and has been for more than a fortnight. He is married to a woman he loves, and nothing you do or say will force him to relinquish her now."

Lady Catherine eyed her daughter warily. "What do you know about it, Anne?"

"Darcy wrote to you months ago, Mother. Since you always have me read his letters to you because his handwriting is 'too difficult' for you to read yourself, I simply did not read out those portions of the letter. I did not wish for you to interfere with my cousin's happiness."

The matriarch was taken aback at this realisation. While it should have been abundantly apparent that this journey to London was pointless, she was still determined to go to make her outrage known. Nothing her daughter could say would stop her, and she was determined to ensure her nephew knew exactly what she thought about his treachery.

She spent the carriage ride fuming about her recalcitrant nephews and obstinate daughters who were unwilling to comply with her plans. Their disobedience weighed heavily on her mind, overshadowing the scenery passing by outside the carriage window. The rhythmic clatter of the horses' hooves seemed to echo her frustration, amplifying her discontent with each passing mile.

The further she travelled, the more determined she became. She intended to confront Darcy and force him to do as she wished. However, she was uncertain how to make him comply with her plans, and it seemed that her brother would be no help in this matter. Regardless, she intended to let her entire family know of her displeasure.

Lady Catherine's carriage rushed toward London, passing through the town of Maidstone without stopping, completely unaware of the carriage colliding with another in her wake as it swerved to avoid the fast-moving carriage. Though had she been aware of her demand that her driver "make haste" had caused an accident, it probably would have done little to change her resolve.

It was mid-afternoon, and the couple was resting in the library, enjoying a brief respite from the responsibilities of managing their home and business. Both were informally attired since they had no intention of seeing anyone other than their servants. They were surprised when they heard a strident voice demanding to see her nephew, and Darcy rolled his eyes expressively when he recognised his aunt's voice.

"Lady Catherine," he informed his wife unnecessarily.

Elizabeth cocked her head at him. "You wrote to her of our engagement and intended marriage, did you not? The marriage announcement was only recently published, I know, but I thought your uncle was to write to her as well."

Darcy nodded before taking a deep breath and preparing himself for whatever was to follow. He had thought it odd she had not at least written before now, but since he did not want to invite problems, he had not worried about it.

Finally, the door was flung open as the harried butler attempted to do his duty in announcing the guest. Darcy merely shook his head at the man, indicating that he should go on about his business.

"What is the meaning of this, Darcy? How dare you defy me by marrying someone other than my Anne. She was formed for you, and your mother and I planned for your match in your cradles," she said, seething at the couple's informal attire and obvious familiarity with each other.

As he stood belatedly, Darcy shook his head in disbelief at her coming to object now. "Madam, you might have wished for it, and my mother might even have agreed that it was a pleasant thought, but that is all it was—an idle thought of two mothers almost twenty-five years ago. No contracts were ever signed and neither of my parents approved the match, a fact of which you are well aware since my father wrote to you about it on several occasions before his death. Anne did not desire to wed me any more than I wished to marry her. Furthermore, I am now married to a dear woman of my choosing. You are too late to do anything about the matter. Now, if you will allow me, I will introduce you to my wife."

"I have no desire to meet your so-called wife. Why would I want to meet such a low-born trollop who would deliberately come in between you and your betrothed?"

Darcy cut her off at the insult. "Madam, you will speak respectfully of Mrs. Darcy, or you will be thrown from this house. Mrs. Darcy is my wife and will be the only Mrs. Darcy in my lifetime. You have been told time and again that I would not marry your daughter. Your presence here is unwanted and I think it best you leave now."

Lady Catherine took a step back, surprised at the vehemence from her nephew. Yes, both he and Anne had said often enough that they would not marry, but she had always brushed such objections aside.

"I will not leave," she insisted.

"You will not remain unless you consent to an introduction to my wife, apologise for your unfeeling words, and speak civilly to both of us," Darcy informed the angry lady, his own temper strained.

"You cannot force me to leave my sister's house," the lady demanded.

"I can, and I will," Darcy retorted, stepping to the door and calling for the butler and several footmen. "Hobbes, escort my aunt to her carriage. She is not to be permitted entry again until I say otherwise."

"I will go to my brother. He will …" She stopped abruptly as another commanding voice interrupted her from the doorway.

"Do absolutely nothing to assist you in your unreasonable demands. Darcy is married and out of your reach. It is time for you to accept your fate and cease telling untruths about an engagement between Anne and Darcy. You are the only one who wanted them to marry–they certainly did not wish to do so, and you know very well that George Darcy denied his consent for such a union in writing several times and that our sister never made any agreement with you about the children marrying each other. Now, I will permit you to stay at Matlock House exactly one night, and then I will send you back to Kent. Once you return, you will say nothing to anyone about Darcy's choice of wife or an engagement between Darcy and Anne. Am I understood? Now desist with this foolishness. Come with me, Catherine, or I will allow Darcy's footmen to carry you out of this house."

With a huff, she did as ordered and left the house on her brother's arm. Lord Matlock glanced briefly at his nephew. "My wife desires that the two of you come for tea tomorrow. We expect you to call at two 'o'clock to discuss this." He paused and chuckled slightly before continuing. "My wife intends to discuss her plans for your social schedule. Be prepared to have your every moment dictated for the next month."

Darcy groaned while Elizabeth laughed at her husband, knowing his distaste for society and its events. He had endured them during the season but had not hesitated to remind her frequently that he attended only so he could be seen with her on his arm. Grinning at him, she teased: "It will be little different from when we were courting, will it not? You will attend, if only so you might be seen accompanying me."

Suppressing the sigh that threatened to escape, Darcy instead pulled his wife into his embrace and returned her teasing grin. "I suppose knowing that you will be my reward at the end of an evening spent in tedious company might actually improve my enjoyment of the event." He paused for a moment, and when he continued, his voice was husky. "Or make me more desirous of ending it early."

Elizabeth giggled when her husband pulled her into him more tightly and the two soon retreated to their chambers where they spent the rest of the evening.

Chapter Twenty-Seven

The day Mr. Collins was expected to arrive at Longbourn came and went without that momentous event taking place. Mrs. Bennet fretted and wondered if he had somehow learned of the breach of contract and was already seeking the advice of a solicitor to sue the family.

Following his usual practice, Mr. Bennet ignored his wife's fretfulness. That his cousin had yet to arrive was of little concern to him. More and more, he regretted sending his daughter away all those years ago and giving in to his wife's insistence that she take responsibility for their daughters' education. She had not liked how much time her husband spent with her eldest two girls when they were small and believed that it had been Elizabeth's influence that led Jane to agree to learn such unladylike subjects.

Before Elizabeth's banishment, his two oldest girls spent countless hours in his study, delving into subjects beyond the typical accomplishments for young ladies. Mr. Bennet immersed them in a variety of books, fostering discussions and debates, and imparting knowledge of scientific matters and mathematics well beyond societal expectations for women. Mrs. Bennet had not liked how much time her husband spent with them and constantly complained that he was making them unmarriageable by teaching them unladylike things.

The incident with Jane in the stables had served as a catalyst for Mrs. Bennet to persuade Jane to distance herself from her sister by convincing her that Elizabeth was to blame for the entire ordeal. In her vulnerable state, Jane believed her and had acquiesced in staying away from Elizabeth. It had not taken Jane long to recover from her injury, but by that time, it was too late. Elizabeth had already gone to London.

As her mother fretted about the absent heir, Jane pondered what had been said to her by Charlotte Lucas and her aunt. The most mortifying was recalling her behaviour with her sister's husband. However, anger and frustration lingered in her mind for her mother had always told her she was the most beautiful daughter. Jane was a classic beauty, willowy and blonde, nothing like Elizabeth's more buxom figure. Surely, she would shine in London, she thought, but it became apparent that Elizabeth wanted little do with her family.

She was angry at what Mr. Darcy had said to her about being beautiful on the inside as well as outwardly. Jane knew she was beautiful in appearance, but after receiving so many chastisements, she was uncertain if any man would find her beautiful on the inside as well.

All these revelations coming at once unsettled Jane, leaving her feeling increasingly disillusioned and not a little abandoned. She no longer knew what to think about anyone or anything and she followed the example that had been set for her throughout her childhood—she took to her bed.

While Jane contemplated these matters, Mary spent more time with the Allens. She began to accompany Mrs. Allen on her visits to parishioners, paying particular attention to what needed to be done for the tenants of Longbourn who lived in poor circumstances indeed.

As Mary walked alongside Mrs. Allen during the second week of these visits, thoughts swirled in her mind about what she could do to improve the lives of the tenants and what the master owed them.

"Mrs. Allen, do you think there is anything I can do to improve the living conditions for the tenants at Longbourn?" Mary asked, her voice laced with concern.

Mrs. Allen smiled warmly at Mary, impressed by her growing empathy for those less fortunate. Although it had been many years since the present Mr. Bennet's mother died, while she lived, the tenants had all they needed. She had already begun training Jane and Elizabeth to take over her role, but they were not old enough to care for the tenants when their grandmother died, and the present Mrs. Bennet had no interest in aiding the tenants. "I believe there is always something we can do to help, Mary. Let us make a list of their needs and discuss how we might address them."

After this discussion, they began visiting the homes of the tenants, listening to their grievances and noting their most pressing needs.

"It is heartbreaking to see the hardships they endure," Mary remarked, her heart heavy with the realisation that her family ought to be doing more.

Mrs. Allen nodded in agreement. "Indeed it is, Mary. But with your determination and compassion, I have no doubt we can make a difference in their lives. Someday, you will do well as the mistress of an estate or the wife of a cleric."

As they continued these visits, Mary felt a sense of purpose blossoming within her. She could not wait to write to Elizabeth about it.

Just a few days earlier, Mr. Phillips had delivered a reply from Elizabeth to Mary, indicating her tentative acceptance of Mary's desire to begin a correspondence. She discussed the matter with Mrs. Allen who advised her to maintain a friendly tone in her letters without requesting favours. Following this advice, she replied in a manner that was both light and friendly yet maintained some distance.

Mrs. Bennet emerged from her bedroom a sennight after taking to her bed. Since they had received no word from Mr. Collins, Mrs. Bennet proceeded as she always had and began making her usual visits in the neighbourhood. As long as they heard nothing from Mr. Collins, they had no reason to fret, and perhaps she could find a way to get another of her daughters married before that event happened. Moreover, she had heard very little gossip since that ungrateful daughter of hers had caused her to take to her bed, and she needed to learn all she could about her new son.

On one of these visits, Mrs. Bennet was aghast to hear the ladies speaking well not only of Elizabeth, but of Mary for her efforts in helping Mrs. Allen with the parish poor. She immediately began to criticise her plainest daughter for what she considered unladylike pursuits.

"Mary, what is this I hear about you gallivanting about with Mrs. Allen instead of attending to your duties at home?" Mrs. Bennet exclaimed, her disapproval evident.

Flushing, Mary lowered her gaze, accustomed to her mother's harsh words. "I am merely assisting Mrs. Allen with her charitable endeavours, Mother. It is a noble cause and one that I think is beneficial," she replied quietly, her voice tinged with defensiveness.

"Noble cause or not, a young lady of your station should not be traipsing about like some common servant. You are a gentlewoman and should be seen to act like one," Mrs. Bennet retorted, her frustration growing.

Sensing the tension between the two, Mrs. Allen interjected gently, "Mrs. Bennet, Mary's assistance has been invaluable. She has shown remarkable compassion and dedication in helping the less fortunate. Surely you would appreciate her desire to make a positive impact in our small community. Likewise, Mary's help eases your own burden in educating your daughters to be proper mistresses of an estate. Aiding the poor is one of a gentlewoman's responsibilities, one that is greatly popular among the great ladies in London."

Mrs. Bennet waved her hand dismissively. "Compassion is all well and good, but a young lady's place is within her own home, attending to her domestic duties and preparing herself for marriage, not gallivanting about the countryside."

Mary's shoulders tensed at her mother's words, but she remained composed, silently vowing to continue her efforts to help those in need regardless of her mother's disapproval. The conversation shifted with Mary adding nothing more.

However, Mrs. Allen had a different idea and spoke to Mary about it the next day. "Mary, while I do appreciate all you have done to help me, I feel that your mother will soon forbid you from taking part. Mr. Allen has heard back from his friend, and they have invited you to come for a visit to see if you can be of aid to their daughter. They live on a small estate near Maidstone below London. It is slightly larger than Longbourn and is well managed, and I think you could learn much while you are there. The family's name is Winters and the daughter for you to befriend is Amelia. She is just fifteen, near your sister Kitty's age."

"I am uncertain that my parents will allow me to go if I ask. Do you think Mr. Allen might suggest it to my father? Perhaps departing without Mama learning of it will make it easier for me to leave?" Mary suggested.

"We will do all we can to arrange it. Mr. Allen has already suggested his friend send a carriage to collect you at the beginning of next week."

"Thank you so much, Mrs. Allen. Mama has been displeased with me ever since she learned of my visits yesterday afternoon. The heir presumptive never appeared as scheduled, nor did he send word of his delay, so she is even more vociferous than usual. I would like to get away from her since I am a frequent target of her ire. I do worry what will happen to Kitty if I go, for she will inevitably become the next target."

"Tell Miss Kitty to seek me out if she needs help. She is entirely too inclined to follow Miss Lydia wherever she leads, and the two will wreak havoc on our small town and your entire family if they are not restrained somehow," Mrs. Allen said.

"They are too young to run wild as they do. However, Mama will not hear a word spoken against Lydia, saying she is only lively and young."

Mrs. Allen patted the girl's hand to reassure her. "Perhaps we can find a way to reach them as well. Do not worry too much right now since they are very young."

"Yes, but Mama indulges Lydia and permits her to do whatever she likes. She is just thirteen years old, yet she attends events as though she is out. The neckline of her dresses gets lower and lower and is scarcely appropriate for a girl in the schoolroom," Mary insisted.

Mrs. Allen sighed. "I know, my dear girl. While you are gone, we will see what may be done. Perhaps if she senses the censure of the neighbourhood, she would be inclined to make a change."

Mary hesitated to scoff at such a suggestion from her mentor, knowing better than to underestimate the power of social opinion. However, she doubted that her youngest sister would be influenced by what their neighbours thought of her. Mrs. Bennet seemed blissfully unaware of anything she did not wish to acknowledge, content to invent reasons to justify her perception.

"I hope that to be true, Mrs. Allen. Thank you for your assistance and please let me know if Mr. Allen is successful in convincing Papa to allow me to go to your friend."

Soon, their calls for the day were completed, and Mary made her way home. Since she returned home well before her mother arrived downstairs, nothing was said about her visits, but she knew it could not last.

Chapter Twenty-Eight

A few days later, plans were finalised for Mary to travel to Maidstone. Mr. Allen came and made the offer to Mr. Bennet, who realised the whole thing would be arranged with little expense to himself and agreed without bothering to consult his wife. Therefore, on Tuesday of the following week, a carriage arrived early in the morning to collect Mary and convey her to Maidstone.

Mary had never been outside of Hertfordshire having travelled but once to St. Albans and never through London. As the carriage passed through the outskirts of London, Mary was taken aback by everything she saw. Stopping once to rest the horses allowed her a brief chance to look around, together with both the maid and manservant who had accompanied the carriage. The carriage finally reached the Winters' estate late in the evening.

"Welcome, Miss Bennet," the matron of the home greeted their guest as Mary stepped down from the carriage with the assistance of the footman. "Mr. Allen had so many pleasant things to say about you, and we are so glad you could come stay with us for a time. Here, come into the house and meet my daughter."

Mary greeted her hostess and accepted the introductions. Mrs. Winters seemed a jovial sort of woman, very different from her own mother and, apparently, happy to have her there. She entered the drawing room where she was introduced to a girl a year or two younger than herself.

"Amelia, I would like to introduce you to Miss Mary Bennet. She will stay with us for a month or two and I hope the two of you will become friends."

Amelia glanced up for a moment, briefly connecting with Mary's eyes before lowering them to the floor again. Her greeting was quiet, so much so that Mary strained to hear her. Mary deduced the girl was shy, perhaps made more so in her grief. While Mrs. Winters wore the colours of half-mourning, Miss Winters still donned her black attire. She recalled what Mrs. Allen had told her of the girl's loss and wondered what she might do to aid the poor girl.

"I am pleased to make your acquaintance, Miss Winters. I hope you do not think it too forward of me, but since we will reside in the same house for the next several weeks, do you think we might do away with some of the formality and address each other by our Christian names? If you prefer, you may address me as Miss Mary if you are more comfortable with that."

"I would be delighted to address you by name, Miss Mary," the girl murmured. "Mrs. Allen told my mother that you play." She allowed the unspoken question to hang in the air between them.

"I play some, but not particularly well. My parents never hired a master to help me improve, so I have learned only what I could manage myself. Mrs. Allen plays a bit, and she taught me some of the basics." This was a sore point for Mary since she had frequently asked for a master, at least for a brief time, to help her improve, but the request had always been denied. Both her parents always claimed there was a lack of funds, but then they would purchase a new dress or a new book.

"I have a master who comes weekly, and I am certain that he would not mind assisting you as well," Amelia said quietly. "My sister and I used to practise together and play duets. She was a far better pianist than I, but since she left us, I have spent more time practising by myself. I miss having someone to share it with."

Mary smiled gently. "Then I would be delighted to practise with you, Miss Amelia. I have longed for a sister to practise with as well. I have three sisters at home, but none of the others were ever interested in playing."

Conversation continued in this vein until Mrs. Winters reappeared and informed Mary that if she wanted to change for dinner, her trunks were waiting for her in her room. Both Winters ladies showed Mary to her room and Mrs. Winters was pleased at how quickly the girls seemed to take to each other.

She said as much to her husband while they dressed for dinner. "I think that Miss Bennet will be exactly what Amelia needs. Both girls were a little awkward at the start, but Miss Bennet began with a request to address each other informally, and I think that helped Amelia feel more comfortable. They have progressed to addressing each other as younger sisters and have not quite settled into the informality, but it is a start." She then began to share that Amelia invited Mary to take part in her music lessons and even offered to practise duets together.

Mr. Winters agreed, stating, "That's an excellent beginning. I apologise for not being here when she arrived, but some business kept me later in town. Have you heard anything about the carriage accident last week?" When his wife shook her head indicating she had not, he continued. "There were two men in a hired carriage, which was clipped by a carriage passing too quickly through town. The driver and the elder man were killed almost immediately, but the younger man was thrown clear. He is injured, but so far, he is still alive. They were also passing through as well, and from their luggage, we have determined he is a Mr. Collins, although we are not certain if he is

William or Patrick. We have not looked through the papers too much, but we did find a letter with a return address to Longbourn which is Miss Bennet's family estate. Perhaps tomorrow you might ask her if she knows the gentleman?"

Mrs. Winters nodded, and the two returned downstairs to meet the girls for a family dinner. The evening passed pleasantly, and even Amelia appeared in better spirits during the meal. After dinner, both girls played the pianoforte for a brief time before they all retired.

The following morning, Mary came downstairs late, finding the entire family had already breakfasted.

"I apologise for rising so late this morning. I am usually up far earlier," Mary said when she came upon Mrs. Winters and her daughter sitting in the morning room sewing.

"You have no need for apologies, Miss Bennet. I know how tiring travelling can be and asked the maids not to disturb you. I am pleased you got the rest you needed. Now, come sit with us, and I will ring for a servant to bring you tea and some pastries. We typically break our fasts at half past eight although my husband is often up and away earlier than that. Amelia has begun visiting tenants with me, and I understand from Mrs. Allen that you have been doing the same with her."

Mary nodded her reply, and the three discussed how they conducted their visits and the schedule the ladies kept. Mary quickly learned that Mrs. Winters was a diligent mistress of her estate and concluded that she would learn much from her example while here.

After Mary had eaten and Amelia sent to her studies, Mrs. Winters brought up the injured man housed in their village. "Miss Bennet, do you know of a Collins family? There was an accident involving two men and a driver recently, and we found letters identifying the men as Patrick and William Collins. We also noticed a return address of Longbourn in Hertfordshire on several letters and wondered if you knew the men."

"Mr. Collins is the heir to my family's estate. It is entailed on the male line, and he is the next in line. I have heard only the elder mentioned, but I am not sure of his Christian name," Mary replied. "Are they well?"

"The elder gentleman died in the accident, and the younger was seriously injured. He had been unable to speak thus far, so little is known about him. Do you know if either man is married?" Mrs. Winters asked.

"I know the elder was not. His wife died some years ago. I have heard nothing of the younger Collins," Mary replied.

"When you write to your family, will you mention the death?" Mrs. Winters asked.

Mary sighed heavily. "I do not know. Mama will not react well to this news. I ..." she sighed again, uncertain how much to reveal. The Winters had been kind and were friends of the Allens, so she thought they might be able to assist. "My mother would likely have attempted to force me into a marriage with the elder Mr. Collins in order to guarantee her ability to remain at the estate. I do not know what the Allens may have told you about my family, but ... it is not a happy home most of the time."

Mrs. Winters reached over to pat the girl's hands that were clasped in her lap. She could see the knuckles turning white from how tight she held herself. "Mrs. Allen wrote to me and told me about your family. She mentioned some problems, including the proposed marriage to a much older heir, but did not mention the gentleman's name. It is one reason we acted so quickly to bring you here."

"Thank you, Mrs. Winters. I do appreciate your willingness to help a stranger," Mary said, gripping her hands more tightly in her lap and not looking her hostess in the eye.

"You are also helping a stranger by befriending my daughter. I do not know if you realise it, but you have already helped her. I think your friendship will be good for both of you." Mrs. Winters already liked the young lady who had come to stay with them and felt protective of her. From what Mrs. Allen had written, it seemed unlikely that Mary had ever experienced any form of motherly affection. She had an abundance of the feeling and did not hesitate even a little to provide a little to this poor child who was now in her care.

"Now, Miss Bennet, since this Mr. Collins is a relation of yours, once he is recovered, would you like to be introduced to him? It may be best for my husband to write to Mr. Allen to inform him of the death of the elder Mr. Collins so he can inform your father. Do you think that is best?"

Mary was not used to being consulted in these matters, but knowing what she did of her mother, she thought it best that Mr. Allen informed her father in person. Then, Mr. Bennet could share the news with Mrs. Bennet. Regardless of how she learned of the death of the heir presumptive, she would react poorly. Mary was uncertain of the legalities of the matter and thought to write Mrs. Allen and Mr. Phillips with the news as well.

Chapter Twenty-Nine

In London, the Darcys were settling into a new routine. The couple attended the tea at the Matlocks, first sending a note to confirm that Lady Catherine had departed before they arrived.

"Darcy, Elizabeth, we are pleased to welcome you back to London." The ball celebrating your wedding will occur in just under a fortnight so we must do what we can to prepare. I know, Elizabeth, that you are not unknown in the *ton*, but you will still need to be introduced as Mrs. Darcy," Lady Matlock said in greeting.

Darcy frowned. He tolerated most society events but, right now, he wanted little more than to return to Pemberley with his wife. "Aunt, I agreed to the ball, but we intend to depart for Pemberley early in December. We will spend the holidays at my estate."

A frown appeared on his aunt's face. "I know that was your intention, Darcy, but before you depart, you should spend a week or two doing the rounds to establish your wife in society. You would not want anyone to think you are ashamed of your wife."

"Of course I am not," Darcy snapped. "But we do not wish to remain in town for much longer than that, and I intend to spend far more time at Pemberley over the next few years. Georgiana has several years before her come out, and while we may be required to spend a few weeks in London each year, I am married now. Surely, there is even less of a reason for me to attend society events since I am no longer seeking a bride."

"You cannot forgo all society now that you are wed. Even if Georgiana will not come out for several more years, you must maintain your contacts so Georgiana can make an acceptable match. You will also need to handle business matters occasionally, and you take pleasure in attending certain events in London," Lady Matlock objected.

Elizabeth stepped in. "We will attend some of the musical evenings we are invited to, along with the theatre and the opera. We will not forsake town entirely, but I doubt we will spend more than a month or two here each year. There is no reason for us to attend a full season until Georgiana is ready for her debut in society. Once she is successfully launched, it is likely we will spend little time in London until it is time for our own children to enter society."

Lady Matlock was displeased but recognised the futility of saying anything else now. She believed she could more easily persuade her new niece to stay longer each year once she learned to enjoy her status as Mrs. Darcy.

Darcy spoke again, recognising the look on his aunt's face and wanting to turn to conversation to what he wanted to discuss. "What happened with Lady Catherine last evening?"

All could see Lord Matlock roll his eyes. "'There is no fool like an old fool'" he quoted. "My sister grows more obstreperous with each passing year. You and Anne both repeatedly rejected the idea of the marriage. Your father explicitly stated there was no engagement at least twice in my presence, and I told her the same thing. I believe she thought by saying it enough, she could force you to bend to her will. Anne kept the letters from her announcing your engagement and marriage and waited until you were wed before allowing her to find out. I cannot say that it was the best idea, but Anne chose to reveal it this way."

"I suppose there was no way to prevent Lady Catherine from having her say at some point, but I had hoped for a few more days of solitude," Darcy replied, sighing in resignation

---

SEVERAL DAYS LATER, Elizabeth received yet another letter from her sisters. She responded to Mary's letter the same day she received it. She had not yet replied to Jane and was surprised to receive another letter already. However, once she opened and read it, she understood a little more why Jane had written again.

She sighed heavily, causing Darcy to look up at her across the breakfast table. "Is everything well at Longbourn?"

"Not really," she replied. "Mr. Collins has not arrived as expected and Mrs. Bennet has become hysterical yet again. The heir to Longbourn and his son were expected four days ago, but they have not arrived, and no word has been received from either man. Of course, Jane does not express it quite that way, but Mrs. Bennet has taken to her rooms yet again to cry and complain about what will become of them when Mr. Bennet passes away. Mary's last letter said she also did this after we left since I ruined their plans for me to wed Mr. Collins. Jane says that Mr. Bennet seems unaffected by this, but given what we have learned of him, that is no surprise."

"Have they had any word from Mr. Collins? Is anyone inquiring about what has happened to him?" Darcy asked.

"Jane does not know. Perhaps Mary's letter will say," Elizabeth replied, turning to look down at the other letter in her hand. After a moment, she looked up. "Mary has been invited to visit a friend of the rector's wife in Maidstone. She said Mrs. Bennet has become unreasonable in the time since we left and has begun to blame Mary for the problems, that is, when she is not finding me at fault for the problems at Longbourn. Apparently, my absence for nearly a decade is the cause of all the problems at the estate, or that is what Mrs. Bennet insisted at the height of her hysteria."

"That is utterly ridiculous," Darcy inserted, his brow furrowing in anger.

"Mrs. Bennet is not known for her logic," Elizabeth said with a shrug. "It is a ridiculous notion. However, I will send a note to both my uncles. Perhaps one of them can determine what has happened to the heir. If I recall correctly, he has a son so if something has happened to him, the son would inherit, would he not?"

"It is probable, but Mr. Phillips would be more familiar with the estate and the entail. He would be the logical choice to pursue this matter, but Gardiner may have more resources to find out what has happened. Do you know where this Mr. Collins is from?"

"I want to say the letter I saw had a return address from somewhere in Kent. I am not particularly familiar with that area and do not recall much else," Elizabeth offered. "I think Uncle Phillips would know since I believe he has corresponded with the man on occasion."

"I will write to Mr. Phillips, if you will write to Gardiner. I think you are right; Gardiner will have resources that Mr. Phillips will not. He may be able to discover more quickly what has happened. Mr. Phillips might have already begun to search since it is not unlikely that all of Meryton is aware of his failure to show."

Elizabeth nodded, not really wanting to reply, but knowing he was probably correct. They finished their meal and then went into Darcy's study to write their letters. While they would eventually choose to work separately one day, for now, they enjoyed the opportunity to spend time in each other's presence even while working.

WHEN LOVE IS TRUE

IT DID NOT TAKE LONG to receive a reply to their letter to the Gardiners. Her uncle promised to send out runners to find out what they could. Surprisingly, Gardiner knew much about the heir to Longbourn already, having exchanged letters with Phillips about the man several times over the last fortnight.

Two days later, they received the answer to their inquiry from Gardiner in person. Several days earlier, on the very day that Lady Catherine had arrived at Darcy House, the carriage conveying the Collinses had been in an accident. A larger carriage, one moving too quickly as it journeyed toward London, had passed the slower conveyance near the town of Maidstone. As it passed, the larger carriage jerked and knocked into the other vehicle, with enough force to cause it to crash along the roadside

The elder Mr. Collins died immediately while the younger was injured and was unconscious. A family had taken the young man into their home and was attempting to nurse him to health although the doctor was unsure of his recovery.

"Is Mary not in Maidstone?" Elizabeth asked when her uncle explained what he had learned. "Perhaps she can make the young man's acquaintance, and the Bennets could help him recover, assuming that he will recover," she said questioningly, looking at her uncle for confirmation.

His face was grim. "It is uncertain," he replied. "The doctor believes the longer he is insensible, the less likely he is to recover. I do not know how near Mary is, nor how willing her hosts will be to allow her to visit the young man. He is her cousin, yes, but they are distantly related and have never met before now."

"Do Mr. and Mrs. Bennet know about Mr. Collins' fate?" Darcy asked.

"I sent a letter by express to my brother Phillips. I have asked him to inform Bennet of the matter and to find out what will happen should the younger Collins pass from this world as well," Gardiner replied.

Darcy nodded at this, and all three were momentarily lost in their thoughts. Finally, Gardiner broke the silence. "I understand, Elizabeth, that my sister is still rather upset with you. She has written to my wife accusing her of turning you against the family. It is sheer ridiculousness, given that she was the one who has not contacted you in many years, but somehow, I expect little else from her. However, I want you to know that I fully comprehend your reasoning for refusing her demands and even those of your sisters that you invite them to visit."

"I know, Uncle. I spoke to my aunt about this same matter a few days ago and have shared with her some of what was said at Longbourn. Jane has written to me twice now, the first time to complain about Mrs. Bennet's fretting and to subtly hint at an invitation, and the second to inform me of the situation with Mr. Collins. I have as yet not responded to either letter. William and I need to discuss matters before I do so."

Gardiner nodded at his niece. "You are wise to continue to distance yourself from them, Elizabeth. If my sister thinks you will eventually comply with her demands, she will become more vehement that you do as she wishes. She has always needed someone to take a strong stance with her; my father would not after our mother died, and Mr. Bennet certainly has not. They did not do her any favours. Only our mother was ever able to handle her, but she died when Fanny was near Georgiana's age."

Elizabeth sighed, not wanting to continue this conversation. "I will write to Mary to tell her what we have learned. I doubt Mr. or Mrs. Bennet will say anything to her; in fact, given what I know about the man, I doubt he will say anything at all to his family about Mr. Collins's fate."

With that, Elizabeth turned from the gentleman and retreated to the mistress' study that she had been shown only a few days before. She rarely used it, but just then, she preferred to be on her own.

Chapter Thirty

Nearly a week after Mary arrived at the Winters' estate, and a fortnight after the accident occurred, the younger Mr. Collins was awake and able to receive visitors. He had not fully recovered yet, but he was now able to sit up and dress, though he still required assistance with both tasks.

Mr. William Collins was in his early twenties and had read for his university degree a year ago. He intended to become a rector but had yet to find a position as a curate. Though he had met with several prospects, none seemed willing to grant him a position. His father had taught him that grovelling would often get what he desired, but that had not worked thus far.

Additionally, he did not care to play the fool, and at each of these meetings, that was how he felt. He might not be the most intelligent man, but he did know the scriptures well and believed he would do a good job of caring for those who needed him.

He was surprised when he was introduced to his cousin. Since this was one of the cousins he was on his way to visit, he wondered why she was not at home, and if she had come all this way to see him. She quickly informed him that it was simply a matter of chance.

"I was very surprised to arrive at the estate of a friend for a visit and learn that you were in the same town. While I knew your father was expected to arrive soon at my family's estate, I am not certain my father ever mentioned you. I wish to offer my condolences on the loss of your father," Mary said.

"Thank you, Miss Bennet. I find myself uncertain what to do when I recover. I believe my father intended to move into Longbourn or at least the dower house, once he married your sister Elizabeth. I have been looking for a position as a curate somewhere, and I have no place to go when I leave here," Collins answered.

Mary looked at him as she contemplated what she ought to do or say. "I think you would be welcome at my family's home for a visit, and I can ask Reverend Allen if knows of anyone who is looking for a curate. Perhaps after meeting you, he would be willing to help you." Mary was uncertain if Mr. Allen could do anything to help but thought that letting him know of the need could not hurt matters.

"I thank you, Miss Bennet. Perhaps you ought to write to your father to ask if he would be amenable to my staying there for a short time and I can figure it out from there," Collins replied, his face revealing his gratitude for the offer of help.

Smiling at the man, Mary felt pleased to offer assistance in this way. It may not be exactly the sort of help Mrs. Allen and Mrs. Winters spoke to her about, but it was doing a good turn for someone who appeared to need it.

The visit that day was short, as Mr. Collins could not sit up for long without tiring. However, Mary continued to visit daily for the next fortnight as he recovered, and each day the visit lasted longer.

After that first visit, Mary sat and wrote a letter to her father, which she did not expect him to answer, and then letters to both her Uncle

Phillips and Reverend Allen. Since Mr. Winters had written to her uncle about the accident so they could ensure Mr. Bennet knew about it, Mary thought she should let him know what she had written to her father. Additionally, she wrote to Mrs. Allen to inform her of the conversation she had with Mr. Collins and to ask for any assistance in finding him a position as a curate.

To no one's surprise, Mr. Bennet did not reply to Mary's letter, but her uncle and Mrs. Allen did. Mrs. Allen wrote that her husband was looking for a curate, and if Mr. Collins seemed a good fit, they would consider him. Mr. Phillips also responded, letting her know that he had spoken to Mr. Bennet about Mr. Collins and that the Bennets were happy to extend an invitation for him to stay for a time after he recovered enough to travel.

Mary and Mr. Collins developed a camaraderie during the weeks of his recovery, engaging in lively conversations on various topics. Despite occasional differences in opinion, Mary's willingness to challenge Mr. Collins was met with receptiveness. He found it intriguing to exchange ideas with a lady, considering it a refreshing departure from his usual company which primarily consisted of his father and others of his ilk.

Mrs. Winters chaperoned these visits. Mary was "out" in society, and though she believed the girl too young to marry, did not want any negative talk to circulate that would affect her reputation. While she remained quiet in most of the conversations, she did occasionally insert an opinion when it became necessary. Often, these comments required both parties to reconsider an opinion.

Through these conversations, both became a little less dogmatic in their beliefs. Mrs. Winters' presence helped maintain propriety and added a layer of practicality that one or the other might have occasionally lacked.

One afternoon, they spent the entire visit discussing the value of novels. Mr. Collins had been taught that women ought not to read such texts, having been told they were vulgar and endangered women's delicate sensibilities.

"You see, Mr. Collins," Mary remarked, "I believe that novels have the power to broaden our horizons and deepen our understanding of the human experience. They allow us to explore different perspectives and empathise with the characters. Yes, they can also teach us what is right and wrong and should be balanced by reading other texts that will teach us what is moral."

Mr. Collins, initially sceptical of her argument, replied, "But Miss Mary, is it not better to spend your time in more edifying pursuits? Novels often indulge in frivolous sentimentality and distract us from our moral duties."

Mary smiled patiently, ready to defend her position. "While it is true that some novels may lack moral depth, many offer profound insights into human nature and moral dilemmas. They can inspire us to reflect on our own lives and strive for personal growth. Again, I am not suggesting that is all a lady should read, but it does not harm us to read one now and then."

Their conversation continued, with Mary advocating for the value of literature, while Mr. Collins listened intently, gradually opening his mind to her perspective. In fact, on her next visit, Mary brought a book written 'by a lady' that she read a portion of to Mr. Collins. At the end of her visit, he asked to borrow it, and the two discussed the book at a later visit.

Mary's horizons were being broadened by not only her growing friendship with her cousin, but by several other relationships as well. Amelia and Mary had become fast friends as they practised the piano together, but it was Amelia's influence that had encouraged Mary to embrace novels. Prior to coming to Maidstone, Mary had been sceptical of their value, but Amelia and Mrs. Winters had been reading one together and encouraged Mary to participate in the conversation. In the end, Mary had stayed up late into the night to catch up with them in the book as she found it far more interesting than she initially thought.

Her piano playing was also improving. Amelia's teacher had easily included Mary in the lessons despite their different levels, and having a friend to encourage her was invaluable. Since Mary was the only one who played at home, there was no one with whom to speak about music, and most of what she had learned was self-taught.

Mrs. Winters was motherly in a way Mrs. Bennet had never been, at least not with her. In truth, the way Mrs. Winters was with both Mary and her own daughter was nothing like the way Mrs. Bennet parented any of her daughters. Mary had been visiting for almost a month before it dawned on her what the difference was: Mrs. Winters was (almost) entirely unselfish.

It was a startling realisation. Mrs. Bennet preferred the daughters who she thought most likely to assure her own security. While it did not say much for the relationship between her parents, she knew her mother's greatest concern was what would happen when her father died. Since Mr. Bennet had presumably done nothing to ensure his family would be provided for after his death, Mrs. Bennet was justly worried about her future. With that in mind, she pushed and encouraged the daughters who were most like her, the ones she thought most likely to make a match that would provide for her in the future.

Even trying to force Elizabeth to marry Mr. Collins was an attempt at self-preservation. Having one of her daughters married to Longbourn's heir would have—at least in Mrs. Bennet's mind—assured her welcome at Longbourn for her lifetime. Of course, knowing what she now knew about her sister, she realised that would never have been true. Had Mrs. Bennet forced Elizabeth to marry, Elizabeth would have had few qualms about sending Mrs. Bennet into the hedgerows upon Mr. Bennet's death. Whether the late Mr. Collins would have supported this decision was a different consideration.

After a mere month at Maidstone, Mary was a completely different girl compared to the one who had arrived there. All these realisations had helped her to mature and her discussions with her new friends and the letters she exchanged with Elizabeth had encouraged her to look at the world in a different light. She was also learning what the mistress of an estate ought to do and wondered how many of these practices she could put into effect when she returned to Longbourn.

To her disappointment, Mary was expected to return home before too much longer. Unfortunately, she had already received and ignored several letters from her mother demanding her return. Initially, she had been unsure why her presence was needed, but it soon became apparent that her mother had learned about the elder Mr. Collins's death and the imminent arrival of the younger. She did not seem to know that Mary had already met the gentleman, but she wanted Mary to return home before he came. Since Jane was destined for a wealthier man—Mrs. Bennet decided Jane deserved a husband even better than the one Elizabeth had managed to get—Mary was now expected to marry Longbourn's heir.

Mary did like Mr. Collins and enjoyed their conversations, but she was only sixteen and felt she was in no way prepared for marriage. Neither was Mr. Collins, given that he had no home and, at the moment, no prospects. If Mrs. Bennet got her way and the two did wed, where would they live and who would support them?

But that was not a concern for Mrs. Bennet. She wanted her daughter married and her own security assured, regardless of the cost to anyone else. Realising this, Mary first spoke to her hostess and wrote her mother a letter informing her that she had been invited to stay until spring. Since she could not in good conscience reject such a kind invitation, Mary accepted it, letting her mother know she could not possibly return before Easter.

Chapter Thirty-One

Mrs. Bennet was displeased.

All of her plans to ensure her security had fallen through. She had intended to have a daughter married before Christmas which she did, but that daughter was not married to Longbourn's heir. That terrible Elizabeth was married, and she had managed to marry far better than she deserved, the matron thought. Moreover, none of her other daughters had any suitors. No one in Meryton was worthy of her most beautiful daughter Jane, for there was a lack of wealthy men. Despite her efforts, the Gardiners were unwilling to let Jane visit them after her disastrous visit several years before.

She has been disappointed when Elizabeth did not show up as expected, willing to marry Mr. Collins. Instead, she showed up married, and, according to gossip, married very well. Gossip in town reported that Mr. Darcy had a large estate in Derbyshire and had titled relatives. However, Mrs. Bennet knew nothing firsthand; all her letters to the Gardiners and Elizabeth went unanswered.

Now, she learned that Mr. Collins was dead and his son, the next in succession, was injured. She began to worry about what would happen if this man died, but then she heard he was recovering. Jane was to marry higher, so Mr. Collins would have to do for Mary. She wondered if her husband would think Mary too young to marry at just sixteen, or if they would have to wait. If nothing else, she could ensure the marriage contracts were signed immediately, and the pair could marry when Mary turned eighteen.

However, Mary was away from home. She had been at first incensed at her daughter's letter stating that she had accepted an invitation to remain where she was for several more months, but soon decided that it was serendipitous since it would allow her to make plans without her daughter's inference. Perhaps, Mary's absence was not the problem she initially thought it was. If she could get Mr. Collins to sign the contracts before Mary returned home, he would not be put off by her looks, forgetting that Mary had already made the gentleman's acquaintance.

She burst into her husband's study to inform him of the plans she had made. "Mr. Bennet, when is Mr. Collins going to arrive at Longbourn?" she demanded.

"In a sennight. I understand from his letters he is mostly recovered and will be well enough to travel in a few more days. He is looking for a position as a curate so he can take orders when he comes of an age to do so," Mr. Bennet answered, slowly setting down his book and looking at his wife, trying to figure out what she was hoping for.

"When he comes, he must be made to marry Mary."

"Mary is but sixteen, and Mr. Collins cannot afford a wife at present unless you would like them to move into Longbourn. Perhaps that would be advantageous for then you can teach Mary how to be mistress of the estate," Mr. Bennet replied, his voice dripping with sarcasm.

Mrs. Bennet either ignored or missed his tone. Instead, she wrung her hands in apparent frustration at his failure to understand. "I am not suggesting they marry immediately, merely that you have him sign the marriage contracts. They can marry when Mary is eighteen. Then, we must see about convincing my brother to host Jane with them in London. If Lizzy could manage to catch such a wealthy husband, then surely Jane will do better. Now that Lizzy is married so well, she could even introduce her sister and then Jane can marry a peer."

Mr. Bennet stared at his wife in surprise at her audacity. "Your brother will not host Jane, nor do anything else you demand of him. You might ask, but as I recall, you recently complained that they had not answered your letters."

"Now that Lizzy is not living with them any longer, they can have no objection to hosting Jane for a time. If they will not, perhaps Lizzy will. We will send Jane to town, and they would have little choice but to keep her at least for a brief time."

Mr. Bennet could only shake his head at her lack of understanding. "At your insistence, we sent Elizabeth away. You wanted nothing to do with your second child, and I did not argue with you." His tone was resigned. "Elizabeth might be willing to make amends with her sisters, but I do not think your demand that she host them in London will bear fruit."

"Of course she will host her sisters in London. Why would she not want to? She must want to help her sister find a match at least as good as her own," Mrs. Bennet cried.

"Jane has written to her already. Elizabeth will not invite Jane to town but is willing to correspond with her. Jane told me about the letter she received, and while she was disappointed, she did eventually come to understand what you apparently will not. Elizabeth has absolutely no reason to want to assist the family that cast her aside. I received a message from her husband, demanding that you cease sending letters to her and the Gardiners."

"How do you know all this, Mr. Bennet?" his wife asked, her tone demanding and shrill.

"Jane and Mary both came to me not long after Elizabeth left Meryton. They both wrote to her in secret and received replies in return. Jane did much as you would have done and asked for Elizabeth to host her in town. Elizabeth agreed to continue the correspondence, but not to host her sister. She is newly married and establishing her own self in society, nor do she and her husband intend to remain in London for long. They will spend the holidays at their estate in Derbyshire."

Mrs. Bennet scowled at that. "She should remain in London to host her sister. Jane deserves a much better match than her ungrateful sister has managed."

Shaking his head, Mr. Bennet ceased his attempts to explain to his wife. "Regardless of what you think she ought to do, she and her husband have determined to act as they will. I will sign no more marriage contracts unless both the groom and my daughter agree to the match. I cannot and will not force Mr. William Collins to marry one of my daughters unless he wishes to. He is also in mourning and will be for six months to a year. As I understand it, his father left him little, and until he finds a position, the gentleman is in no position to marry."

"What does that matter?" Mrs. Bennet waved away her husband's protestation. "You must encourage him to wed Mary, preferably before she returns home, and he can meet her. He will not want to marry her if he sees her first since she is not as beautiful as Jane. If only Lydia was older and of a suitable age to marry. She is a very pretty girl, and I have little doubt she will be just as beautiful as Jane. She is far more lively, taking after myself as a girl, and I am certain she will have all manner of beaux when she is older."

Mr. Bennet repeated that he could not force Mr. Collins to accept any of his daughters and coldly sent his wife from his room, shaking his head at her foolishness before returning to his book.

Chapter Thirty-Two

JUNE 1809

Throughout the winter and spring, many letters travelled back and forth between Elizabeth and Mary. In those letters, Mary shared first of her growing familiarity with the new heir to Longbourn, Mr. William Collins, a young man of just twenty-three who was waiting to take his orders to become a rector. Mary and her cousin formed a friendship, and Mary recommended him to the Allens in Meryton who might help the young man find a curacy.

Since he was not yet of a proper age to take orders, Mr. Allen was able to offer him the position of curate for his church in Meryton. This pleased the young man, who enjoyed the company of his cousin. The two were frequently in company as their friendship continued.

Initially, he stayed at Longbourn, though Mrs. Bennet's shrill complaints and her vocally insisting that Mary and Mr. Collins wed "to save the family" grew taxing on everyone. When Mr. Allen offered Mr. Collins not only the position as curate but also a small cottage for him to live in, he gladly accepted. He earned enough to hire a maid to help with the cleaning and washing, and he knew enough to brew a cup of tea and prepare a few simple dishes. Mrs. Allen often invited him for meals, and as he became more involved with Longbourn's tenants and the parish's less fortunate, the number of invitations to meals and social events steadily increased.

It became widely known that the young curate was the heir presumptive to Longbourn, which made him an eligible catch by many of the women of that small village. However, most of these ladies seemed to want to bide their time, for they saw where and how he lived and were not quite ready to suffer the hardships of being a curate's wife, regardless of his future prospects.

Mary's letters indicated a growing regard for the gentleman although it was evident that she viewed him as a friend and brother, not as a future husband, much to her mother's frustration.

Toward the end of April, not long before Elizabeth's nineteenth birthday, two critical events came to pass. The first was that Elizabeth discovered she was with child after emptying the contents of her stomach every morning for nearly a fortnight. Both she and Darcy were concerned by this until a casual reference by the housekeeper reminded Elizabeth of a conversation she had with her aunt before her marriage. She sent a note to Mrs. Gardiner asking her to visit and related the symptoms she was experiencing. It did not take long for Mrs. Gardiner to confirm what Elizabeth already suspected and when she informed her husband of the cause of her so-called illness, he was delighted. The two would become parents before the year was out.

The second event was much more upsetting. A letter from Mary informed the pair of a smallpox epidemic spreading through Longbourn village. It had begun with the tenants and servants and quickly spread to the family, with each member of the Bennet family suffering from the illness in varying degrees. Mary returned to Longbourn, and as she remained unaffected, took up nursing the rest of her family. The least ill of the servants assisted her in this, as did Mrs. Allen and several others from the neighbourhood who had smallpox as children and were therefore at less risk. Mrs. Hill, the housekeeper, was one of these as was Charlotte Lucas, and these three proved invaluable in assisting those who needed it.

Jane was not particularly ill though she was perhaps the most affected by the rash. This was enough to keep her confined to her room for the duration, believing what her mother had taught her, that her only value came from her appearance. Therefore, she did not want anyone to see her when her body was marked by the sickness. When anyone entered her room, she would cover her body with the bed clothes and refused to be seen. This frequently made caring for her more difficult, while, as usual, she did not seem to realise how her actions affected others.

Though Mrs. Bennet, Kitty, and Lydia were all ill, they recovered reasonably quickly. It was Mr. Bennet who was the sickest in his family. Mr. Allen came frequently to speak to the gentleman, as did the apothecary and Mr. Phillips, all who had fallen sick from the illness in their youth. Each of these conversations was serious, and they provided guidance in the only way they could: Mr. Allen tended to him spiritually, Mr. Jones medicinally, and Mr. Phillips spoke to him of his family's future.

Unsurprisingly, none of these conversations were pleasant. Mr. Bennet was angry with himself, his family, God, pretty much everyone, blaming each in turn for the illness that befell him. He had little to say to Mr. Jones, though he did listen to his advice. However, Mr. Bennet's health only grew worse. It was Mr. Phillips who heard the worst of his anger. Mr. Bennet had done nothing to plan for his eventual demise, and Phillips could barely disguise his disapproval at this lack of foresight, leading to several arguments between the two men.

As Mr. Bennet declined further, Mrs. Bennet took to her own bed, demanding attention from her daughters. She could not help but bemoan Jane's altered appearance, lamenting the small scars from smallpox near her right ear. Though minor and confined to a small area, Mrs. Bennet acted as if Jane was now hideous. All the praise she had once heaped upon her daughter for her beauty turned into cries of lost chances.

Therefore, Elizabeth was mostly unsurprised a little over a week later when she received a black-edged letter from Longbourn announcing the death of Thomas Bennet. She was still in London, and while a part of her wanted to pay her final respects to the man who had given her life, neither she nor Darcy were willing to travel to Hertfordshire for the funeral. As a female, Elizabeth would not be permitted to attend, and neither wanted to be party to the inevitable complaints from the Bennet matriarch when they would not give into Mrs. Bennet's demands to provide for the rest of the Bennet ladies.

They had fortunately met Mr. Collins a few months earlier when he visited London on Mr. Phillips's behalf. He was a good man; they had heard good things about him through Mary's letters, and knew she considered him almost as a brother. Despite Mrs. Bennet's insistence that Mary and Mr. Collins wed, neither had any intention of doing so, especially now that the Bennet family was in mourning.

When they met, Mr. Bennet had been healthy although Darcy and Collins had spoken of what might transpire upon the event of that gentleman's demise. Collins agreed with Darcy that since the Bennets had cast Elizabeth from their home at the tender age of eight, that she owed nothing to her parents, particularly her mother. Due to his friendship with the middle daughter, Collins reassured Darcy and Elizabeth both, along with Mr. Phillips and Mr. Gardiner, that he would not cast the Bennet family from their home immediately upon Mr. Bennet's eventual death. So long as Collins was unmarried, he would allow the family a minimum of six months to mourn their father before even attempting to claim the estate as his own, though he would begin managing it as soon as he could. However, he was comfortably situated at present in his little cottage, and so would not do as Mrs. Bennet feared and "cast them into the hedgerows."

He also agreed that, as long as he could, he would assist the widow and her daughters financially, ensuring they had enough to live on. When it came time for him to claim Longbourn as his, he would allow Mrs.

Bennet and her daughters the use of the dower house. However, he did ask Darcy for some assistance in ensuring the dower house was suitable for residence since he was uncertain of its condition at this moment.

Darcy and Elizabeth agreed since it was unlikely to cost as much as what Mrs. Bennet might demand; Elizabeth felt assisting her sisters in this way was the least she could do for them. She did not offer it on Mrs. Bennet's behalf, but truly, most of it was done for Mary since she was the only sister who had continued a correspondence with Elizabeth that did not consist of demands for new clothing, ribbons, or trips to town.

After Mr. Bennet's death, Elizabeth received a letter from Mary. She was very surprised to find a second letter addressed to her inside. She did not recognise the handwriting and opened it.

> *My Dear Elizabeth,*
>
> *It hardly seems fair to you to call you dear now, though I did want you to know that you were, in fact, dear to me. You were my always favourite child, little though I showed it, and I missed you dreadfully when you went away. However, by that time, I had spent the last decade giving into my wife's demands, without thinking of what it may cost me. Losing you was a much larger cost than I fully realised.*
>
> *I doubt even Mary knows it, but I have read each letter you sent her and know more about your life at present than I have any right to. You have been generous in your advice to her, and, frankly, generous in continuing to correspond with her at all, given what Mrs. Bennet and I have forced you to endure. We wilfully threw you to the side when I ought to have stood up to my wife. What happened to Jane that day was not your fault, and I think Mrs. Bennet must realise that as well, though she would never admit to it.*

Our family suffered much when you went away. I tried even less following your departure, and we spent every bit of the income from Longbourn selfishly. Because I would not stand up to my wife on the issue of you, I found myself giving in to my wife's demands over and over again. Now that I am dying, I realise far more of what I have done.

Longbourn is in worse shape now than it was when I inherited it. I think my young cousin Collins is a good man though perhaps not well versed in estate management, but I think he will be a more diligent master than I have been. He will do a better job than me, that is for certain, but mostly because few could do worse.

In the months following your return, I managed to set aside small amounts of the estate income. I had intended it to serve as a dowry for my daughters eventually, but with this illness, I believe that it is insufficient to aid as it should. I should have been taking these steps all their lives, yours included, to ensure they would be protected at the end of my life. However, it seems as with most things in my life, I have waited too long. There is nothing for it now, for it seems that I will shuffle off this mortal coil much sooner than I would have liked. I truly believed my wife would have gone first, with all her nervous flutterings and complaints, but it seems that it will be me. At least the heir appears to be a good man so perhaps my wife and daughters will be cared for, despite my lack of effort in that direction.

It is hardly adequate for an old man now on his deathbed to offer an apology. I feel certain it cannot make up for what you have suffered in being sent away from your family, but perhaps you had a better life than what we would *have offered you. Had I raised you, you would have no doubt been full of conceit and sarcasm, just as I am, and unwilling to stand up for what is right, as I have done. I would have made things far worse for you. Though perhaps having you home would have helped me to be a better man and made me less indolent.*

Regardless, there is little point in exploring these ideas now, but I do want to tell you how sorry I am for not being a better father and a better man. By all accounts, you have married an excellent man, and when the time comes for you to bring a child into this world, he will no doubt prove to be all I am not and chose not to be. I hope that this letter will help you, if even a little bit, to forgive me for my failures.

Sincerely,

Your Father, Thomas Bennet

Elizabeth shook her head as she read the letter through a second time. Part of her would like to find it in her to forgive the man, but even his apology was worthless. To wait to tell her now that she was 'dear to him', when he had made no effort in his lifetime to act remotely like a loving father, or even a concerned one, felt almost like a slap to the face instead of the apology he believed he was making. Like everything else in his life, he hoped to ease his conscience so he could die in peace. He might have felt better after writing this letter, but instead of evoking feelings of love or even of sympathy, instead she felt anger and annoyance.

Darcy saw these emotions as they flashed across her face and moved toward her. "Dearest, are you well?" he asked, his voice soft and filled with concern, as he sat on the settee beside her, drawing her into his arms.

Elizabeth shook her head, her movements slow at first as though weighed down by the heaviness of her thoughts. Then, with a suddenness that startled him, she shook her head again, as if trying to dispel the cobwebs clouding her mind. "My fa … Mr. Bennet has died."

Darcy's arms tightened around her. "Oh, Elizabeth …" he whispered, his breath warm against her hair.

Her voice was steady, though the weight of sorrow pressed upon her words. "Mary's last letter indicated this was not far away. Of the family, he was the most ill. Then I received this," she paused, holding up a letter, her father's handwriting unmistakable on the pages. "In the days leading up to his death, he wrote this … apology for not doing enough to protect me as a child."

She looked at Darcy, her eyes searching his face as though trying to find the words to express the tangled emotions within her. "In it, he claims to have loved me. He read my letters to Mary—probably all the letters I wrote to my sisters—and thinks he knows about me and my life from those."

Darcy's brow furrowed as he listened intently, his heart aching for her, though he remained silent, not wishing to interrupt the flow of her thoughts.

"Truly, I am sorry he is gone, which means we can never be restored," Elizabeth continued, her voice tightening with unshed tears, "but I am not certain we ever could have been. He is … was too selfish to truly love anyone besides himself."

Her words hung in the air, and Darcy could feel the truth in them. The resentment she had harboured for years, the pain of neglect, all seemed to spill out, raw and exposed.

"If there is one thing I have learned from my aunt and uncle," she said, her voice softening, "and from my relationship with you, it is that love is unselfish and wants the best for the object of its love. This claim of love from Mr. Bennet is selfish and is more about appeasing his conscience than any real affection for me. If he truly loved me or any of my sisters, he would have done more for us and not waited until he was dying to try."

Darcy's chest tightened at her words, and he instinctively pulled her closer. He could feel her tremble, the weight of her grief pressing against him. Yet, there was little he could say. He agreed with her, deeply so, and he thought she knew that. Still, finding the right words to comfort her felt beyond his reach.

Instead, he held her, hoping she would feel the depth of his love in his embrace. His hand gently stroked her back as she nestled into him, her head resting against his chest.

For a long moment, they sat in silence, the crackle of the fire in the hearth the only sound in the room. Darcy's thoughts flickered briefly to her condition, worrying that the stress and grief would worsen her health. But as if sensing his concern, Elizabeth shifted slightly and looked up at him, her gaze steady despite the sorrow lingering in her eyes.

"Do not fret, my love," she whispered, her hand coming up to rest against his cheek. "I will be well. I promise. It was merely the shock of receiving first Mary's letter and then his."

He kissed her forehead, his lips lingering there as he whispered, "I know, dearest. I know. There is a finality to death, is there not? We might have wished for something different, something better, but now it is impossible."

Elizabeth nodded, acknowledging his words, but she did not wish to dwell on the matter any longer. Instead, she leaned into his embrace, allowing the steady warmth of his presence to soothe her as she grappled with the multitude of emotions swirling within her—grief, anger, regret—all threatening to overwhelm her. Darcy held her close, offering his silent support, knowing that words were no longer necessary.

Chapter Thirty-Three

As planned, Elizabeth and Darcy left a few days later for Pemberley. By mutual consent, they had not spoken again of Mr. Bennet's death although Elizabeth received another letter from Mary, and Darcy received one from Phillips and another from Collins.

Mary's letter indicated that Mrs. Bennet had done as expected and taken to her room, bemoaning the loss of her husband. She missed him far less than she regretted that his death meant she no longer held the social status she experienced as wife of the largest landholder in the area. While Netherfield was larger, the owner did not live there, giving Mrs. Bennet primacy of place in the local society. With Mr. Collins taking over as the master of Longbourn, and her being banished to what amounted to a cottage, she would no longer have the same standing in the local society.

"William," Elizabeth began as she entered her husband's study on the morning they were to depart, "have you heard from Uncle Phillips or Mr. Collins? Mary says her mother is hysterical over being sent away from Longbourn. No one at Longbourn seems to know that they will not be forced out of the house immediately; surely someone must tell them if they have not already done so about the agreement you made with Mr. Collins."

Darcy searched on his desk for the letters he had just read. "Yes, dearest. In fact, I just had a letter from both of them which I planned to read once we were on the way north. I assumed there was nothing particularly urgent in the letters, and since we intend to stop in Hertfordshire briefly on our way, we could speak to them about when we arrived."

"From what Mary says, Mrs. Bennet is more displeased about the loss of her status as mistress of the estate than the loss of her husband. In truth, she has been a poor mistress, at least according to Mary and Charlotte, and was mainly concerned with hosting and attending parties. She insists that Mary wed Mr. Collins immediately so she does not have to leave her home. Mary likes Mr. Collins but does not wish to marry him."

Struggling not to roll his eyes at the thought, Darcy merely grimaced in what he hoped was a sympathetic manner. Elizabeth did not hold back and did roll her eyes at him. "While I have little sympathy for their situation, we have been helping Mr. Collins refurbish the dower house. It is not large, but it is sufficient for the five of them. However, they will not have to move for several months and will have time to arrange things to their satisfaction. I am concerned that Mrs. Bennet will continue to push Mary toward Mr. Collins. At least, according to Mary, Mrs. Bennet has given up any thought of Jane marrying well, now that she is supposedly 'disfigured' by the scars from smallpox."

"There was little chance of any of them marrying truly well, for neither Mr. nor Mrs. Bennet put any effort into making them marriageable. Mary is more so, now that she has begun to better herself; the time she spent with the Allens and Winters has benefitted her greatly. Jane has not changed at all, and still seems as bland and selfish as she was when we first began to write. However, Mary indicates that she is quieter now although I am not certain why. I have not had a letter from her since the illness first started, and Mary seems to think that it has affected her. The younger girls did not escape without some scarring, though Mary says they are confined to less visible parts of the body which is why Mrs. Bennet has not dwelt upon those."

"If Mrs. Bennet is decrying Jane's beauty as lost as a result of her scars, then perhaps she will be forced to look at herself more closely. Without her 'beauty' to recommend her, she will need to face the fact that there is more to a person than that. Perhaps this will be a good thing," Darcy replied. This was a conversation they had exchanged several times in the last few weeks ever since Mary first wrote of the epidemic in the area. Elizabeth had struggled to build relationships with any of her sisters other than Mary, for she was the only one interested in knowing her sister as a person and did not ask for gifts or trips to London.

The presence of smallpox in the vicinity nearly prevented the Darcys from stopping briefly in Meryton on their way to Pemberley and led to the couple's most significant spat as a married couple thus far.

"Absolutely not, Elizabeth," Darcy said sternly, pacing back and forth in their shared sitting room when she had brought the idea up. "We will not risk your health nor that of our unborn child by venturing into an area where smallpox has been reported."

Elizabeth, seated calmly by the fireplace, looked up at her husband with a mixture of exasperation and determination. "Fitzwilliam, I understand your concern, but you are overreacting. The epidemic is confined to Longbourn and its tenants, not sweeping through the entirety of Hertfordshire. It is perfectly safe to visit Meryton where no one has been sick."

Darcy stopped pacing and turned to face her, his expression softening but his resolve unchanged. "My love, your safety is paramount. You have never faced this disease before, and I will not take any chances."

Elizabeth's eyes flashed with irritation. "Actually, I have. I was sick with smallpox when I was ten years old, and therefore I am not in danger of catching it again."

Darcy's brow furrowed in confusion and concern. "Why did you never tell me this before?"

"Because it never seemed necessary," Elizabeth replied, her tone softer but still firm. "And it does not change the fact that it is safe for me to visit Meryton. We can avoid Longbourn entirely."

Each had expressed their point of view vehemently, neither willing to yield. The tension in the room was palpable until their housekeeper, Mrs. Whitmore, unusually placed herself in the middle of their disagreement.

"Mr. and Mrs. Darcy, if I may," Mrs. Whitmore began, her voice calm and respectful but with an air of authority that immediately commanded attention. "You both need to consider the other's perspective for a minute."

Darcy and Elizabeth turned to her, slightly taken aback by her intervention.

"Mrs. Darcy is correct," Mrs. Whitmore continued. "Having had the illness before likely means she will not get it again as has been the case with many who have survived smallpox. If the illness is indeed confined to Longbourn, it should be safe for you to visit the village of Meryton."

Elizabeth smiled gratefully at the housekeeper, but Mrs. Whitmore was not finished.

"However," she said, turning to Elizabeth, "since you are carrying a child, you do need to be more careful than usual. Even if you are not at risk, we cannot be certain how any potential exposure might affect the babe."

Elizabeth's smile faded slightly as she considered this.

Darcy stepped forward, taking Elizabeth's hand in his. "My dearest, I want only what is best for you and our child. Can we not find a compromise that ensures both your safety and your peace of mind?"

Elizabeth looked into her husband's eyes and saw the depth of his concern. She sighed, squeezing his hand. "Very well. We will avoid Longbourn and ensure that our visit to Meryton is brief and cautious."

Darcy nodded, relieved. "Thank you, Elizabeth."

Mrs. Whitmore smiled at the couple, pleased that her intervention had helped them find common ground. As the Darcys prepared to continue their journey, the tension between them had eased, replaced by a renewed understanding and respect for each other's perspectives.

Feeling as though they had disappointed a much-loved mother, Darcy and Elizabeth were forced to concede that the other's point of view held merit and soon reached an agreement to visit Meryton on their way to Pemberley. Gardiner also promised his support for his sister's family but would not attend the funeral. A decade before, when Bennet set his child from his home, Gardiner had lost all respect for his brother. In truth, had it been only his sister who needed support, he would have refused outright, but felt that his nieces should not suffer because their parents had been neglectful.

Therefore, one day early in June, the Darcys arrived at Mr. Phillips's office in Meryton just before noon. They left London early in the morning and arranged to meet both Mr. Phillips and Mr. Collins in the former's office when they arrived.

They were surprised to discover Mary Bennet was present. "Mary, how good it is to see you," Elizabeth said upon entering the office. "From your letters, I expected you to be too busy at Longbourn to come to Meryton."

Mary sighed heavily before answering. "Mama is insufferable. Between her fears of the hedgerows—a fate she has been informed multiple times will not be hers—and her insistence that I disregard mourning entirely to marry Mr. Collins immediately, she spends her days in bed, demanding that everyone attend to her. It upsets the house entirely. My father has been dead and buried for nearly a fortnight. We are assured of a home in Longbourn for the entirety of her mourning period, and the dower house is being renovated to accommodate us when it is done. Mr. Collins has promised a measure of support for all of us, provided Mama does not attempt to be too extravagant. I have a feeling he will be hard pressed to restrain her spending, especially when so much of the estate's funds will be needed to restore the estate to what it ought to be after my father's indolence in the matter."

Elizabeth nodded thoughtfully. "When we wed, William gave me control over my dowry. We have discussed the matter and want to offer our assistance to you, Mr. Collins, to restore Longbourn, particularly its stables. It would be an investment—one that would be repaid over the next decade as you are able." When the man began to speak, Elizabeth held her hand up to stop him. "I know that Longbourn has the potential to be far more profitable than it is at present. We are family, if distant, and I would like to see my family estate returned to what it once was. As I said, it is an investment, one which would be repaid."

Darcy and Elizabeth had discussed this matter several times over. Through their correspondence, Mary and Elizabeth had grown close, and Elizabeth knew the difficulties the family would face in the next months as Mr. Collins attempted to restore the damage Mr. Bennet had done to the estate through his neglect. It would be a significant undertaking, one that would be made easier if Collins did not have to worry so much about the funds needed to both support the Bennet family and make the needed improvements.

"I ... I am ... I am uncertain what to say," Mr. Collins stammered. "I feel I cannot refuse, but I would like Mr. Phillips to write up a contract to ensure the terms of the repayment are entirely clear. I will accept an investment, or a loan, as long as it is not an outright gift. There is much work that needs to be done on the estate."

Mr. Phillips agreed. "I will write up the contract. I presume it will not be much different than other investment contracts," he said before asking a few questions about the details. Darcy answered most of those, being familiar with investments, as was Mr. Phillips, and within the hour, the two had a contract written to everyone's satisfaction and signed.

"If I understand correctly, Mrs. Bennet is aware of what Mr. Collins has agreed to about the family remaining in Longbourn for the present?" Elizabeth finally broached the subject that had brought them to Meryton in the first place.

"Yes, she knows although she still believes the only thing that will keep her from the hedgerows is for me to marry Mr. Collins. I will be seventeen in a few months; I do not feel old enough to marry anyone. While I like Mr. Collins very much, we have discussed this, and neither of us wishes to marry the other. I suppose that could change in a few years, but I am not willing to commit myself in marriage to a man towards whom I have only brotherly feelings," Mary stated firmly.

"Your Uncle Gardiner and I are now your guardians. Neither of us will force you into a marriage you do not wish for," Mr. Phillips said to reassure his niece. "Despite what my sister might say, none of you will be forced to marry Mr. Collins. We hope all our nieces, and even you, Mr. Collins, will eventually find someone to marry you can love and respect. Between all of us here and my brother Gardiner, we will support you in whatever decision you make."

Mr. Collins sighed heavily. "I am most concerned about Mrs. Bennet and the youngest girls. Miss Catherine and Miss Lydia need to be separated from their mother's influence, else they will turn out quite wild. Miss Catherine will soon be sixteen and Miss Lydia will turn fourteen in a few months. Neither is prepared for entering society, not even in Meryton, and Miss Catherine is all too willing to follow her youngest sister's bad example. Unfortunately, my youngest cousin has been allowed far too much freedom, and she has already begun to complain about wearing black and not being permitted to have visitors or to visit."

"Would it be unseemly for them to be enrolled in school so soon after our father's death?" Mary asked.

"Not at all, Miss Mary," Darcy said. "In fact, I think it would be easily understood. They could not attend until the next term which would not begin until near Michaelmas. While they would still be expected to wear mourning clothes for the full mourning period, they would at least be able to socialise a little more than they might at home. They would not have the same reminders of home which might benefit them both. I would also suggest they attend separate schools if one is easily influenced by the other."

Everyone nodded their agreement as they considered this. "I will pay for the two youngest girls to attend school," Darcy said after a moment. "It will be my gift to my sisters. I will also allow them to purchase two new dresses suitable for mourning and another two for half mourning if they have a successful first term. Perhaps that can be an inducement to them to behave and to work hard at school."

"Since I am one of the girls' guardians, I would agree. Please write to me and to Mr. Gardiner about whatever arrangements you need me to make on your behalf. I have also wondered if Kitty would not benefit from being separated from Lydia sooner; perhaps she could go to London with the Gardiners. Mary, if you wish to return to the Winters's home, you may do so at any time. My wife and I will speak to Fanny and make her see reason. With fewer of the girls about, perhaps she will find it easier to do," Phillips replied.

The group chatted a bit longer about estate matters before the Darcys needed to take their leave so they might arrive at the inn before it grew too late to travel.

Chapter Thirty-Four

Several days later, the Darcys drew nearer to Pemberley. They had taken the journey slowly, making frequent stops to ensure Elizabeth's comfort, as she found travelling by carriage increasingly uncomfortable now that she was with child. Though she had visited the grand estate before, this was her first arrival as its mistress, and the realisation filled her with a quiet sense of awe.

Elizabeth gazed out at the sweeping landscape as their carriage approached the familiar estate, taking in the rolling hills, the manicured gardens, and the grand façade of the house itself. It was a sight that had once taken her breath away, and now, knowing it was to be her home, it stirred something even deeper within her. She was aware that she was stepping into a new chapter of her life, one where her influence and presence would shape the lives of those who lived on the estate.

Darcy, sitting beside her, sensed her reflection and reached for her hand. "I can see your thoughts turning, my love," he said gently, his thumb brushing over her knuckles. "What is on your mind?"

Elizabeth turned to him, offering a soft smile. "It is strange to think that this place is now my home. I am eager to begin my role as mistress, but I would be lying if I said I was not nervous."

Darcy's expression softened, and he squeezed her hand reassuringly. "You will be wonderful, Elizabeth. The household will thrive under your care, and you will bring life and warmth to Pemberley in a way it has never known before. My mother was a remarkable woman, but you ... you are something entirely different. The people will love you."

Elizabeth's smile grew, her heart swelling at his words. "I hope you are right. I shall do my best, for your sake and for the sake of all who depend on us."

As the carriage pulled to a stop in front of the grand entrance, the staff stood in neat rows, waiting to greet them. Elizabeth took a steadying breath and glanced at Darcy, who offered her a reassuring nod. Together, they stepped out of the carriage, and as soon as Elizabeth's feet touched the gravel, she was welcomed with curtsies and bows from the assembled servants.

"Welcome home, Mr. and Mrs. Darcy," the housekeeper, Mrs. Reynolds, said warmly, her eyes shining with pride as she curtsied deeply.

Elizabeth smiled and nodded in return, her heart lifting at the sound of those words—home. After exchanging a few pleasantries with Mrs. Reynolds, Darcy led Elizabeth inside, his hand resting protectively at the small of her back. As they entered the grand hall, Elizabeth was struck once again by the beauty of the house—the high ceilings, the elegant mouldings, the rich tapestries that adorned the walls. Yet this time, it did not feel intimidating. It felt welcoming, and she could already envision the life she and Darcy would build within these walls.

As they made their way toward the drawing room, Darcy leaned in close and whispered, "Are you ready for the tour, Mrs. Darcy? I want to show you every corner of your new domain."

Elizabeth laughed softly, glancing up at him. "Admittedly, it has been a few years, but I believe I have seen most of it already."

"Ah, but not from this perspective," Darcy replied with a playful grin. "Everything looks different when you know it is yours."

Elizabeth squeezed his arm, her heart lighter now. "Then I look forward to seeing it all again, through new eyes."

Together, they wandered through the halls of Pemberley, Darcy pointing out small details and telling her stories of his childhood and family. Elizabeth listened intently, her love for him growing deeper with each story he shared. By the time they reached the gardens, the sun was beginning to dip toward the horizon, casting a golden glow over the estate.

Darcy stopped and turned to face her, his eyes full of quiet affection. "You belong here, Elizabeth," he said softly. "I have always believed it, and now that you are here, it feels complete."

Elizabeth smiled, her gaze sweeping over the land before settling on him. "Yes, Fitzwilliam. I believe I do. Now, there is one room in the house that I was never permitted to see before, and I would be interested in seeing it now."

"Which room is that, Elizabeth?"

"The master's chambers, Fitzwilliam. Do you think I could see that room now?"

SEVERAL WEEKS LATER, Darcy sat in his study after dinner, reviewing ledgers and estate accounts. It has been a long day, full of meetings with his steward and a few of Pemberley's tenants who were having issues of some sort. To his surprise, Elizabeth entered, carrying a few documents of her own.

"I have been thinking," she began, settling into a chair across from him, "about the tenants at Ashford Farm. When I spoke with them today, it became clear that their cottages are in need of repairs, especially before winter. I would like to see them improved."

Darcy glanced up, surprised. "You met with them today?"

"Yes," she replied calmly. "I have been trying to get around to introduce myself to all of the tenant families, and today I spoke with several of the women."

Darcy set his pen down, the line of his jaw tightening. "Elizabeth, it is not that I do not appreciate your concern, but you should not feel it necessary to involve yourself in the estate's daily business. That is why I employ a steward. I manage those affairs myself."

"But I am part of this estate now," Elizabeth countered. "As its mistress, I should be involved. The tenants, particularly the women, should feel comfortable coming to me, and if I can help, why should I not?"

Darcy's brow furrowed as he leaned back in his chair, clearly trying to temper his reaction. "Elizabeth, you have a kind heart, and I admire your wish to help. But estate management is complex. It is not just about listening to grievances and making decisions on the spot. There are processes in place, and changes cannot be made without considering the long-term impact."

Elizabeth bristled. "I am not asking to make decisions on the spot. I am merely suggesting that improvements are needed, and I would like to work with you on them. I do not want to be shut out of these matters, Fitzwilliam."

Darcy sighed, running a hand through his hair. "I am not shutting you out. But you must understand that this is how estates have been run for generations. The master handles these matters, and the mistress oversees the household. It is not about denying your involvement but about maintaining order."

"Order?" Elizabeth's eyes flashed with indignation. "So, I am to sit by and mind the house while you make all the decisions? That is not the marriage I thought we agreed to."

"Elizabeth, that is not what I meant," Darcy said, exasperation creeping into his voice. "You are my equal in every way that matters, but some responsibilities are—"

"Are yours alone?" Elizabeth interrupted, her tone sharp. "I did not marry you to be relegated to hosting dinners and arranging flowers while you govern all that is important. We are supposed to be partners, Fitzwilliam, not master and mistress in the old sense. Even when I visited all those summers ago, your father and you appreciated my help with the tenants and in training Georgiana to assist with them."

Darcy paused, realising the depth of her frustration. He had not meant to belittle her involvement, but he could see now that his words had unintentionally done so.

"I did not intend to make you feel less than my equal," he said quietly. "But Pemberley's management has always been a burden I carry alone, and it is difficult for me to share it. Georgiana did help in small ways, but she never visited tenants, not after that summer with you."

Elizabeth softened slightly, but her resolve remained. "I understand that this is difficult for you, but I want to share that burden. I love this place, just as you do, and I want to contribute to its success. I will not be content to sit in the drawing room while you make all the decisions. We promised to be partners, and that is what I intend to be."

Darcy studied her for a long moment, his expression thoughtful. "You are right, my dear," he finally admitted, his voice filled with the quiet sincerity that always accompanied his more profound reflections. "We are partners, and I should not have assumed you would be satisfied with a lesser role. Let us discuss these matters together from now on."

Elizabeth smiled, relieved that he was willing to compromise. "That is all I ask. Together, we can ensure Pemberley thrives."

Darcy nodded, standing to join her by the fire. "Together, then," he agreed, wrapping one arm around her shoulders, while gently caressing the small bump that was becoming more obvious on her abdomen. "I love you, Elizabeth. Forgive me?"

"Of course, William. I love you as well." Leaning up, she kissed him, and as always seemed to be the case, their passions quickly rose, leaving them with little else to discuss that evening.

Chapter Thirty-Five

Mary and Mr. Collins left together, headed toward Longbourn. Mr. Collins had begun to spend more of his time at the estate, learning all he could about its management. Mary occasionally helped with her limited knowledge about its workings. She did, however, know much about the tenants and their needs, and she still frequently visited the tenants to provide what assistance she could.

Mr. Collins was already familiar with the tenants through his position as curate. Since he first arrived in the area, he made particular efforts to come to know Longbourn's tenants, preparing for his eventual position as master of the estate. He had become master far earlier than anyone had expected, for no one had anticipated an outbreak of smallpox affecting the estate and claiming the disinterested former master so soon after his arrival.

"Mama will not be pleased about the decisions made today. She has scarcely left her room since Papa's funeral. Even after you and Uncle Phillips came to tell her that we would not be immediately forced from Longbourn as she feared, she has not been content. She continues to speak of our marriage as a foregone conclusion and berates me when I try to put her off. I am afraid that my only escape will be by going to Maidstone to the Winters again for a time although I hate to impose myself upon them. Is it not improper of me to beg for a visit so soon after my father's passing?"

"Perhaps in some instances, but, truly, Miss Mary, you can only benefit by being with a friend during your grief. I know that your father was not the father he ought to have been, and perhaps your grief is more for what you wish could have been rather than what was, but no one who knows you can fault you for wanting some separation. Despite your short acquaintance, Mrs. Winters is more of a mother to you than your own has been. You can only benefit from some time with her," Collins said.

Mary nodded, and the two walked in silence for several minutes. "I will write to her as soon as I arrive at home to ask for a short visit at least. I should return before Kitty and Lydia leave for school, and I have little doubt that Mr. Darcy will ensure they both receive the education they so desperately need. I think Kitty will improve with a little attention, but Lydia might prove more recalcitrant."

Collins chuckled briefly. "I do not envy the uncle who will have to take her to school when the time comes. I am pleased that Mr. Darcy offered to fund the endeavour—I think I might have managed it, but it is good not to have the need to find the funds. Perhaps without them at Longbourn, it will be easier to set money aside for what will need to be done."

Agreeing, the two finished their walk in companionable silence. As usual, only Jane was below stairs when Mary and Mr. Collins arrived at Longbourn. Mr. Collins joined the young ladies for tea before going into the study to continue to sort through the papers on Mr. Bennet's desk as he attempted to understand what condition the estate was in.

This had proven to be a more difficult task than he expected. Due in part to Mr. Bennet's illness before he died, he found several unpaid bills that needed to be settled, but at the moment, Collins lacked the funds he needed to ensure they were all paid. The next quarter day was approaching, but since several tenants had been sick, he was uncertain what he would be able to collect from them. One of the biggest problems was that the former master was not particularly diligent in keeping records of who paid what and when the money was collected.

So many papers and receipts cluttered the desk that it was difficult to tell exactly what was important and what was not. In the days following Bennet's death, Collins spent several hours each day going through the desk and the papers that surrounded it. He let out a cry when he discovered an account book that appeared to be the most current one. It was shoved in a drawer and covered by several papers.

Eagerly, he opened the book and began to examine its contents. Mr. Bennet's record keeping was haphazard, and the ledger was at times difficult to read, but the book detailed the rents received and expenses paid over the past year. It was still a significant improvement over the random notes and loose receipts he had been dealing with. As he painstakingly deciphered the entries, Collins began to piece together the financial situation of the estate more clearly.

He could see that more than one tenant had fallen behind on their rent, particularly in the last few months. The accounts also showed that the estate had been running at a deficit with expenses regularly exceeding income. This was troubling news, but at least now he had a clearer picture of what needed to be addressed.

Collins decided he would need to speak with the tenants personally to understand their circumstances and to encourage them to pay what they could. He also made a note to consult with his cousin Darcy, whose advice and financial support could prove invaluable in navigating this difficult period, and Mr. Phillips, who might know of another account that could be used to cover some of the estate's debts.

As he continued to work through the account book, Mary entered the study quietly and observed him. She had seen how diligently he was working and felt a mixture of pity and admiration for him. Though she had never held her father in as high regard as some of her sisters, she knew how much his neglect had burdened the family and now Mr. Collins.

"Mr. Collins," she began softly, "I see you have found the account book. Is it helping you make sense of things?"

He looked up, a little startled, but then smiled gratefully. "Indeed, Miss Mary. This book is a godsend. It will take time, but I believe I can bring some order to the estate's finances with its help."

Mary nodded. "If there is anything I can do to assist, please let me know. I am not well-versed in such matters, but I am willing to learn and help where I can."

Her offer was genuine, and Collins appreciated her kindness. "Thank you, Miss Mary. Your support is most welcome. Perhaps you could assist by organising these papers into categories. It would make my task much easier."

Together, they set to work, sorting through the piles of documents. Mary's methodical nature proved to be a great asset, and soon the study began to look more orderly. As they worked side by side, a quiet camaraderie grew between them.

By dinner time, Collins and Mary had made significant headway in understanding the papers they found. On a few occasions, they discovered accounting errors that were actually in their favour. Some expenses had been recorded twice, and mistakes had been made in calculations. These errors, though small, added up and provided a glimmer of hope to the new master, who had been worried about how to keep the estate afloat given the poor management of its previous master.

The most significant find came a few days later. As Collins was continuing to clean out his desk, he found a drawer with a false bottom. When he lifted the false bottom away, he found a stash of cash and coin which amounted to a little over five hundred pounds. This money was not accounted for in any of the ledgers, as far as Mr. Collins could tell, and provided the estate with enough income to see them through the end of this year. The tenants needed relief after the outbreak, and many were struggling to pay their quarterly rent. With this influx of funds, Collins could afford to forgive at least a portion of the debt owed for those who could not pay.

Just after the quarter day when this was announced, Mary departed for Maidstone. Mrs. Bennet had begun to venture from her room more often, frequently berating Mary for her continued refusal to marry Mr. Collins. Even when Mary attempted to explain that would not be the case, Mrs. Bennet insisted that none of her daughters could possibly take her place as mistress.

When Mary had enough arguing with her mother, she wrote to Mrs. Winters to beg for an invitation. Mrs. Winters sent a carriage with her reply, offering Mary refuge at their estate for as long as she wished. In fact, the invitation stated if Mary wanted to pass the remainder of her mourning with them, she was welcome to do so.

WITH MARY AWAY FROM HOME, Jane began to do more to assist the tenants of Longbourn. Jane had not thought much of the idea when Mary first presented it to her sister, choosing to believe her mother's words that Jane would marry well and did not need such accomplishments. However, the three small scars which now marred Jane's otherwise lovely face were enough to cause Mrs. Bennet not only to cease praising her daughter, but to decry her as 'disfigured' and unlikely to ever make a match.

WHEN LOVE IS TRUE

Without the usual effusive compliments, Jane began to pay more attention to those around her. She saw the work that Mary did and recognised that many in Longbourn, Meryton, and the surrounding areas spoke well of Mary for her actions toward others. Soon, Jane realised that Mary had more friends than she, both in the community and without, for no one had come forward to offer her refuge from her family during this time.

Realising this, Jane began to do far more for Longbourn, working with Mr. Collins for the betterment of the estate. She took an active role in overseeing the welfare of the tenants and ensuring that their needs were met and their grievances heard. Jane overcame her selfishness and began to display kindness and empathy toward the tenants, which quickly endeared her to them. They had not expected any of the Bennet ladies to help with Mary gone, so they appreciated this new concern for their well-being and prayed it was genuine.

One afternoon, as Mr. Collins was reviewing the accounts in the study, Jane came in to ask a question and happened to note a discrepancy in the records. "Mr. Collins, it seems that the entry for Mr. Thompson's payment has been recorded twice," she noted gently, as she scanned the ledger while she waited for Mr. Collins to finish. Among other things she had been doing that autumn, she had been working with both Mrs. Hill and Mr. Collins to learn about the accounts.

Mr. Collins peered over at the ledger she was looking at, squinting at the handwriting there. "Indeed, Miss Jane, you are correct. I am most grateful for your careful eye. Such an error might have gone unnoticed and caused no end of trouble when I attempted to reconcile my accounts at the end of the quarter."

Jane smiled, feeling a sense of accomplishment. "I am happy to help. Perhaps I could assist you by double-checking the rest of the entries for similar mistakes while you take a brief respite. It is very tedious work, is it not?"

"An excellent idea," Mr. Collins agreed. "Your assistance has already been invaluable. I must admit, I would be quite overwhelmed without your help. When Cousin Mary left, I had not thought you would be interested in assisting, or I would have invited you to do so before now."

As she immersed herself in the management of Longbourn, Jane found a new sense of purpose and fulfilment. She no longer felt defined by her beauty or her prospects for marriage. Instead, she discovered a deep satisfaction in contributing to the well-being of the estate and its tenants, and a growing tenderness toward her cousin. Despite his awkwardness and tendency to ramble, Jane saw his genuine effort to manage the estate responsibly and unfailing kindness toward others.

One evening late in the autumn, after the other two girls had been away at school for some time, Jane sat with Mr. Collins in the drawing room chatting while Mrs. Bennet sat in one corner of the room, working on her sewing. "I think it would be beneficial to establish a small school for the tenant children," Jane suggested. "A little education, at least knowing how to read and write, could greatly improve their futures. Mrs. Allen mentioned it was a need in the area."

Mr. Collins nodded thoughtfully. "It would be a worthy endeavour, Cousin Jane. I believe we can allocate some funds for that purpose in the spring. The partnership with the Darcys has enabled me to get our stables up and running, and we have brought on a few additional workers to help. There are several new families who have come to replace some of the older tenants, and a school would be a worthwhile investment in the community."

Mrs. Bennet, overhearing their conversation, put down her sewing and looked up. "A school? For the tenants' children? What an odd idea, Jane. You should not waste your time on such an endeavour."

"Not so odd, Mama," Jane replied gently. "Educating them could help improve their lives and, in turn, benefit the estate. Literate tenants can manage their affairs better and contribute more effectively. Mrs. Darcy has written to me of the school at Pemberley for their tenants that was started by her husband's mother."

Mrs. Bennet huffed softly but returned to her sewing, muttering something about Jane spending too much time on such matters, especially if they were suggested by 'that ungrateful girl.' Jane and Mr. Collins exchanged a glance, and Jane gave him an encouraging smile.

"Cousin Jane," Mr. Collins began, "your compassion and forward-thinking are truly admirable. I must confess, your influence has greatly benefited Longbourn these last months."

Jane blushed at the praise. "Thank you, Mr. Collins. I believe we make a good team."

Over the next few months, they spoke of their plans for establishing a school in the spring once the planting was finished. One afternoon, as they walked through Longbourn village to check on a few of the new families who were setting in, Mr. Collins turned to Jane. "Cousin Jane, I cannot express how much your presence and assistance have meant to me and to Longbourn. You have a rare gift for bringing people together and inspiring them."

Jane smiled warmly. "I have simply followed my heart, Mr. Collins. I am glad to be of service."

He hesitated for a moment, then spoke with uncharacteristic sincerity. "Jane, I must admit that my feelings for you have grown beyond mere gratitude. Your kindness, intelligence, and beauty have deeply affected me. I would be honoured if you would consider ... perhaps, a closer partnership."

Jane was taken aback by his candour but felt a warmth in her heart. "Mr. Collins, I am touched by your words. Let us continue our work together and see where our path leads. I value our partnership greatly."

Chapter Thirty-Six

Over the course of the summer and autumn, a number of letters were exchanged between Pemberley and points south. Elizabeth wrote to all four of her sisters regularly, though she only received responses from three of them. Though she had been mistress of an estate for only a short time, Jane was full of questions about what was necessary beyond the walls of the estate, for Mrs. Hill had successfully managed the house despite Mrs. Bennet's interference for nearly two decades.

Mrs. Hill helped Jane with the running of the house, allowing Jane to take the lead wherever possible. Both allowed Mrs. Bennet to think she was the one in charge, but truly, most of the work was done by Jane. With the house in mourning, she was able to make significant savings in the funds required to keep the house running, easing the burden on Mr. Collins. That, combined with Catherine and Lydia away at school, allowed Mr. Collins to invest more into the estate. Jane and Collins spent considerable time discussing how to rein in Mrs. Bennet's spending once her mourning period ended, especially since she would no longer be the mistress of Longbourn once she was moved into the dower house.

WHEN LOVE IS TRUE

Though Mrs. Bennet had been widowed for several months, she had not ceased her complaints about the loss of status she would suffer once she moved to the dower house. She was constantly attempting to cajole the new master into giving her additional funds for anything that struck her fancy despite the fact that she was in mourning. So far, that excuse had been grudgingly accepted, but Collins expected Mrs. Bennet to be far less easy about the matter when that was no longer the reason. Collins was willing to assist the family to a point, but he had no intention of doing as his predecessor and giving into the lady's every whim. She would have the income from her dowry, but for the first time in her adult life, Mrs. Bennet would learn to live within her means.

This fact did not surprise the Darcys when they read of it in the letters from both Collins and Jane although Elizabeth was surprised to read of the growing familiarity between Jane and their cousin. The infrequent letters Jane had sent her sister prior to her illness had been highly critical of the man, but as the two spent more time together it became apparent to Elizabeth that Jane had become fond of him. From Mr. Collins's letters to her husband, Elizabeth believed the sentiment was returned and discussed the matter with Darcy one afternoon as they sat in his study drinking their tea.

"William," Elizabeth began, her tone reflective, "I have been reading through Jane's recent letters and noticed a change in her sentiments toward Mr. Collins. I believe she has developed a genuine affection for him. I wonder what Mrs. Bennet thinks about this development since she once thought Jane too beautiful to 'waste' on Longbourn's heir."

Darcy looked up from his book, his expression thoughtful. "Indeed? That is unexpected. Jane was so critical of him before her illness." Darcy thought for a moment. "However, in his last letter, Collins mentioned the two have been spending a great deal of time together. I thought perhaps it was one-sided, but I think they could be an excellent match."

Elizabeth nodded. "She mentions several conversations they have had about the estate, and it appears they go for daily walks that have little to do with the business of the estate."

Darcy leaned back in his chair, considering this new information. "It seems that their time together has fostered a bond that neither I nor you anticipated. Jane's change of heart is quite remarkable."

Elizabeth continued, "Mr. Collins's letters to you are filled with admiration and respect for Jane. He speaks of her in a manner that suggests he holds her in the highest regard. It seems he has come to value her companionship more deeply than I would have imagined."

Darcy's brow furrowed slightly. "If this is indeed the case, it could be a positive development. Jane has been learning to become a proper mistress of an estate while Collins is trying to do all he can to prove a good master. He has done well so far in spite of not having had enough time to truly make that much of a difference."

Elizabeth smiled. "I do hope they are able to make the estate successful. From what I have been told, neither Mr. nor Mrs. Bennet were willing to put forth the effort required to see the estate be successful, and I am pleased that Jane is now trying to change that, along with Mr. Collins. I would wish my sisters to all be happy and to make good matches. If Mr. Collins indeed cares for her, and she for him, then perhaps their union could be beneficial for both parties."

Darcy reached for Elizabeth's hand, giving it a reassuring squeeze. "We should support them if we can. It is clear that their relationship has evolved in ways we did not foresee."

Elizabeth nodded, feeling encouraged by Darcy's understanding. "I agree. However, I will not say anything, for I think they need to discover these feelings for themselves. I wonder if they have realised their growing fondness for each other yet."

Later that evening, Elizabeth penned a letter to Jane, expressing her pleasure at the positive developments on the estate and answering all the questions Jane posed about Elizabeth's responsibilities as mistress. She would encourage her sister in any way required and was pleased to see how Jane had changed in the last months.

JANE WAS NOT the only sister who had improved in the months since their father's passing. Catherine benefitted greatly from being separated from her mother and younger sister. The girls at school referred to her not by the diminutive of her name but called her Catherine, making the girl feel older and more mature, and she soon found she liked it better.

At first, Catherine was taken aback to receive a letter from her elder sister, one whom she barely remembered. Her only clear memory was of the day Elizabeth had answered their parents' summons to discuss the attempt to force her into marrying Mr. Collins. Catherine had not fully grasped all that had transpired in the drawing room at Longbourn that day. Although her sisters had tried to explain the events to her, Catherine was still unsure about the specifics, yet she responded warmly to the overtures from this sister she hardly knew.

Unlike Lydia, whose infrequent letters complained of how dull school was, Catherine fully embraced the opportunities afforded to her there. Not only was she away from the influence of her mother and Lydia, but she also delighted in the opportunity to learn accomplishments such as drawing and painting. Catherine had always been artistic, but such pursuits had not been encouraged at Longbourn.

Through the exchange of letters, Catherine came to know more about her second eldest sister. After the confrontation, she and Lydia had written to Elizabeth at their mother's direction to beg for presents of clothing, ribbons, or funds while still demanding for an invitation to town. Elizabeth had responded, ignoring the requests while asking her sisters questions about themselves. Lydia had not bothered to respond after that, but Catherine had. However, she stopped when Lydia found out about the exchange and teased her about it.

Once at school, she was pleased when Elizabeth wrote to her again. Their letters grew in frequency and length through the term as the two established a closeness they might not have managed if they had all remained at home. There was no Lydia and no Mrs. Bennet, to interfere or to insert themselves into the conversation. Catherine had also begun to see, based on her observations of the other girls at school, that the behaviours so frequently demonstrated by her mother and sister were not appropriate for polite society. Catherine was a follower and naturally a quiet girl, but over the last few years she had followed Lydia's lead in whining to get her way. At school, she quickly learned this behaviour would not endear her to anyone, and Elizabeth's letters reinforced these lessons.

In particular, Catherine was delighted to learn she would soon be an aunt and nearly begged to be allowed to see her niece or nephew as soon as it could be arranged. However, Elizabeth encouraged her sister to embrace her opportunity for an education, inviting her to visit them at Pemberley in the summer. Mary had already been invited, and Elizabeth thought bringing both sisters to Derbyshire would benefit them.

Unlike her sister, Lydia was unhappy at her school. Used to being indulged, she quickly found that she could not manipulate the headmistress or the other students to do as she wished or to give in to her complaining. If she "borrowed" something from her roommate or another girl without asking, there were consequences. Within the first month, Lydia had been prohibited from venturing into town for the entire Michaelmas term along with losing other privileges. Her handwriting had improved significantly from the frequent writing of lines or notes of apology for taking what was not hers and other offences. Since each of these had to be perfect, the first few had been written several times before they met the strict expectations of the headmistress. Lydia soon learned she would be better served by writing these as neatly as possible.

She did write frequently to her other sisters and her mother, complaining of her unfair treatment. Other than Mrs. Bennet, no one in her family believed she was being treated poorly, and Mrs. Bennet took to bed yet again to decry the fate of her "poor baby" each time she received one of these letters.

"My dear, dear Lydia should not be made to suffer so," she was frequently heard to say. "It is simply too cruel of my brothers to force her to attend school and at such a distance from her mother. No one understands Lydia's liveliness, and they will encourage her to become just as dull as Mary or as boring as Jane has become. Now that Jane's looks are gone, she cannot possibly make a good marriage; I must rely on my darling Lydia to do what Jane ought to have done, had that terrible disease not ruined her appearance. Oh, it is too much to bear."

Such comments were ignored at Longbourn while Jane and Mrs. Phillips, the most frequent recipients of these complaints, did their best their best to placate the matron by reminding her of the accomplishments Lydia was no doubt learning and how much better the girl would marry once she was properly educated. This reminder did little to alleviate Mrs. Bennet's frustration though she would usually allow herself to be redirected into thinking about the peer Lydia would no doubt marry once she was introduced into society by the Darcys. Both ladies had long since given up on telling Mrs. Bennet how unlikely that was to occur so they contended themselves with rolling their eyes behind her back when possible while doing what they could to pacify the mulish woman.

Mrs. Bennet also found much to complain about in the growing familiarity between Jane and Mr. Collins. After several months of unofficially courting, Mr. Collins approached first Jane, then her uncle Phillips about a formal courtship between the two. Jane's period of mourning would end early in the new year, and Collins spoke to her uncle about the possibility of his proposing once it was complete while waiting to marry until Mrs. Bennet's mourning period was over.

He believed this would placate his future mother, though Mrs. Bennet was little pleased about her daughter settling for the new master of Longbourn. Despite frequently lamenting Jane's loss of beauty from her scars, she still expected her to marry well, at least as well as Elizabeth had. The bitterness toward her second daughter had not faded; she resented Elizabeth for marrying such a wealthy man and for refusing to recognise her authority. Mrs. Bennet remained unaware that the Darcys were paying for her youngest daughters to attend school and assisting Mr. Collins with the estate, both financially and with advice.

Chapter Thirty-Seven

DECEMBER 1809

"But, Jane, how can you settle for marrying Mr. Collins? He is only the master of Longbourn, and you were meant for so much more. You must go to London to stay with your uncle for surely, he will introduce you to someone at least as wealthy as that man Lizzy ensnared. Surely you will manage to meet a peer, and he will fall madly in love with you. It is too bad that you are not the beauty you once were, but still, you should be able to marry better than your sister," Mrs. Bennet remarked to Jane one morning not long after learning about the courtship.

"Mama, Mr. Collins and I are well-suited to each other. He makes me very happy, and I do not wish to go to London. I will be quite content as the Mistress of Longbourn and do not want to marry someone in the peerage. Nor would I want to inconvenience my aunt and uncle and show up uninvited at their house again," Jane replied, frustrated by her mother's repeated suggestion. This was not the first time they had a similar conversation, and they had only grown worse now that the courtship was publicly known.

"You could do so much better, Jane. With you as the mistress of the estate, then I would not have to move out of Longbourn and into the dower house. Perhaps it is for the best that you will be mistress here. If Mary were to take my place, she would attempt to restrict my spending. You will ensure that my allowance remains quite healthy, will you not, Jane?" she pleaded.

"Mama, should Mr. Collins offer for me once my mourning is complete, you will still be expected to move into the dower cottage. There cannot be two mistresses of the estate, and when my sisters return from school, it would be better for you to live together. Mr. Collins has already offered to cover reasonable living expenses so you are not required to do that out of your allowance, but you will be expected to limit your spending," Jane informed her mother.

She and Mr. Collins had discussed this matter on several occasions as they discussed their courtship. Jane remembered how her father had always given into her mother whenever she had demanded additional funds for whatever she felt was necessary at the moment. At the time, Jane had not thought much of these conversations, thinking that if the income was available, why should they not spend it? However, after months of assisting others, she was now acutely aware of how much better off they would be if her parents had considered the future more carefully. Were it not for the generosity of Mr. Collins, and to a large degree that of the Darcys, Jane and all her sisters would be in a far worse position.

Initially, Jane had not realised just what Mr. Collins was giving up to by allowing the Bennet women to remain in Longbourn while the dower cottage was being renovated. However, several events had transpired over the last few months that made her more aware.

After Mary left for the Winters' estate, Jane began accompanying Mrs. Allen on tenant visits. Initially reluctant to take on this responsibility, she felt compelled to step in when Mr. Collins mentioned specific needs of the tenants, a duty that Mary had previously fulfilled. Once she overcame her initial reluctance, she found she enjoyed the visits. The tenant children flocked to Mrs. Allen who frequently brought them small gifts though not on every visit. Regardless, they adored her and soon warmed to Jane as well. Initially shy around the children, she quickly became more comfortable and engaged with them naturally. Though her mother fussed over these visits, Jane had learned to tune out most of her complaints, realising she was much happier for it.

A second catalyst for these changes in Jane related to the gossip in Meryton. It struck a chord in Jane because the situation was so similar to what she had faced. In October, a widow and her two daughters had moved into a small house on the outskirts of their village. Jane had not encountered them since they tended to keep to themselves.

According to local gossip, they had recently lost their father, and their half-brother had inherited the family home. His wife had not wanted to share her new home with its former mistress and had *encouraged* her husband to force them into a different situation. From what was being said around town, they were used to far better but had been forced into reduced circumstances. The two girls each had a small dowry, significantly more than Jane could claim, yet they were now in a precarious situation. Mrs. Allen helped Jane realise that this could have been her own situation, for Mr. Collins was not obligated to allow the Bennet ladies to remain in Longbourn or to restore the dower cottage to make it habitable.

"My dear, Mrs. Gordon and her daughters were forced into genteel poverty due to the selfishness of Mr. Gordon. The son, not the husband. Perhaps Mrs. Gordon's husband could have done more to ensure his son would care for his second wife even though gossip seems to indicate he extracted a verbal promise from his son. However, the new mistress of the estate is reported to be a rather uncharitable person and likely did not want the former mistress or two lovely girls to remain in her home. It is understandable, I suppose, though the Gordon estate is healthy enough to support the three. I have spoken with our town's newest resident, and she is resigned to her situation. Understandably, she is grieved over the loss of her husband, and that is made worse by the need to relocate so far from home," Mrs. Allen explained when Jane asked for confirmation of the gossip.

Jane nodded thoughtfully as she sipped her tea, finally speaking several minutes later. "We are fortunate that Mr. Collins was not already married when he came to Meryton. If he had a wife, he would not have been as willing to allow us to remain in the house for so long. I also am aware that Mrs. Darcy is significantly responsible for the renovations to the dower cottage. Mary indicated that she assisted not only with that, but with arranging for Kitty and Lydia to go to school."

It was Mrs. Allen's turn to nod as she sipped. "Yes, the Darcys are paying for your youngest sisters to attend school. It is not terribly expensive, and your uncles paid for the clothing they needed so the entire burden did not fall on your sister and her husband. Elizabeth wants to do well by her sisters, for she understands that your parents neglected your upbringing. I know she and Mary write to each other often, and I am aware you write to her on occasion though you have not become close. Much of that is your own fault, and I think you are aware of that."

Jane blushed a little at that. "I was resentful of her when she first came back into our lives," she admitted. She was quiet for a moment longer, then sighed heavily. "The distance is mostly my own fault. Elizabeth has been far more generous than I deserve, given that I was the one who broke our relationship first. She did try to correspond with me after she left, but I allowed Mama's words to colour my impressions. I resented that she was away from home, writing to me of all the interesting things she was doing with our aunt and uncle while I was stuck at home. Mama only spoke of my beauty being so important, encouraging me to do little other than gossip about our neighbours. She spoke of my future marriage, despite the fact that I was only a child, telling me that it was my responsibility to save our family. All the while, Elizabeth was in London learning things, visiting museums, even travelling on occasion. I was jealous of what I thought was her good fortune."

"She might have been given much, but that could not make up for the fact that she was sent away from her home and family at such a young age, nor was she permitted to return home. Her aunt and uncle were good to her, but they were not her parents, and I daresay she could not forget that fact," Mrs. Allen pointed out.

They sat in silence for several moments. As a rector's wife, Mrs. Allen knew when to remain quiet, allowing Jane the space for reflection that she clearly needed at that moment.

"I need to write to Elizabeth to ask for her forgiveness; I am uncertain how willing she will be to grant it after all this time. She was initially willing to, but I cannot be certain that I have not ruined that possibility. I ... I have been selfish, I suppose, and only recently have considered that my demanding things from her was not helping our relationship—if I can even claim we have one at this point. She responds to my letters, but without the openness of her letters to Mary. I am not certain I have been a good sister to any of mine, for I have lately considered how differently Mary seems to write to me compared to how I know she speaks of Elizabeth. They have managed to form a relationship, and I know that Mary has been invited to visit her at Pemberley next summer."

"How is Elizabeth? Mary mentioned she is with child; do you know when the child is expected to come?"

"Soon, I think. Sometime before the end of the year. I admit that I have avoided the subject, and Elizabeth has not mentioned it in her letters either. We tend to avoid personal subjects, and I am not sure why. Perhaps I can inquire in my next letter to ask if we can begin to come to some sort of ... rapprochement. At the very least, I would like to build a better relationship than we currently possess," Jane confessed.

"That would be wise, Jane," Mrs. Allen agreed and soon turned the conversation in a different direction.

Chapter Thirty-Eight

As the time for Elizabeth's confinement drew nearer, Darcy grew increasingly anxious about the impending birth. He had taken to hovering near her at every moment, aided by many of Pemberley's servants, who felt it was their duty to remain close to the mistress during this crucial time.

Winters in Derbyshire were not always kind, and this particular year brought a relentless series of biting cold days and snowfall that blanketed the estate in a thick layer of white. The winds frequently howled, rattling the windows of Pemberley, and the unpredictable weather only heightened Darcy's nerves. He worried not only for Elizabeth's well-being but also for the safety of their child.

The weather compounded Elizabeth's discomfort as well; she had quickly adapted to country life and relished spending time outdoors. However, the current conditions made this nearly impossible, and her daily walks—essential for alleviating her discomfort—became increasingly difficult to manage.

"Are you certain you are comfortable, my love?" Darcy asked one evening, his voice laced with concern as he adjusted the blankets around Elizabeth, who was seated by the fire. She looked radiant, her cheeks flushed with warmth, but he could still see the signs of fatigue etched on her face.

Elizabeth smiled reassuringly, though she could sense his growing agitation. "I am quite well, William. I promise you, I have been in worse discomfort. The fire is warm, and I am enjoying your company."

Darcy frowned, unconvinced. "But what if the baby arrives tonight? I cannot bear the thought of you enduring any hardship. Perhaps we should summon the midwife to check on you, just to be safe."

Elizabeth chuckled lightly, amused by his overprotectiveness. "You would have her at my side every hour of the day if you could, would you not? It is only a few more days, I assure you. You need not worry so. I shall tell you immediately if I feel any changes."

He shook his head, determined not to relent. "I cannot help but worry. You mean everything to me, and the thought of anything going amiss is unbearable. You deserve all the care and comfort I can provide."

"William, I appreciate your concern, truly. But I have faith that all will go well. Our child will arrive when it is ready, and we must trust in that," she said, patting his hand.

Darcy's expression softened at her words, though he could not entirely quell the unease that coiled in his chest. "You are far more courageous than I, Elizabeth. I wish I possessed your strength. All I can do is stand by your side and hope for the best."

"Your love is my strength," she replied, reaching for his hand and intertwining their fingers. "We shall face this together, just as we have faced everything else."

As the days passed, the anticipation in the household grew palpable. Servants moved about with purpose, preparing the guest chamber for the arrival of the midwife and ensuring that all was ready for the birth. As the end of Elizabeth's confinement drew closer, Darcy had implored the midwife to stay at Pemberley, adding another set of watchful eyes to ensure Elizabeth's care and comfort.

Elizabeth remained composed, but even she could not deny the flutter of nerves she often felt. She wished her Aunt Gardiner could have been with her, but it was far too difficult to travel all this way.

Late one evening, a sudden storm swept through the area surrounding Pemberley, the wind howling fiercely as thick, swirling gusts of snow fell outside. Elizabeth lay in bed, wrapped in blankets, her heart racing as she sensed that the moment she had been waiting for was drawing near. She glanced at Darcy, who was finally sleeping soundly after a night of fretting when she had grimaced in response to a pain.

"Fitzwilliam, wake up," she urged, her voice steady despite the whirlwind outside. "It is time to fetch the midwife."

Though it took a moment, Darcy slowly came to consciousness. "What … what did you say?"

Elizabeth felt a wave of discomfort wash over her. She inhaled sharply, her eyes widening as she clutched her belly. "You need to fetch the midwife and Mrs. Reynolds. I believe it is my time," she said, her voice steady yet laced with urgency.

Darcy shot upright in bed, instantly alert. "What do you mean it is your time?" he asked, his brow furrowed with concern. "Are you certain?"

"Yes, Fitzwilliam, I am certain," she replied, forcing herself to remain calm despite the tightening sensation. "The contractions have begun. I need you to act quickly."

He scrambled from the bed, throwing on some clothes in haste, his hands trembling with a mix of anxiety and determination. "I will be back in a moment. Just stay here and breathe. I will not be long."

As he rushed out of the room, Elizabeth took a deep breath, trying to quell the rising tide of discomfort. She focused on the flickering candlelight, its warmth a small comfort against the storm raging outside. She could hear the wind howling, echoing her own nervous anticipation.

A moment later, Darcy returned, his face pale but resolute. "Help is on the way, Elizabeth. And I am here. I will stay by your side if you wish it. You do not have to go through this alone."

"I want you to stay with me if you can stand it," she replied gently, her eyes sparkling with mischief. "And I need you to breathe with me. We cannot have you passing out and becoming one of the patients."

As another wave of discomfort washed over her, she squeezed her eyes shut, breathing through it. Darcy moved closer, taking her hand and holding it firmly, her pain appearing to give him strength. "You are incredibly strong, Elizabeth. We will get through this together."

She nodded, finding strength in his words. "I know. I have faith that we all will be well."

Just then, the door opened, and the midwife entered, her face a picture of calm amidst the chaos. "Mrs. Darcy, I am here," she announced, her voice soothing. "Let us prepare for the arrival of your little one. Mr. Darcy, I must ask you to leave."

"No," he replied, "Elizabeth wishes me to stay with her."

"You can return after we have her settled," the midwife replied. "There are several things we need to do to prepare Mrs. Darcy for the birth, including moving her into the birthing chamber. Let us do what we need to and then you rejoin your wife."

Reluctantly, Darcy moved to do as he was asked, but only after receiving a patient smile from Elizabeth. He stepped out into the dimly lit hallway, taking a deep breath, trying to calm the storm of emotions swirling within him. He leaned against the wall, straining to hear any sounds from the room, praying for Elizabeth's safety.

Finally, after what seemed like an eternity, a servant came out into the hallway from the mistress's chamber. "Mr. Darcy, you may come back in now."

Darcy entered the room and went directly to his wife's side. Her face was glowing although she was clearly weary. The midwife and other servants worked efficiently at the foot of the bed, arranging the necessary items, while Elizabeth's breathing quickened with each contraction.

"Elizabeth," Darcy whispered, brushing a strand of hair away from her forehead. "You are doing so wonderfully."

As another wave of discomfort washed over her, Elizabeth gripped his hand tightly, her nails digging into his palm. The midwife's voice was calm as she said, "Just a little longer, Mrs. Darcy. You are almost there. Focus on your breathing."

Darcy watched as Elizabeth breathed through the pain, her brow furrowing. "William, I—" she began, but another contraction hit, cutting off her words. She closed her eyes, trying to push through the discomfort. He squeezed her hand, attempting to reassure her.

Minutes passed like an eternity. Soon, the midwife guided Elizabeth through the final steps of childbirth, and they heard her announce, "Congratulations, you have a son."

Tears of joy sparkled in Elizabeth's eyes as she cradled the tiny, squirming bundle against her chest. "William Edward," she whispered, her voice filled with love.

Darcy leaned closer, overwhelmed by the sight of his wife and their newborn son. "He is perfect," he murmured, emotion thick in his voice. "Just like his mother."

Elizabeth smiled, her exhaustion forgotten as she looked down at their child. "Look at him, Fitzwilliam. He is the best part of both of us."

"Yes, he is," Darcy replied, his heart swelling with pride.

Once Elizabeth was helped into clean clothing and settled back into her chambers, the maid returned, cradling the now washed and swaddled babe. "Here you are, Mrs. Darcy," she said, her eyes sparkling with warmth.

"Thank you," Elizabeth replied, her voice barely above a whisper as she reached for her son.

Darcy joined her on the bed, his heart racing as he took in the sight of his wife holding their child. Elizabeth's face lit up as she cradled little William against her chest, and Darcy could not help but smile at the beautiful scene before him.

"Can you believe he is ours?" Elizabeth asked, her eyes shimmering with wonder.

"I can hardly comprehend it," Darcy replied, wrapping an arm around her shoulders and pulling her close. "He is everything we have ever hoped for and more."

Elizabeth looked down at William, her expression softening. "He is so small and fragile," she murmured. "I want to protect him from everything."

Darcy nodded, understanding her sentiment. "We will do everything in our power to keep him safe. He is our greatest responsibility now."

FOLLOWING her conversation with Mrs. Allen, Jane wrote to her sister to apologise for her previous attitude, acknowledging the insights she had gained in the weeks since their last exchange. This letter led to a thawing of relations between Jane and Elizabeth, bridging the gap that had formed between them. Jane was overjoyed to learn that Elizabeth had given birth to her son, William Edward Darcy, just a few days before Christmas.

Elizabeth congratulated her elder sister on her courtship with Mr. Collins and expressed her delight that the two would likely marry the following summer. Despite the invitation to attend Jane's wedding, whenever it might occur, Elizabeth had to decline. With a newborn to care for, the Darcys had no intention of travelling to London until after William's first birthday. The thought of navigating the bustling city with a young child seemed daunting, and Elizabeth wished to create a serene environment at Pemberley for their son's first year.

However, in a gesture of goodwill, Elizabeth extended an invitation for Jane and Mr. Collins to visit Pemberley in the autumn. Elizabeth hoped it would be a delightful opportunity for their families to bond, and she was eager to introduce her son to his aunt. Jane, touched by the invitation, promised to discuss it with Mr. Collins, but since their future together was still uncertain, she neither accepted nor declined the offer.

As the days passed, Elizabeth embraced her new role as a mother, cherishing every moment with her son. The winter season brought its own magic to Pemberley, with snow blanketing the grounds, and the warm glow of the hearth filling the house with a comforting light. Elizabeth would often find herself gazing out the window, dreaming of the adventures that awaited William in the years to come.

In her letters to Jane, she shared stories of the baby's milestones—the first time he smiled, the way he cooed when she sang to him, and how Darcy could spend hours simply watching their son, his heart full of love and pride. Elizabeth's joy was infectious, and Jane found herself swept up in her sister's happiness, longing to hold her nephew and share in the laughter that echoed through Pemberley's halls.

While the invitation to Pemberley remained an open promise, Elizabeth felt assured that no matter the distance or the time apart, the bond between sisters would continue to strengthen. Their hearts were woven together by love and shared experiences, each anticipating the moments that would unite their families in the future.

Chapter Thirty-Nine

JANUARY 1810

Just after the new year, Collins proposed to Jane and was accepted. Initially, the two planned to wait to marry until summer when all her sisters would be home, but Mrs. Bennet made it necessary for the marriage to occur sooner. Her insistence that the wedding be some grand event that surpassed all other events in Meryton was a constant cause of strife at Longbourn. After only a month of this, Collins and Jane came to a decision.

By marrying while Longbourn was still technically in mourning, they would be able to settle the argument about the extravagant wedding and move Mrs. Bennet into the dower cottage earlier. When Mrs. Bennet was informed of these plans, she had been incensed.

"Mother, I no longer wish to argue about my wedding," Jane began, glancing at her intended, Mr. Collins, and her aunt for support. They had decided to be present to help her confront Mrs. Bennet.

Mrs. Bennet smiled, thinking Jane was ready to yield to her insistence for a grand wedding. But Jane continued, "Mr. Collins and I have decided to purchase a common license and marry as soon as possible. Mr. Allen has agreed to perform a quiet ceremony. Since you are still in mourning, we will forgo a celebration, especially since you have not listened to our suggestions for a wedding breakfast. After we marry, you will move to the dower cottage. The renovations are complete, and you will have two maids, a cook, and a manservant. You will manage just fine with this staff."

Mrs. Bennet's smile faded. "What of my allowance, Jane? Am I to pay for the servants out of my pin money?"

"Longbourn will cover the servants' costs. The home farm will supply your food, but you will need to pay for anything extra out of your own pocket," Mr. Collins explained.

"What about my clothing and other necessities?" Mrs. Bennet pressed.

"Those will also come from your own funds. I have approved three new dresses for June when your mourning ends. Jane will accompany you to the dressmaker to discuss what we will cover," Mr. Collins replied. "The estate's income is improving, but unlike the previous master, I will not be coerced into spending more."

Mrs. Bennet flailed her handkerchief. "You cannot mean to do this to me, Jane. You will need me to manage Longbourn. I am an excellent hostess, and my counsel is invaluable."

"Mother, I have been managing Longbourn since Papa died. Mrs. Hill taught me how to run the household, and Mrs. Allen showed me how to be a proper mistress. You have ignored my efforts while pressuring me to host a grand celebration. You declared me ruined due to my scars, and it seemed what I did mattered less after that."

"Your rapid marriage will disgrace the family," Mrs. Bennet protested.

"Enough, madam," Mr. Collins interrupted. "We are tired of your complaints. The best solution is for Jane and me to marry and for you to move to the dower house. No one will be surprised by our decision, given how difficult you have been."

Seeing her future son-in-law was resolute, Mrs. Bennet resorted to wailing and crying. Instead of receiving comfort, she was roughly carried upstairs to her room. Her cries ceased when she realised no one would indulge her tantrum. Accepting the smelling salts brought by the housekeeper, she fell asleep on her bed.

When she awoke, clarity washed over her. Her life had unravelled since Elizabeth arrived at Longbourn, ruining all her plans. Lighting a candle, she sat at her small writing desk—rarely used since she preferred the one in the drawing room. Determined, Mrs. Bennet began writing a letter to Elizabeth.

IN THE MIDDLE OF FEBRUARY, Elizabeth received a slew of letters from Meryton. As usual, she sat in her husband's study, their two-month-old child in a bassinet near the fireplace that had been brought down soon after Elizabeth had been released from her rooms. The couple always enjoyed their time together, and while Elizabeth had a study of her own, she could often be found in her husband's when reading her letters.

She smiled upon recognising the handwriting of two of her sisters. The tenor of the letters from Jane had changed over the last few months, and it seemed to Elizabeth that the two might be able to be something like friends again. They would never be close, not after the way Jane had acted in the past years, but perhaps they would be able to exchange letters and see each other on occasion. Elizabeth would remain wary of her, particularly given the way Jane flirted with Fitzwilliam that night in Meryton, but since he had offered to host the newly married Collinses in the autumn, Elizabeth could only hope the apparent change in the letters equated to a real change in her oldest sister.

Opening the letter from Jane first, she read the account of the confrontation with Mrs. Bennet and then about the wedding. Elizabeth was surprised to learn how the wedding came to pass and, knowing what she did about the former mistress of Longbourn, she supposed the result was not that unexpected. Still, Elizabeth was pleased to learn the two were able to be married sooner than they originally planned, and it seemed they would do well together at Longbourn.

Mary's letter informed her that she had returned to Longbourn for a brief visit. The Winters were very kind to her, but without Mrs. Bennet at home and with Mr. Collins now married to Jane, it seemed best to return home at least for a time. The Gardiners had invited Mary to London, and they would collect Catherine from her school on their way north for the summer. It would be the first time her sisters had visited her new home as well as the first time she had spent a significant amount of time with them since she left Longbourn all those years ago. Elizabeth looked forward to spending this time with her sisters, and hoped the visit would go well.

The last letter was written in an unfamiliar hand. Immediately upon opening it, she scanned down to the end to read the signature. She gasped audibly, causing her husband to look up in alarm. "Are you well, dearest?"

"I am. Mrs. Bennet sent me a letter, and I was surprised."

Darcy's face darkened, and his voice was cold. "You do not need to read it, Elizabeth, not if you do not want to. That woman has no claim on you."

Elizabeth stood, moving to stand directly in front of her husband. He leaned back to give her room and immediately wrapped his arms around her. "I know, Fitzwilliam. There is little doubt in my mind that she intends to complain about Jane marrying and relegating her to the dower cottage on the estate. Jane opted to marry without a fuss and has refused to give in to her many complaints and demands. I will read what she wrote, but her words no longer have the power to hurt me. She is a lonely woman who seeks to blame others for problems she herself has caused."

His hold on her tightened. "I cannot suppose it has always been this easy for you to ignore her, but I suppose you have had years of practice by now. May I read the letter with you?"

"Promise not to get upset at anything she might say?"

Sighing, he nodded, so she moved to perch on his lap. Together they read the missive:

> *Lizzy Bennet,*
> *How is it that you are still creating problems for me all these years after I had your father send you from Longbourn? I thought that would fix things, but you cursed me so I could never have a son. Then, years later, I finally found a way to keep Longbourn in the family by promising you in marriage to the heir when somehow, you managed to trick a man into marrying you before you arrived home though I doubt it is the love match your uncle tries to claim. No, I still think you ensnared him somehow, for why would such a wealthy and handsome man want you? It is a shame he did not have the chance to meet Jane first, for she would have made a far better mistress of an estate than you. It is shameful that you have not invited any of your sisters to join you in London for the Season.*
> *To add insult to injury, not only did you manage to claim such a husband, but you gave him a son on your first attempt. I do hope that nothing happens to the child, for you know that many children do not survive to adulthood. It is best you give your husband a spare as soon as possible ...*

Darcy snatched the letter away from Elizabeth's hand. "Dearest, I cannot continue to read such drivel. She seems almost mad in her ramblings. Are you certain she is well?"

Elizabeth shuddered. "I cannot be sure, in large part because I cannot and will not spend any time in her presence. She is bitter, unable to see her own role in her present unhappiness. We can toss the letter into the grate and be done with her. If she sends any other letters, I will throw them away unread. Perhaps you can suggest to Mr. Collins that any letters she attempts to send to me are discarded before they even make it into the post."

Pressing a kiss to her head, Darcy sighed and tightened his hold on his wife. "She is a fool, and it seems she will never learn any better. What of your other sisters?" he asked, turning the conversation toward more pleasant topics.

Chapter Forty

Unlike Elizabeth, Lydia was pleased to receive a letter from her mother. The two exchanged letters frequently, complaining about those who denied them what they most wanted. Lydia hated being made to wear mourning, but now that she was no longer in mourning, she complained about not having the funds to purchase new dresses. The dresses she had been provided to wear were too plain, too simple … ugly. School was boring—the dancing lessons were enjoyable, but what was the point in learning to dance when no gentlemen were nearby to dance and flirt with? There were no parties to attend, and no one at school seemed to care for the spoiled girl. Lydia could not understand that her lack of friends had more to do with her and less to do with the others.

Her letters to her mother were full of complaints about how the girls were mean to her, refusing to share their belongings with her, even when she asked nicely, nor did they give into her whims. The headmistress expected her to clean up after herself and regularly took away her privileges when her room was left a mess. Despite there being servants at the school, all the girls were expected to keep their rooms and clothing reasonably tidy. At Longbourn, it was not uncommon for Lydia to tear her room apart in search of a particular gown and then expect the servants to clean up after her. The first time she had done this at school, she had been severely reprimanded by the headmistress and while she had not done that again, her room was rarely as tidy as the other girls'.

This feeling of mistreatment seeped into all of Lydia's letters to her mother, who was the only one to sympathise with her. As Lydia's return home drew near, the two began to hatch a plan to free themselves of their wardens.

> Mama,
> My uncles expect me to return to school in the autumn, but I do not wish to do so. Surely there is something you can do so I will not have to. I would much prefer to remain home with you, although from what you have said, it is just as boring at Longbourn now that Cousin Collins is in charge. It is unfathomable that he will not give you funds for additional clothing for any of us. Since he was a clergyman, I suppose it was expected for him to be somewhat miserly, but I did not think he would be so bad as to forbid us new clothing. What of my allowance? I have not had one since I left home so I am due those funds ...

Her letter continued in this vein for some time, mirroring the tone of her correspondence with her sisters. She sent one letter to Elizabeth requesting funds, along with an accusation of "casting their mother from Longbourn." To Jane, she made a similar request and included complaints about their mother's situation. Her letter to Kitty was filled with grievances about school, her eagerness to return home for the summer, and her disappointment that Elizabeth had not invited her to Pemberley. She demanded that Kitty insist on her inclusion in the trip. Finally, she wrote to Mary to lament the Collinses' treatment of her and their mother, claiming they were forced to live in a dismal cottage at the back of the property, seemingly oblivious to the fact that it had been updated and redecorated to make it pleasant and comfortable.

Lydia returned to Meryton in June, furious that none of her family had come to fetch her from school. Instead, the Gardiners had sent a maid and a manservant to escort her home on the post coach from Leicestershire. In contrast, Catherine's school was closer to London, so Mrs. Gardiner collected her and took her to Longbourn, where she would stay for a few days to help everyone settle in.

All three girls had been given the choice to join Mrs. Bennet in the dower cottage or to stay at Longbourn. Mary had already chosen to remain with her elder sister, the two having formed a tenuous friendship they had not managed before. As with Elizabeth, it had begun through letters, but now that they were living in the same house, Jane and Mary had grown much closer to each other.

Catherine chose to stay at Longbourn for the short period between returning home from school and her visit to Pemberley later in the summer. One of the reasons Mrs. Gardiner accompanied her home was that Catherine requested her assistance in explaining this decision to her mother and youngest sister.

"Lydia will not be happy with me; she has written to me to complain already about not being invited to Pemberley this summer. I am afraid she will view my decision to stay at Longbourn as a betrayal. While Jane and Mary will support me in my decision, Lydia will abuse me for it, and I would prefer to have your support, Aunt," Catherine explained to her aunt during one of her visits to her aunt and uncle's home. During this last year, Catherine had visited her London family often during holidays and school breaks, growing close to her aunt in particular. Given her father's indifference, Catherine was often uncertain how to be in company with her uncle although she adored spending time with her aunt and cousins.

Mrs. Gardiner looked at her niece for several moments. "I will accompany you, but I admit, I find it difficult to be in Mrs. Bennet's presence after what she has done and said. If you prefer it, you may stay with us in London until we head north to Pemberley. That may only delay the confrontation that will inevitably occur, depending on your plans after our visit. You are sixteen now, Catherine, and may do well to remain at home this coming year instead of returning to school. If you prefer to attend another year, you might."

Catherine nodded at this. She knew what her options were but had not made any decisions just yet. "I want to spend this next month at Longbourn before I make any decisions. Elizabeth has introduced me to her sister by marriage through letters, and I have been corresponding with Georgiana Darcy. The two of us want to see how we get along, but she has invited me to stay with her at Pemberley. We have not discussed it with Elizabeth or Mr. Darcy, but she thinks we can share her companion and do our lessons together."

"And Elizabeth and William do not know about this plan?" Mrs. Gardiner repeated.

Catherine flushed slightly. "No, we wanted to wait to see how well we got along before we mentioned the idea to them."

Mrs. Gardiner smiled at her niece. "That seems wise. Well, when we are at Pemberley, I will see what I can do to forward the idea if I think it is sound after seeing the two of you together."

"Thank you, Aunt," she gushed. It was still such a novel notion to have someone want the best for her, something she now realised her parents had never done. Both Mr. and Mrs. Bennet had been far more concerned about themselves than ensuring their children had the support and education they needed.

When Catherine arrived at Longbourn, she was met by her two elder sisters. "I am sorry, Catherine, but Lydia sneaked into the main house yesterday and overheard us speaking of your intention to remain here with us. She was annoyed, certain we were lying, and I am afraid she will not receive your news well. We did not truly expect her to—she appears to have become more selfish at school rather than less—but I am afraid overhearing us has made her even less accepting of your decision."

Catherine and Mrs. Gardiner both frowned at this news. After a moment Mrs. Gardiner looked at her nieces and shrugged. "I suppose it is for the best. They likely have gotten over the worst of their reaction by now, surely."

Jane cleared her throat. "I do not think they have. They are rather upset that no one is willing to give into their demands. Lydia arrived home a few days ago and truly believed she would be able to move her and Mama back into Longbourn. She also expected me to hand the reins back over to Mama, allowing her control of the home and the funds. Since arriving, she has visited multiple times each day, attempting all manner of stunts to get what she wanted. She sneaked into mine and Mary's rooms and went through our clothes, hoping to abscond with some dresses and other items. Each time, she was encountered by a servant, and now all the servants are aware of her intent. She surprised us yesterday when she arrived in the parlour, just as we were all sitting down to tea, which is how she learned of your plans." She looked at Catherine as she said this, who appeared surprised at her youngest sister's audacity.

"Lydia's letters were full of plans. She was certain she would be able to work on you and Mr. Collins to obtain the dresses and other items she wanted. Several letters complained that she had not received an allowance since she had been at school, and I know she expected to be given those funds upon her arrival so she could purchase whatever she wanted," Catherine answered.

"Well, she cannot make any purchases in town without ready cash—neither can you nor Mary. I apologise for what may seem an inconvenience, but it was easier to make it a requirement for all my sisters and mother rather than to make it seem as though I were singling out those at the dower cottage," Jane told her.

"Are there funds in the study that Lydia can get to? I would not put it past her to take what she wants," Mrs. Gardiner suggested.

Jane shook her head. "The study is kept locked, and Mr. Collins keeps the key on his person. Additionally, the household funds are kept in a safe which is always locked. Mrs. Hill has a small purse that she keeps in her pocket for the post and other small expenses."

"I think that someone should keep an eye on Lydia and the dower cottage," Mrs. Gardiner said, her brow creased with concern. "We cannot be certain what she might attempt, especially if she has already attempted to steal into the house and take things that are not hers. What has Mrs. Bennet said about any of this?"

"My husband escorted Lydia home after she was caught with the dresses and other items from our rooms. Mama excused her behaviour, claiming that Lydia was taking what she was owed since she had not been given her allowance in the last year. She also said that Longbourn was Lydia's home, and that we could not prevent her from entering the house if she wished."

Mrs. Gardiner shook her head sadly. "I am unsure what it will take for those two to see reason, or if they can even be persuaded to understand the truth of the situation. Jane, would you please send a note to the Phillipses asking them to visit? Mr. Phillips is Lydia's guardian, along with Mr. Gardiner, and perhaps together they can address Lydia's behaviour. She will only get worse the longer she remains with her mother. Surely there is a school where she can attend year-round until she learns to behave properly. If not, we may need to hire a companion whose sole responsibility will be to prevent Lydia from committing a crime or running away."

Before Jane could do as asked, Lydia appeared in their midst. "I will not go back to school. You cannot make me," she yelled.

Chapter Forty-One

For a moment, silence fell over the room as everyone listened to Lydia rant. Suddenly, Jane reached over and slapped her youngest sister, silencing her hysterical demands. "You are a fool, Lydia. Despite everything you have been given, you still do not understand how easy your life has been so far. It could be far worse, especially if others had not taken pity on you, your mother, and your sisters. People have paid for your schooling, your clothing, and everything you need, and yet you continue to demand more. You seem to believe you have a say over what happens to you, forgetting that you are penniless and have yet to reach your majority. Our uncles are your guardians, and they can send you wherever they choose. You have complained about not receiving your allowance, but you were informed before you left for school that you would not be receiving one, nor did you need one."

"In fact, you were informed you would only receive an allowance if your behaviour at school was acceptable," Mrs. Gardiner inserted. "Your uncle has been in regular contact with the headmistress; even if you had received an allowance, you were not permitted to venture from the school to spend it anywhere. According to reports we received, you were on restrictions more often than not for your refusal to comply with the most basic of instructions or to complete assignments. Even had you wanted to, you could not go back to the school where you were."

"What do you mean by that?" Lydia bit out.

"The last letter your uncle received from the headmistress just before your departure informed him that you were not welcome back. Neither the instructors nor your classmates wish for your company."

Lydia scowled at that. "Why would I care about them? Lizzy will take me to London and help me find a spectacular match. If she will not, surely Jane and Collins can do so."

Mrs. Gardiner laughed at that. "No one will take you anywhere, child, nor are you ready to participate in London society. You would be laughed at if you behave there the way you do everywhere else. You are far too young to even contemplate marriage."

"I will be the youngest of my sisters married. Maria Lucas wrote to me that a company of militia soldiers will spend the autumn in Meryton; one of them will wish to marry me and take me far away from all of you. We will be happier and livelier, and I will have the best of everything."

Such a foolish statement earned laughter from all gathered in the room. Mrs. Gardiner was the one who chose to address it, being the only one to whom Lydia might listen. "There are several things wrong with that statement, Lydia, though I wonder if anyone is able to help you see the error of your ways. When those militia officers come, know that none of them are acceptable suitors for you; none of them can give you the life you think you deserve. Those men typically have barely enough to live on themselves and will not be able to keep you in pretty dresses. Nor will you attend parties nearly as often as you think, for you will be too busy with the cleaning and the cooking to attend. Once children come, you will be kept even busier."

Lydia shrugged off such concerns. "La, you cannot stop me from doing as I wish. I will marry an officer who will adore me and give me everything I want."

The housekeeper came into the room then, followed by Mr. and Mrs. Phillips. Though the letter had not been dispatched, Mrs. Gardiner had been expected, and the two hoped to speak to her about the exact issue that was presently being addressed.

"Ah, Sister, you are already here, and since Lydia is in the room, I must assume you already know what we wish to address with you. Something must be done about the girl before she completely ruins herself," Mrs. Phillips said as she entered.

Lydia looked outraged but knew better than to speak as she had been doing in her uncle's presence. The conversation after she had "borrowed" her sisters' dresses had been uncomfortable, and she did not wish for a repeat of it.

"Lydia, you should return to the cottage you share with your mother. We will discuss what will be done about you, but I assure you, we can and will stop you from ruining yourself and the rest of your family along with you,' Mrs. Gardiner said, before turning toward the housekeeper. "Mrs. Hill, can you ask my groom and manservant to escort Lydia to the cottage and remain there with her to ensure neither she nor her mother leave it?"

Pouting the whole way, Lydia complied with her aunt's commands, especially when she saw the rather large footman who had been brought for this purpose. While she was escorted out, the rest sat down to speak.

"Catherine, can you tell all of us what Lydia has said in her letters to you? You mentioned some general concerns to me in London, but I would like the whole group to hear what she has said," Mrs. Gardiner began.

Taking a deep breath to steady herself, Catherine spoke up, revealing what she had kept to herself for months. "Lydia has been complaining endlessly. She is convinced she is owed an allowance, and when I told her otherwise, she accused Mr. Collins of being stingy and keeping what she believes is rightfully hers. She has even hinted at gathering enough funds to leave, possibly taking Mama with her although it seems more likely she intends to find someone to marry. Lydia also believes that Mr. Darcy has set aside a dowry for her and is under the impression she will gain access to it as soon as she marries."

"No doubt her mother's influence," grumbled Phillips, for they all knew that Mrs. Bennet did not need the facts when she was convinced of something. "Lydia cannot be permitted to remain with her mother. Everyone will be better off if the two are kept apart. Nor do I think that any of us will be able to handle Lydia in our homes on a daily basis. No, I think it is best Lydia be sent to a school for difficult girls, one that will keep her there year-round. If after a year or so her behaviour improves, it is possible she can return home, but it may be best to find her a small cottage in an isolated place and set her up with a companion who is capable of keeping her under control. She obviously cannot be trusted right now."

The others nodded their agreement, and further plans were made over the next several days. Four days after her arrival, Mrs. Gardiner returned to London accompanied by Lydia. The girl would be placed in a school as quickly as it could be arranged for Mrs. Gardiner intended to use her connections in town to find a place for the rebellious child.

OVER THE NEXT MONTH, Mrs. Gardiner was kept busy making arrangements for Lydia to be placed in a school. The school was in the Cumbrian region of England, so Mr. and Mrs. Phillips arranged to take the girl west while the Gardiners travelled north with Kitty and

Mary. Lydia remained defiant and often complained about the perceived ill-treatment by her relations.

"I cannot understand why I am being sent away in this manner!" Lydia protested loudly one evening, her arms folded across her chest. "I am not a child, and yet I am treated like one. Everyone in this family is conspiring against me to prevent me from making the match that I deserve. You are all jealous of me."

Mrs. Gardiner, with a calm but firm tone, replied, "It is not punishment, Lydia, but rather an opportunity. This school will teach you skills and discipline you will come to appreciate in time."

Lydia huffed; her face flushed with indignation. "Skills? I already possess all the accomplishments I need. You simply will not allow me to seek a suitor who is worthy of me."

"Lydia, you know it's not true. We just want what's best for you, truly, and hope that you can, in time, come to realise what you need to do to act as a proper lady."

"I don't need anyone deciding what's best for me," Lydia snapped, her voice laced with frustration. "You will all be sorry when I return and marry far higher than any of my sisters."

The Collinses were to remain at Longbourn for the present, delaying their intended wedding trip to Pemberley and the Peak District as they sought a way to deal with Mrs. Bennet. In the month since Lydia had departed, Mrs. Bennet had grown increasingly agitated with the three daughters who remained nearby. They took turns visiting her, most often in pairs or accompanied by Mrs. Phillips or Mrs. Allen since her complaints and vitriol grew increasingly difficult to bear.

"Oh, why must you all torment me so!" Mrs. Bennet cried out during one of her frequent tirades. "First Lydia was sent away to some awful school—my poor, innocent girl—and now I am left here to rot, surrounded by ungrateful daughters!"

Mary, attempting to console her mother, tried to reason with her. "Mother, Lydia's absence is for her own good. You must understand—"

"Understand?" Mrs. Bennet interrupted, her eyes filled with indignation. "You all treat me like a fool, but I see what is happening. You and your sisters plot against me, just as you did with poor Lydia. If only Mr. Collins was more generous and Jane more of a dutiful daughter, I would not be stuck in this rundown cottage with barely any company, not nearly enough to eat, and no entertainment."

Catherine, who had accompanied Mary on the visit, sighed softly. "Mama, no one is plotting against you. My sisters and I visit you regularly, along with several ladies from town, although your complaints tend to frighten them away. You are well cared for in this house and attend nearly every event to which you are invited. Just because Jane and her husband do not cater to all your whims does not mean you should feel slighted. You need to find peace and contentment in your situation, just as the rector has advised."

Mrs. Bennet threw her hands up in exasperation. "Peace? I shall never know peace again! Not until all my girls are properly married—and not abandoned to that godforsaken school like my poor, poor Lydia."

Then, Mrs. Bennet called for her salts and Longbourn's housekeeper, only one of which was offered to her. The two girls helped settle Mrs. Bennet above stairs with a maid for company before returning to Longbourn.

That night, after dinner, Mary and Catherine told the others about their encounter. "I am afraid Mama is quite undone and am concerned our continuing to visit her is doing her no good. Catherine and I are scheduled to leave soon, and then visiting Mama will fall on you, my dear sister. She grows increasingly upset each time we visit, and I am afraid the staff will leave soon due to her outbursts. The maid who sat with her after her diatribe today was clearly unwilling to remain for long and has mentioned seeking other work."

Jane and Collins looked at each other and sighed. "I spoke of this with Aunt Gardiner when she took Lydia. I am concerned that the upheaval in her life over the last year or so has caused her to go a little mad. At the moment, I do not think she is a danger to anyone, but my aunt mentioned that if she progresses in her madness, she could become such," Jane said.

The two younger girls gasped at that thought. "Do you truly think so?" Catherine asked.

Collins cleared his throat before replying. "I am uncertain what she is suffering from, but it appears to be some type of melancholia or perhaps hysteria. My wife and I have spoken together and thought it best to consult with the apothecary, Mr. Jones, first, and then, if needed, seek the opinion of a physician. I do not think she is fit for Bedlam, nor would I wish for her to be treated in such a way. If Mr. Jones believes some action to be necessary, we can hire a companion who will also serve as a nurse. Should that become necessary, we will make a decision then about her remaining in the dower house or whether another location would be better for her."

For half an hour, the four of them discussed the various options and the concerns associated with each. However, by the end of their conversation, they remained no closer to a decision. They agreed to wait for the apothecary's report before proceeding, and they also planned to consult Mr. Phillips. Collins wrote letters to both Mr. Phillips and Mr. Gardiner, informing them of their chosen course of action and seeking advice on the next steps. He also requested the name of a doctor in London who could be consulted, should it become necessary.

Chapter Forty-Two

JULY 1810

When the Gardiners, along with Mary and Catherine, arrived at Pemberley late in July, they were pleased to see Elizabeth once again. It had been more than a year since most of the sisters had been in company with each other even though they regularly corresponded.

Through these letters, Elizabeth had developed a close bond with Mary, although she had also formed a friendship with Catherine. The differences in their ages and circumstances made it a bit more challenging, while Catherine and Georgiana found much more in common with each other.

Therefore, the sisters, both by blood and by marriage, were excited to see each other. Even young William Darcy, safely ensconced in his mother's arms, waited on the steps at the front of the house as they awaited their guests. When the carriages arrived, footmen quickly assisted everyone as they disembarked, and for several long minutes, chaos reigned as greetings were exchanged.

Finally, Darcy's voice sounded over the overlapping noise. "Come inside, everyone, and join us for refreshments. That is, unless you would prefer to see your rooms first."

When no one wished to rest, they all settled into the saloon that had large windows opened over the park. Before long, the Gardiner children and young William, who by this time was beginning to droop from all the excitement, were escorted to the nursery. With that, the groups moved from more general conversation and drifted into groups. The two gentlemen settled into conversation about business ventures while Elizabeth and Mrs. Gardiner discussed the children.

Initially a bit awkward, the three unmarried ladies soon grew comfortable with one another, aided by the letters they had exchanged.

After a few tentative glances and polite smiles, Georgiana spoke first. "Miss Catherine, you mentioned in one of your letters that you enjoy reading poetry. Have you come across anything new that's captured your attention lately?"

"Mary shared a copy of Lyrical Ballads with me, and I was reading it on the way here. She and I discussed it a little during the journey, and I confess I am most intrigued by Samuel Coleridge's contribution about the sailor," Catherine answered.

This led to a discussion of the poem that eventually caught the attention of the others. Nearly an hour later, when it became necessary for them all to seek their rooms to dress for dinner, the friendship between the three younger girls was fully formed.

Gardiner waited until the following day to speak to Elizabeth and Darcy about Mrs. Bennet. "She has become increasingly hysterical over the last few months, to the point that her daughters no longer want to visit with her. Before they departed Longbourn, Mrs. Bennet was becoming increasingly abusive in her language toward them. She has not been violent, but Phillips wonders if it is possible that she may become so one day. He asked me for suggestions for a physician who might be able to treat her if it becomes necessary."

Darcy nodded. "My family physician in London would be helpful in this matter. He assisted my uncle after our marriage in dealing with Lady Catherine. They have her tucked away in a house at the seashore to help her recover from her nerves. The physician specialises in cases where the mind has grown troubled and could offer a similar course of treatment for Mrs. Bennet, should it become necessary."

Elizabeth's face grew pale at the mention of her mother's condition. "I hate the thought that she has gone mad. I wonder if she has always been this way, or if by always giving into her demands, Mr. Bennet made it worse."

"My sister was always selfish, even as a child. My parents did not always acquiesce to her demands, but when they did not, she would raise such a fuss that it made her difficult to live with. Likewise, Mr. Bennet gave in to her because it was easier, but it is possible she would have been this way regardless of who her husband was," Gardiner replied, patting Elizabeth on the hand. "Your Aunt Phillips was often her target, which is why the sisters are not particularly close now. Both she and her husband believe she will grow worse with time, and it has become difficult for anyone to visit her. She is demanding and hateful, not to mention combative. As we said, she is not violent, but there is concern that she could become so."

Elizabeth and Darcy look at each other, silently communicating with each other. "What do you need from us?"

Gardiner looked at them in surprise. "Nothing," he paused for a moment. "Well, perhaps an introduction to the physician you mentioned, but my brother and I will handle everything else. Collins will continue to contribute the same amount he is currently giving her, and that, along with the interest from her dowry, should take care of most of her expenses. Phillips and I will cover anything above that."

Darcy nodded. "Please let us know if you need anything else. I have an estate in Scotland, and my uncle has one in Northumberland. If you need a more remote location for her, please let us know and we will see what can be arranged."

Reaching out, Gardiner took his nephew's hand to clasp it. "We do appreciate your offer of assistance. I know that you and Elizabeth have little reason to do anything for my sister at this point, given her actions over the years."

Elizabeth shrugged. "Truly, we offer to make things easier for *you*, not for her. I do not wish her ill and I want nothing to do with her, but I do not want your children or my aunt and uncle to suffer when we have the means to offer assistance."

"And we appreciate your offer. I will let you know if there is anything we need. Have you heard from Lydia at all?" he asked, changing the subject.

Scoffing, Elizabeth shook her head. "No, I have not. She has not written to me since the last time I replied to a request for funds with an emphatic 'no.' It is good she is no longer under Mrs. Bennet's influence, but I am uncertain she will ever learn her lesson."

"Your aunt had a time with her while she stayed with us," Gardiner confirmed. "Like my sister, she has no problem throwing a tantrum when she does not get her way. My wife did not give into her demands, and there were several occasions when we were forced to lock her in her room. At five years of age, my children were better behaved than that girl who believes herself ready for marriage."

Elizabeth sighed heavily. "Forgive me, but I have had enough of this conversation. I am grateful that I now have a relationship with three of my sisters even if they are primarily conducted through correspondence. Now that Mary and Catherine are here, I look forward to the opportunity to get to know them even better while they are in residence at Pemberley, more so when I saw how well they and Georgiana got along. However, I am certain you gentlemen have business to discuss, and I need to meet with Mrs. Reynolds before I search out my sisters so we can enjoy some time together."

With that, Elizabeth stood and departed the room, leaving her husband and uncle behind her.

It did not take long for her to finish the necessary conversation with the housekeeper and then to seek out her sisters. All three were settled in an upstairs sitting room, speaking quietly about a novel they had each read. Elizabeth joined in the conversation happily and spent the next several hours enjoying time with her sisters. They fawned over little William who joined them about half an hour after Elizabeth did, and the Gardiner children followed shortly after.

The rest of the visit was spent in a similar fashion, and when it came time for Gardiners to depart, several plans emerged. First, Catherine would stay in Derbyshire with the Darcys, and Catherine and Georgiana would benefit from each other's friendship. It had not taken either Gardiner or Darcy long to agree to their request since it was obvious the two girls had become close during the three weeks of the visit.

Mary would also remain, at least for a time since she had met a gentleman in Derbyshire who had piqued her interest. Fortunately, she had piqued his as well, and only a day before she was scheduled to depart, a neighbour of Darcy's called at Pemberley to meet with Gardiner about the possibility of her remaining for a time so the two could visit, and possibly court, should they decide to move forward.

The Darcys and the gentleman, Thomas Linley, would likely travel to London around the same time in the autumn, and any relationship begun at Pemberley could continue there. Mary was a few months before her eighteenth birthday, and her sister and aunt were making plans to introduce her to society in the spring. Georgiana and Catherine would travel to London with them as well to learn from masters in music and art, and to experience a taste of the culture that could only be found in town.

Over the months that followed, the sisters grew closer together. Mr. Linley became a fixture at Pemberley in the months between the

Gardiners' departure and the Darcys' planned trip to London as Mary slowly came to know the young man. She celebrated her eighteenth birthday in early October, and it was on that day that Mr. Linley formally asked to begin a courtship. Mary hesitated only briefly, relieved that he had chosen this path rather than rushing into a proposal.

She confessed her anxiousness to her elder sister. "A part of me feels that I am unprepared for marriage. The example of our parents makes me afraid of someday finding myself in a relationship like theirs. I have seen how you and your husband are, and the Gardiners, and even the Winters and the Allens, so I know that such good relationships are possible, but still I worry."

"Our parents were selfish people, Mary, who were incapable of loving their children as they should have. You are nothing like our parents; you clearly are capable of loving others. If you and Mr. Linley decide to marry one day, make sure he is someone you can love completely. More importantly, once you wed, you will have to choose to love each other every day. No matter what anyone else says, love is a choice that you make. You have seen how aggravated I can get at William, and you are by now well aware of how stubborn I can be. However, we have chosen to love each other and to put each other first. That is something our parents did not do, either for each other, or for their children."

Mary could only sigh and agree, but she continued to go slowly in her relationship with the young man. He was content to allow her to set the pace, escorting her to the theatre and other events she was allowed to attend before her official debut, but that was as long as his patience lasted.

Leading her to a small alcove in the ballroom, still in sight of the others but giving them the privacy they needed, Mr. Linley confessed his love to Mary Bennet and begged for her hand in marriage. With tears in her eyes, Mary admitted to her own feelings and happily accepted.

Chapter Forty-Three

APRIL 1811

After such a long courtship, it was decided that the wedding would not be delayed. The wedding would take place at the chapel in Longbourn since Mary wished for her friend, Mr. Allen, to preside over her wedding. Now that William Collins was her brother, along with having been her friend, she asked him to walk her down the aisle, a decision both her uncles seconded.

Since the previous summer, Mrs. Bennet had been confined to her cottage and a nurse was employed whose primary responsibility was to keep the lady content and to provide companionship. This woman knew not to trust her charge or to allow her to leave what had essentially become a very well decorated gaol. Among other responsibilities of the nurse, she had a special blend of herbs to give her patient three times a day. These herbs, recommended by Darcy's physician the previous summer, were intended to keep the lady calm and to prevent outbursts.

Out of a sense of duty, Jane continued to visit her mother at least once a week. Upon hearing the news of Mary's wedding, Mrs. Bennet had grown angry since the gentleman Mary had wed had a larger estate than Longbourn, and Mrs. Bennet was still upset at Jane for marrying

Mr. Collins. This anger grew when she overheard that Jane was with child.

Following this outburst, Jane ceased her visits, and the physician was called again to assess her condition. Before he arrived, Mary returned to Longbourn to prepare for her wedding, and somehow Mrs. Bennet learned of the impending arrival.

No one was quite certain how the next event happened. When Mrs. Bennet was supposed to be resting, she managed to sneak out of the house and make her way to Longbourn to meet the carriage that Mary arrived in with her Aunt Gardiner.

Mary had barely set foot on the gravel when her mother's shrill voice reached her ears.

"Mary! Oh, Mary, how could you let them do this to me?" Mrs. Bennet wailed, rushing toward the carriage. Her face was flushed, her hair slightly askew, and she clutched at her gown in a way that suggested she had dressed hastily. "My own daughter, coming home with no thought of visiting me! They have locked me away, treated me like some old hag, and you—you have forgotten your poor mother!"

Aunt Gardiner stepped forward, her voice calm but firm. "Sister, this is not the time nor the place. Mary has only just arrived, and you are in no state—"

"No state?" Mrs. Bennet cut her off, her eyes wild as she rounded on her. "Of course, I am in a state! Left to rot in that dreadful cottage while my children abandon me! How could you allow this? How could you let them shut me away?"

Mary, who had stood frozen in shock, finally found her voice. "Mama, please. We only did what was best for your health. No one has hurt you and you have everything you need."

Mrs. Bennet's gaze swung back to her, narrowing. "My health? My health would be perfectly fine if I had not been treated so shamefully! No one cares for me, not even my own daughters. First Jane abandons me, and now you too, Mary? And you have allowed them to send Lydia away to some terrible school and she is not even allowed to write to me."

"Mama," Mary began, her voice growing firmer in her resolve, "you know that it is not like that. Your family is trying to care for you and to do what is best for you; for all of us. You will exhaust yourself if you continue as you are."

Mrs. Bennet threw her hands up dramatically. "Exhausting myself? I am merely trying to live my life. But what do any of you know of exhaustion, hm? Living in comfort while I am kept away from society—no one to speak with, no carriage to take me where I please! I am a prisoner in that awful place!"

Aunt Gardiner made an attempt to calm the situation. "You must return home and rest, Fanny. Mary and I intended to visit you once we were settled in Longbourn." This was not completely true; they had intended to visit with her briefly during their stay at Longbourn, but it likely would not have happened that day.

"You were going to visit me?" Mrs. Bennet spat. "As if I wanted to see you after what you have done to me these last few years. I need to be freed from that prison of a cottage. I am suffocating, I tell you! I should be at Longbourn, hosting guests and keeping my house as I have always done before. But you—" she pointed an accusing finger at Mary, "you refused to marry Collins and are now marrying the man who Jane ought to have had. You have stolen from her the chance to marry a man of wealth. Jane barely visits me anymore, and I know that it is due to your influence." She turned and moved her finger to point at her sister instead of her daughter.

Mary's expression grew pained, her composure slipping. "Mama, I have not taken anything away from Jane. Mr. Collins and I were only ever friends, and he and Jane fell in love. She wished to marry him; I did not. Neither did he ever ask me to do so since I have only recently reached an appropriate age to marry. Your entire family has done everything they can to make sure you are comfortable in your cottage, but you have continued to make it difficult for people to do anything for you, Mother. Please stop now and return to your cottage. Please do not make things harder than they already are."

Mrs. Bennet paused for a moment, as if the thought had finally registered. But instead of softening, she grew more indignant. "Harder? Harder on you? Well, let me tell you, Miss Mary Bennet, it is hard on me to be left alone as I have been. And now you are to marry some wealthy gentleman while I am left with nothing and stuck in this cottage, without even my Lydia for companionship. I have no fortune, no house, no respect. It is always the same with you girls, thinking of yourselves and never of your poor mother!"

Before Mary could respond, Aunt Gardiner stepped in more forcefully, her patience finally wearing thin. "Fanny, this is enough. You are clearly not well, and this behaviour is unbecoming. We will not continue this conversation out here. Go to your cottage and rest, or I will have no choice but to send for the apothecary to come and sedate you immediately."

Mrs. Bennet looked between them, her chest heaving with fury, but Aunt Gardiner's steady gaze seemed to quell her outrage—for the moment, at least. With a final huff, she turned on her heel and began storming back toward her cottage. A groom from the stables followed her to ensure she made her way back safely and to let the nurse know she had escaped.

Mary watched her go, her shoulders sagging in defeat. "That was worse than I expected from her in some ways, but not as bad in others. She still believes she could have forced me to marry Mr. Collins and is still upset that Jane did not simply allow her to remain as Longbourn's hostess. Despite the fact that she never truly acted as the mistress of the estate, she liked being the hostess of the largest estate nearby and the social status she gleaned as such."

Her aunt nodded and placed a comforting hand on her shoulder. "I believe you are correct, Mary. She is the type of person who will never be satisfied with what she has been given. For now, it is best that we enter the house and tell Jane and Mr. Collins what has transpired on their drive. It is obvious that your mother is ill, but you must not let her overshadow your future. We will manage her, as we have been doing." She gave Mary a reassuring smile.

Mrs. Hill stood at the entry; her eyes wide at having witnessed the confrontation. "You were expected, ladies, but Mr. Collins was called away this morning by a tenant and has yet to return. Mrs. Collins is upstairs resting since she has not been well this morning. She asked me to convey her apologies to you for not being down to greet you and requested that you be shown directly to her private sitting room. However, if you prefer to be shown to your rooms, she said she would wait upon you later."

Not needing to rest after such a short journey, the two asked to be shown directly to Jane. They quickly related their encounter with Mrs. Bennet to their hostess, and Jane could only sigh. "I have had to stop visiting her myself. Since she is now aware that I am with child, her behaviour has only grown worse. The physician should arrive within the next few days to evaluate her and give some suggestions about what can be done about her. Honestly, I am worried about what will happen if she learns that Elizabeth and her husband are to arrive soon for the wedding. They are leasing a house nearby for the weeks before and after the wedding."

Mary nodded, remaining silent for several moments. "Fitzwilliam told Uncle he has an estate in Scotland where there is probably a cottage that could house Mrs. Bennet and any servants necessary to care for her and maintain the house. I doubt it would be any more expensive to hire servants in Scotland than it is here; the only extra expense will be the journey."

The others agreed and they began discussing possibilities for Mrs. Bennet's care; however, the conversation soon turned to a letter Mrs.

Gardiner received from Lydia's school. "I am afraid Lydia will eventually need to join her mother although I have suggested that the headmistress give Lydia a tea similar to the one that Mrs. Bennet takes. It seems to help when she takes it first thing in the morning. However, they have noted that when Lydia goes for a vigorous walk in the morning, her energy levels and ability to focus improve. With a suitable companion to encourage her to maintain these habits regularly, she may eventually be able to return home."

This was met with another round of nods as they all considered what they had been told. "Given her treatment of her sisters over the last few years, I am uncertain any of us will be very willing to spend much time with her unless she has truly changed. I think she could do well with Catherine and Georgiana—they would provide an example of proper behaviour for her—but I am afraid she would become jealous of the close relationship between the two and seek to be the centre of attention in whatever way she can," Mary stated

"I agree," Mrs. Gardiner said. "The headmistress reports her behaviour is the same as it always has been except she is somewhat more cooperative when she takes her tea and has exercise. She is still difficult to get along with and tries to intimidate her schoolmates into giving her what she wants."

Jane and Mary both sighed at that. "I am afraid she would not be welcome here either. There is no one in the neighbourhood who would be willing to befriend her due to her previous actions, and I am worried about how she would treat me. Given that I am with child, I think it would be unwise to have her here. I am afraid if she is not at the school, she will need her own establishment someplace where her interactions can be monitored," Jane finally said.

"But she cannot be with Mama. If the two are together, they will make each other worse instead of better. I do believe Mama is truly ill, perhaps a little mad, but with a proper example, I would like to think Lydia could be better," Mary replied.

Mrs. Gardiner tutted. "You are borrowing trouble. At the moment, Lydia is well established at the school and will remain there for some time. The school is year-round, and Lydia will not need to return home any time soon. When that time comes, we will determine what needs to be done then. For now, let us focus on what needs to be done for Mary's wedding."

Chapter Forty-Four

The physician arrived a few days later, suggesting a change in the herbal tea that Mrs. Bennet drank each day. A small amount of laudanum was added to a tonic for her to take each morning as well—not so much as to make her sleep, but enough to keep her docile and more biddable. He had not wanted to give her laudanum before now, but after the verbal attack on Mary and Mrs. Gardiner, he decided that it would be for the best.

When the Darcys arrived, their first visit to Longbourn occurred without issue. Though she had sworn to never return, Elizabeth was pleased to see how Longbourn had changed from what she remembered as a child and even from her brief visit a few years before. With a master and mistress who were diligent in their care of the estate, it was thriving, and the funds that Elizabeth had invested with Collins after he inherited had been used to add to the stables.

Upon their arrival at the house, they were greeted by the family as their carriage arrived in the drive. As soon as they disembarked, the master of the house strode to them with a smile, calling out "Mr. Darcy! Mrs. Darcy! What an honour it is to welcome you both to Longbourn."

"Indeed, Mr. Collins. The estate is thriving, and I commend you for the improvements you have made. Perhaps you and I can visit the stables later," Darcy replied, greeting his host.

Jane smiled at her guests as well. "But first, you must come and take tea with us. I am looking forward to meeting my nephew and hearing first-hand about the events you have attended in town. We expect Mr. Linley on the morrow, and I am equally anticipating making his acquaintance. Please, come inside."

A few minutes later, they were all settled in the drawing room. Jane moved to sit next to her sister Elizabeth and her husband. Speaking quietly, she offered an apology for her actions upon their long-ago first meeting. "Elizabeth, I know I have offered you both my apology and my reasoning behind my actions when we first met, but, Mr. Darcy, I have never had a chance to apologise to you. I was raised to think so highly of myself and of my appearance and to think poorly of others, particularly Elizabeth, and I was jealous that she was married when I was not."

Elizabeth and Darcy exchanged a look that spoke volumes between them. "I forgave you long ago, Mrs. Collins. Elizabeth told me of your apology to her along with the explanation of what you were experiencing at the time. I think the incident is best forgotten at this point."

With a grateful smile, Jane patted her sister's hand, and the three joined the conversation about the wedding that would occur in just under a week. After tea, the gentlemen walked out of doors to visit the stables, successfully avoiding as much of the talk over dresses and wedding decorations as they could manage.

The rest of the week passed without incident. Mr. Linley arrived the following day as expected, accompanied by his family and several of his friends. Catherine and Georgiana arrived on that same day, accompanied by Colonel Fitzwilliam. Longbourn was full of visitors as they finished the preparations for the wedding, and the houses taken by the Darcys and Linleys were likewise full of their own guests.

On a bright Tuesday morning in May, Mary Bennet was joined in marriage to Thomas Linley. Her marriage was witnessed by both her aunts and uncles, three of her sisters, and many friends she had met over the last few years, including Mr. and Mrs. Winters and their daughter Amelia, who stood up with Mary. The rector, Mr. Allen, conducted the ceremony and felt nearly as proud as a father at seeing her make an excellent match. Yes, Mr. Linley was wealthy, but of far more importance, the man adored his new bride, a fact that was obvious in the way he could barely pull his eyes from his bride to repeat his vows and the slight shake in his voice as he spoke them.

Jane and Elizabeth sat next to each other, their husbands on their outsides, as they watched their younger sister marry. Each seemed to realise how different their lives were now and understood the influences that had both hurt them and helped them, as they cried happy tears upon seeing the ceremony conclude.

The wedding breakfast was equally pleasant for its invited guests. Many in the neighbourhood were pleased to see a third Bennet daughter marry so well, especially knowing what they did about the girls' parents and their indifference over the years. They recognised the influence of others in their lives and were glad that most of the girls seemed to have overcome their upbringing.

The Gardiners departed for London soon after the wedding breakfast ended along with many of the Linley family and the friends of the groom who came for the wedding.

However, the Darcy family remained and were often found visiting Longbourn and some of their friends in the neighbourhood. Those connections were not as strong as they might have once been, but Elizabeth and Darcy made an effort to spend time with her aunt and uncle and the Lucases because of their kindness to them over the years.

After another sennight in the country, the Darcys elected to forgo the rest of the Season to return to Pemberley. Little William was over a year old now, and Elizabeth had recently begun to suspect she was once again with child, so her husband sought to remove her from the bad air of London as quickly as possible.

Though Elizabeth was not concerned about the air affecting her or her child, she always preferred the country to town, and they had been in London far too long for her liking.

DURING THE DARCYS' visit, Collins and Darcy discussed plans for transporting Mrs. Bennet to his estate near Ayr in Scotland. One thought had been to take Mrs. Bennet there by ship, but they were concerned about possible seasickness during the journey. It was decided that yet again, Mr. and Mrs. Phillips would provide escort for a Bennet who needed to be sent far away. The couple actually looked forward to the trip, for it gave them the opportunity to travel far beyond what they might have been able to do otherwise. Their journey was funded by a mutual effort between the Gardiners, Collinses, Darcys, and Linleys.

As a reward for agreeing to take on the task, the couple would travel there as quickly as they could manage in a large comfortable travelling coach owned by the Darcys, and then return much more slowly, allowing them to visit and tour wherever they wished. Phillips had a clerk who was nearly ready to take over for him, and so Phillips had little concern about leaving his law office in the clerk's care for the month their journey would likely take.

They would also stop in Derbyshire on their return to visit with both of their nieces in the north, for Mary had opted to forgo a wedding trip in favour of returning to her new home where she would take her place as mistress.

Of the Bennet daughters, all but Lydia were content in their situations. Lydia was only allowed to write letters to Mrs. Gardiner. However, she could include notes for her sisters, and Mrs. Gardiner would forward them if they were deemed appropriate. Most were not, and while her sisters did occasionally write to her, they took care in their letters to say as little as possible about what was actually taking place in their lives to prevent Lydia from becoming even more jealous. News of Mary's wedding was not well received, for Lydia still believed that she ought to marry before at least one of her sisters, and the letter she wrote to Mary following her wedding had gone straight into the fire upon Mrs. Gardiner receiving it.

In the years that followed, Lydia remained consumed by resentment and jealousy toward her sisters, convinced she deserved more than she had. Shortly after reaching her majority, she was moved from the school to her own establishment near Newcastle. Like her mother, she received a calming tea each morning but was also encouraged to take long walks with a footman and a maid. These walks exhausted her enough to make her more manageable in the afternoons, allowing her to sit quietly and sew while her companion read to her. Additional cups of tea in the afternoons and one with supper helped her fall asleep and stay asleep through the night.

Catherine and Georgiana debuted together the spring after Georgiana turned eighteen. Though Catherine had reached a similar age the previous spring, she elected to wait to enter society until Georgiana could join her.

The two were widely regarded as excellent catches. All three of Catherine's brothers and her uncles had contributed to her dowry, which, while not as large as Georgiana's, was still respectable. Both girls were equally determined to marry for love and endured two full seasons before finally finding matches toward the end of their second.

Georgiana met and fell in love with a young viscount who had only recently gained the title. He had been the second son but inherited the title and estate upon his elder brother's death in a duel a few months previously. Darcy was at first unconvinced about the wisdom of the match, but quickly came to realise the young man truly held his sister in affection and was of a very different sort than his elder brother who had been something of a rake.

Surprisingly, Catherine met and fell in love with a young rector she met in town. Arthur Sinclair, third son of an earl, had chosen to go into the church rather than the army. Though he had only recently taken orders, he was in London visiting his family just after Easter and had encountered Catherine in the park. Colonel Fitzwilliam was accompanying the young ladies, along with Georgiana's suitor, allowing the young man to request an introduction to the rest of the party. He knew both gentlemen from Gentleman Jack's as well as White's and had attended Cambridge with the viscount.

Sinclair was intrigued by the lovely dark-haired lady in their party, and upon learning that she was not being courted by either of the gentlemen in the group, requested permission to call. When he heard that she was living at Darcy House, he nearly wavered, but visited anyway and soon found the lady agreeable to his attentions. In the weeks that followed, Sinclair travelled from his rectory in Northampton to London as often as he was able to visit the young lady. At the end of the season, he requested a courtship and permission to exchange letters with Catherine so they could continue to come to know each other.

Gardiner agreed to the request, and letters were sent included with the correspondence exchanged with Mr. Collins. Catherine had chosen to spend part of the summer at Longbourn to assist Jane after her second confinement. She planned to travel to Derbyshire later in the summer with the Gardiners for Georgiana's wedding, making a stop in Northampton along the way.

During that visit, Sinclair asked for Catherine's hand in marriage, and was accepted, with the wedding to occur later that autumn. Like her sister Mary, Catherine opted to wed from Longbourn, despite that not truly having been her home for many years. However, she still wished to have the friends and family she had grown up with around her when she married.

In October of that year, the entire extended Bennet family—except for the matriarch and the youngest daughter—gathered at Longbourn to celebrate Catherine Bennet's marriage. It was a pleasant occasion with more children present than at Mary's wedding. The sisters were happy to be reunited although such gatherings became more challenging as their families grew. Mary and Elizabeth, now living near each other, were perhaps the closest, but all four Bennet sisters were far more at ease with one another than they had been on that fateful day when a summons to Longbourn had upended their lives and fates.

Epilogue

Over the years that followed, the extended Bennet family made it a tradition to gather together every summer. Most often, these reunions took place at Pemberley, the only estate large enough to accommodate the entire family and conveniently located for many members. The estate, with its sprawling grounds and welcoming atmosphere, became a cherished backdrop for the family's summer holidays.

A few years after his marriage to Catherine, Sinclair was granted a living closer to Lambton, making it easier for their family to join the summer festivities at Pemberley. The Collinses, the Linleys, and the Wyndcliffes—formally known as Viscount Andrew and Viscountess Georgiana Liverstone—also made it a point to attend whenever possible, often squeezing in visits between their time spent in London during the social Season. The house would come alive with laughter, games, and shared stories, creating a vibrant tapestry of familial bonds.

However, there were occasions when some family members could not attend the summer gatherings due to various reasons, such as one sister being close to childbirth. The extended family steadily grew, with new additions almost every year for two decades. Each new baby brought joy, but it also meant that the gatherings became increasingly crowded, stretching Pemberley to its limits as the next generation began to marry and start families of their own.

Amidst these joyful reunions, life also brought sorrow. Mrs. Bennet passed away after more than a decade spent at Darcy's estate in Scotland. Her nurse sent regular reports to the lady's brothers about her deteriorating condition. During this time, Mrs. Bennet held onto her grievances, never forgiving Elizabeth for what she perceived as mistreatment, and blaming her daughters for "allowing" her to be treated poorly. Occasionally, the nurse would include one of the many letters Mrs. Bennet wrote to her daughters—letters filled with complaints and exaggerated accounts of her suffering—none of which were ever sent to their intended recipients.

When the news of her death reached the family, neither Gardiner nor Phillips felt compelled to travel to pay their respects to a woman they believed did not deserve such courtesies. The timing of her death, in the midst of summer, compounded the indifference, as the letter informing them arrived long after she had been laid to rest. Gardiner took it upon himself to inform his nieces of their loss, though they had all long agreed that they would not mourn for a woman who had not truly acted as a mother to any of them. Instead, they chose to remember the summers spent together, the love and laughter that defined their family gatherings, and the bonds that continued to grow stronger in Mrs. Bennet's absence.

RICHARD FITZWILLIAM, after a distinguished career as a Brigadier General in the Army, settled down to manage a horse farm he jointly purchased with his friends Darcy and Linley. This new venture allowed him to immerse himself in the daily rhythms of farm life, where he took pride in breeding and training horses sought after by nobility.

During a visit to Pemberley, Richard met Charlotte Lucas, a spinster and cherished friend of the Darcy family. While their relationship lacked the fervour of passionate romance, it was built on genuine fondness and respect. They enjoyed long walks in the gardens and meaningful conversations, finding comfort in each other's company. Their courtship blossomed into a solid partnership that both families embraced.

To everyone's surprise, a few years after their marriage, Charlotte announced she was expecting a child. When their son was born, they named him William, honouring Charlotte's father and Richard's dear friend Fitzwilliam Darcy. This choice reflected the deep connections in Richard's life.

FITZWILLIAM AND ELIZABETH DARCY maintained a deep friendship throughout their lives, a bond that deepened as they faced the many challenges life threw their way. From the early days of their marriage, they leaned on each other for strength and support, creating a partnership that would weather both storms and sunny days. Their journey was marked by trials common to any couple, but rather than allowing these challenges to create rifts between them, each obstacle became a stepping stone toward greater intimacy.

In the years when Pemberley faced lean times due to poor weather or as the nation transitioned from an agrarian society to one driven by industry, the Darcys remained united. They tackled each challenge together, discussing strategies late into the night, making decisions that would benefit not only their family but also their estate and tenants. Their mutual respect and love fortified their resilience, allowing them to navigate even the most tumultuous times with grace.

During the first fifteen years of their marriage, Elizabeth welcomed six children into the world, though their joy was marred by the loss of one precious daughter, little Anne, who succumbed to a childhood illness shortly before her third birthday. Her passing cast a shadow over their household, and they mourned together, finding solace in each other's arms as they reflected on the fleeting nature of life. Darcy's heart ached not only for their lost child but also for his wife, who bore the burden of their grief with quiet strength. Each subsequent pregnancy filled him with anxiety, reminding him of his own mother's tragic fate, who had died giving birth to a child that also did not survive. Yet, through this fear, Elizabeth's determination shone bright, and Fitzwilliam admired her tenacity in the face of uncertainty.

Ten months after Anne's death, Elizabeth brought joy back into their lives with the birth of a little boy, whom they named Richard after Darcy's beloved cousin. Richard was a bright light in the Darcy household, embodying the same jovial spirit and fearless nature that characterised his namesake. His laughter echoed through Pemberley's halls, reminding them of the joy that life could still bring despite their previous heartache. Fitzwilliam and Elizabeth revelled in their son's antics, finding in him a renewed sense of hope and purpose.

As the years rolled on, the Darcys nurtured their growing family, cherishing every moment while honouring the memory of little Anne. With each child, their bond deepened, grounded in love, shared experiences, and the mutual understanding that life's path would inevitably bring both joy and sorrow. Through it all, their friendship remained a constant, the foundation upon which their family was built—a testament to the enduring power of love and companionship.

About the Author

Melissa Anne first read Pride and Prejudice in high school and discovered the world of JAFF a few years ago. After reading quite a few, she thought perhaps she could do that, and began writing, first on fan fiction sites, and then began to publish as an independent author. Melissa Anne is a pen name.

She began her career as a newspaper reporter before becoming a middle school English teacher and then a high school English teacher. She presently lives and works in Georgia, although she grew up in East Tennessee and claims that as home. Melissa has been married to a rather wonderful man (something of a cross between a Darcy and a Bingley) for nearly two decades, and they have three children.

Contact her at melissa.anne.author@gmail.com

- facebook.com/melissa.anne.author
- instagram.com/melissa.anne.author
- bookbub.com/profile/melissa-anne
- amazon.com/stores/Melissa-Anne/author/B0C54C1BNF
- youtube.com/@MelissaAnneAuthor

Also by Melissa Anne

Darcy & Elizabeth's Dreams of Redemption

Worthy of Her Trust

Hearts Entwined

Responsibility and Resentment

A Different Impression

Finding Love at Loch Ness

What Happened After Lambton

The Accidental Letter